W9-BDV-036

MAR   2003

Primitive Secrets

Primitive Secrets

Deborah Turrell Atkinson

Poisoned Pen Press

First Edition 2002

10 9 8 7 6 5 4 3 2 1

Library of Congress Catalog Card Number: 2001098499

ISBN: 1-59058-017-6 Hardcover
ISBN: 1-59058-046-X Trade Paperback

Poisoned Pen Press
6962 E. First Ave., Ste. 103
Scottsdale, AZ 85251
www.poisonedpenpress.com
info@poisonedpenpress.com

Printed in the United States of America

"One of the beliefs of the early (Hawaiian) peoples was that the spirit of a dead person entered into an animal. These spirits, or 'aumakua, became helpers of the people."

From *Ancient Hawaiian Civilization*, A Series of lectures delivered at the Kamehameha Schools. Revised Edition. Charles E. Tuttle Company, 1965. From the lecture by C.H. Edmondson, page 289.

'Aumakua. 1. Nvt. Family or personal gods, deified ancestors who might assume the shape of (animals) and plants. A symbiotic relationship existed; mortals did not harm or eat 'aumakua (they fed sharks), and 'aumakua warned and reprimanded mortals in dreams, visions, and calls.

Hawaiian Dictionary. Hawaiian-English, English-Hawaiian. By Mary Kawena Pukui and Samuel H. Elbert. University of Hawaii Press, 1986.

Acknowledgments

Many people participated in the birth of this book. In fact, running my eyes over the list of co-conspirators and plotters brings a grin to my face. It was a lot of fun sharing experiences, conceiving, shaping, and putting together the story behind *Primitive Secrets*. *Mahalo nui loa* to all of you.

Thank you to my agent, Lynne Doyle Thew, for staying with me. It's been a long time. My editor, Barbara Peters, had critical input, comments, and advice. Thank you for your patience and expertise.

My sister, Claudia Turrell, and friends Francis Mukai and the Honorable Evelyn Lance gave direction and advice as to the wheels and cogs in a legal office. Robert Atkinson, M.D., and Reid Manago, M.D., helped with pharmaceutical information and the hospital scenes. Major Butch Robinson of the Honolulu Police Department and Justin Bridges, a retired Houston homicide cop, outlined police procedure with unattended deaths. Frank and Karen, investigators with the Honolulu Medical Examiner's office, explained their work after the body is found. Dr. Randall Baselt, of the Chemical Toxicology Institute in Southern California, shared his knowledge of drug scans and toxicities. Puakea Nogelmeier and Sahoa Fukushima corrected my Hawaiian language errors.

Thanks to fellow writers and editors Michael Chapman, Karen Huffman, Jim and Janet Mozley, Karyn Koga, Boni Gravelle, Honey and Lisa Pavel, Michelle Calabro

Hubbard, Kelly Cook, and Egen Atkinson for their comments, guidance, and enthusiasm.

Despite the best efforts of the fore-mentioned professionals, any mistakes or misstatements in the book are mine. Though the towns mentioned in Storm's tale are real places, all characters are fictional. Thank goodness, neither my friends nor I encounter bodies at Storm Kayama's rate.

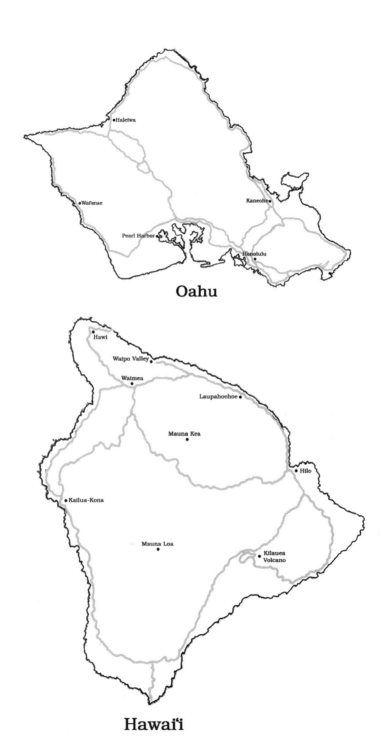

Oahu

Hawai'i

Chapter 1

Miles Hamasaki stood at his picture window and looked, unseeing, over the azure depths of Honolulu Harbor where graceful Coast Guard cutters passed like swans and tugs pushed squat freighters from the Orient. He thought about two big problems. One was business and he would squash the greedy sonofabitch like a cockroach in the next forty-eight hours. A smile twitched at the corner of his mouth, then faded. The other was personal, and would be much more difficult to resolve.

Hamasaki walked back to his desk, sank into his big leather chair, and ruffled through the legal contract he was preparing. Age had taught him to put aside worries he couldn't solve until he had the information he needed. Patience was a formidable ally.

Right now, he wanted to get this contract ready to review with Storm in the morning. His eyes crinkled with pleasure as he thought about how she, the adopted daughter of a dead friend, was turning into a terrific lawyer. If only his own sons were as promising. Sadness passed briefly over his features and was replaced almost immediately with resolve.

Hamasaki's secretary knocked lightly on the door, then pushed it open. "Dr. O'Toole on line two, Boss. I'm *pau* work, so I'll put your calls through to the office."

"Thanks for coming in on a Sunday afternoon, Lorraine. Hey, if you and Ben go to that Keanu Reeves movie tonight, I want a review tomorrow." He grinned at her.

Lorraine's gray hair shook with laughter as she set a cup of tea on Hamasaki's desk. "Yeah, sure. When Bitsy gets back from visiting her sister on the Big Island, go yourself."

Even though he'd slowed his practice, he and Lorraine still spent thirty hours a week together. When they'd first opened the law firm, she'd stood by sixty to eighty hours a week. They knew each other better than they knew their own spouses.

Hamasaki picked up the phone and spoke soothing words to his old friend O'Toole. A few minutes after he hung up, the managing partner, Edwin Wang, tiptoed into the office. Hamasaki stifled a sigh at the interruption and looked up. "How's your mother?"

"I'm trying to keep her out of a nursing home. It's difficult right now."

Hamasaki glanced at his watch, made a note on the contract, let a few seconds elapse. "Alzheimer's is a tragic disease. We should all worry."

"I'd like to speak to you about some things."

"It'll have to be tomorrow morning. Nine o'clock."

Wang nodded and backed toward the door. "Thank you."

Hamasaki watched the door close. Frowning at both his old man's need for the toilet and Wang's obsequiousness, he stood up and headed for the washroom. Hamasaki knew Wang's behavior had nothing to do with his mother's illness. He wasn't ready to talk to Wang yet, though. The managing partner would be as malleable as a child if he had to stew in his anxieties a little longer, plus Hamasaki wanted to check on one more detail before tomorrow's meeting.

A half-hour later, Hamasaki didn't look up from his papers when he heard footsteps in the hall. O'Toole had said he'd try to drop by to talk. Hamasaki was a little surprised when the door opened without a knock. It was unlike O'Toole, but these weren't normal circumstances. He finished the note to Storm in the margin of the contract.

Hamasaki glanced up, then sat back hard in his chair with a sharp intake of breath. His eyes narrowed.

"You have to listen to me."

"What do you mean, have to?" Hamasaki threw down his pen. "What excuses can be made for degeneracy, dishonesty, and preying on the...the..." he gritted his teeth, "naive!"

"I told you, you misunderstand."

Hamasaki watched the depraved wretch struggle with what he wanted to say. He began to pace before Hamasaki's desk. Rings of sweat blackened the purple of an orchid-patterned shirt. Hamasaki found it hard to hide his disgust. He unclenched his teeth and took a sip of his tea and a deep breath, which he stifled midway.

"Okay, you've got my attention. If you're going to attempt to justify yourself, at least sit down." He waved his hand at the chair facing the desk. Maybe the locker room aroma would stay confined to the other side.

The visitor sat on the edge of the chair and sputtered a string of self-justifications. Hamasaki took another couple of swallows of tea and leaned back in his chair. Total bullshit. Time to end this pretentious monologue. He tried to stand and dismiss the moron, but felt his gaze slipping. He was so tired, so damned tired.

Storm Kayama struggled with the doorknob. She gripped a steaming mug of dark tea in each hand and had a bag filled with two fat cherry turnovers clamped in her teeth. She was trying very hard not to drool down the side of the pastry bag. A client folder clasped under one elbow inched along the silky fabric of her blouse.

She was early, but it looked like Uncle Miles, as she still called him in private, was here. Her father and Miles Hamasaki had been boyhood friends on Maui, fought in the 442nd Infantry together, and had vowed to take care of each other's families in the event that one didn't return. Decades later, Uncle Miles had kept his word.

Storm got the knob turned and kept her eyes on the swaying surface of the tea. A big drop had already splatted, fortunately onto the toe of her shoe instead of the plush beige carpet. She kept going, though; she had a great joke for him this morning. Uncle Miles said lawyers needed to start the day with a laugh because few people visit their attorneys with a smile.

Storm let the pastry bag slide from her mouth into the crook of the arm that did not hold the slipping file folder. "Uncle Miles, did you hear about the guy who went into the psychiatrist's office wearing only cellophane shorts?" Storm chuckled and kept her eyes on the mugs. He was going to love this. "The shrink said, 'Well, we can clearly see you're nuts!'"

She stopped sliding her feet across the carpet and looked up. He should have been hooting.

But he had his head down on the desk and his fingers entwined in the handle of one of his brightly colored mugs. Storm had never seen him nap in the office.

"Uncle Miles? Uncle Miles?"

Chapter 2

Morning sunlight sliced through the branches of the monkey pod trees and burned away the morning mists that still hovered in the deep Manoa valley. Storm Kayama plodded up the sidewalk and regarded the cracks in the concrete. The steamy world around her paralleled the one she'd lived in before she found Miles Hamasaki's body. But she was alone in this new surreal one. Miles' friends and colleagues gestured to her, made conversation as if they stood next to her, but they didn't. They were outside the shimmering curtain of incredulity and grief that isolated her.

Heavy incense rolled from the wide temple doors, bringing her other memories of death. Buddhists offer incense as a ritual of purification, a perfume to discourage the departed soul from taking a member of the living with him. Storm felt halfway to the nether world, as numb as she'd been at twelve when her father had lit the incense at her mother's funeral.

Inside, banks of lilies and cattleya orchids surrounded a portrait of Hamasaki that sat on the altar. At least two hundred people were here at Miles' *shonanuka*, the first of his memorial services. Storm mumbled excuse-me's and jostled her way through a mass of bodies to the family pew, where she dropped into an empty space next to Bitsy Hamasaki. Despite her pallor and the rice-paper thinness of her skin, Bitsy still managed to smile at her husband's friends and business associates.

Most of the observers knew the family, but a stranger would have noticed that Storm was not of the same gene pool. Though her father had been Japanese, Storm had the larger stature and wide, almond eyes of her Hawaiian mother. At five-eight, she was taller than anyone in the entire Hamasaki family. Instead of smooth, ebony hair, Storm had wavy mahogany hair that she pulled into a French braid in an attempt to tame it.

A blurred three hours later, Storm stood in the foyer of the Hamasakis' oceanfront home and said goodbye to friends and colleagues who had come to help the family mourn. Mountains of food, vegetarian in the Buddhist funeral tradition, had been catered by David and Michelle Hamasaki's classy downtown restaurant. A group of Bitsy's women friends had formed a support group, or *kumiai*, and they flitted about the house, picking up after the dispersing guests.

Martin Hamasaki, the youngest son, had arrived from Chicago a few days ago. He gave Storm a hug. "Get something to eat before you leave."

"Can't," she whispered back and wondered how, under the circumstances, he managed to look so tanned and rested. She knew she looked like she'd lost a battle with the specter of insomnia. Not only were people doing subtle double takes at her, this morning her eyes in the bathroom mirror had reflected a dark tragedy so evocative of her mother that Storm had buried her face in the sink and spit toothpaste with vehemence. She would not let the black hole of depression overtake her. Not her, not ever.

Martin nudged Storm. "Look, there's Dr. O'Toole. Never thought he'd outlive Dad." O'Toole was dressed in bright green polyester linen-look slacks. His green and yellow flowered aloha shirt accentuated his swollen red nose. They both could see the tremor in O'Toole's hand when he reached for his car keys.

"That's his golf outfit. The one that matches Dad's," Martin whispered.

His comment dispersed a cloud of Storm's gloom and she stifled a smile. "Be nice. He wore it out of respect."

"I wouldn't mind having their lives." Martin's voice held a note that surprised Storm. She shot a glance at him, but he was saying goodbye to a family friend.

Martin's life couldn't be so bad. He looked great. A wave of loss passed over Storm with a force that hurt. She had never been as close to David or Michelle as she was to Martin. Martin was thirty, three years older than she. Michelle and David were six and eight years older, and seemed like they were from another generation. The real problem, though, was a rivalry she felt stemmed from David and had burgeoned over the last four or five years. Now Hamasaki was gone and Martin would soon return to Chicago. She would miss both of them terribly.

Martin turned back to her. "Get some rest and we'll have lunch tomorrow, okay?"

Storm nodded and made her way out the door. On the sidewalk, she stopped and took a deep breath. It hurt; the old stone of loneliness sat on her chest again. She couldn't imagine life without Hamasaki. Irrational as it was, she felt as deserted as she had when she was twelve and her mother had died.

When her father died four years later, the pain was not as severe. He had wasted away with kidney disease, and though she was angry and alone, she had seen it coming. Now her chest burned as it had fifteen years ago. Despite what anyone said about her mother's problems, her mother had abandoned her. She had chosen her death.

Storm balled her hands into fists and glared down at the front walk. Hamasaki's departure had brought back emotions she thought she had outgrown. She needed to remind herself that in most people's eyes he was elderly, a full forty-four years older than her thirty-three year old mother had been.

Storm sighed. It was not good to wallow in this sadness. Hamasaki had already been cremated and candles for the forty-nine day mourning period sat at the home altar to give light and direction to his wandering spirit. Though Storm had not been raised in the Japanese tradition, Aunt Bitsy followed it with steadfast faith. Dwelling on thoughts of the dead brought bad luck. The departed might take a friend or family member with him.

Chapter 3

The prospect of going home didn't appeal to Storm at all. She'd end up staring at the walls and wondering how to deal with going to work the next day. She would be better off facing the office now. The place would be peaceful and air-conditioned. No one would be there, especially after the service. She could tie up a few loose ends on the contract Hamasaki had prepared for her, or look around the office library for his old leather briefcase, the one in which he carried all of his current work.

The office staff had their collective eyes out for the battered old attaché case. Hunting for it was nothing new; Hamasaki was famous for mislaying it. Storm and Bitsy once told him they were going to replace it with a neon orange tote bag, with a flag attached.

No one was worried, though it did contain files that needed to be passed on to other lawyers in the firm. It would turn up and since Storm had been doing most of Hamasaki's clerking, the other partners expected her to find it. She had already called the Lexus dealership where he'd had his car serviced last week, the post office in his neighborhood, and the University of Hawai'i law library. People wished her luck.

Even as she unlocked her office, Storm pondered checking his barbershop and the dry cleaner. She murmured a scolding to Hamasaki, wherever his spirit might be, changed it to a request for help, and then felt silly talking to herself and glanced around the hallway. The light was on under Hamlin's door, but every other office, including the receptionist's area, was dark. Storm was glad Lorraine had gone home after the service. Lorraine had leaned weakly against her husband Ben during the short time they visited the Hamasaki home. Usually the most efficient person in the organization, she'd been a ghost of herself since Hamasaki's death.

Storm sat at her desk and rummaged around for the phone book. A couple of fruitless calls later she put the receiver back and listened to muffled voices in the hall. She got up and popped her head around the doorjamb.

Ian Hamlin, the newest associate in the firm, was walking a handsome, burly man in frayed denim jeans and a buttery suede shirt down the hall. Storm did a double take; he was worth a second look. She recognized the man from publicity photos. Hamlin must have a good reputation. The client was Christopher DeLario, a sculptor renowned for his sensual bronzes. DeLario did larger-than-life interpretations of men and women with musculature that one New York critic had compared to Michelangelo. Around O'ahu, he was better known for his wild parties and the thirty-year-old custom Harley he rode. People gossiped that the radiant bronze Aphrodite at the art museum was modeled after a lover who had left him for another woman, and that she'd posed during a party that swirled with flakes of cocaine and clouds of ice.

DeLario looked haggard, though the droop of his shoulders didn't hide their powerful breadth. Storm didn't believe everything she heard; she knew that people love to color in the empty spaces around fame. Her eyebrows bounced in appreciation at the sight of the men and she went back to her desk. In one of the drawers, she dug out a slightly crushed package of peanut butter and cheese crackers and stuffed one in her mouth. She had passed up all that delicious food a couple of hours ago and now her stomach rumbled with hunger.

She opened the laptop case that she used as a briefcase and rooted for the papers she'd taken home a few nights before Hamasaki had died. Until the old man's attaché turned up, these were among the few files available to pass on to the other partners. Edwin Wang had asked her twice already.

Storm stopped chewing and batted at crumbs that fell into the case. The folder wasn't in there. She went through the bag again, then dumped the computer and all the papers out on the desk.

She forced herself to sit back in her chair and take a deep breath. Okay, she'd been preoccupied lately, but she'd looked through some of this last night. She pawed through the mess again, more quickly. The folder was missing. With a flash of insight, she remembered it resting on the kitchen counter, where she'd set it this morning when she went back inside to feed the cat. Storm let her breath go in a hiss. "Son of a bitch!"

"And good afternoon to you, too." Hamlin stood at the door, grinning.

Storm looked up, startled. "Oh, hi." She wiped her mouth with the back of her hand. "I didn't mean you. I—"

"I refuse to take offense. One of my dearest childhood companions was a Labrador Retriever." He dropped into the chair facing her and set a cup of coffee in a Wild Bill Hickock mug on her desk. "How are you doing? I'm surprised you're here."

Storm could see the varying shades of hair in his mustache; some of them were graying, and she liked the overall effect. It gave him a renegade appearance despite the well-cut, double-breasted navy suit, which he wore with a white shirt. His tie was some tropical flower pattern in red and orange. Hibiscus, maybe. She looked at the portrait of the poker-playing marksman on his mug and almost laughed. Hamlin resembled him.

"I'm okay." She held the package of crackers out to him. "Was that Christopher DeLario I saw leaving your office?"

"Yeah." Hamlin took a cracker. "Thanks. I didn't feel like eating at the memorial service."

"Me either. I still expect Hamasaki to walk in here and tell me a joke. Or give me advice."

"Yeah, I know. But I hope I live as long and happily."

"You seen his briefcase anywhere? Maybe in a kitchen cupboard or a partner's office? You could hide a body under the journals on Cunningham's bookshelves."

"No kidding," Hamlin chuckled. "You talked to Lorraine?"

"She's the first person I asked."

Hamlin helped himself to another cracker. "When do you take the bar?"

"I did last month." Storm shrugged. "We'll see if I get to be a real lawyer or continue gophering."

"Sometimes it feels like there's not much difference."

"Hey, for a guy with clients like Christopher DeLario, I'm surprised you feel that way."

"I've known him a long time," Hamlin said quickly and bit into a cracker. "That was a nice service. Are you Buddhist?"

Storm lifted an eyebrow at him, then shifted gears. "No, my mother was Episcopalian and my father rarely went to church. I know about this stuff from living with the Hamasakis, though Martin and I used to make fun of some of the rituals." She smiled at the memories of Martin's impertinence. "Despite his irreverence, Martin went with Aunt Bitsy to *obon* memorial festivals until he left for the mainland. Sometimes I went along and said a prayer for my parents." She pushed a pile of paper clips around on her desk and wondered why she'd brought up the issue of her parents. The funeral, she supposed.

"Martin's the youngest son, right?" Hamlin asked. "I was in Hamasaki's office a few weeks ago when they were talking on the phone. Sounded like long distance."

"Yeah, Martin lives in Chicago."

"They were discussing business and something about a party Martin had, but Hamasaki sounded serious. He was using his lecturing voice. You know the one."

"Uh-oh." Storm's forehead creased. Though in the past, Martin had partied too much for his parents' tastes and could still be rebellious, she had always felt that he had inherited his father's strong set of ethics.

"Well, he had this authoritative tone. It was the end of the workday for us, must have been night in Chicago. They were discussing the financial records of some company whose stock Martin wanted to buy. Hamasaki said he'd check something out and call him back."

"He's really proud of Martin. And of David and Michelle, too."

"He was proud of you, too." Hamlin cocked his head at her.

Storm heaved a sigh. "Hamasaki probably saved me from reform school. It had to be hard to take in an angry teenager when you had three kids of your own."

"You were angry?"

"Yeah." Storm went back to pushing the paper clips around on her desk.

"And Hamasaki tamed you?" Hamlin grinned at her, his eyebrows high arcs above gray-green eyes.

"Hardly." Storm suppressed a snort, but forged on to cover her discomfort. "He'd been hanging around in the background when my dad was dying. He didn't have to take me in, but it was funny, I felt like he really understood me." She frowned. "More than my dad. And my mom was long gone." She clamped her lips closed. She couldn't believe she'd said as much as she had.

Hamlin got up and examined a photo Storm had on her shelves. Storm's best friend Leila McShane and her son Robbie clowned on the beach. Hamlin avoided looking at Storm. "It was my dad who ditched out on my family."

"No kidding. How old were you?"

"About sixteen, the third of four kids. Unlike the others, I stayed home until I finished high school, used my anger to do well in school."

"You were smarter than I was."

"Maybe I was madder." Hamlin squinted into his coffee mug.

"I doubt it. My first day on O'ahu, I dyed my hair purple and got a tattoo."

"No shit. Show me."

"In your dreams." They both laughed.

"You didn't want to move to O'ahu?" Hamlin asked.

"No, I wanted to stay with Aunt Maile, my mother's sister. She's a healer on the Big Island. I wanted to learn to be a healer, too, and practice *lapa'au*, traditional Hawaiian medicine."

"But you came."

"Well, yeah." Storm frowned and carefully examined the handle of a coffee mug on the desk. "Your parents live here?"

"My mother lives in Detroit. So does my sister."

"And your dad?" Storm asked. Pain or contempt, she wasn't sure, streaked his face before he lowered his lips to his coffee cup.

A rap on the doorframe startled both of them. Edwin Wang stepped into the office. "I'm looking for some notes of Hamasaki's. That briefcase turned up yet?" He took off his gold-rimmed glasses and wiped them on a monogrammed handkerchief.

"No to the briefcase, but I've got some notes lying around. Most are at home."

"I need them," he said. "I have to call clients, tie up loose ends."

"I'll bring them in tomorrow."

"Thanks." Wang gave his glasses another wipe, then replaced them. "There's a meeting for partners and associates tomorrow afternoon. Storm, you're invited, too, since it concerns the repercussions of Hamasaki's death." Light glinted off the lenses of the glasses. "His office is unlocked now. You should look around and see if there's anything you want. Bitsy said she wanted the furniture and artwork, but to let you look over work-related items."

Hamlin drained his coffee and stood up. "I'm going to miss the old guy."

"Me, too," Storm said.

She packed her laptop and a few assorted papers into her carrying case, slung it over her shoulder, and headed down the corridor. She couldn't help but glance toward the closed door of Hamasaki's office.

She had gone out of her way to avoid entering his office since the morning she'd found him. A few times she needed one of his books, but she kept finding ways to keep from going in. The longer she put it off, the more skittish she got. Her feelings were confused. Part of her was frightened that she would relive finding him lifeless at his desk; the rest of her wanted to be alone in his sanctuary, where they had shared professional confidences, family secrets, and good jokes. By the time she pushed the elevator button to the underground garage, she had decided that she'd face it tomorrow morning.

Her battered '72 Volkswagen Beetle sat alone on the dark, sloping floor of the garage. That's what you get when you leave after six. A couple of weak fluorescent lights reflected from the oily concrete floor. Not even the maintenance people were around.

Storm rummaged in her bag for the car keys. A package of mints fell to the grimy floor and she let them roll under the car. Where the hell were those keys? She always put them in the outside pocket of the laptop case. Except, oh yeah. She had been carrying her purse when she drove back from the memorial service. Storm shifted the laptop case on her shoulder and felt like a pack mule readjusting her load. She swung her purse onto her right hip and concentrated on digging to the very bottom of the black bag.

She smelled him before she heard him, old garlic and strong, nervous sweat. When she heard the glutinous lisp of rubber soles immediately behind her, she twisted toward the noise, her hands still rooting in the depths of the handbag. He slammed her into the side of the old Beetle before she could raise her head.

Chapter 4

The car rocked with the impact and Storm hunched against its rounded side. She instinctively tried to protect her face and head, even though a pain so piercing that she was stupefied emanated from her frontal sinuses. A yowl that she didn't recognize as her own voice echoed through the garage.

The shock of the attack disabled her for a few moments and she curled her body around the laptop case and purse as if they were life preservers in a forty-foot sea. Then some primeval and irrational belligerence surfaced within her. Her face hurt like bloody hell and she was pissed. What kind of vicious desperado attacked women in parking garages? Especially one trying to get into a rusting '72 VW?

She brimmed with a snorting, bull-charging, red-hot rage that wanted to flatten this scum-sucking stump-dick. How dare this scrotum-faced bottom-feeder attack people he perceived as weaker? Storm roared and swung her purse hard at the side of a stocking cap mask. He grunted and made a grab for the purse with one hand while his other grappled for the laptop case.

This brought his foul-breathed visage to within about four inches of Storm's throbbing nose. His chest was nearly touching hers, but she knew (from a few close calls in her wilder teen years) that this was not a bad position in which to have a guy, his arms spread like a crucifix.

Awareness of the gratuitous pose gave her extra strength. With a yell muffled by closing sinuses, Storm hammered her right thigh to the vicinity of where his legs met and felt a satisfying mass of soft flesh.

The guy gargled with pain. He bent over and made gagging noises while he struggled with the balaclava he wore. One ear and a few tufts of black hair poked from an eyehole. He retched and heaved and clawed with one hand at his crotch and the other on the black mask.

This was a good start. Experience had taught Storm that most guys have an enormous advantage over women, even fit ones, in terms of brute strength. Women need to be faster and smarter. He could still have a surge of agony-driven fury and flatten her for good. She would be safer if he were blind, disoriented, and in disabling pain. Unconscious would be ideal.

She wasn't going to give up her brand new laptop easily. No fucking way. She'd just paid it off.

She raised her knee into the guy's face and felt what might have been a crunch. But the stocking mask padded his face and he was still standing, so she raised the laptop case over the back of his head. She had centered her weight over the bent-over figure to let him have it with whatever she could when a man's voice shouted from a distance.

"Storm!" Heels clattered across the concrete floor.

The attacker, doubled over, scuttled away like a crippled crustacean. Storm lowered the laptop and leaned against the car.

"You just saved my computer," she said to a gasping Hamlin.

He dropped his own briefcase and reached for her. "Jesus! Are you okay?"

Storm slumped against him for a minute. The adrenaline was fading and she was left with shaking knees and a face pounding with pain. Hamlin put his arm around her for support, but she struggled upright. "I'm all right. Really."

Hamlin held her at arm's length. "What's all over your blouse, then?"

Storm looked down. "Shit," she mumbled.

"Fortunately, it's only blood. I got my nose creamed like that once, too." Hamlin took her gently by the arm. "Come on, you need to be looked at. Who's your doctor?"

"Same as yours, probably. Remember, Wang got a corporate rate at that new HMO." Storm stopped and looked around. "Maybe we should call the police."

"Let's do it from my car."

Storm sagged in the leather bucket seat of Hamlin's Porsche. Her adrenaline rush had waned and all the energy had left her limbs. She didn't feel as if she could lift a finger, but when Hamlin handed her a cell phone, she took it and managed 911.

After explaining to the cops that they should meet her at the emergency room, she hung up and looked over at Hamlin, who was jamming his parking card into the exit slot for employees. "Mind if I make another call?" she asked. "I was supposed to meet my friend Leila and her son Robbie for dinner."

"Huh? I hope you're canceling."

She answered Hamlin with a mute nod and spoke into the phone. "Hi Leila, I got mugged." She could hear the fatigue in her own voice. "No, you should see the other guy. Really. Okay, I'll see you later." She handed the phone to Hamlin. "They're meeting us at the ER, too."

Leila and Robbie burst through the wide glass door to the emergency room two minutes behind Storm and Hamlin, who were standing at the admissions desk.

"Geez, Storm," Robbie said with wide eyes. "You look *bad.*"

Storm pulled away the ice pack an ER nurse had given her and peered at him from slitted eyes. That comment had multiple meanings in ten-year-old speak.

He grinned and touched the ice bag. "I mean, you're gonna have two black eyes. Way cool. I've only ever had one."

Leila dragged him away by the neck of his tee-shirt. "Tomorrow, you're going to look much bet—"

"Worse. You're gonna look like you went skydiving without a parachute." An ER doctor loomed over Storm and squinted at her. "Come here and sit down, please."

He poked at her nose and stopped a whole two seconds after she yelped and tears crowded her eyes. Then he shone a light into her blurred and sensitive orbs. She had to tell him how many fingers he held up and who the Vice-President was. "You'll start to look better in about a week. At least your nose isn't displaced. We don't have to set it."

So much for bedside manners. Storm tried to glare him down, give him stink-eye that would tell him what she thought of his alleged compassion, but he'd moved on to another patient in the hospital assembly line.

The police had waited through the examination to ask their questions. Storm spoke to them for a few minutes, trying to describe the attacker using acceptable language, and realized how little information she could give them. Black hair, she thought. Jeans, black tee-shirt with no distinguishing marks, tennis shoes, mask. She could picture his posture, the way her hands slipped on the sweat of his arms, the garlic on his breath, but how to get his essence across? From what she could tell the police, the attacker could be one of hundreds of guys.

The police were closing their notebooks when a handsome blond man in scrubs hustled into the room. She cracked a fat lip into a half-smile. "Rick. I thought you worked the morning shift. That's why you couldn't come to the memorial service."

"Yeah, but I got called back in. We're short-staffed. I heard what happened. You okay, babe? You look terrible." He stroked Storm's arm while he leaned back to assess the damage. Leila and Robbie moved off a few discreet steps.

"I'll take you home," he said.

Hamlin turned to leave. "Storm, I'll pick you up tomorrow for work if you like. About eight?"

"Sure." Storm nodded. "Thanks for all your help, Hamlin." She looked back at Rick, who was scrutinizing a bruise on her cheekbone. "Leila can give me a lift, Rick.

I'll call you tomorrow." Rick looked a bit disappointed, but Storm wanted the comfort of being with Leila and Robbie, who, unlike Rick, never commented on makeup or designer handbags. Right now she didn't want to worry that she looked a wreck. Heck, Robbie even seemed to admire it.

Leila avoided potholes and made all her turns slowly on the way home. She and Robbie tried to talk Storm into spending the night at their house, but Storm convinced Leila that all she wanted to do was go straight to her own bed.

Storm waved at them through her screen door, let in the cat, and marveled again at how Fang drooled a puddle on the floor at the mere sound of the can opener. When the cat was purring over her dish, she filled a glass at the sink and took a Tylenol with codeine, pondered but decided not to take two, then barely made it to her bedroom to pass out with an ice pack on her face.

When her radio alarm went off, she hauled herself upright and opened her gritty eyes. She felt as if weights had pressed her into the mattress during the entire night, but then maybe it was Fang. She was sitting on Storm's chest, rumbling like a '67 Corvette.

Storm let the cat out and stumbled back to the bathroom, where she moaned at the apparition in the mirror. Makeup wasn't going to fix this problem. Her nose was fat, her lips were scabby, and her dark eyes were highlighted in upside down arcs of fuchsia and violet. They gazed back with a hurt wonder that reminded Storm, with a pang, of her mother. She looked away quickly and took a very long shower.

Chapter 5

When Hamlin knocked on her door, Storm swung it open and grappled for her computer case, shoes, and keys, which were still scattered from last night. He looked right at her fat nose. "Remind me never to argue with you, counselor."

"Yeah, right." How in the world was she supposed to face people this morning? She wished she had at least pulled off the attacker's stocking mask. Then she'd have had a chance of hurting him in the courtroom and of taking him off the street.

"From what I saw, he forfeited fatherhood."

Storm started to grin at him, then grabbed at her split lip. "Ow, don't make me laugh."

Once at work, she crawled into the privacy of her office, closed the door and fired up the espresso machine. If she'd driven herself, she would have stopped at Leila's popular downtown bakery and bought a couple of scones, maybe even a wonderful, sugary Portuguese *malassada* or two to soothe her battered soul. She wished she'd never looked in the mirror this morning.

When Edwin Wang knocked on her door and it swung open, his jaw dropped. "Oh!"

"Don't worry, I look worse than I feel. Luckily, I don't have to see anyone today. Thought I'd go through Hamasaki's office like you suggested."

"Good idea. Glad to hear you're not hurt too badly." Wang took off his glasses and wiped them, probably to avoid looking at her face. "Did you bring in those papers we talked about?"

"I forgot! I'm sorry."

A little tic twitched under Wang's right eye. "Please have them tomorrow." He smoothed the front of his perfectly tailored Hong Kong suit and marched out the door.

Storm wilted in her chair and shook her head at her forgetfulness. She'd had a tough week, but it was time to stop letting it affect her work. She drained her coffee cup and was bracing herself to head down the hall to Hamasaki's office when Meredith Wo, the youngest of the partners, popped her head around the corner. Her eyes opened wide.

"Wow! What happened to you?" Meredith exclaimed.

"I got mugged in the parking lot," Storm said. "You picked a good week to be gone. When did you get back?"

"Last night. I'm lagged." Meredith's perfectly lined almond eyes became somber for a moment. "I'm going to miss Hamasaki. Geez, I couldn't believe it when Lorraine called me in Sydney."

Storm didn't feel up to commenting on Meredith's important travels for the firm. "Yeah. We just have to live every day with gusto."

Meredith raised a curved eyebrow. "Maybe you should take it easy on the gusto for a few days. Hey, have you found Hamasaki's briefcase yet? You know if there were any cases in there for me?"

"No, but he would have given any medical cases to you," Storm said. All the malpractice cases in the firm went to Meredith. Hamasaki hated them. He always said he couldn't tell the good guys from the bad and that everybody except the insurance companies and the lawyers lost. He preferred finding shelters for people's money by discovering loopholes in tax and estate laws. The IRS was a worthy opponent and his clients were mostly happy, healthy, and wealthy.

"Keep looking, okay?" Meredith tried to hide a glance at her watch. She squared her thin shoulders and strode from the room.

"Right." Storm stared at the doorway for a minute, then drew a deep breath and stood. She headed down the corridor to Hamasaki's office.

She forced herself to turn the doorknob and push open the door. Just inside, she stopped and let her eyes rove over the room. The police, who had come when she called the ambulance, had moved some things around, but the office looked essentially the same. She felt her neck relax. The worst was over. The room brought good memories instead of the bad one she'd feared. It felt different, though. Deserted. The mug he'd gripped was tipped over on the desktop. A pen lay in a dried stain that spread across the blotter.

Storm walked over to the desk and picked up the mug. He had a set of four in brightly painted ceramic from a trip to Tuscany. She wouldn't mind having those; they brought back happy memories. They'd shared his favorite teas together on many a late afternoon.

She wandered over to the glass-fronted antique bookcase that glinted in the sunlight streaming through the picture window. He treasured his old books, for their contents more than the fact that many of them were valuable first editions. She'd love to have some of his Mark Twain and Ogden Nash volumes, the ones they'd chuckled over together. Tears blurred her vision and she reached out for the back of a nearby chair. She needed more time. It would be better to look through the office with Aunt Bitsy when her grief was not so raw.

Storm wrote some notes down for Wang's sake and went to his office. "I'd like to go through some of his things when the family can get together, if you don't mind. Maybe next week?" she asked.

"Next week's fine. We won't start moving things around until then anyway," Wang said.

His secretary popped her head in the door. "Senator Maehara is here."

"See you at the meeting later, Storm," Wang said.

Storm walked away and once in her own office, closed the door and slumped at her desk. Hamasaki's office felt empty of his presence, the way a house does when the realtor shows it after the family has moved away. Dust motes were already dancing in his absence.

A few minutes later, Storm blotted at her eyes and took a deep breath. She walked back down the carpeted hall to Hamasaki's office where she gathered up the four gaudy mugs and took them back to a cluttered corner of her own domain. She closed the door, picked out a clean one, and made herself a cup of Hamasaki's favorite tea from his stash in the office kitchenette. With her feet up on her desk, she gazed at the back of the door and felt incredibly alone.

Chapter 6

The telephone interrupted her contemplation. "Hello," Storm mumbled.

"I called to see if we could cheer each other up."

"Martin! Can you get away for lunch?"

"That's why I called. David can drop me at the office in a half hour if you'll give me a lift home."

Martin was just what she needed. In the past, they had always been able to bring each other out of a slump or get one another out of trouble. When Martin was a junior in high school, he got suspended for designing book jackets that were funny as hell, and usually obscene. It was a huge family crisis: shame, shame. Hamasaki nearly sent Martin to military school. But Storm loved Martin's clever, raunchy sense of hilarity and she had finally been able to point out the humor in the situation to the distraught father.

It was the least she could do for Martin; she hadn't told Hamlin what happened after she got the tattoo. She never revealed to anyone that she had hidden a bottle of narcotic painkillers from her dad's long illness in her underwear drawer. The day after her sixteenth birthday, when she'd cut her hair a half-inch long and dyed it purple, Martin had burst into her new bedroom. He'd marched right by the unpacked boxes and tipped the glass of water she held over the pile of pills she held in her hand.

Forty minutes after his call, Martin pushed open the door. She dropped her pen, stood up, and threw her arms around him without the restraint they'd had to show at the memorial service. They held each other tighter than usual, then both stepped back, stifling tears.

He pressed on his eyes with a thumb and forefinger and punched her in the arm with the other fist. "Stop it. Dad wouldn't want us to be morose. He'd be happy to pre-cipitate a family reunion. By the way, you look like shit."

"Gee, thanks. You don't. Where'd you get that tan? Has Aunt Bitsy scolded you about it?"

As teenagers who liked to surf, Storm got very brown and Martin got freckles, which was unusual for a person of Japanese ancestry. The Nisei, or second generation Japanese in Hawai'i, still prided themselves on pure, white complexions. Even before the data was out on skin cancer, Bitsy had followed her children around with bottles of sunscreen.

He waved off her question with a self-conscious chuckle. "Hey, Chicago has beaches, too."

"I'm glad you've got time to enjoy them."

Martin took her arm. "How long do you have for lunch?"

"I can get away with an hour or so. The whole place is still moving in slow motion."

"Me, too."

A note in Martin's voice made Storm examine him more carefully. Though he was tan and healthy, his eyes seemed sad, preoccupied. His hair was short and neat. Hamasaki would have approved; he probably would have liked the tailored black kidskin vest, even over the neat black jeans. But he wouldn't have liked the two small gold rings in Martin's ear. She, however, smiled with approval. "I thought you'd be in a pin-striped suit."

"I am, sometimes. But a lot of our work is done by computer or phone." Martin marched her through the reception area. "Can we get outta here and find someplace near the ocean? Damn, I can't get enough of it."

"Let's walk down to Aloha Tower Marketplace. We can find a good sandwich there." She paused along with him when he stalled to take in the busy downtown square, with its people bustling about or perched eating their lunches beside the sculptures and fountains.

"I left for a couple of years and everything's bigger," Martin said.

"Yeah, the city's growing." They strolled down the bustling sidewalk toward the piers. In a few blocks, the aquamarine promise of water shone through a gap in the skyscrapers.

Arm in arm, they trotted across Ala Moana Boulevard at a crosswalk and entered a shaded parking lot overlooked by the old Aloha Tower. Martin looked up at the landmark, whose clocks on the square edifice gazed in four directions. "Can you believe this used to be the tallest building in the state? It's ten stories."

"No kidding. Last century?" Storm pulled him toward a line of eating establishments, all perched within twenty feet of the azure water that sucked at concrete pilings.

"No, only seventy years ago." He took a deep breath. "God, I've missed that salt smell."

Storm led him to an open sandwich shop and they took seats, which looked directly onto a shipping lane. A Coast Guard cutter glided by, lean and graceful.

"What about your beaches on Lake Michigan?" Storm squinted across the harbor.

"It's not the same. Smells, looks, tastes different. Look, there's a Chinese freighter—and a Russian one. In Chicago, the cargo ships are huge, named for big men who, like the ships, look a lot the same. Their sailors wear heavy black wool and the dark, cold aura of the North." He leaned back in his chair and let the sun bathe his face.

"How's work going?" Storm asked.

Martin sat up. "It's exciting. Certain industries are changing so fast, fortunes are being made in days."

"Yeah? You getting in on any of it?"

He shrugged. "Takes a lot of money, but there are opportunities out there. Dad and I were discussing one of the new health management organizations, which has a big branch here. They're diversifying into medical equipment sales. You know, PET scanners, dialysis machines. Mega-bucks stuff."

Storm straightened in her chair. "Is that Unimed?"

"Yeah, you know it?"

"I was there last night." She pointed to her black eyes. "They're the biggest game in town, and advertising everywhere." Storm cocked an eyebrow at him. "So he was looking into investing in them?"

Martin looked out at the water. "He wanted me to check on what kind of equipment Unimed was going to broker and where it was made. Things like that."

Storm sat back and crossed her legs. "Doing research before he bought the stock?"

Martin grunted. "Yeah, you know Dad. Wanted to check all the angles, first."

"What's the rush?" Storm asked.

Martin pressed his lips into a thin line. "Money is made and lost in seconds."

"And it's legal for you to invest in something like this?"

"Depends on who you get the scoop from. In this case, it's legit. You interested?"

"I'd like to take a look at some of the data."

"You sound like Dad." Martin chuckled.

"Without the money. I'm still paying off school loans."

A waiter cast his shadow over them and recited a list of seafood specials that made Storm decide she'd redis-covered her appetite. The food came quickly and they devoured mahi mahi sandwiches on Portuguese sweet-bread buns with homemade garlic basil mayonnaise.

The time passed too quickly. " I'd better take you home," Storm said. "I've got to get back to the office."

They strolled back to the office parking lot. When she drove into the sunlight from the dark underground ramp, Martin looked around her car and grinned. "Some things haven't changed. You not only have the same car that you had years ago, you have the same stuff in it." He craned his neck over the back of his seat. "Did you realize that you've got two tennis racquets, three tennis shoes...and what year is that *Time* Magazine—"

Storm threw a sock that had been on the front seat at him. "Now you sound like your dad."

She pulled to the front of Hamasaki's house and when Martin opened the door to the car, he threw the sock back at her. "You may be a slob, but I still love you. What are you doing for dinner? Michelle and David invited us to the restaurant."

Storm's smile faded. "You need time to yourselves."

"Come, now." Martin narrowed his eyes at her. "This is not the time to get aloof on me. I'll call you this afternoon."

Storm examined a hangnail on her thumb. "Okay, I'll talk to you later."

She backed out of the driveway. Sometimes the chattering of the Hamasaki family members, the intra-family bickering, the layered conversations without a rest between topics, tired her. She'd had too many years of solitude after her mother died. Her dad, already a quiet man, had grown more reticent in his grief and the pain of his illness and had left her to herself for long periods of time.

When Storm got back to the office, the receptionist handed her a message that Rick had called. "Call before two," it said.

Not a bad idea. She'd like to talk to someone not so close to the events of Hamasaki's death. Rick could give her some perspective and a strong shoulder to lean against.

She also had another motive. Rick was chief of physical therapy at Unimed. It was a new job; a few months ago, he'd been lured away from another Honolulu hospital. She'd like to hear his thoughts on patient care and the operation of the HMO. He'd have some insight into how fast the organization was growing, what the future plans of the place might be. Maybe she could get some inside information to share with Martin.

It was one-fifty and his answering machine picked up. No matter, he'd get the message when he got off the afternoon shift. "Hi Rick," she said to the tape recorder. "I just got your message. How 'bout if I come over tonight and grill? I'll bring a good wine and whatever the fresh catch is." She hung up and dug into some paper work on her desk.

At three o'clock, Storm went to the conference room. Ed Wang sat at the end of the long table. Meredith Wo, to his left, was reading through work she wouldn't set aside until the meeting began. She dug into an elegant tin candy box that sat next to her briefcase and popped a mint into her mouth without taking her eyes from the page. Wang ran his eyes over notes, but without Meredith's level of concentration. Sometimes when a meeting began, someone would have to nudge Meredith to drag her from whatever vivid personal injury scenario she visualized on those dry sheets of paper.

Meredith was probably the most disciplined person Storm had ever met. She was only a few years older than Storm and was the firm's youngest partner and possibly its highest biller. Storm admired her, but wasn't sure if she would have sacrificed her own adventures for the same professional advancement.

Cyril Cunningham, the other senior partner, had draped his suit coat across the back of the chair to Wang's right, yet he stood, leaning against the windowsill. The afternoon light gleamed in his silver hair and intensified his tanned, craggy face. He smiled at Storm when she entered the room.

Wang stood, motioned Storm and a couple of the associates into chairs, then began the meeting. He told the group that a formal reading of Hamasaki's will would be done with the family the next morning, but that Hamasaki had written certain stipulations for the benefit of the firm, in addition to the formal partnership agreement, to be read in the event of his death.

Wang's face was smooth as an eggshell. He read paragraphs that ensured Storm's position as a law clerk until she had passed the bar. At that time, the firm was to consider her employment as an associate. Nice try, Uncle Miles, she thought. Except that no one here is bound legally by this document and you, my main defender, are gone.

Lorraine was to stay employed until her seventieth birthday or until she wanted to retire, whichever came first. Certain cases, procedures, and employment details were discussed. He even recommended a system of checks and balances among the partners. At the conclusion, everyone in the room seemed thoughtful. They went back to their offices with little interaction.

Storm waited for Wang. "When did he write this?"

Wang looked down at the cover sheet. "About two months ago. Not long after you were hired as a full-time clerk." He put the papers into a file folder. "He has, I mean had, some good ideas."

"Yes, he understood a lot about people's needs."

Wang's hands stopped and he looked carefully at Storm's face. "I agree."

Storm dragged her feet down the corridor to her office. For the last couple of years, she had worked part-time at the firm to defray law school expenses. She was the gopher, paper-filer, copier, and firm librarian. Two months ago, she had begun to work full-time, with real benefits like health insurance. Yet Uncle Miles had thought it necessary to issue a directive protecting her and Lorraine, and implementing certain procedures at the firm. Storm had never seen any interpersonal fireworks at the firm, but now she wondered if Hamasaki had known about competition and insecurities among the partners that were hidden from the staff.

Do lawyers learn to anticipate the unexpected, cover themselves for contingencies? Maybe the elderly begin to prepare for their absence as if they were putting the dog at the vet's for a long vacation. Or had Hamasaki known, somehow, that his days were limited?

Chapter 7

Storm was buried in files when the phone jerked her attention to the present. She nearly knocked over a cup of cold coffee in her grab for the offending receiver.

It was only Martin's voice on the line that kept her from barking with impatience at the interruption. "I'm calling to remind you of your dinner date."

"Would you think I was a rat if I begged off tonight? I'm still full from lunch and if I don't get in touch with my boyfriend, he'll forget my name."

"He's not worth your time if he does," Martin said. "But okay. Mom's pretty tired. I think it'll be a quick bite."

"You know Cunningham is going to read the will tomorrow?" Storm asked.

"Right. We'll see you at ten-thirty, then?"

"You bet." Storm hung up and looked at her watch. It was five-fifteen and her eyes burned from reading and fatigue. She picked up the phone and dialed Rick's number. His answering machine picked up again and she told it that she'd be there around six-thirty. All he needed to do was heat up the grill.

Storm looked out her small window toward the Waianae mountain range, where the sun flamed vermilion and lavender in its descent to the ocean. She'd see the Hamasaki family in the morning. It would be nice to see Rick, get away from the office reminders of Hamasaki's death.

Storm stuffed papers into her computer case, hit the lights, and paused in the hallway. The light was on under Meredith Wo's door and Hamlin's. Hamlin emerged from his office and waved to her, then turned in the opposite direction toward Wo's office. He had the sleeves of his white dress shirt rolled up and the collar unbuttoned. Storm watched the door close on his tailored behind. Not bad. She snorted softly at her own reaction. Driving home, she reflected, not for the first time, on how a brush with death forged attachments to the basic functions of life. The sight of a nice *ōkole*, like Hamlin's backside disappearing into Wo's office, could give a soul an infusion of juice.

Storm picked her footing along the flagstones to the cottage and watched Fang trot toward her. She grinned at the cat. Having a warm fuzzy greet her after work was pretty nice, even if it was hungry. "Hey, girl." Storm leaned down to stroke the purring creature.

The cat followed her into the house and headed directly for the kitchen. Storm stopped in the sitting room, where she dumped her laptop and satchel on the sofa and noted with relief that Uncle Miles' folder sat on the floor by her reading chair.

She hustled into the kitchen, where the cat stood, meowing in front of the refrigerator door. "Good grief, I'm coming." Storm swung open the refrigerator door. The half-full milk carton definitely smelled funky, but behind it hid a chunk of cheddar. Except for one cracked and dry side, it was in pretty good shape. "You'll have to work on this until I get home with some real food." She put it down in front of the cat.

"Mrrowww." Fang picked up the cheese and walked off to a corner of the kitchen, where she lay down with the orange cube between her paws and began to gnaw. Crumbs scattered around her.

"Out." Storm held open the front door. The cat, cheese morsel clamped between her teeth and drool seeping down her lower jaw, ambled outside.

Storm changed into a dark red silk tank top and a pair of black jeans. She looped a jade pendant on a black silk cord around her neck and seized her purse. When the phone rang, she considered letting her answering machine get it, then picked it up. "Hello?"

No answer. Probably someone on a cell phone who forgot that Diamond Head blocked transmission of radio waves. Storm grabbed her keys and headed for the car. Whoever it was could try again and leave a message.

At the grocery, Storm picked up a chocolate dobash cake, put it at the far end of the cart where she wouldn't be tempted to sample the frosting, then headed for the fresh fish counter. A big chunk of ahi sat on ice. She had the butcher cut two filets, then picked up a bottle of Yoshida's Teriyaki sauce on the way to the produce section. Rick would have rice; all she needed to get were green onions and sesame seeds for the teriyaki sauce, arugula and avocado for a fresh salad. Oh yeah, that would be good with some mandarin orange slices and she'd better get some sesame oil and balsamic vinegar for the dressing. Her own vinaigrette would be better than the three bottles of Ranch that Rick usually had in his fridge.

She went to the wine section of the store and faltered. She wasn't confident in choosing wine and didn't have time to call Leila. With a touch of frustration, she put a bottle of Chardonnay and a Merlot in her basket and walked away. Almost at the checkout stand, Storm made a U-turn and headed for the pet aisle. She had nearly forgotten Fang.

Fifteen minutes later, Storm was climbing the stairs to Rick's house in upper Makiki, arms laden with dinner supplies. He shared the house with a couple and their young daughter; they had the lower floor and he had the upper, complete with a small kitchen of his own. She had been a little worried that he had not retrieved her message after work, but his car was sitting out front.

When Storm knocked at the door, all was still. She waited a moment, knocked again, then opened the door and walked inside to the kitchen. "Rick?" she called out. Maybe he'd lain down for a nap. No answer, but there was a big pot of chili simmering on the stove. It smelled great, and Storm set her groceries down and peered at it, momentarily disappointed. Oh well. Chili was better the next day. They could still cook the filets.

"Rick? Hello?" she said. She wandered a few steps into the hallway and heard the sound of the shower.

When she heard a high-pitched giggle, Storm stopped dead. There must be some explanation. Maybe the family below was having a plumbing problem and borrowed Rick's facilities. She walked six more feet to the bedroom, nearly tripping over lacy underwear lying on top of some flowered garment and a man's shirt just outside the door.

Storm peeked inside, then stopped. She felt as if someone had hit her in the chest with a bag of hot charcoal. The king-sized bed was unmade, blankets were strewn to the floor, and twisted sheets formed a rumpled playground. Sweat and sex perfumed the air.

Storm ran back to the kitchen and braced herself against the counter. Her shaking elbow knocked the grocery bag against the hot chili pot. The merlot bottle bounced to the floor and its long neck broke off at the shoulders. Red wine bled across the linoleum.

Storm pushed the remaining groceries across the counter, away from the stove, and looked at the chili pot with narrowed eyes. She clenched her teeth and pulled the ladle out of the pan. Some of the hot sauce dribbled across her left arm, and she flung the ladle toward the sink with a yelp. Beans scattered along the path of the clattering utensil. Sauce splattered as high as the white cabinets.

Fury blotted out all thought except confronting the self-serving, two-timing, lie-spewing boob she'd called a boyfriend. She picked up two oven mitts from beside the stove and grabbed the handles of the big kettle. The mitts were a bit thin and the heat from the pot stung, but the pain was just bearable and it drove her on, down the hall, past the noisy, steam-filled bathroom, to the bedroom.

Her hands were shaking so badly that when she paused in the doorway, chili slopped over the side of the kettle onto the lovers' underwear and onto a corner of the trailing sheet. Until that moment, she was mad as a screaming teakettle, but without a plan. She'd had some vague concept about announcing to Rick that she'd come to dinner, also.

The chunky blotch on the sheet triggered a notion. She marched to the bed and upended the chili over the middle of the mattress. Lumpy sauce dribbled across the clothes and continued to the bedding on the floor. With a final burst of wrath, she flung the pot onto the mess and hurled the mitts on top of the steaming pile.

"Take that, you red-hot asshole!" She stomped down the hall. At the door, her hands trembled so badly that she required three slippery tries at the doorknob. A couple of kidney beans stuck, crushed, on the white paint of the door. Halfway down the stairs, she turned and stormed back into the ravaged kitchen, gathered the remains of her groceries, and slammed out again.

Two miles and ten minutes later, stuck in rush hour traffic on H-1, Storm burst into tears. She cried all the way to the Koko Head exit, barely keeping her eyelids apart so she could see the line of red-starred brake lights in front of her.

This was too much on top of Uncle Miles' death. How could Rick betray her on the heels of Uncle Miles' desertion? Desertion? A whiff of self-knowledge brushed her. The raging tears were more for Uncle Miles than for Rick. And they came from even deeper, from when her mother had left.

Lani Kayama's desperate, tear-spotted note of explanation to a twelve-year-old Storm couldn't wring understanding from a forsaken adolescent. Storm, the adult, still felt the wounds and anger of abandonment.

From Twelfth Avenue to Diamond Head Road, Storm drew deep, shuddering breaths. When her eyes stopped streaming, she clenched the steering wheel and forced herself to count twelve more deep breaths.

What was commitment, anyway? Hadn't Rick deserved that mess? Was it just her idealistic fancy that once you slept with someone, you were faithful until at least telling

the other person otherwise? And what was the commitment of a parent to a child?

Her mind skittered around that thought and she gladly
steered the car to the curb in front of her home. Maybe
she had been too buried in law books to keep abreast of
social conventions among the single crowd.

She was feeling a touch of remorse about the chili.
Maybe it would have been better to fling open the bathroom door and watch them cope with her contemptuous
glare. Some choice expressions flitted through her mind.
She could always think of something she should have said
after the moment. In fact, she could be brilliant a day later.

Storm was stumbling along the flagstones to her door
when Fang met her halfway, wailing. "Oh, yeah, the
groceries. I promised you cat food for dinner." Storm
plodded back to her car, opened the passenger's door, and
rummaged around in the front seat. In her anger, she had
thrown the grocery bags on top of one another and items
now rolled around on the floor of the car. Storm dug out
the food and carefully stacked everything into the bags
so the greens wouldn't be any more crushed than they
already were. The cake box had frosting stuck all over the
cellophane lid. Maybe she'd just eat the bloody cake for
dinner, her hips be damned.

Rational behavior was returning in sporadic bursts,
although she stamped up the walk with anger toward Rick
in every footfall. Behind her, in the jungle of plumeria and
papaya trees that made up her front yard, she heard a
door slam. The neighbors traveled so much, she never
could keep track of their comings and goings. Fang
followed about six feet behind. As Storm made her way
to the door, the cat bawled again, louder.

"Don't be pushy. I'm not in the mood." Hands loaded,
she swiped at her cheek with a shoulder to satisfy the itch
of a droplet of sweat running down the side of her face.

The cat turned and trotted away from the house, looked
back, and jogged back to Storm. She meowed again,
drawing out the noise like an alley cat.

"I told you, stop scolding." Storm felt around for her house keys, glad that she'd stopped earlier to change her clothes and get out of her heeled pumps. The silk of her shirt clung to her back and sides.

The cat got on the front step and wailed. Storm set down one bag and opened the outside screen door. It wasn't until she had the keys pointed toward the lock of the inside door that she realized it already stood ajar.

She froze, trying to recall what she'd done when she'd left. She'd locked the door. Fang was quiet, now, and looked up at her with eyes that glowed yellow in the fading light.

Chapter 8

"Let's get the hell out of here," Storm said to the cat. She set the grocery bags down next to the front door and jogged back to the car.

She drove straight to Leila's house, where Robbie gleefully called 911. Leila insisted on going back with Storm to meet the police.

Two cops arrived and asked Storm, Leila, and Robbie to wait outside for a few moments. After about five minutes, they called for Storm. "He's gone. Take a look around and see if anything is missing. We'll dust for prints, but unless the kid's got a record, it won't do us much good," the younger man told her.

"Kid?"

"Yeah, break-ins like these, it's usually kids lookin' for money, jewelry, something they can sell quick."

Storm stared at him. She'd mentioned the mugging yesterday, but neither cop seemed to think this event was related to it. "Have there been other burglaries on my block?"

"We'll check, ma'am." He turned to one of the uniforms that had just arrived and sent her off to poll the neighbors. "Ask if they saw any unfamiliar cars or kids wandering around."

Storm walked around her living room in a daze. The emotional slam of the last hour made it hard for her to see details. What she felt most strongly was that the safe ambiance of her home had been defiled. Furniture still sat where it should, but the room was growing dark and though the temperature was near eighty, the place felt chilled.

The police began to pack up their tools and fingerprint powder. They told Storm that the burglar had picked the lock, a bit unusual for kids, but these things were happening more these days. The older policeman, who talked a stream while he filled out his report, expounded on the availability of catalogues and websites that sold lock picks, night scopes, and whatever espionage gear your everyday maniac desired. He clucked his tongue and wagged his head from side to side, then pushed his glasses up on his nose and recorded a few more notes. A few minutes later, the police left with a promise to call Storm if they got any fingerprint matches or leads. She was to call them if she noticed anything missing.

Storm and Leila looked at each other across the violated living room. "Leila, I don't like this. Not after yesterday."

"You're going to spend the night with us," Leila said. "Robbie, wait." He was heading down the short hall to the bathroom.

"No one's here, Leila. The police checked everywhere." Storm's voice was a monotone and she stood unmoving by the sofa. "I think I will spend the night with you guys, though."

"Let's see if anything's missing, then we'll go," Leila said.

Storm walked back to her bedroom. Drawers were dumped on the floor and her jewelry box was upended so that her little pile of costume jewelry looked like a tray at the Salvation Army thrift shop.

She felt the need to make noise and shouted back to Leila. "Take a look around the living room again, will you? Is the VCR still there? It's brand new."

Robbie came out of the bathroom, the toilet flushing behind him. "No one was in there. You left the top off your toothpaste."

When Storm came out of the bedroom, Leila was standing in the living room again. "Nothing missing in the kitchen and your VCR is right where it should be. Looks like you scared him off."

Storm stood next to her friend, frowning. "Yeah, maybe. The three twenties I left on the dresser are gone, but I dropped my work clothes in kind of a heap on the floor and my good pearls are still at the bottom of the pile." She looked around. "I left my laptop in the car and...Hey! The file's gone!"

"What?" Leila and Robbie looked at her with wide eyes.

"I brought home some of Uncle Miles's papers. They were lying on the floor in a folder." She pointed to the spot on the sisal rug next to her reading chair.

"You sure?" Robbie asked.

"Positive. I saw them when I came home from work earlier." Storm dropped to the floor, cross-legged, and sank her head between her hands. "Wang is going to fire my ass."

"Just your ass?"

"Robbie!" Leila barked at her son. "Go watch TV." She turned her attention back to Storm. "We need to call the cops back."

"This has been a really shitty day." Storm stomped toward the kitchen phone and tried to ignore the buzz that was beginning in her ears.

She called the police and reported the missing file, then came back into the living room and dropped into a chair. "They're going to call me back." She rubbed her temples. "Wanna know how bad my day has been? I walked into Rick's apartment this evening and he had another woman there."

"No!" Leila's eyes grew round. Both she and Robbie gaped at Storm, then Leila turned up the TV, grabbed Storm's arm, and dragged her into the kitchen.

"That sonofabitch," Leila hissed. "When did this happen?"

"Right before I got home."

"I guess he didn't know you were coming. Rick, that is."

"No, but he was." Storm tried to laugh, but her voice wavered. "Bad joke. My night for surprising people, huh?" She turned away, opened the refrigerator and rummaged inside, clinking bottles together. Leila stared at her.

Storm mumbled inside of the refrigerator. "Want a glass of wine? I could use some. Matter of fact, I could use some food. You won't believe what I did—"

The phone interrupted her. Storm reached for the receiver at the same time that someone knocked on the door. Leila went to the door and got there with Robbie.

"Hi. I met you at the hospital last night." Hamlin offered his hand to Leila, then Robbie. "Is Storm all right? I was jogging and saw police cars outside."

"She's okay. Have a seat, I'll let her tell you about it. She's on the phone." Leila led him to the living room.

Two minutes later, Storm walked in. "Hi, Hamlin. Want a drink?" Storm set the bottle down. Three stemmed glasses rattled in her hands. Hamlin took them from her, sat down on the sofa next to Leila as if he'd been there a dozen times, and pulled the cork.

Storm dropped into a chair and looked at Hamlin and Leila. The buzzing in her ears was louder and her head was starting to ache since talking to the cop, who had rattled papers over the phone, grunted a few syllables, and said goodbye.

Storm's eyes traveled back to Hamlin. He was in running shorts and was answering a question Leila had apparently asked him. Leila's face was tight and pale. Her gaze went back and forth between Storm and Hamlin like a spectator at a tennis match, oblivious to the fact that Robbie was glued to *The Simpsons*, which she didn't allow him to watch.

Storm wanted to laugh at the absurdity of the situation. This could not be her life; she was boring. She was the type who didn't even know when her boyfriend was cheating on her. Funny that Hamlin had shown up when he did. Those legs were something. They could go a long way to cheer a woman up.

Leila's hand, offering a glass of wine, distracted Storm from the legs. Storm reached out and smiled in what she hoped was a pleasant expression of coping. If she got the giggles now, Leila would have her back at the hospital, but in the psychiatric ward. She took a deep breath and kept her eyes above Hamlin's shoulders. "Did Leila tell you that some papers were stolen?" She thought she sounded as if she were speaking down a long pipe, but Leila and Hamlin didn't seem to notice.

"Yes." Hamlin poured a glass for himself.

Storm repeated that the only thing she could find missing was sixty dollars and the file. "The cops think it's a bunch of kids. They think I frightened them away before they were finished."

"Maybe," Hamlin said.

"Why would kids want a bunch of papers?" Leila asked.

Hamlin shrugged. "The police are probably asking themselves the same question. Problem is, unless there's something to tie this burglary to others, or unless the investigator has some solid clues as to who broke in, he can't justify an allotment of manpower to look into what looks like a random B & E. They've got murders, arson, and accidents to check out, too."

"So I'm on my own." Storm's face hardened.

"Not entirely. They'll run prints and see what turns up. They're just spread a little thin." Hamlin grinned at her. "You have Leila and me."

This is when she might have at least chuckled, but Storm's sense of humor had departed like Fang fleeing the neighbor's rottweiler. She took a healthy belt of her wine and didn't even remember to enjoy his legs. This whole week was looking like hell. Her headache and ear buzz fused into a piercing throb.

"What were those papers anyway?" Hamlin asked.

"Nothing I saw looked important." She looked at Hamlin. He knew that Hamasaki handled sensitive issues. "Some beef about Hamasaki's neighbor's seawall and some notes on the prices of old folks' homes." Storm sighed. There had been two hand-scribbled, barely legible pages breaking down the cost of private home care for the elderly versus one of the swanky local nursing homes and a note with Sidney O'Toole's name and some phone numbers. Storm hadn't looked twice at that one. O'Toole was his golf partner, after all.

"And you've had them since he died?"

"Yeah." Storm did not feel like sharing the fact that Hamasaki had given them to her last Friday. She was supposed to have discussed them with him Monday morning. However, she'd spent the night at Rick's after a dinner with a bit of wine and hadn't finished reading them. As a consequence, she'd been a little late to the office Monday. When she arrived, she'd found Hamasaki cold in his chair. Even though the medical examiner stated that Hamasaki died Sunday night, Storm felt guilty. And she still hadn't gone through all of the papers as carefully as she'd have liked.

Leila set her wineglass down on the coffee table with a click. "You should move in with us for a while."

"Good idea," Hamlin said. "Stay with Leila for a few nights. You'll feel better."

Robbie walked over to them with Fang in his arms. *The Simpsons* must be over.

Leila looked at her watch. "It's nine o'clock. Storm, I'll help you pack some things. We'll load your car and you can follow us home."

Hamlin stood and gathered the glasses. "I'll rinse these for you." He gave Storm's shoulder a squeeze with his free hand. "Call me if you need help, okay?" He looked over at Leila. "You, too."

"I'll go throw a few things in a bag," Storm said.

When Storm came out of the bedroom, Robbie was asleep on the couch. Lying on his tummy was Fang, her head in the curve of Robbie's neck. Storm could hear the cat's purr from across the room. "You mind if we bring the cat, too?" She twisted her mouth into a smile.

"Wouldn't think of leaving her," Leila said. "After the initial shock, Pua will enjoy the company." Leila referred to her aging English bulldog.

Storm followed Leila and her drowsy passenger to Leila's house, several miles away on one of O'ahu's mountain ridges. Once they tucked Robbie in, Leila insisted that Storm have a sandwich. The women sat together, Storm hunched over a plate, her gaze out the window on the twinkling lights of the city below.

"I have to tell you something. Rick might call here when he can't find me at my place."

"Huh?" Leila snorted. "After what that asshole's done—"

Storm's words were muffled by bread and she kept her eyes on her plate.

"Chili?" Leila's eyes widened. "I love it!"

Storm peered up at her friend and let a smile twitch the corners of her lips. "Yeah."

Leila chuckled. "Why didn't I ever think of that?"

"Their underwear was in the hall. Like they couldn't wait." Storm giggled. "I dropped a big blob on her sexy g-string. That was an accident, but it gave me the idea."

Leila grinned. "You did the bed?"

Storm's face was bright red. "Just in case they were planning to return."

Leila threw her head back and guffawed.

Storm sputtered on breadcrumbs. "I was so mad I acted like Pua playing tug-of-war. You know, when her eyes roll back in her head?"

Leila wiped her eyes. "Don't ever get mad at me, okay?"

"What do you think she'll do?"

"The new girlfriend? If she's got any brains, she'll call a cab and never look back."

"He'll tell her he's being stalked."

"So what?" Leila took Storm's empty plate to the sink.

Storm followed with the glass and noticed that the buzzing in her ears and the headache were nearly gone. "Says a lot for my intelligence."

Leila laughed again. "I've been there, too." She gave Storm a push. "We've got to get to bed, or we'll be zombies tomorrow. Especially after the day you've had."

Storm nodded her head in agreement. As she brushed her teeth, she wondered who would risk breaking and entering for a lousy sixty bucks and a bunch of trivial papers. On top of Uncle Miles's death, the burglary of her house and his papers weighed on Storm. She swallowed a hard knot in her throat and remembered how Uncle Miles had looked at his desk, as if he were asleep. Had death crept upon him without any warning whatsoever?

Chapter 9

Storm slept like she'd been drugged and woke to the smell of rich coffee. Six-thirty and she could hear water running. Plenty of time for a shower and a cup of coffee with Leila before she headed out. Maybe she would have two. She was going to have to face Wang and tell him that not only had Hamasaki's briefcase not turned up, the file he'd requested for the last two days had been stolen.

When Storm walked into the office, the receptionist gave her a big grin. "There's a packet on your desk," she said.

Storm nearly dropped her laptop. "Good news or bad? I can hardly stand any more surprises."

The woman's expression was reassuring. "We think it's good," she answered.

We? Storm hurried into her office and dumped her computer case and files on a chair. A flat manila envelope with the Hawai'i State Bar Association return address was positioned so that when she sat down, she couldn't miss it. Storm didn't bother to sit down. She ripped it open and looked at her bar certification with tears pooling in her eyes. She was a real lawyer, now. If only Uncle Miles could have seen it. Well, who knows, maybe he could. Her lips curved into a smile that quivered a little bit.

A soft knock on the doorframe caused her to look up. Hamlin was standing just outside the office with two coffee mugs in his hands. "I would have brought champagne, but I'd fall asleep during this morning's deposition.

Then I had the idea you might let me treat you after work. So I brought coffee."

"How'd you know it was good news?"

"It's like college. When you don't get in, you get one of those skinny white envelopes." He cocked an eyebrow at her. "So what do you say?" He handed her a mug.

"Yeah, that sounds good." Storm sat down on top of a stack of papers on her chair. She stood up. "What time?"

"Come get me when you're done." Hamlin raised his mug to her and left.

Storm pulled a sheaf of papers from her in-box that one of the partners had left for her to research. When someone knocked on the door, she came up for air, wondering if she'd forgotten an appointment.

Wang walked into her office. "I wanted to extend my congratulations. We're all proud of you."

"Thanks." Storm set her mug down on her desk and squared her shoulders. "Mr. Wang, my house was broken into last night and Hamasaki's files were stolen. I—I'm sorry."

A look of what might have been fright on Wang's face turned to concern. "Were you home? Was anything else stolen?"

"Some money."

"Any idea who did it?" he asked.

"The police think it was addicts."

Wang nodded. "Probably. You should get your locks changed. Get dead bolts, too." He turned to go, then stopped. "The Hamasaki family is meeting in forty-five minutes for the reading of the will."

Storm gave him a few seconds to get down the hall, then sagged in her chair with relief. She'd given him the bad news without even setting his tic off.

The phone dislodged her thoughts and a voice with a businesslike tone identified himself as Roy Tam. The name sounded familiar. Oh yeah, Tam was the head of a local labor union. Storm sat up straighter.

"Ms. Kayama, I wanted to let you know how sorry we are about Miles Hamasaki's death. We're sending a donation in his memory to a foundation Bitsy...er, Mrs. Hamasaki named."

"Thanks for your concern, Mr. Tam. It's been quite a shock."

"Of course," Tam said. Storm could hear him rattling papers. "Hamasaki was working with us on a bid for a highway renovation out by the airport. I'd like you to take over the job, if you feel up to it."

Storm set her coffee cup down, sloshing some onto her desk. She knew the case; Hamasaki had shown her some of the proposals. "Are you sure you don't want a lawyer with more experience?"

"This is straightforward. You've got to start somewhere."

"Thanks, Mr. Tam. Sure, yes. I'll give it my full attention."

Storm hung up the phone very carefully, got up, closed her door, and did a dance around the desk. Then she did the Hallelujah Chorus under her breath. Either Uncle Miles or Aunt Bitsy had pointed some heavies in her direction. A second later, Storm stopped and gazed across the small room.

Tam must know that she passed the bar. The coconut wireless was operating at full tilt and the speed of it was making her dizzy. Uncle Miles had taught her that information was power. Even Hamlin had known about the theft of the file minutes after she'd discovered it. She needed to pay more attention to what the people around her were doing.

She had a half-hour before the reading of the will. With a pencil, she first doodled a comical picture of Fang, then wrote down the subjects of the papers in Hamasaki's file: seawall, nursing homes, Dr. O'Toole's phone numbers. None of these notes seemed significant. What had she missed in that file folder?

Storm sketched leafy vines between the three topics. Whom could she trust to keep her confidence, yet share information? Storm squinted into the distance; a gray head passed by her partially open door. Lorraine looked a little better than she had at Wednesday's memorial service, though she had aged a decade in the last five days. But Lorraine would help, if not for Storm's sake alone, then out of loyalty to Hamasaki.

Someone tapped on the frame of Storm's door. Meredith Wo peeked around the corner. "I need to ask you some questions," she said.

"Sure."

Wo perched on the edge of the seat facing Storm's desk and held out a little tin of imported candies. "Mint?"

"Sure, thanks." Storm popped the hard sphere into her mouth and regarded Meredith. The woman seemed fidgety. Her hair was limp and she had a pimple on her shiny nose. She looked like she was working too hard. Not that Storm felt cocky; Meredith earned a few hundred grand a year and didn't have two black eyes.

Wo crunched one of the candies between her teeth. "You're going to the reading of the will, aren't you?"

Storm glanced at her watch and nodded.

"Have you seen it? When he was alive?"

"Not recently, but I don't expect many surprises. Uncle Miles was straightforward about money. He wanted all his kids to be economically self-sufficient."

"That sounds like him." Wo also looked at her watch. "Did Hamasaki ever tell you about a cancer patient? I can't remember the person's name and was hoping you might know."

"A malpractice case?"

"I don't know. Hamasaki told me he wanted me to look over some medical charts on a guy. I got the impression he didn't know if the patient had a case or not." She sighed. "I never heard any more about it."

"I haven't seen a reference to a patient in any of his papers." Storm thought of the paper with Dr. O'Toole's name and phone numbers, but didn't mention it. Not only had Hamasaki and O'Toole been old friends who golfed together twice a week, but Hamasaki had helped O'Toole with a rancorous divorce a few years ago. The notes could refer to anything.

Wo got up to go. "I guess it was one of Hamasaki's passing thoughts."

"Wish I knew something." Storm got up and walked down the hall with her. Wo's office was across the corridor from the conference room.

Wo looked sideways at Storm. "How's Cunningham treating you?" she asked.

"He hardly ever talks to me. Wang can be a little tough, though," Storm said.

"He's a detail man." Wo nodded toward the room. "Looks like everyone's there. I'll see you later." She headed into her own office and closed the door.

Storm entered the conference room, gave Aunt Bitsy a hug and shared embraces with Michelle. She had to explain her black eyes to the women. David stood up and nodded while Martin pulled the chair out next to his.

Lorraine fussed in the corner with a coffee and teacart, and when Cunningham entered, she headed toward the door. Cunningham smoothed one side of his carefully arranged silver hair and motioned Lorraine to an empty chair. "Please join us," he said. "You're mentioned in the will, also." He stood at the end of the long table and smiled down on the small group. "Let's get started. It's not a complicated will and most of you probably know what's in it."

For Storm, the will held a few surprises, mostly good ones. The first was that Hamasaki's estate was bigger than she had expected. With the oceanfront home, which had appreciated astronomically over the last twenty years, he left his wife a combination of assets worth over twenty million dollars. His pension fund, mostly in blue-chip stocks, was worth about four million and he also had quite a bit tied up in commercial real estate properties.

Storm sat back in her chair, a little smile on her face. He'd mentioned interest in a few shopping centers and office buildings, but she hadn't been paying full attention to his low-level flow of information. He had also left Lorraine ten thousand a year in a mutual fund for the three decades of what he called their "partnership." It was worth well over a million dollars, now.

Storm knew that when the Hamasakis took her in at sixteen, they had established a trust fund for her as they had for each of their natural children. David's, Michelle's, and Martin's were started at birth and the Hamasakis had put together well-rounded portfolios that had appreciated over the years to hundreds of thousands of dollars per child. Storm's, of course, was smaller than the others' because it had been started later, but she still was left almost two hundred grand.

When Cunningham read the dollar amounts of the funds, everyone smiled with pleasant surprise. It's hard not to be pleased when someone bequeaths you a small fortune, no matter what the circumstances. Cunningham stifled a smug smile as the bearer of good news and read the last sentence about the trusts. "The funds will be available to each individual on his or her fortieth birthday."

His lips were parted to continue, but David bounced to his feet, shaking the table and the floor with his weighty momentum. "Fuck!" He struck the table with both fists, which spilled coffee that everyone was too stunned to notice. Then he stomped to the window and stood facing the glass, arms folded across his belly. Michelle chewed on her lip and looked at Bitsy with tear-glazed eyes.

Storm followed Michelle's gaze to Bitsy's face. Bitsy looked into her lap and murmured, "Oh, dear." Martin looked pale and still. Storm looked back at Cunningham, who tried not to appear perplexed.

David caught her movement in his peripheral vision. He jerked his head toward her and a shock of black hair fell into one eye. He snarled at Storm. "*You* wouldn't understand."

Bitsy still stared at her lap, so Storm looked at Martin. His eyes were black with anger, and he shook his head at her, apparently in warning. Cunningham gazed around the room at each of them. A strand of his silver hair had fallen across his forehead, but he pushed it back with a small snort. With utmost dignity, he read the last sentences of the will, technicalities nobody listened to. Then he snapped his briefcase closed and strode from the room.

Lorraine slipped out with him. Bitsy Hamasaki and her three children clustered at the window with their backs to Storm.

Storm sat stunned in her chair for a second, then duplicated Cunningham's and Lorraine's swift exits. A headache pounded behind her left eye. She headed for the solitude of her office cubbyhole.

Chapter 10

Storm dropped into her office chair and stared at the back of the door she'd closed carefully behind her. She'd always been sensitive to the fact that she wasn't a full-fledged member of the family. Still, she had at least felt like she could share her problems with them and they would do the same. But it appeared that Hamasaki had been the glue that held her in the family orbit.

Storm picked up the phone. "Hi, Lorraine. Can you come to my office?"

Lorraine sounded worn and a little apprehensive, but she was at the door in less than a minute. She looked like she hadn't slept in the last week. Her hair was in disarray and her eyes had lost their light. She looked like an ill, elderly woman.

Storm offered the older woman the more comfortable desk chair, which she had pulled to face the other chair in the room. She sat across from Lorraine, close enough that their knees almost touched.

"I'm glad about your inheritance. You deserve every cent," Storm said.

"Thank you. Mr. Hamasaki took good care of Ben and me." Lorraine twisted her wedding ring and kept her eyes directed toward her lap. "I wish I had…done some things differently."

"I wish I had, too."

Lorraine looked at Storm quickly with an expression almost like hope, then looked down again. "Did Mr. Hamasaki show you his recent work?"

"A little, but I've lost some of his papers. Do you have any duplicates?"

Lorraine slumped a fraction more in her seat.

Damn, she'd put the poor woman on the spot. Hamasaki always was trying to teach patience, a sense of timing. "I was just hoping you might be able to help me with some of the documents that were stolen."

Lorraine spoke cautiously. "A man came and started Mr. Hamasaki looking into some things. He was sick." She looked up at Storm. "Was this why you called me?"

"Uh, not exactly. Do you remember his name?"

Lorraine pressed her lips into a tight line. "He told me his name was Mike Oshiro, but that wasn't his real name." She sat up straighter. "Why did you call me?"

"I was surprised at David's reaction to the will. You have any idea what's going on with him?"

Lorraine clamped her hands together and looked down at them with an unhappy expression. Storm wanted to ask a dozen questions, but forced herself to lean back and take a deep breath. Lorraine certainly knew more than she was saying. Storm looked at the older woman's tiny white hands, which she'd twisted tightly together, and suddenly understood that the woman was afraid. Lorraine wanted to talk, but was anxious about something.

Storm's mind raced. Learning whether Lorraine worried about a family or a business issue would depend on how she could put the woman at ease.

"I'm trying to figure out if I did something wrong," Storm said softly. "Even Martin shut me out of the conversation after Cunningham read the will." She let the sadness show on her face. "I also wanted to ask you about Hamasaki's briefcase. Maybe if I knew where he was Sunday, who he spent time with, I could find it."

"Maybe his late appointment has it," Lorraine mumbled.

"He met someone on Sunday?"

"Yes, Bitsy was visiting her sister on the Big Island, so he was getting some extra work done. He had an appointment that afternoon."

Storm sat back with surprise. He hadn't said anything to her about it. "Who'd he meet?"

"I don't know. I'd come in to do some filing and he told me not to wait, that he wouldn't be long. Dr. O'Toole called, but he says he never came to the office."

Storm blinked rapidly. Uncle Miles used to tell her over and over that one had to pay attention to more than words. He knew better than most that she operated with her head in the clouds. He also understood that almost everyone lied.

"You answered his private phone line for him, didn't you?" Storm asked.

Lorraine nodded slowly. "Yes, most of the time."

Storm leaned toward the older woman. "Maybe if we put our heads together, we could figure out who he met. Or where he left the briefcase." Storm searched Lorraine's face. "Do you think you could make a list of people he talked to last Friday and any calls to the office during the weekend?"

Lorraine nodded. "I could try."

Lorraine's eyes flitted from Storm's face to the desk to the hands folded tightly in her lap, then she stole another glance at Storm.

Again, Storm had the feeling that Lorraine wanted to share something. "I can help with Friday. I drove him to work after we dropped his car for an oil change," she said.

"Oh yes, you two came in together. And not long after he went to his office, Bitsy called." Lorraine started twisting her wedding ring again and avoided Storm's eyes. "Some of his problems were family ones."

"You know, until this morning, I thought I was part of the family." Storm's voice quivered a bit.

Lorraine sighed. "You probably know some of this, anyway. I overheard part of the conversation when I dropped some contracts in his office to be signed. He was practically shouting." Her face reddened. "He was telling Bitsy that David's financial problems were his own fault and loaning him money wasn't going to teach him to stop his champagne and truffle parties. It sounded like Bitsy thought David's worries were hurting his health." Lorraine dropped her voice. "She told me a few days ago that he'd gained more weight and his insulin requirements have gone up. He has to give himself at least two shots a day, now." Lorraine looked at Storm. "He's gained weight, hasn't he?"

Storm nodded. "And Hamasaki was tough about money. He was determined none of us would depend on our trust funds as a livelihood. He'd pay for four years of college, but you had to make it from there. " She put a hand to her mouth. "David resents me for having a job in Hamasaki's firm, doesn't he?"

Lorraine looked quickly down at her lap. "Well, no one else went to law school. I don't know what they expected."

Storm swallowed. "I see."

The older woman looked at Storm's face. "It's easy to forget how hard another person has worked." She gave Storm's knee a soft pat and stood up to leave.

"Um, Lorraine?" Storm asked. "What happened to the man that came to see Uncle Miles? That Mike Oshiro?"

"I don't know, except that he looked very ill and he didn't want anyone to see him in the office." She frowned. "Miles might have sent him to see Meredith, but—" Lorraine was interrupted by loud knocking, then Cunningham opened the door and popped his head in.

"Am I interrupting something?" He smiled and smoothed his hair. "You girls having a coffee break?"

"We wish," Storm said. "I'm following up on some of Hamasaki's business." She smiled. "Thanks, Lorraine. Come in, Cyril."

Storm stood and started to roll her office chair back around behind the desk.

Cunningham put his hand on her arm. "Don't bother moving things around. Have a seat. I wanted to congratulate you on passing the bar."

Storm sat in her office chair and gestured for him to take the other chair. He scooted it closer to her. She gave him what she hoped was a professional smile: no teeth showing and dead-on eye contact. But he was sitting a little too close and he kept smiling. She could smell his aftershave. Too much cologne on men always made her wonder what they were covering up.

"Thanks," she said. "Interesting meeting this morning, wasn't it? I was a little surprised that Hamasaki moved the age of acquiring the trust up to forty years. The last time we talked, it was thirty-five." She shrugged. "That was about four years ago, though."

"He asked me to change it a few months ago."

Storm leaned back in her chair. Cunningham moved so that his knee touched hers. She tried to scoot the chair back without appearing obvious, but the wheels wouldn't turn in the pile of the carpet. "You have any idea why David was so upset?" she asked, backpedaling.

"No idea." His knee slipped between hers.

Storm could feel her face burn. She stood up. "It's probably the stress of losing his father."

"Yes, I imagine you're right." He rose from his chair and put a warm hand on her shoulder. "I'd like to get together with you and discuss your aspirations with the firm. Losing Hamasaki as we did was a real shock to us all. We need to talk."

Storm stared at his blue eyes. She could see capillaries around the fading iris, red against the yellowing sclera. The odor of last night's scotch was on his breath. Or had it been a more recent cocktail? She took a step back. "Good idea. Why don't you call a meeting with Wo and Wang? I'll make it fit into my schedule."

The smile faded from his face. "Fine. We'll be communicating soon." He turned and left the office.

Storm shoved her chair back behind the desk and fell into it. She had noticed her stomach growling during her talk with Lorraine. Now it was roiling with disgust. Her lower lip quivered with despair, a combination of this morning's ostracism and Cunningham's behavior. She clamped her jaws together and glanced at her watch. After two and she hadn't had lunch yet. What she needed was to take a walk and clear her head, maybe stop for a bite where, hopefully, she could be alone to think. .

On the way through the reception area, which was busy with staff returning from lunch and waiting clients, Lorraine handed her a sheet of paper. "It's a start. Check with me when you come back," Lorraine said.

"Thanks." Storm glanced at the list and shoved it into her purse. She walked away as Wang and Meredith Wo approached Lorraine.

Warm, humid air drifted up Bishop Street from the ocean. A thick cloud layer lay over the city. Storm took a deep breath. She could smell the ocean; the breeze was from the south, instead of the northeast trade winds. Locals called them Kona winds, which meant storms and still, sultry air. She didn't mind; it reminded her of lazy summer days on the Big Island.

Storm wandered into the pedestrian area of Fort Street Mall, where fast food places lined the sidewalks. The smell of Chinese noodles, garlic and fresh ginger tickled her appetite. Her stomach growled again and a frozen yogurt stand caught her eye. Storm ordered a chocolate shake with walnuts. It was delicious, even though chunks of nuts clogged the straw. Maybe she'd have stir-fried noodles after she finished the drink.

She sat on the edge of a fountain and watched a pair of mynah birds fight over half of a Big Mac someone had dropped on the cement. The sandwich was big enough for ten birds, yet the two squawked and carried on in a racket that attracted passersby. The birds quarreled as if their lives depended on the victory, rather than the food. Not unlike humans, Storm reflected. She slurped the rest of her shake and took a deep breath of briny air mixed with spray from the fountain.

What she really needed right now was a trip to the Big Island. She needed to be in the small town of Pa'auilo with family who wouldn't judge her. Life was simple there. She smiled at the memories of running a bit wild with cousins and second cousins of her mother's. She could go visit them, see their kids, and spend time with Aunt Maile and Uncle Keone.

There, everyone watched everyone else's children and the kids darted through koa forests in the mists that drifted down from Mauna Kea and brought a coolness that never reached the hot southern part of the island. They rode old, rusty bicycles, probably the same ones their parents used to ride, along the cane haul roads. Drivers of the huge, muddy trucks knew to watch for them, and the sugar cane itself, with its great prickly leaves, kept them out in the open where they could be seen. The kids, like their parents before them, rode the bikes to the edges of the cliffs that jutted hundreds of feet above the ocean. There, they could watch the occasional humpback whale cavort with its mate in the indigo swells.

Nothing was wasted. Storm remembered happily accepting a cousin's faded overalls for school. Most weekends were spent with extended family; the adults supervised kids' games from old lawn chairs while they shared a keg. There was usually a reason for at least a potluck, if not a *lū'au*.

The very thought of an imu-roasted pig, *lomilomi* salmon, and *laulau* made Storm's mouth water. She got up and threw her empty paper cup into a nearby trashcan. The wrapper of the sandwich the mynah birds had torn apart drifted against her foot and left a grease spot on her shoe. She needed to get out of the city.

It was Friday, why not? A pay phone perched on the side of a building at the corner of Queen Street, where the traffic around the pedestrian mall resumed. Storm picked up the receiver, got someone at the Aloha Airlines desk just as a bus bellowed by, spewing a diesel cloud in her direction. Storm coughed. "When's your next flight to Kona? Or Hilo? I'll take either."

The person at the airline desk chuckled. "Sounds like you're downtown. Next one to Kona is at 3:55. There's one to Hilo at 6:30. Which one ya want?"

She'd never make the 3:55 and the drive from Hilo was a bit shorter than from Kona. "Hilo, thanks." Storm leaned against the side of the little open phone box and read off her credit card number to the agent.

Storm hiked briskly up Bishop Street back to the office. The sidewalks were crowded with people leaving work to avoid the Friday afternoon rush hour traffic. Storm felt herself jostled, but didn't turn around. It wasn't until she heard her name that she glanced behind.

Hamlin's face was flushed. "I've been trying to catch you for three blocks."

"You were having a late lunch, too?"

"Yeah, I got held up in a meeting, then a long-distance phone call, and then Cyril dropped by to tell me about the reading of the will."

Storm glanced at Hamlin, who now matched her steps, and wondered if Cunningham had told him about their private meeting. Hamlin didn't appear to be hiding anything, but he probably practiced nonchalance in front of the mirror.

"From what I heard, Hamasaki's kids were pretty upset." he said.

"I was surprised by that, too. David took it hard."

"David strikes me as the type who might not share with his little sister."

"No kidding. Not the adopted one, anyway."

Hamlin looked over at her. "Don't take it hard. I doubt if he talks much outside his circle of friends. Cyril told me Mrs. Hamasaki seemed taken back by his behavior, too."

Storm nodded. If Cyril had overheard the phone call from Bitsy Hamasaki to her husband, he might have interpreted her reaction as disappointment rather than surprise. Perhaps Lorraine was the only one in front of whom Hamasaki could argue with his wife. Somehow, that detail was reassuring to Storm.

Hamlin held the front doors for her. "Was Martin disappointed, too?" he asked.

"I'm not sure." Storm had wondered about the expression on Martin's face. She pushed the button for the elevator, still thinking. "He wasn't happy, but it may have been because of David's reaction."

"I could understand that." The elevator glided to a stop and they got off. Hamlin pushed open the door to the office.

Storm preceded him, looking over her shoulder. "Uh, Hamlin, I was thinking of taking off this weekend. Could we have our drink next—"

Meredith Wo rushed toward them. "Excuse me, Storm. Ian, you didn't have your cell phone on. I've been looking all over for you." She grabbed his arm and pulled him in the direction of his office.

Storm stood in the waiting room, with the eyes of several clients, one of them a familiar suit that she couldn't place, and two secretaries on her. "She's been a little antsy for the last hour," one of the secretaries said.

Storm raised an eyebrow. "I see." She went to her office and closed the door. It had been a long week.

Chapter 11

Storm looked at the files stacked on her desk, then glanced at her watch. It was three-thirty; with the lines at the airport these days, she didn't have much time to straighten up and think about what work she needed to take with her.

She picked up the phone and dialed Aunt Maile. Her aunt was thrilled to hear her voice.

"We'll have dinner ready, my dear."

"I won't be there until late, Aunt Maile. The plane leaves here at six."

"A cup of tea, then. Drive carefully."

Storm punched in Leila's number. When she got the answering machine, she realized that her friend was picking up Robbie and doing afternoon errands. "Hi, Leila. Would you guys keep Fang over the weekend for me? I'm going to Pa'auilo to see Auntie Maile. I'll call you later."

Storm leaned back in her chair and tried to think. The events of the week were like a pile-up on the freeway, with grief and frustration jumbling any sense she might be able to make of all that had occurred. She still rankled from Rick's betrayal, so Wo's appropriation of Hamlin was especially irritating.

Frowning, Storm shuffled some papers piled next to her laptop. Her earlier cartoon of Fang peeked out from under one of them; the words *seawall, Dr. O'Toole,* and *nursing homes* were scribbled beneath the little caricature.

Old habits were what you fell back on when you didn't know what else to do: list the events, make an outline. She added *cancer patient?* and Hamasaki's name, then balked at writing the word *death*. Instead, she penned *theft*. Twice, if she counted the attempt on her laptop.

She sat back. The burglaries, a meeting the night Hamasaki died, plus the elusive and sick client were disturbing loose ends. Storm dug around in her laptop case for the phone number of the detective that had come to the office after she'd found Miles's body.

"Sergeant Fujita here."

"Hello, this is Storm Kayama."

"How you doing? I heard about your break-in last night."

"That's partly why I called. Did you know that someone tried to steal my laptop the night before?"

She heard him rattle through papers. "No, that's not in the file yet." He paused. "That's not good."

"Um, Detective Fujita, did you see anything suspicious when you came to the office Monday morning?"

"What are you getting at?"

"A man who gave a false name visited Miles a few days before he died."

"Do you know what he wanted?"

"No, but Miles's secretary saw him and said that he looked very ill. Plus, Hamasaki had a meeting with someone the night he died." As she spoke them, Storm's words came back to her as a bit paranoid. Hamasaki had a lot of meetings, and still often worked long hours.

"Those thefts would bother me, too. If you find out who this man was and what he wanted, I want to know." Storm could hear him ruffle through papers. "But right now, we don't have any hard data. Just hunches, which I respect, but we can't run an investigation on so few facts."

"I see," Storm said. And she did. The detective was being kind.

"Ms. Kayama, please be careful."

Storm hung up the phone. Lorraine had laid a fat labor union file from Hamasaki's office right next to Storm's laptop where she wouldn't miss it, bless her heart. Storm jammed it into the case. She would review it over the weekend and give Roy Tam a call on Monday to set up a meeting.

She went out to the front desk to check and see if Lorraine had anything else for her. Diane, Wang's secretary, was talking to Lorraine.

"I'm taking off," Storm said. "Do either of you know if Wang has anything for me to look at over the weekend? He's already upset about Miles's briefcase and the papers that were stolen."

Diane smiled at her. "Don't you worry about him. His bark is worse than his bite." She glanced around and spoke in a near-whisper. "He's just moody because of his mother."

"What happened to her?"

"Her Alzheimer's is getting worse. She's pretty helpless, she wanders out of the house, and he still won't put her in one of those homes."

Diane exchanged a concerned look with Lorraine. "He says the patients are tied up, or locked in their rooms."

"What does he do during the day when he's at work?" Lorraine asked.

"He has a private nurse, but at night he takes care of her himself. Gets up and gives her all her medications and everything. He told me about it when the nurse was late one morning."

Storm shook her head with sympathy. "You never can guess the extent of another person's troubles, can you?" Diane and Lorraine tsked and agreed.

All three of them looked up at Hamlin, who approached. "Storm, have you got a moment?"

"About half of one. I've got to catch a plane."

Lorraine and Diane exchanged a glance and headed toward the kitchenette.

"I'm sorry about Meredith dragging me off like that," Hamlin said. "She can be high-strung."

"I've noticed."

"You going to the Big Island?"

"Yes, I thought a few days where I don't have to wear shoes, where I can watch the sun set over the ocean without any buildings in the way, would be a good break from last week."

Hamlin looked wistful. "Sounds nice."

"It is." Storm felt a wave of sheepishness for taking her frustration about Meredith's rudeness out on him. He could have refused to go, but that would have caused a scene in front of clients. Bad form, for sure.

"Will you tell me about it next week over that glass of champagne?"

"Sure." She smiled at him.

By the time Storm was running through the VW's gears on the ramp from the parking garage to the street, she figured she had all of a half hour to get home, change, and throw some clothes in a duffel in order to get to the airport in time to deal with the long security lines.

Two minutes after she walked in the front door, the phone rang. She ignored it and continued throwing tee-shirts into her bag. When Leila's voice on the answering machine drifted back to the bedroom, Storm picked up. "Hi, Leila, I'm here."

"You're late, aren't you?" Leila asked and both women laughed. "I just wanted to let you know I got your message. Fang is fine and Robbie is thrilled. Relax and give Auntie Maile and Uncle Keone hugs for Robbie and me."

"Thanks, I'll call you Sunday."

Storm jogged to the car and threw everything into the back seat. She zoomed down the freeway entrance, only to jam on the brakes at a line of cars forming behind some idiot who thought stopping at an on-ramp was the way to merge. She winced as she heard the contents of her purse clatter to the floor behind her.

Something rolled forward and hit her foot, then retreated as Storm accelerated with the car in front of her to slip into a slot in the column of traffic. If it was the pink lipstick that turned orange, then it could roll around until it fell through a rust hole in the floor, but if it was the

Montblanc pen Uncle Miles had given her for graduation, she needed to rescue it.

There was no way she could reach it as she wove through the rush hour traffic, so she waited until she'd found a parking place in the multistoried airport lot. She did not have time for this, what with the long lines at the ticket counter and the thorough security check. She cursed the top-heavy purse for falling, then herself for careless driving.

She jumped from the car, jammed forward the driver's seat, threw aside a tennis racquet and some old Sunday newspaper want-ads that had been sliding around for days, and gasped with surprise. There was Uncle Miles's briefcase.

He must have left it Friday morning, when she'd helped him drop his car off at the Lexus dealership. Was this what the thieves were looking for? Or something in it? She regarded the case as if it were newly unburied treasure.

A noise brought Storm back from her mental wanderings and plucked at stretched nerve endings. Footsteps echoed in the cement chamber of the parking structure. She scrambled to stuff things back in her purse, then dropped to her knees on the floor of the garage and struggled to reach under the front seat.

It had been the Montblanc rolling around, of course. She could see its black and white tip, nestled into the sliding mechanism of the seat. Storm pushed against the back of the driver's seat with the side of her head and reached out her fingertips. Not quite. She couldn't reach over the damned briefcase.

The footsteps got closer. Storm jerked the attaché to the garage floor and bent into the back of the car again. Her face stuck to the vinyl of the seat with the heat of her exertion. She felt like her rear end was waving in the air like a Coast Guard buoy in the channel. She stretched forward.

Under her arm, she could view the stealthy approach of a tall, dark-skinned man in khaki pants and boots. Her heart thumped throughout her whole contorted body. For a split second, Storm considered diving into the cramped back seat for protection. But then she'd be bottoms-up and ass-backward. An octogenarian could mug her.

The man walked to a pickup truck in the next aisle. Storm let go of breath like a leaky balloon. She was dizzy with relief. Or hypoxia, she wasn't sure. A rivulet of sweat trickled down her temple. The last couple of days were getting to her. She needed to get her feet on the ground again. In more ways than one.

She backed out of the car. If anyone really had been watching, she would have heard howls of laughter. Her derriere, the only visible body part, had been bouncing around during the entire struggle to dig the pen out. She had probably looked like a one-woman volleyball game in a bushel basket.

Storm heaved a sigh and steadied her weak knees. Okay, all she had to do was get on the plane. In the commotion, Lorraine's list had fallen out of the purse and down beside Hamasaki's leather case. Storm crammed it into one of the zipper pockets on the outside of her duffel because her handbag was filled so haphazardly that she couldn't close it. Then she locked the car and bolted for the ticket counter with the duffel, the laptop, her purse, and Uncle Miles's briefcase flapping on her thighs. She felt like a camel loaded for a Sahara crossing.

Storm was the last one on the plane, but she made it. Like buses, the inter-island flights had open seating. The only remaining seat was in the last row by the window, next to a toddler. With a sigh of relief, she crunched her duffel into the overhead bin, clambered over the kid and woman in the outside seats, and since bending over in the tiny space was impossible, shoved her purse and laptop case under the seat with her feet. She buckled her seat belt and wiped her face with the back of her hand. It came away streaked with grit. She kept Uncle Miles's briefcase clasped in her arms.

The child next to her stared, then offered a gummy graham cracker without cracking a smile. The mother, who sat like a boulder on the aisle, faced stonily ahead. Her eyes darted, probably trying to catch the attention of the flight attendant in order to report a grimy, suspicious passenger.

A flight attendant advanced, checking seat belts. She turned toward Storm and the frowning mother and tilted her head with a puzzled look. "Storm Kayama, right?"

Chapter 12

"Becky?" Storm did a double take, then grinned. She and Becky Allegrino had shared the same homeroom throughout high school. They'd sat next to each other in chemistry and passed notes about the professor, who was also the football coach. They agreed that he'd probably banged his head against too many goal posts. Though they'd shared giggles then, Storm hadn't seen Becky since graduation. "I've wondered what you've been up to."

"Yeah, me too. How are you?" Becky's smile faltered. "How'd you get those black eyes? And you've gotta stow that briefcase. I'll do it for you, if you want."

Storm held onto the case. "Can I put it under the seat?"

"Sure, if it fits." Becky looked around, then lowered her voice. "Have you got time when we land to go get dinner and catch up on things? I'm off duty until tomorrow."

The mother on the aisle glared at the two women. "Sure, that'd be great," Storm said. People were less rushed on the rural neighbor islands than in Honolulu. Old friends and family were important there; it would be rude to refuse her old friend. Plus, this would be a good beginning to a relaxed weekend.

"I'll meet you at baggage claim, then." Becky left to prepare her passengers for take-off.

Storm sat back and took a deep breath. She was on her way. From the window, she watched the receding coast of O'ahu and marveled, as always, at the brilliance of the waters and the shadows of the coral reefs beneath them. She watched a sailboat, tiny as it crashed through the swells of the Moloka'i Channel, and felt the tension seep from her shoulders. When the plane passed over the island of Moloka'i and she could see the two mountains that made up Maui, she closed her eyes and let her mind wander.

She thought over the last few days. Events had piled up so fast that she was having trouble fitting them into a bigger picture. Lorraine had told her of an argument between Aunt Bitsy and Uncle Miles on the day he died. They weren't saints, but a quarrel was pretty unusual. And she would never have imagined the family's behavior at the reading of the will. Horrible to think that Hamasaki's death might have been welcomed by one of them.

This last week, was forcing her to reevaluate how the entire Hamasaki family related to one another. To her knowledge, Uncle Miles had never promised any pots of gold; she couldn't imagine any of his children counting on it. But now she suspected she had been excluded from a number of family discussions.

Storm's throat tightened. She had believed for years that she was family. Today she had learned that the family had secrets they kept from her. Lorraine had even alluded to jealousy on the part of her step-siblings because Hamasaki had given her a job. Storm didn't know how to deal with that problem. She'd have to ask Martin what he thought. And hope he would tell her.

Meanwhile, she was practically sitting on the missing attaché case, which she hoped would reveal to her the identity of Hamasaki's visitor Sunday afternoon. For a moment, she wondered if maybe she'd better give it to Aunt Bitsy first. No, it had to do with legal work. Jealousy or not, that was still her domain. And Hamasaki had left it with her, in a way.

Also, if the attack in the parking garage and the theft of Hamasaki's papers from her home were related to Hamasaki and what he had been working on, then she was involved to a dangerous degree. The briefcase was definitely her domain.

As Hamasaki had tried to teach her, information was power. She needed the answers to a number of questions in order to protect herself. Who was this sick client? Could he have been the person Hamasaki met on Sunday? Though her concerns had resonated with fear and conjecture when she'd shared them with the detective earlier in the day, she was beginning to suspect that Hamasaki had been murdered.

Storm stared down at the blue ocean and pondered this idea. Abstract as it was, the very thought of someone snuffing out Hamasaki made her flame with anger.

Storm knew Hamasaki. Accustomed to victories in boardrooms and the offices of the powerful, he would have confronted any person he had suspected of wrongdoing. It was his way. Though there were no hard facts to support her suspicions, she wasn't just being paranoid. Everyone knew that she and Hamasaki worked closely together. If this person suspected Hamasaki of keeping documentation, then it would be reasonable for him to suspect that Storm had possession of it now.

Storm chewed on her lower lip. The attacks in the garage and on her home had not been directed to her person as much as to obtaining papers and material Hamasaki might have given her. If there was a killer out there, it seemed likely that he—or she—didn't suspect Storm of having any personal knowledge. She swallowed hard. The killer was right.

It also appeared that this person knew of Storm's lack of attention to detail and considered her a lightweight. This thought stoked both her anger and grief at Hamasaki's death.

She had one advantage: no one knew that she had the briefcase. The papers stolen from the floor of her home may not have given the thief what he had sought. Storm's eyes followed the shadow of the plane on the sea's surface. Though the answers were not obvious to her at this point, they might lie in the briefcase, or on Lorraine's list, presently stuffed in the overhead bin.

Just about everyone in the firm, in addition to several clients, delivery people, and a repairman who had been standing around, had seen Lorraine hand it over. A number of those people were probably interested in the attaché, too. Storm shook her head. She had information someone was desperate to obtain, but did not have enough data herself to guess what it was.

She leaned forward. The case was a big satchel style and she struggled to pull it from under the seat. The woman on the aisle gave her stink-eye that would have curdled milk. Storm ignored her. She rested the case on her legs in the too-small plane seat with the gaping mouth of the case at her chest level and popped open the catch. It wasn't even locked.

She didn't dare stick her elbows into the territory of the kid next to her. The person in front of her was just about lying in her lap, so she couldn't tip it over, either. Since she couldn't see six inches past the top, she just plunged her hand in and rummaged.

She gulped. The first thing her fingers encountered was an article she could identify without even seeing it. It was Hamasaki's appointment book.

Storm let the small leather book fall open. Not long ago, he'd filled these familiar pages with his scrawl. Just seeing his handwriting sent a pang through her.

On Friday, two days before his death, notes covered the page. On the 7:30 a.m. line, he had written *Bitsy, Aloha #272, Hilo*. Flights ran to the outer islands like the downtown buses went to the O'ahu suburbs, only a little more reliably.

Maybe he'd taken Bitsy to the airport early that morning. That was the morning Storm had picked him up at eight to drop his car off and take him into the office. He probably would have mentioned having already been to the airport and back, but he hadn't said a word. Okay, David or Michelle could have taken Bitsy. Storm tapped the page with her finger. Wonder when that phone call, the argument Lorraine had told her about, had taken place? Bitsy must have called from the Big Island.

Lorraine probably had made a note of the phone call on the list she'd handed Storm. But the list was in her duffel in the overhead compartment. Storm sneaked a look next to her. The toddler had dozed off. His gluey graham cracker was crumbling against Storm's shorts and the mother was reading *Cosmopolitan* with a look of grim satisfaction on her face. Probably looking over the article on multiple orgasms. Storm decided not to disturb her. She trailed her finger down Hamasaki's Friday schedule. A couple of court dates, lunch with Roy Tam, and a note to call Sherwood Overton. Oh, yeah, that was Wang's and Cunningham's new client. He was a big wheel; she remembered Hamasaki introducing her to him a week or so ago. As the CFO of the big local health management organization, he was an important customer. For Saturday, there was a memo to tell Meredith something that Storm couldn't decipher, some reminders to phone people, and a note to pick up the dry cleaning.

The Sunday page was empty except for one note. On the six-thirty p.m. line, Hamasaki had written *S.O.* Storm sat back in her seat. Sherwood Overton?

She would have to wait to get back to O'ahu to check if Overton had met with Uncle Miles. Since Lorraine hadn't mentioned it, she might have to call Overton's office and finesse some information from his secretary.

She turned the page to Monday and frowned. Uncle Miles had written *Bitsy, Aloha #23, arr. 10:15* on the morning schedule. Storm remembered Sergeant Fujita checking to see when she was expected to arrive, since he was reluctant to give her the news of her husband's death over the phone. Fujita had mentioned that Michelle was planning to pick her mother up that afternoon.

Which didn't jibe with Hamasaki's notebook. It was possible that Aunt Bitsy had arranged to stay longer and have a more leisurely morning with her sister. With more careful questions, Storm could probably find out.

The rest of the notes in the planner were routine appointments with familiar names, though Uncle Miles had *root canal!#*scheduled for Monday afternoon. Poor Uncle Miles. Storm flipped through the rest of the book. Nothing else rang any bells.

She put the calendar book back in the satchel and pulled out the first two files her fingers grasped. She flipped open the one on top and found some info on Roy Tam's highway project. Great, she could look that over this weekend and be prepared for the meeting on Monday. The second file had the name Tom Sakai typed neatly on a tab that did not match the ones Storm usually saw in the office. When she opened it, she read a letter from Sidney O'Toole, M.D. that addressed the board of directors of Unimed. Storm knew that name; it was Sherwood Overton's company and the ER where the assembly line doctor had checked her nose. It was also the new employer of Rick, the philandering asshole.

The letter was cc'ed to the Utilization Review Committee. In it, he pleaded the case of Tom Sakai, a local plumber and a charter member of the health management organization. Sakai had multiple myeloma, a virulent cancer of the bone marrow. His only hope of recovery lay in having a bone marrow transplant. Storm blinked with surprise. This had to be the guy who came to see Hamasaki.

O'Toole appeared to be responding to a previous rejection of Sakai's request for the transplant by the utilization review managers. He pointed out the long-term financial benefits for the HMO in terms of public relations in a community where word travels faster than radio waves. Storm appreciated O'Toole's reference to the coconut wireless as a stab at levity, but she knew his plea was completely serious.

He proposed that the HMO cover the cost of Sakai's therapy, which with plane fare to Seattle and his treatment at a private hospital would add up to a couple hundred thousand dollars. People would hear about the organization's caring efforts toward their patients and their subscribers would increase. Even if Sakai died, which was possible in spite of the transplant, O'Toole promised that large establishments, like law firms and state offices, would know of the organization's heroic efforts to save this man's life and enlist their employees in their health system. Especially since the HMO planned to develop its own high-tech oncology center and cancer clinic.

Storm sat back and reflected on what she knew about the operation of health management organizations. They were hierarchies run by business people who watched the bottom line and made sure the company turned a profit. An internist like O'Toole was called a capitated doctor, which meant that he practiced in a group of doctors that was paid a set monthly fee by the HMO to examine patients. One of his jobs was to decide which patients needed to see specialists or to be admitted to the hospital.

O'Toole's group held back part of this fee every month to cover their own operating costs. What was left went to specialists (like oncologists) and to the group's own physicians as monthly salary, or capitation fee.

Specialists and extra treatments for a patient came out of this set-aside fee. Consequently, when O'Toole referred to a specialist or asked for special treatments, he cut into not only his own income, but also that of his colleagues. In addition, like all capitated doctors, O'Toole had signed an agreement called a "gag order," which meant he wasn't allowed to inform Sakai or any other patient that he had any options other than what the HMO offered him.

The organization had both O'Toole and Sakai by the short and curlies. O'Toole was stuck between being a bouncer, maintaining his income and reputation, and being the patient advocate the Hippocratic oath commanded. Sakai fought for his life and depended on O'Toole, as his primary physician, to refer him for the treatments he needed.

Storm let her head flop back on the seat and tried to read between the lines in the letters she held. O'Toole had approached Hamasaki because he trusted Hamasaki's confidence, but probably also because O'Toole needed some muscle behind his words. Hamasaki had enough clout with local law firms and state organizations to influence the employee health plans that would be chosen.

O'Toole's request for more extensive therapy for his patient had been rejected once already. The letter Storm held was a second try. Storm imagined that O'Toole had come to Hamasaki before he mailed the second letter. In his favor, he just couldn't stand to stay silent and watch the young man die. But Unimed could ruin O'Toole. They could curtail his pay, fire him, sue him, or smear his reputation if he spoke outside of the HMO. As for Sakai, no other health insurance establishment would take him on. The HMO could hold him to the treatment they wanted. Storm shuddered. Poor Tom Sakai.

She wasn't sure if O'Toole or Sakai legally had a chance. Sakai, when he joined the HMO as a healthy thirty-year-old, had signed a contract with them for the medical care they offered. Even if he had read the small print, he probably wouldn't have cared that the HMO didn't offer bone marrow transplants. What thirty-year-old believes that he'll need one? What sixty-year-old does?

Storm swallowed hard. Still, tens of millions of dollars would be at stake if Sakai started a lawsuit. Juries like to side with people like Sakai. Sadly, if Sakai died in the middle of the proceedings while being refused treatment by the HMO, the family could get even more for the anguish they'd endured.

If they knew about it, the executive board had to be very nervous. Storm had a bad feeling that they did.

She looked again at the letter. O'Toole wrote that the palliative treatments, the methotrexate for chemotherapy and rodding of the bone fractures, were not working. Sakai was in pain and growing weaker.

The next couple pages in the file were photocopies of Sakai's medical history. He was thirty-five. Storm's stomach flip-flopped; he was so young. He had gone to see a general practitioner at the HMO, the one running the clinic that day, because he had recurrent pains in his thighs. It had grown so bad that he couldn't continue to throw a ball with his seven-year-old son. The GP punted

Sakai to O'Toole, who was the next level up in terms of specialists. O'Toole called in the oncologist.

O'Toole and the oncologist supervised a round of chemotherapy for a year with decent results. Then Sakai relapsed. His wife was three months pregnant.

Storm checked the date on that note. Eight months ago, so she'd had the baby. O'Toole's last written comments were that the patient was seeking traditional Hawaiian therapies. O'Toole was encouraging it, as long as Sakai also continued his chemotherapy.

The final paper in the file was a confidential letter from the HMO board to O'Toole. He was reminded not to discuss the possibility of treatments not offered by the organization with Sakai or his wife. The bone marrow transplant was out of the question. The last sentence said that perhaps when the HMO underwent their planned expansion and had their own cancer treatment center, they would be in a position to help Sakai.

Storm shook her head sadly. Except that Sakai would be dead. A bunch of MBAs had handed down a death sentence to a thirty-five-year-old father. The file drooped in her grip while questions stampeded her mind. O'Toole had to have informed Sakai before he'd copied his chart and shown it to Hamasaki. If he hadn't, O'Toole would be betraying his patient-physician confidentiality, and that didn't sound like old Dr. O'Toole. O'Toole must have gone ahead and told Sakai about getting treatment not covered by the HMO, too, or Sakai would never have gone to see Hamasaki. Perhaps the doctor had suggested the visit, perhaps not. O'Toole was certainly walking a minefield of personal, moral, and legal uncertainties.

Just whom had Hamasaki contacted on Sakai's or O'Toole's behalf? Where had he asked his questions? The theft of Hamasaki's file from her living room floor stuck in Storm's mind like a raspberry seed in a molar. O'Toole's name had been scribbled in it, but nothing else, she was sure.

The announcement came for passengers to prepare for landing. Storm rubbed her burning eyes, then slipped the file back into the briefcase. She wrestled it under the seat, raised her seat back, and gazed out the window at Hilo Harbor. The fragility of life was particularly apparent to her at that moment. Usually, takeoffs and landings were nail-biters for her. Storm watched the ground approach with a thrum of anxiety that, this time, had nothing to do with the aircraft.

She wondered again about the incidents of the last few days. The letter in the briefcase might be what the thief was after, and this person was someone with enough clout to hire thugs to do the dirty work. There was a chance that Hamasaki had stroked out over the stress of keeping the secret, but Storm didn't think so. The man thrived on secrets. So had he been killed for threatening to reveal the details of Tom Sakai's sad story?

Storm yawned to pop her ears and clear her mind. None of this made sense. The HMO treated thousands of people; Sakai wouldn't be alone in this struggle. Health maintenance organizations would have their legal eagles lined up to defend the company against many of these lawsuits. And Hamasaki would have known this.

She stared out the window. She was still missing a large chunk of information. Information that someone might have killed to find.

Chapter 13

When the plane banked to make its approach, the sun on the water sparkled like rare jewels on blue velvet, a reminder of beauty in the world. Storm tried to dispel the cold breath of eternity prickling her neck with a wish for dry weather on the serpentine two-lane highway that ran from Hilo to Pa'auilo.

That particular drive demanded a person's full attention. There are wetter places in the Hawaiian Islands than the northeast coast of the Big Island, but Storm hadn't seen many. Weeks could pass when one didn't see the sun peek through the clouds and mist. But when the sun shone, the emerald green of the tropical foliage against the matte black of ancient lava flows startled with its splendor.

Hilo was surrounded by waterfalls, plants with leaves the size of her VW that bore flowers as big as her head, and orchid farms whose exotic blooms were extolled worldwide. If one were to wander from the well-traveled paths, the silence and aroma of jungle were omnipresent. Decomposing leaves, fragrant blossoms, and lushness so thick that walls of plant growth confronted the explorer. It was not hard to believe in *menehune*, or the Hawaiian version of leprechauns.

Hilo itself was a city of about forty thousand people, populated with families who had been there for generations. In the past, many had worked in the sugar cane industry. The last several years, people switched to farming various products like macadamia nuts and coffee. Because of its rainy climate, tourists came through Hilo on the way to Volcano National Park, ate a fast lunch, then hightailed it back to Kona on the sunny side of the island.

Storm, however, found Hilo's water-blurred edges more conducive to tranquility than the blades of sunlight reflected from the white sands of Maui or O'ahu. Standing at the covered, open-air luggage claim, she took a deep breath of the humidity. Water dripped from the eaves of the building onto blooming anthurium plants. Men in rubber slippers slapped one another's backs and women hugged each other. All around her, people smiled. Storm relaxed; this was the Big Island, where everyone knew someone who knew you or your parents. She could unwind now.

Becky rushed by. "I'll meet you here in fifteen minutes. I've got to check out."

Storm had time to pick up a car at the rental booth, then call Fujita to tell him that she'd found the appointment book with its entries about Hamasaki's activities the days before his death. She struggled with whether to tell the detective about the briefcase, but then realized she'd have to reveal Sakai's medical issues and O'Toole's conflict of interest. She decided not to mention it yet, because of the potential damage to both Sakai and O'Toole. She'd talk to O'Toole first.

Sure enough, Fujita wanted to see Hamasaki's appointment book. An officer would meet Storm at the airport, package it, and send it back on the next flight. "Don't leave, now. He'll be there in ten minutes," Fujita said.

Storm looked at her watch. Nearly seven-thirty. He couldn't be too late; the last plane to O'ahu left in an hour. The small, outer-island airports tucked in early, just like the rest of the businesses, except for the bars. She and Becky would have no trouble finding a cozy place to have a bite, especially if it had good beer on tap. Local folks liked their happy hour.

The police officer, who turned out to be a no-nonsense woman, showed up before Becky arrived. Hilo is not a big town, but she must have been only a few blocks away. She pulled her squad car to the curb, got out, walked to Storm as if she were the only person standing around, and gave Storm a receipt for the notebook with an efficient thank-you.

"Tell Fujita that I'd like it back, eventually. Please?" Storm called after her.

The officer turned with a half salute and a nod. "Will do." And she disappeared into the terminal area.

Storm phoned Aunt Maile to tell her that she'd be late, threw her bag and Hamasaki's briefcase into the trunk of the car, then leaned against the door to wait for Becky. She wondered if Becky had access to passenger lists. Storm knew from experience that airline personnel wouldn't usually release passenger information to the general public. She felt a pang of guilt at wanting to check up on Aunt Bitsy. Did it matter if the flight time Hamasaki had written didn't jibe with when she had arrived? Storm wasn't sure, and the loose end bothered her.

She caught sight of Becky, who had changed into jeans and was dragging a small bag on wheels.

"Oh, good," Becky said when she saw Storm's car. "I was hoping I could bum a ride from you. My fiancé can pick me up at Haunani's Grill."

"Sure. I have a favor to ask." A story spun out of Storm's mouth before she could reconsider. "My aunt lost her trifocals on a plane from Hilo last Wednesday. I thought we could look for them."

"What flight was she on?"

"I'm not sure. Can you find out?"

"I think so." Becky led Storm into the terminal. Except for helping a straggler trying to make the last plane, the attendants were beginning to close up. Becky asked a clerk whose computer terminal was still lit to check the passenger lists for Elizabeth Hamasaki.

He typed, then waited a few moments. "She was on flight twenty-eight, the two-forty. Let's see...lost glasses." He looked at Storm. "What color were they? We've got two pairs."

"Two in the afternoon? From Hilo? Uh, they're blue."

"No, twenty-eight leaves from Kona. Hmm...One's gold-rimmed and the other pair's green, it says. Kona sent them over. Wanna see 'em? Green and blue could be mixed up. Heck, some of the baggage guys wouldn't know the difference."

Storm had to force her mouth closed. "Er, no thanks." She showed her teeth in what she hoped looked like a grateful smile. "I'll call her first. They're probably in the bottom of this huge purse she carries. She loses them twice a week in there." Storm hoped she didn't look as flabbergasted as she felt. Her mind whirled. Why Kona? Bitsy's sister lived in Hilo. It was a winding, arduous drive of at least two hours from one town to the other.

The clerk returned her smile, and Storm backed away before he could notice her lips quiver.

Chapter 14

Storm tried to focus her attention on Becky's happy chatter. Fortunately, Becky rambled on about her fiancé and Storm could savor the chicken long rice and spicy *tako*, a raw octopus dish, without having to do much more than nod and grunt in the right places. The food was great and Storm was ravenous despite her preoccupation with the Hamasakis.

Becky had taken her to a local tavern known for its home-made Hawaiian food. When Storm had lived on the Big Island, she was too young to be allowed inside, though in high school she'd used a fake ID a couple of times. The place looked different now, but the changes were due to an adult perspective, that of one who wasn't as fixated on checking out the construction workers' tight jeans.

Though no longer exciting and forbidden, the Grill was still dark, woody, and filled with the yeasty odor of beer. It was just what Storm needed, a departure from the Caesar salads and double lattes of the city. The single room was comfortably dim. The tables, which filled the floor adjacent to a bar crowded with the same type of guy she'd ogled a decade ago, were lit with those candles in the plastic net-covered globes. The one on Storm's table was faded red and gave Becky's cheerful face a ruddy glow.

Storm relaxed and drank the beer she'd allowed herself with dinner. Becky was on her second, but the beloved Donnie was picking her up.

By the time Donnie showed up, the women were up-to-date on life after high school. All their old friends had been discussed; who'd had how many babies and divorces. Storm pushed her plate away with a contented sigh and ordered haupia pudding for dessert, even though she'd have to work off all that coconut milk tomorrow. Becky and Donnie shared Keoki coffees and nuzzled each other. The jukebox had gone from a ballad by the Cazimero Brothers to a Willie Nelson love song.

It was time to hit the road; this romantic stuff was making her lonely. She thought about Hamlin's legs in his running shorts and how he had seen the police cars at her cottage and dropped by to see if she was okay. It seemed like a long time ago, now.

Storm excused herself and went to the women's room. She passed down the narrow hallway lined with a couple of pay phones. A lean, muscled fellow let his eyes run down her body, then turned his back to her and cradled the mouthpiece in one hand. He wore low-slung, baggy jeans. She could see a hint of the crack in his bottom. Ten years ago, she might have enjoyed his flirtatiousness, but tonight she kept her eyes straight ahead, thinking that she'd rather anticipate someone's unclothed physique than see it slouching in a bar.

When she returned, Becky and Donnie were nearly sitting in each other's laps. It was definitely time to go. Storm gave Becky a hug and told her to call when she was on O'ahu.

Storm started her rental car, a metallic blue tin can with an engine. At least it didn't have any holes in the floor, which is more than she could say for her own car. It also didn't have cockroaches that dove for cover when the interior lights went on, which wasn't bad for a Hawai'i rental car. The air conditioner and defroster appeared to work well, too, for which she was grateful. Rain had begun to fall and the night was as dank and murky as the inside of a just-swilled Budweiser bottle.

Storm hadn't driven Highway 19 along the northern coast of the Big Island for several years. Laupāhoehoe, Pa'auilo, Honoka'a: all were scenic post office crossroads with the majority of their inhabitants on welfare since the sugar refineries had closed. Big Island people were rich in spirit and culture, but hurting economically.

Headlights glimmered about a half-mile behind her. Though it was nice not to feel alone on the highway, it would probably be safer to maintain her distance from the driver behind if he'd been drinking with his friends. This road, with its blind hairpin turns and narrow viaducts, was known for deadly accidents. Most of them involved people who had been drinking.

Storm wished it were day, or at least a moonlit night. She would be able to see the depth of the chasms she crossed and the ubiquitous waterfalls that crashed into the streams hundreds of feet below her. Now, the only way she could tell that she was on a bridge was by the glowing guardrail and the impenetrable void beyond the scope of her headlights.

The lights of the car behind her flashed in the rearview mirror. Storm gave her own car a bit more gas; the driver had gained on her while she'd been peering into the dark and slowing down on the muddy curves. She was almost to a straight part of the road, though by the solid double yellow line and the vanishing guardrail, she knew it wouldn't last long.

The driver behind crept up steadily. Storm slowed down. Maybe the idiot would just go around her.

He gained ground. Soon he was just a few feet behind her, his lights blaring into her rear window. The car seemed larger than hers, some kind of full-size, older sedan. She squinted. There was no way she could see its color, let alone the driver. Storm reached up and flicked the rearview mirror to the night setting. Better in terms of glare, but she still couldn't see into the car. She waved her hand in a drop-back motion.

The jerk. Hurrying on a road like this doesn't get you there faster. It gets you dead. Storm steered into a curve marked only by the sinuous path of the double yellow line and the flash of guardrail reflectors on her right. The reflectors disappeared to the left in a sharp curve, then flickered through the mist.

The rain fell harder. Storm slowed to a crawl. The driver behind flashed his high beams directly into her car.

Storm drew in a sharp breath. His bumper was mere inches from hers. This was not only stupid and dangerous, it was pissing her off. Storm reached for her cell phone, which was in her purse. It would take the cops a half hour to reach her, but dialing 911 would make her feel better. And maybe seeing the phone at her ear would make this moron back off. At the same time, she rolled down her window and yelled into the night, "Pass me, asshole!"

His bumper thumped hers. At first she couldn't believe it; she thought she'd driven over a rock in the road.

He bumped her again, hard enough to jolt her car toward the edge of the narrow road.

"Jesus," Storm whispered. She dropped the phone onto the seat. With cold fingers, she grabbed the steering wheel with both hands. Slowly, she lowered her foot on the accelerator.

Her own headlights revealed only a few feet of slick black pavement ahead, but she couldn't help glancing into the rearview mirror for a glimpse of the car behind. His bright headlights were not weaving, as she expected a drunk's would. Their brightness flooded her car with the intensity of a searchlight. She could barely see the road ahead.

She sped up. The tailing car sped up, too. Storm went faster; the car came within inches of her bumper, then fell back a foot or two. For a second, she reached out with one hand for the phone, which had moved across the seat toward the passenger side door.

A low silver guardrail glinted ahead at a right angle to her path. The road veered sharply to the left, making another hairpin turn over a chasm. Storm could hear her own tires wail on the pavement. She seized the steering wheel and struggled to ease it into the turn. The rear wheels slid toward the guardrail and she clenched her teeth and prayed. Her foot lifted instinctively from the gas pedal and she felt the car respond to her control. She let go of a pent-up breath.

The pursuer's engine raced toward her. Oh, God, I can't take another hit, she thought. The guardrail's a foot from my outside fender.

The car butted her bumper. Storm's body jerked forward against the restraint of the seat belt.

Her rental compact hopped ahead, its wheels out of contact with the road. The phone fell with a tiny thunk into the space between the seat and the passenger door. "No!" she screamed, her voice thin and lonely.

Afraid to slow down and too petrified to speed up, she drew close to the sharp turn on the other side of the gorge. Her hands clenched the steering wheel like a lifeline on a sinking ship. Cold sweat trickled down her torso and seeped from her palms. Her breath rattled in her throat.

The little car gripped the road again and Storm whimpered with relief. The road straightened for a hundred yards, then the double yellow line veered right. Another bottomless abyss loomed beyond the scope of her headlights like a black wall filled with the confetti of falling raindrops.

The bright lights behind filled her car as the big sedan shot toward her. With a moan of terror, she jammed her foot onto the accelerator and prayed that the curve ahead was a gentle one. She was too afraid to breathe. Her sweating hands slipped on the steering wheel.

She gained a car's length on the sedan and sped toward the turn. The road glistened; mud blurred the yellow lines. Her windshield wipers batted ineffectually at the water streaming across her vision. She couldn't see more than five feet in front of the car's hood. She had to slow down.

Storm tapped the brakes. Once, then again, as she followed the weak flicker of the guardrail reflectors around a steep curve. Her own headlights bounced back to her from the falling rain, unable to penetrate the black night. When the sedan slammed her, Storm's head whipped forward. Instinctively, her foot played the brake pedal despite the confusion of all her senses. Brakes squealed, and she couldn't tell if they were hers or those of the car on her tail.

Storm gasped with terror and stomped on the accelerator. With a shudder that carried through the car, the little car's tires screamed on the muddy road. Her hands clutched the steering wheel like a hawk's talons on its prey. The car fishtailed toward the cliff. Storm strained at the steering wheel, willing the car toward the yellow line, away from inky oblivion.

Behind her, the big sedan sped up, then rammed her again. Closer to the rail at that moment than Storm, he grazed the outside corner of her bumper. Pushed by the mass of the pursuing vehicle, Storm hurtled across the lane for oncoming traffic, fighting now to keep her car from smashing into the wall of glistening rock on the other side of the road.

She overcompensated and skidded back across the road into the path of the sedan. His engine roared, and then his car crashed into her left rear fender.

Storm lost control. For a moment, time slowed while she cranked the wheel and stood on the brake. Her tires howled and the car pounded the guardrail, then ricocheted and spun. Storm screamed.

The sound of tortured rubber and the snarl of the sedan's engine sped toward her.

She leaned into the car door with every fiber of her body and mind, trying to force the wheel away from the cliff. Her car had spun to face the other car, which careened across the road in front of her. Storm punched the accelerator so that her car hopped closer to the cliff in a last-ditch effort to avoid a head-on collision. Two inches from the vertical wall, she swerved into the oncoming lane, then overcorrected in a skid that rammed her front fender into the sedan's rear quarter panel.

The sedan slammed into the bent guardrail. The rail had held against impact once, but the second time and the bigger car were too much. The metal tore with a shriek that shredded the fabric of night. Then all was quiet. Silence and blackness closed over the road.

Storm let her car crawl to a stop. She turned off the key and sat with the car straddling the yellow lines, unable to move from the middle of the road, gasping softly while her headlights pointed two feeble beams out over the ocean.

It was a while before she heard the surf beating the cliffs below. A sliver of moon peeked through a gap in the clouds. Rolling waves glinted faintly out at sea.

The rain had stopped and the night was silent but for the sound of her own ragged breathing. If the broken edges of the guardrail hadn't swayed gently against the night sky, she would have wondered if she'd lost her mind.

Terrified of the edge of the cliff, Storm's eyes strained into the blackness beyond the guardrail. She put on the emergency brake as hard as it would go and forced herself to get out of the car. One step at a time on quivering legs, she tiptoed toward the gaping hole in the rail. Nothing was beyond; no little ledge with a branch like in the movies. Clouds covered the moon again. She could see no further than a few feet below her, a view that was as unfathomable as the depths of space.

Chapter 15

Storm's hands shook so that she could hardly turn the key in the ignition. Tears ran down her face and the reflectors between the yellow lines looked like stars wavering before her. Trembling, she crawled along for an undetermined length of time before she realized that she was lucky her car still ran. When she noticed philodendrons the size of her living room bordering both sides of the road, her mind clicked into a higher gear. She saw a few lights glittering in the distance and sped up to twenty miles per hour.

Good, Laupāhoehoe, a crossroads big enough to pull safely off the road. There it was, a Laundromat, post office, and general store. The store and post office were closed up tightly; one person sat in the Laundromat, spellbound by a supermarket tabloid. Storm rolled to a stop in the gravel parking lot.

She knew her phone was someplace in the bottom of the car. Lying on the seat to feel around on the floor, she felt like curling up in a ball and staying there. The shakes began to roll through her again. When her fingertips touched the rounded, friendly shape of the phone nestled under the passenger seat, Storm moaned with relief.

Her hands trembled so badly that she could barely punch the numbers, but she got through to 911 and reported the accident. She told the dispatcher that she was uninjured and where she could be reached, then hung up.

Then she sat for a moment and stared, unthinking, into the warm glow of the Laundromat. Someone had died on that lonely dark road, the second person in a week with whom Storm had had contact.

The ante had been raised. Surely Hamasaki had been murdered. And whoever was after her thought that Hamasaki had chronicled his concerns, knew that an attorney with Hamasaki's experience and connections would build a case before striking. She, in this person's view, knew what it was. And it had to be big enough to commit murder. She doubted that poor Tom Sakai's case was sufficient. Was it Hamasaki's meeting with S.O.? So what? That only led back to Tom Sakai.

Storm looked around the dark, empty parking lot. The only noise was from the toads belching mournfully in the tall foliage. She searched the briefcase again, but aside from a couple of pens and laundry receipts, the only files were Ray Tam's and Tom Sakai's.

She sniffled. The back of her hand wasn't adequate for her runny nose. Storm turned and rose on her knees to reach into the back seat for her duffel. When she got it in her lap, she flicked on the overhead light and dug for a wad of tissues. Instead, she pulled out a crumpled sheet of typing paper that she had jammed inside.

Lorraine's list. Storm cleared her eyes with the sleeve of her shirt and studied Lorraine's neat script. Even if the list had precipitated the car chase, it hadn't caused the earlier robberies.

Lorraine had written *Friday* at the top of the page, and the first name under it was Mrs. Hamasaki. She'd placed question marks next to the times, but Aunt Bitsy had called twice, once in the morning and again in the afternoon. For the morning call, Lorraine had written *9:30*. That must have been the one when she and Hamasaki had argued.

Lorraine had noted a half dozen or so other people, too. Some of the names were familiar: *O'Toole, Meredith Wo (HK), Cunningham (DC)*, and some clients familiar to Storm from working on Hamasaki's cases with him. He had a meeting with Wang, which was fairly common.

Nothing struck Storm as unusual, though she didn't understand the meaning of the letters following Wo's and Cunningham's names.

Sherwood Overton wasn't on the list. If Storm assumed that Overton was the late meeting, then the call from O'Toole might be significant. She figured that Hamasaki hadn't given Tom Sakai's case to Meredith Wo because he couldn't yet reveal that O'Toole had been to see him. So how had Wo known that a cancer patient had visited Hamasaki? Then again, Lorraine knew it, too, so perhaps information had leaked inside the office.

Storm was going to have to make some leaps of faith. Unimed, the HMO, was a common link between several of the most powerful people on Lorraine's list. It was a good place to start digging for information.

She flicked off the overhead light and listened carefully to the simple, reassuring noises of the night. Aunt Maile and Uncle Keone would be starting to worry about her. Suddenly impatient, Storm looked up the empty, dark highway, started the engine, and skidded from the gravel onto the road. It wasn't far to their home. Why wait any longer for the police in this lonely place? She could call them again later.

The rest of the trip was uneventful, though Storm sped past while visually scouring any dark turnouts along the highway. When she made the left turn to head up the slopes of Mauna Kea to Pa'auilo, she paused at the lonely intersection and peered into the night behind her car. The dark was impenetrable; mountain mists had descended from the cooler heights to stifle sounds and veil all but the nearest lights. Storm would never be able to spot a tail if she had one; she'd have to trust the *menehune* to protect her from here to Aunt Maile's and Uncle Keone's house.

She headed up the half-paved, half-graveled road. Old stands of eucalyptus and koa were the same, but the potholes had multiplied. When she passed the post office and general store, she had two more miles to go. Living room lights of houses perched near the roads endowed the route with the ephemeral characteristics of Brigadoon; Storm could imagine the elves in the clearings.

The people who lived in these woods vowed that certain areas were *kapu*, or forbidden. As a child, even Storm had seen fireballs, a signal that the night-marchers approached, and smelled the sweet warning aroma of gardenias and *pīkake*. Though the diaphanous lights were most likely the result of subterranean methane, the ghosts of Hawaiian warriors patrolling the slopes of the volcano were a myth that even modern folk hesitated to challenge. Too many old-timers told stories about members of their families and the marchers. Most people who had lived on the mountain for more than a generation wouldn't think of doubting the legends.

Storm's eyes scanned the sides of the rutted road, opaque past the arc of her headlights on the stout tree trunks. Despite the chilly mist, she rolled down her window and took a deep breath of the eucalyptus-scented air. Sometimes the trade winds brought a whiff of sulfur from the live volcano on the other side of the mountain, but not tonight. She turned onto a drive barely marked by a beat-up blue mailbox perched in the same old cock-eyed position on its PVC pipe. That was to keep the newspaper from getting wet; Storm doubted that mail delivery had started in the past few years. In fact, most people relied on their trips to the post office. It was how they kept up with local news.

The glow of kitchen lights beckoned. A yellow rectangle widened as the front door opened and a broad silhouette passed through it. By the time Storm was abreast of the house and had turned off the engine, Aunt Maile was beside the car. In the light that reached from the windows, her white teeth gleamed and her dark eyes sparked merriment.

The moment Storm's feet hit the gravel of the drive, the women had their arms around each other. Storm leaned against Aunt Maile. She inhaled the sweet aroma of puakenikeni growing on shrubs beside the house. Maile probably had blossoms in her hair.

"Where have you been, child? We were almost ready to send out a search party."

"I'll tell you when we get inside," Storm said. She took another grateful breath of blossom-scented air.

The inside of the house looked exactly the same. Uncle Keone's worn cowboy boots sat on a colorful braided rug by the door. His newspaper had dropped from his hand and drifted across the floor from his favorite reading chair. He awoke with a few snorts when the women came through the door. Storm reached him halfway across the room and they clasped each other in a tight embrace.

"Kid, you wait too long fo' come visit," he said when he released her. His face creased into deep squint and laugh lines, carved by years of riding the range of Parker Ranch. Uncle Keone, like the other *paniolo* who rode the thousands of acres that reached from the sea up the slopes of Mauna Kea, was proud of the fact that it was one of the largest privately owned cattle ranches in the United States.

Maile gave him a swat with part of the paper that she'd picked up from the koa-planked flooring. "Hey, gotta use bettah English—no pidgin. Practice, you."

She peered at Storm and frowned. "You look tired and pale, almost like one *haole*." She swayed her wide muumuu into the kitchen. "Storm, you want cuppa tea or one beer? Sit and tell us everything."

Storm had only enough energy to follow obediently. Uncle Keone was used to following Maile's directions. He grinned at Storm and they both dropped into chairs at the kitchen table. "Beer, please," Keone said.

Maile cocked an eyebrow at him.

"I'm thirsty," he explained and shrugged at Storm.

"I'll have one too," Storm said.

Maile set two longnecks on the table, then plopped a tea bag into a mug. She lowered her voluminous flowered dress into the chair. "'Bout time you're here. Poor Miles Hamasaki. How he wen' *make*, anyway? A heart attack? Tell the whole story." She slurped her tea, ignored Uncle Keone's glare at her own pidgin for the word "die," and focused her keen black eyes on Storm.

Storm took a long pull on her beer and noted with satisfaction that her hands were no longer trembling. She gave her head a shake to unjumble her exhausted thoughts and looked into their wise, weathered faces. "Someone followed me from Hilo. He ran into the back of my car, then I think he went off the cliff at the turn before Laupā- hoehoe."

"Lord, honey! Was he drunk?" Maile asked. Uncle Keone set his beer down with a thud and sat up straighter in his chair.

Storm nodded. "I thought so at first, but he wasn't. He was trying to force me off the road."

"He'd have to be *lōlō*, crazy screw-loose." Maile sat back in her chair, aghast. "Why would someone do that?"

"I think someone believes I have information they either need or want to hide." Storm gulped from her beer, took a deep breath, then told them about finding Hama- saki's briefcase and the burglary of her home.

"What do the police say?"

"The Honolulu police don't know about the car that followed me tonight. So far, most of them think I've been a victim of random crime."

Both Maile and Keone stared at her. "What's the world comin' to?" Maile whispered.

Storm frowned into her beer. "One detective might be starting to wonder."

"Did you call the police about the accident tonight?" Keone asked.

"Yes, I called 911, but I got tired of waiting."

"Storm, they'll want to talk to you," Keone said.

Aunt Maile squinted at her. "That call will have gone to the Kamuela police. It'll be a while before the Big Island cops and the Honolulu cops put the situations together."

"We gotta talk to them, tell 'em the whole story," Keone said.

"I don't know anything about the guy that was follow- ing me. I couldn't even see his license plates. And even you thought at first that he was some drunk."

"You act jus' like city folk. They never want to get involved." Keone shook his head, disgruntled. "You need to be here, where people take care of each other."

Storm's chest burned with fear, frustration, and loneliness. This was the end of a trying day. "I get here often enough. You sent me away, remember?" She had had no intention of bringing up the past, but the words bubbled out of her mouth, unbidden. She stuck the rim of the sweating Budweiser bottle in her mouth and took a deep swallow.

Aunt Maile looked at her without flinching, her eyes dark and moist with emotion. Storm had the feeling she'd anticipated this for a long time.

Exhausted, Storm's emotions rose to the surface and pricked through the half-healed scars of loss. "Why did you send me off with Uncle Miles in the middle of my sophomore year of high school?" she asked, her throat tight.

Uncle Keone snorted. "That gang you ran with and those *pakalōlo* pl..." He grabbed for his shin under the table.

Storm stared. Oh. They'd known all along about her patch of marijuana plants, ten feet high, covered with sensimilla, tenderly cultivated with Parker Ranch's finest manure. They'd never said a word. She had been going to put a down payment on an old Harley one of the guys in Honoka'a had for sale. Talk about counting your chickens.

Aunt Maile took a sip of tea. "Ah, darlin'. You were one angry *wahine* those days." She set her mug down as if it were the finest porcelain. "Remember the leather jacket you got for Christmas that year, right before your dad died?"

Storm nodded. She had loved it, almost as much as the motorcycle she had her eye on. Maybe more. The bike was a bit scary. "Well, Miles Hamasaki gave that to you," Maile said. "He'd been sending gifts ever since your dad's health really went down hill. Acted like they were from your dad and always said not to tell you."

"Why?" Storm asked, frowning. So they hadn't been from her dad. She didn't feel that gut-wrench of surprise, only an eddy of melancholy acceptance.

"He said you wouldn't like it. You reminded him of himself at sixteen."

Storm took a gulp of beer. He was right. She would have hated it. She had hated most adult attention those days, unless the person had some high-quality blow and a fast bike. She'd hated Hamasaki for taking her away from Pa'auilo, but she'd seen his good intentions in about six months. Plus, by that time she and Martin had established rapport as mutual hell-raisers. And, one more thing. Hamasaki was helping her with her arguments for the debate team at the new school, and they were kicking ass. That's when some of her classmates started to call her "pit bull." And contrary to the core, she loved it. But mostly, she loved arguing and winning.

Aunt Maile sighed softly. "We missed you terribly."

Storm picked at the label on her bottle. "Even after ten years on O'ahu, this is still home."

Maile's eyes filled with tears and Uncle Keone stared at the tabletop while he cleared his throat a few times. Storm reached across the table and took their hands in each of hers. "Look, we'll get to the bottom of this accident. I don't want you to worry too much."

"The police here may not be too sympathetic." Maile's expression was a warning.

Storm sighed. She knew Maile didn't want to bring up Storm's colorful past again. "I know. I'm a little worried about that."

"You'll go talk to them first thing tomorrow?" Keone asked.

"Yeah, I can barely hold my head up now."

The kitchen clock said almost one o'clock. Aunt Maile and Uncle Keone looked exhausted, too.

When Storm woke up, her blinds were drawn and she was sleeping in her underpants and the tee-shirt she'd been wearing last night. Although she had no memory of undressing, her jeans were planted by the bed as if she'd peeled them off and fallen face forward. Aunt Maile must have tiptoed in this morning and pulled the window shades so she'd sleep in. Storm peered at her watch, then looked again. She hadn't slept till eleven o'clock since her late-partying school days. She felt about as bad, too. A headache lingered behind her eyeballs, warning against any quick movements.

A shower and the aroma of freshly brewed coffee improved Storm's energy level. Aunt Maile must have heard her rummaging around, because when Storm made her beeline to the kitchen, her aunt pointed to a mug of strong brew in front of the chair opposite her own. The older woman sat with her own cup and the morning paper propped at arm's length.

"Good morning, dear. Just poured it." She shoved the paper toward Storm and went to the stove. "I don't know how this story got to the press in time for the morning paper. Of course, this is pretty exciting news around here."

> *Kwi Choy of Honolulu, 20, died when the Chevrolet Impala he drove smashed through the guardrail on the Māmalahoa Highway. Ocean currents carried Choy, still inside the car, to Waipuna Stream, where he was discovered early this morning. Hilo resident Tong Choy reported the car stolen at two a.m. from the street in front of his home. Police are seeking more information regarding the accident.*

Storm skimmed the top story on the front page, then looked up at her aunt. "This guy Choy reported his car missing long after the accident. He noticed in the middle of the night?"

"Maybe he had insomnia."

"Right."

Aunt Maile peered over her reading glasses at Storm and shrugged. "Just trying to be the devil's advocate."

"Yeah, or maybe he gets up to walk the dog."

"What?" Aunt Maile looked at her and frowned.

"These guys have the same last name. It's a common one, but I don't like the coincidence. You know many people in Hilo?"

"Some. I'll ask around."

Storm propped her chin in one hand and siphoned off a noisy swallow of coffee. "I told you about Tom Sakai last night, didn't I?"

"Tom Sakai? No, but I know that name. Bebe Fernandez asked me for some special herbs for him a couple weeks ago. They only grow here, high on the slopes of Mauna Kea." Aunt Maile put a plate of scrambled eggs in front of Storm. "Since we learned *lapa'au* from the same *kupuna*, we share ideas on treatment."

"So she's on O'ahu?" Storm set her fork down with a click.

"Sure, in Waianae. She's the best healer in the islands."

"How's Tom doing?"

"He's pretty sick. Doing chemotherapy, too."

Storm knew better than to get into a discussion comparing traditional Hawaiian healing to Western medical techniques. "I found Sakai's file in Hamasaki's briefcase, but he never handled medical cases."

"Maybe he was going to hand the case over to his partner but never got the chance."

Storm nodded. "That's possible. But I don't think he would talk about either Sakai or O'Toole's problems without asking them first."

Maile sat down at the table with a grunt. She picked up her tea without looking at Storm.

"Do you think I could talk to Tom?" Storm asked.

"I wondered if that's what you were getting at." Maile thought for a moment. "Bebe needs those herbs and I could send them with you. It's the safest, fastest way of getting them there." She peered at her niece. "Do you really believe that a sick man can give you any useful information? Enough to warrant disturbing him and his family?"

"I'll be very careful when I tell him about the file. I'll just ask him if he knew Hamasaki."

Maile frowned. "You take those herbs to Bebe, then let her decide." She pointed to the newspaper. "Meanwhile, you'd better go to the police before they come to you."

"Right." Storm ate the rest of her eggs. She would never cook them for herself and they tasted wonderful. After the last bite, she tried to help clean up the kitchen, but Aunt Maile shooed her out.

Storm drove into Waimea, where the principal police station for this side of the island was located. A dark-haired woman in the familiar blue uniform smiled up at her from a desk. "May I help you?"

"Yes, could I talk to you about the accident that happened last night?"

The woman put down her pen. "You need to talk to Chief Mendoza. Let me check if he's free. What's your name, please?" She picked up her phone and pushed a button.

Chief? Shit.

Mendoza stood behind the woman's desk by the time she'd placed her receiver back in the cradle. "Kayama. You're back." His hair was still slicked straight back, but its raven sheen was silvery gray and he'd gained fifty pounds.

"Nice to see you, too, Chief Mendoza." Well, what else could she say?

He exhaled through his nose with a puff that reminded Storm of a Percheron and caused the woman cop's smile to diminish a watt or two. "Let's talk in my office."

The office was bigger than Storm remembered, and the walls were covered with pictures. Mendoza with the mayor of Hawai'i, the mayor of Honolulu, and Jack Lord of "Hawaii Five-O." That one was from the days Storm lived on the Big Island and Mendoza was still a sergeant.

"Have a seat." Mendoza pointed to a chair, then perched his substantial behind on the edge of the desk. He glared down at her and folded his arms. She looked up and noticed that her neck was stiff from the ordeal last night.

"We got your call. Why didn't you stay at the scene?" he said.

"Chief Mendoza, I was so upset, it was all I could do to dial the number. I grew too tired to wait."

"Did you stop when you heard the crash?"

"Yes, but I couldn't see anything. So I drove to Laupāhoehoe, where I could safely pull off the road and call."

"The car Kwi was driving was white. It had metallic blue paint on the front bumper. If I look at your car, will I find that it matches?"

"Of course. He rammed me from behind."

"And you fled the scene of a fatal accident, which is a felony."

Ten years ago, Mendoza's bullying would have terrified her. This morning, it made her mad. She stood up and looked down at Mendoza's seated bulk and folded her arms like his. "Chief Mendoza, I reported the accident. He rammed me, dropped back, rammed me again, and went over the side. The marks on both cars will corroborate my story."

Mendoza narrowed his little black eyes. "We'll see. Why would he do that?"

"Chief Mendoza, I'm reporting not only an accident, but an assault. The why part is your job."

Mendoza stood up. "You have your car outside? I want to see it." He opened the door. "Hamasaki can't get you out of trouble anymore. If you're involved in any of your old shenanigans, I'll bust you flatter'n a cockroach."

Mendoza looked at the rental's crumpled fenders. He walked around the car twice, opened the doors, looked under the front seat, and sniffed around the dashboard, punctuating his search with grunts and snorts. He slammed the driver's side door so hard the car rocked. "Watch yourself," he said and went back in the station house.

Carefully obeying the speed limit while her blood pressure threatened to blow the top of her head off, Storm drove north to her aunt's and uncle's home. No one appeared to follow her. It was hard to know which sight would have upset her more in the rearview mirror, a police car or an anonymous sedan.

Twenty minutes later, she found a note from Aunt Maile on the kitchen counter saying that she was doing errands and would be back in an hour; when the day cooled off, they would go pick herbs. Storm still seethed at the confrontation with Mendoza, but now she realized that what upset her most was the memory of her past put on display. She paced the floor for a few minutes and mentally reviewed the conversation. Mendoza was a jerk, but he was right about her leaving the scene of the accident. Still, she didn't feel that she could ask him for help if she needed it. What she needed was to go for a run, burn off the frustration, and think about the situation.

The gravel roads around Pa'auilo were wonderful for running. There was very little traffic and the few drivers who passed waved with big grins on their faces. The air was humid, cool, and smelled of sweet grass and the faint perfume of, well, cow manure.

Storm found her rhythm in ten minutes, then jogged without fatigue. When she turned around in the middle of the dirt road to head back, she was inhaling deep, cleansing breaths and she had left the conflict of the morning in the dust of the road.

Clearheaded, she reviewed the events of the drive from Hilo last night. When she left the house this morning, dreading the visit to the police, she had the feeling that she'd left something undone. With a jolt, Storm realized that she had intended to call Lorraine. If the whole thing with Kwi Choy hadn't been just a crazy accident, then someone believed Storm knew something damaging. That person might figure Lorraine knew it, too.

Maile was in the kitchen, chopping the tops off carrots and stowing them in the refrigerator when Storm came in sweaty from her run. Maile watched with a wide-eyed, bemused expression when Storm burst into the kitchen and grabbed the phone.

Storm shifted her weight from one foot to the other and counted the rings. From past conversations, Storm knew that Lorraine and her husband went to the farmer's market and Chinatown on Saturdays for their weekly vegetable shopping. It was an activity they enjoyed together and Lorraine frequently related the bargains they found to colleagues at the office. Storm left a message for Lorraine to call her immediately and hung up the phone. "I'll try again later."

"Good idea." Maile put down a peeler and washed her hands at the sink. "You feel like walking with me, picking some herbs for Bebe's patient? We need to go soon. The clouds are coming in and it'll rain in an hour or two."

"I'd love to. Give me five minutes to change my clothes." Storm dashed off to her room.

When they got outside the house, Aunt Maile pressed a piece of carved wood into Storm's hand. Storm smiled. "*Pua'a,* my pig. You still have it."

"Of course, it's your '*aumakua,* your personal guardian. One day soon, I'll give it to you." Maile cocked one eyebrow at her. "When I know you'll take proper care of it."

"It's old, isn't it?" Storm looked at the totem in her hand, gave it a pat, and handed it back to Aunt Maile.

"Yes, it belonged to my father, and his father, your great-grandfather. A *kupuna* carved it about a hundred years ago, when people knew how their ancestral guardians looked out for them." Maile looked at Storm, her smile tinged with solemnity.

"You think I need it today?"

"I think you need it always, but I chant to it from time to time for you. It can take care of you from my house." Now, her eyes had a mischievous sparkle.

"Come on, Aunt Maile." Storm grinned back.

Maile looked up the mountain and started to walk. "The ancients had good reasons for their beliefs. We shouldn't reject so many of their teachings."

"I believe you." Storm recognized her aunt's mood. She knew that while she'd been changing her clothes, Aunt Maile had probably said an Hawaiian prayer for guidance in her search for strong herbs. Like many other Native American cultures, Hawaiians believed they were a small part of a great circle of life; the earth and her gods nurtured and needed to be shown gratitude for their benevolence.

Aunt Maile was a modern woman in many ways, but she believed in the teachings of the ancients. When Storm was a child, Aunt Maile had tied a small *'aumakua* on a thong around her neck before taking their walks on the slopes of the volcano. For Storm, it was tradition, like putting a star on top of the Christmas tree. For her aunt, it was deeper, a plea for a safe journey into the sacred lands that bordered the *kapu*, or forbidden trails of the *ali'i* and their *kāhuna*.

The royalty of old, their priests, and certain gods still wandered among the koa forests and lava fields. Those who saw them said that their feet never touched the ground and their presence was preceded by the aroma of gardenia or *pīkake*. It was said that whenever the sweet perfume of those flowers surrounded a person out walking, this person needed to heed the warning or face death. Tale after tale, even modern-day ones, passed on the omens.

Chapter 16

Storm followed the wide seat of Aunt Maile's overalls up the narrow path that veered from the main road and rose with the slopes of the volcano. Mauna Kea had not erupted for many years, though Kīlauea spewed regularly from the Puʻu ōʻō vent, north of Hilo. Still, Storm could see the lava paths that had flowed hundreds of years ago. A thick layer of lava could take decades to cool, and only then did the hardiest varieties of grass, blade by blade, poke through the convoluted sheets of congealed rock.

Along the edges of the lava flows, koa and *kiawe* grew gnarled by the ceaseless trade winds into skeletal crones that tottered across the grasslands. Storm was always amazed that this same koa tree produced the richly burled wood treasured by the best furniture makers in Hawaiʻi.

She took a deep breath of cool air and watched wisps of clouds dance ahead of them on the path. Aunt Maile bent down and plucked a plant, carefully leaving leaves behind. Storm drew up beside her and tilted her head back to the damp mists that drifted around them like amiable spirits. She'd forgotten how revitalizing it was to hike these pastures. From time to time, a cluster of cows with their spring-born young would low and trudge away from their approach.

"Want me to carry your basket?" She spoke softly, as if the clouds that descended upon these deceptively fruitful lands requested peace.

"Thanks, honey, but I'm accustomed to it. I'd feel like something was missing." Aunt Maile's voice was low, too.

"Aunt Maile, why did my mother use the *pueo* for her *'aumakua*?"

Maile looked at Storm out of the corner of her eyes. Storm saw the glance and knew she'd caught her aunt off guard by actually bringing up the topic of her mother. "She felt closer to the owl, our mother's family's animal guardian. I chose our father's, the pig. Same as you."

"Did she carry it?" Storm knew she was surprising her aunt by discussing her mother, a topic she'd avoided over the years, even when Aunt Maile had brought it up.

Maile grunted, then bent down and poked among some grasses. "No, she didn't." She stood up slowly. "She didn't learn about the old ways as much as I did. She was only twelve when our mother died. I'd had six more years of learning, and that's a lot when you're young."

Storm felt goose flesh creep along her arms. "I was the same age when she died."

Maile looked over her shoulder at her. "That's right."

"But your mother was sick." Storm's voice was brittle and Maile dropped back to her side.

"So was yours." Maile sighed. "If my mother had got pneumonia a few years later, better antibiotics might have saved her life. Eme was no different. There are good drugs these days which might have relieved her illness."

"Like the sleeping pills that killed her?" Storm spat out the words.

Aunt Maile's voice was gentle. "Depression killed her. She had no more control over it than my mother did over pneumonia."

Storm kicked a rock and sent it bouncing along the path. "Didn't any of these remedies help?" She waved her hand in the direction of Maile's basket and quickly stomped ahead of her aunt.

Alone, she sat down on a boulder off the side of the path. Why was she searching for answers about her mother now? Maybe Uncle Miles's death had set it off, or maybe it was just PMS, though she'd never admit the latter out loud. It made her feel like crying.

She was terrified of being like her mother, yet she could still miss her so badly that she ached. One of her childhood memories was of her mother comforting her, saying, "Cry, let it out. Your tears carry away the pain." Why hadn't crying, or something, relieved her mother? Why hadn't her only daughter been able to provide enough light in her life? A wave of pain passed through Storm. Maybe because the daughter hadn't been a very sympathetic adolescent.

Storm shuddered with the recollections of how people had whispered about her, lovely Eme's defiant daughter. Then, later, when Storm was a gawky teenager, the women sitting around would stop talking if she walked into a room and look at her with pity blurring their expressions to mush. It made her furious; the notion still made her boil.

Storm swallowed hard. She seemed to be caught between grief and the fear that depression would be as much her legacy as her mother's dark eyes and wavy hair. She was even further tormented by the scorn that much of society and organized religion heaped on suicide. Storm detested pity, the condescension it implied.

Aunt Maile sat quietly, six feet away on another boulder. She looked up at Storm, her brown face creased with sadness. "I still miss her." Maile picked a flower out of her basket and twirled it between her strong fingers. "Sometimes when I look at you, I see her."

Storm jerked as if Maile had touched her with a hot wire. Awareness passed over Maile's wizened face. "You only resemble her physically."

Storm lowered her gaze. "Was she stubborn, like me?"

Maile chuckled. "No, she was sweet."

Storm glared at the older woman.

"She was impressionable, even as an adult," Maile continued. "Very different from you. You're stubborn, yes, but tough. And generous."

Storm shook her head with distress. Maile walked over and put her hand on Storm's shoulder. "I mean that in a good way. I'm like you. Eme was artistic and sensitive. You and I blaze ahead. To our own detriment, sometimes." Maile smiled. "She did like to walk these same paths, though, just as you and I do."

Tears burned Storm's eyes. She wiped her nose on the back of her hand, then rubbed her hand across her jeans. "I should slow down and listen to people more."

Maile shrugged. "We learn at our own rate." She looked around at the fog that had silently surrounded them. "Storm, the clouds have come down and I need to get one more plant, *koali*, the blue morning glory. I think there's a vine on the pasture fence up ahead. Let's go, then we'll head for home."

"Aunt Maile, I want to sit here for a minute and enjoy the peace. Could you come back this way?"

Aunt Maile paused, then nodded. "It's only about a hundred yards up the path. Stay here, you could get lost in this fog coming."

The thickening mists gradually muffled the sound of Maile's footsteps. Storm raised her face to the coolness that eddied around her, glad for tranquility and solitude. Some of the cloud wisps were cooler than others and carried larger raindrops; they gathered and obscured the path Aunt Maile had taken. The fog cushioned not only the sights and noises of the pasture, but Storm's own bruised emotions. She took a deep breath of the soothing dampness and rested her elbows on her knees, chin in hands. Unlike the city, this was the land of her people, and for her, it held the power to heal.

Chapter 17

Storm had been startled by the upsurge of emotion that enveloped her. She had nearly shouted a protest to Maile's comment about her resemblance to her mother. Her aunt had meant it as a compliment. Family members who dared to bring up the subject of Storm's mother around Storm usually spoke of her beauty or musical ability.

Storm took a deep breath and forced herself to picture her mother. Her memories were still those of an insecure little girl facing adolescence. The sadness in her mother's dark eyes, the translucent pallor of her skin, the slenderness of her waist and wrists, merged into a fuzzy portrait. Storm found this image mixed with a sense of self-loathing.

Though superficially aware that she was, at five-eight, tall and handsome, when she was around other women she still thought of herself as clumsy and robust. She felt as if her hips and breasts were too voluptuous, her fingernails ragged, her feet too large.

In addition to her self-consciousness, she detested sitting in salons. She found herself intimidated by petite women who had perfect makeup and never sweated armpit rings onto their silk blouses, but she sensed she should try to look more like them. In her mind, they mirrored her mother's fragile perfection, an icon that Storm had no hope of duplicating.

People had admired and wanted to care for her mother. In the year before her death, neighbors dropped by with noodles and *manapua*, those tender pork-filled buns, helped with the cleaning, or drove her to doctor's appointments. They sat and drank tea with her in the afternoons after the long nap that was meant to rejuvenate her fragile constitution. Storm remembered the disapproving moues of certain women when she got home from school and let the screen door slam behind her.

One of them, a willowy brunette—Storm now was convinced that she had maintained her stick figure with an eating disorder—snickered at the number of chocolate-covered graham crackers Storm had placed on her plate for a snack. "Eme, you're going to have to watch this child's appetites," the woman simpered.

Storm's mother walked into the kitchen and poured two big glasses of iced guava juice, then sat with Storm at the table and ignored the woman who slipped into an extra chair with them. That day, Storm only ate one cracker instead of the usual five or six. Despite her mother's efforts, her mouth had been dry and the guava juice too sweet.

Her mother was a singer, the one-in-a-million lottery winner of talent who got to leave the islands to study in New York City. She was famous for her promise. One day she darted from the stage after the first song of an important recital. She wandered the icy streets without a coat for hours until she stopped to rub the muzzle of a mounted policeman's horse. It was a breakdown, people said. She was too high-strung.

Storm remembered singing with her mother. Eme had played the piano and encouraged her daughter's reedy voice. She blended her own rich contralto to Storm's in duets. Storm's voice would break with effort and she tried to believe people didn't cringe when she sat beside her mother on the piano bench.

Her mother didn't see it; she would hold Storm's hand against her stomach to teach her better breathing technique. Storm remembered her own dirty thumb next to the perfect one, rising and falling with the deep breaths.

She looked at her thumbs again. Still grubby, though the nails weren't as tattered as she remembered. In fact, they looked more like Eme's.

A rustle brought Storm to the present. "Aunt Maile?"

No answer. There were probably cattle grazing nearby, though she wasn't sure how far away the pasture fence was. Visibility was practically nil. She could barely make out the shape of a good-sized koa tree fifteen feet away. Its shadowy form wavered. A rustling sound came from the tree. Were the branches moving or was something behind the trunk?

Storm squinted and stood up. "Scram." Her voice sounded uncertain in the foggy stillness. She hoped it wasn't an escaped bull.

Maybe only a branch had fallen. She sat back down with a glance up the path in the direction Maile had taken, then looked back at the tree and froze. Something large moved in the deep grass. Whatever it was glided away from the tree, then clouds veiled its form.

The shape was too small for a bull, maybe more the size of a calf. Storm let a breath go.

Momentarily, the mists thinned and Storm saw the shadow again. It stood with a posture like that of a sprinter at the starting block. A creature that stood nearly upright. Or did it? She frowned and strained to see. Clouds drifted between her and the animal, but its shoulders looked higher than its rump. Its arms appeared to approach the ground, though the creature didn't use them to walk. It looked more like a human than a bull.

A hole in the fog drifted by. Through a tunnel of visibility, Storm caught a glimpse of the brown-furred animal. Its small, glittering eyes looked in her direction. She clapped a hand over her mouth with surprise and stood absolutely still.

Long, curved teeth gleamed against its dusky muzzle. It wasn't human, but it was definitely not bovine. The creature paused and swung its dark, boar-like head on muscular shoulders as if scenting the air. Lifting its long snout, it sniffed in her direction. Storm froze to her rock, unable to even lower the hand over her mouth.

The beast glided parallel to the path. It traveled several feet in the direction Aunt Maile had taken, without making a sound in the twig-strewn grass.

Fog wafted between them, obscuring the twenty or so yards between Storm and the creature. Storm drew a shaking breath. God, what *was* that?

The inside of her mouth was as dry as sandpaper. The back of her throat stung from the volcanic fumes, but she was too scared to even swallow, let alone move. She sat like a statue and prayed the animal's small porcine eyes couldn't see any better through the sulfurous vapors than hers could.

Storm stared into the shifting haze until her vision blurred. Something rustled again near the koa tree. This time, she dropped to the other side of the boulder and curled into the smallest ball she could manage. She strained, listening, but either the fog muffled the movement of whatever was there or it had left. Was it another beast, moving toward Aunt Maile?

Aunt Maile was out there, elderly and unsuspecting. Storm unturtled her head from the collar of her shirt and peeked over the top of the rock. Fog swirled around her; the meadow was unnaturally still. No cattle lowed, no birds chirped.

Aunt Maile might come down that path at any moment. Yelling a warning wouldn't help either of them. She had to get to her aunt ahead of this thing. They would be far stronger together than alone.

Storm crouched and peered around at the swirling mists. Her eyes burned with the effort of trying to penetrate the haze and her limbs tingled from fear and immobility. She felt as if she'd sat paralyzed for an hour, but she knew it had probably been only a few minutes.

The fog was still thick, but wetter and less sulfur-laden. An occasional raindrop splatted onto the top of her head and she felt moisture gather into drops heavy enough to glide down her forehead into her eyebrows.

Storm slowly stood. An aroma of gardenias floated on the next wraith of mist. It was a welcome scent compared to the sulfur from the volcano and she raised her chin in the direction it came. Now the perfume was cloying, too sweet, like a dying lei.

The odor wrapped around her with an insistence that made her take shallow breaths. She could practically taste it. Abruptly, she recalled the repeated tales of Aunt Maile's and Uncle Keone's friends. The yarns of people around campfires, folks talking story at family *lū'au*. The old Hawaiians had said, "If there are no flowers around and you smell gardenias, it's a warning. Get out, go away, leave it alone. Go, go!"

Fists clenched, too terrified to breathe, Storm bolted up the path. Once she stumbled on a rock and sprawled facedown in the dirt. Her knee slammed into the ground and she heard her jeans tear. Shakily, she got to her feet and darted ahead, too frightened to check her aching knee. The trail forked a few feet in front of her and one path disappeared behind a thicket of *kiawe*, the other wound around porous black boulders of volcanic rock to higher elevations. It led to thicker mists. Which way had that creature gone? Which way was Aunt Maile?

Storm paused and decided to head toward the thicket, where the fog was thinner. She took a few steps, then came to a standstill. Had the *kiawe* moved?

Storm froze, then saw a form behind the leaves. A dark figure, on two legs, smaller than the beast, she thought. Its arms were shorter and it stood more upright.

Storm smelled the flowers again, cloying, almost gagging her with their sweetness. She bolted for the uphill trail, winding through stands of wizened koa trees. Her chest burned with exertion and fear, but she kept her feet pounding along the trail.

The fog thinned. Gauzy wisps floated by, specters of the thick odorous stuff behind. Storm glimpsed the posts of a fence. Thick, flowering vines wound around the barbed wire between the weathered pickets. *Koali*, the morning glory that Aunt Maile had wanted. Storm sniffed the air. Nothing. The blue flowers were odorless. Nor could she smell the over-ripe gardenias.

"Aunt Maile!" Storm ventured a whisper. Her eyes scanned the fence line. Only the incline of the lava rock-strewn meadow stretched on both sides of the fence. She started to run along its length, then stumbled to a stop. Something had moved ahead, next to the path. A lone cow on the other side of the fence lowed and ambled away from Storm. She moaned with relief.

"Aunt Maile?" Storm's voice wavered.

"Here!" Maile's voice was a distance away, but sounded strong. "Over here."

She walked toward it, still gasping from the mad sprint up the hill. She searched the horizon, but saw nothing but a huddle of cattle. "Keep talking to me," she called.

"Go straight until you see the stream bed, then turn right from the path." Maile sounded close, but Storm still couldn't see her. "Down here." The voice came from so close, Storm stopped and scanned the rise and fall of the landscape.

Between the intermittent banks of clouds, she began to make out the terrain. Twenty feet ahead of her, a thick hedge jerked erratically.

"Where are you?" Shrillness wove through Storm's voice.

A flannel-sleeved arm popped out of the bushes and Storm heaved a whoosh of gratitude. She began to rant to the waving plant. "I've been scared to death. The fog got so thick that I...I saw something very strange." She made her way to the bush. "I think we should go home."

Maile's head bobbed among the leaves. "I know." Her head disappeared and the bushes shook harder. "Honey, I need your help." Her voice got more muffled. "There were these plants I wanted, but someone left a pile of barbed wire and I'm stuck."

A clot of vapors drifted between Storm and the line of vegetation. In its thick moisture was the sulfurous aroma she'd smelled earlier.

Storm skidded down the creek embankment and landed on her rear end in a mini-avalanche of gravel. She nearly collided with her aunt, who had one leg wrapped past the knee in spiky metal teeth.

She sat for a moment, gasping. At her aunt's knee-level, Storm could see rips in Maile's overalls and spots of blood dotting the denim. She pulled at a couple of strands of wire, but tightened a few others around Maile's calf.

"That's what I kept doing," Maile said. She looked down. "I can't sit because I'd land on top of that tangle and never get up. I'm twisted around here all funny-like. You think you could reach the ties of my tennis shoe?"

Storm looked up at her aunt's face, which was perspiring with the effort to stay upright in her awkward position. The air had become heavy around them and wisps of acrid moisture drifted through the creek gully.

"I think so." Storm snaked her hands into the nest of spikes and winced at the gouges, but kept going and snagged one of the laces. After it was untied, she held the shoe down while Maile wiggled her foot out. Storm kept her eyes on the mess in front of her and resisted looking over her shoulder, but the stillness disturbed her.

"Ouch, ouch," Maile muttered. "Gonna have to use some of these plants on myself."

"Aunt Maile, have you had a tetanus shot?"

Maile glared at her niece. "Of course. I believe in modern medicine, too." She shook her head and made a snorting noise. "I'm not takin' any chances on that lockjaw disease. You think I'm stupid or somethin'?"

"Uh, definitely not. Let's just get you out of here." Storm spoke to Maile's kneecap. It wasn't as grumpy. Her aunt's testiness was a welcome switch from the dry-mouth terror of twenty minutes ago, though the hairs on the back of Storm's neck still prickled and rain was starting to fall in earnest. Water crawled across her scalp and snaked into her eyes.

Her hands were occupied trying to push barbed wire in two directions. Maile leaned over and maneuvered her hands opposite Storm's. Slowly, the two women jiggled some of the teeth over one another and gave Maile's leg another inch of space. Storm picked ragged denim away from the catching points. With some hopping, flailing, and muttered curses, Maile wiggled her bare foot up through the tangle.

"Lordy, *auwī!*" Maile rolled up her tattered jeans and looked at her skin. "Ouch."

Storm lifted up the mass of wire to work the shoe free of the nest of spikes. She winced at the narrow rivulets of blood that tracked down her aunt's scratched and punctured calf. "Think you can walk?" she asked.

Maile grimaced and nodded.

"I'll help you. Let's get the hell out of here." Storm stuck the shoe under Maile's bare foot and together they shoved it on. "Hold onto my shoulder," Storm said and stood up slowly.

"Superficial cuts. They sting like the devil, but I can walk." Maile stooped to pick up her basket and a number of plants that had fallen out.

Storm looked around them. Maile watched her.

"Do you know another way down?" Storm asked.

Maile looked at Storm, her gaze dark and serious. "Yes." She grabbed Storm's arm for support and led her across the stream bed in the opposite direction they'd come. Despite her scratches and scrapes, she walked quickly. "What did you see? I need to know."

"Did you see something, too?" Storm gave a little shiver. "The fog distorted my vision. I was getting nervous alone, that's all."

"Tell me." Aunt Maile's voice was low and serious.

Storm's hands became clammy. The creature's shadowy image was so real to her that she glanced behind them on the trail. She didn't want to talk about it.

Maile led them into a forest of eucalyptus and large-leafed plants Storm couldn't identify. The leaves and brambles lay so thick on the ground that only someone who knew the forest intimately could have found the trail.

"I need to hear about it." Maile squeezed Storm's hand as if she were a reluctant child.

Storm told her about the muscular, unworldly creature that moved silently through the meadow.

"I think there was something else, too. I heard a noise, but couldn't see anything. The thing I saw didn't make a sound." Storm swallowed hard. "Then the smell of gardenias, or some sweet flower, got so strong I could nearly taste it. I knew I had to get out of there."

"The thing you saw, did its feet touch the ground?" Storm couldn't read Maile's shadowed eyes in the gloom, but she could see the grim lines in her face.

Storm stared back at her aunt.

"Did they? Did its feet touch the ground?"

Storm looked around, then whispered. "I...I'm not sure. I just know it didn't make any noise. I was scared to death because it was going in the direction you'd taken and you wouldn't hear it."

The lines in Aunt Maile's face deepened. "What did you hear, then?"

"Rustling, but I didn't see what did it. I saw a shape, but I don't know. It might have been human."

Aunt Maile looked at Storm and her eyes narrowed. "Stay with me," she ordered. She dropped Storm's hand in order to wind through the trees. The older woman moved her flannel and denim bulk with less crackling and footfall than Storm. Storm had to trot to keep up.

Her aunt's overalls were a benevolent blue smudge in the woodsy darkness of taupe and moss. The forest darkened as the mist coalesced into heavy clouds that began dropping an earnest rain on the leafy canopy. Sporadic chilly splats found their way through to the ground. Like a ghostly reproach, they tapped Storm's shoulders.

Storm hustled to catch up. "What was it?" She wished her aunt would talk to her.

"I don't know." Maile spoke in hushed tones without looking back.

Storm frowned and glanced at the dense, dripping foliage. The rough scales of tree trunks rubbed against her swinging arms and left their streaky rebuke; briars snagged at the legs of her jeans. She felt like a trespasser in the territory of a spirit who restrained the devilishness of the woods out of respect for Aunt Maile's presence.

When they reached the open field that led to the main road, rain pounded them in earnest. The air temperature rose and Storm stopped shivering despite the water that plastered her shirt to her chest and shoulders and streamed from her wet hair down her back. She drew abreast of Maile.

As if a veil had been lifted from their eyes and a harness from their bodies, relief lightened the air around them. They grinned at each other's appearances, then broke into laughter that caused them to stop walking and turn their faces to the streaming sky.

When they walked through the kitchen door, Uncle Keone rose from his reading chair with a snort, shook his head, and went to find towels. After the women had changed, he helped Maile treat her barbed-wire punctures and scrapes. When Maile put the teapot on to boil, he went back to his reading chair, harumphing gently under his breath.

Storm bent her head gratefully over her mug. The aroma of green tea bathed her in a sensation of safety. She wiggled her toes in Uncle Keone's borrowed wool socks and peered over the rim at Aunt Maile, who sat across from her.

Maile took a sip, then leaned back in her chair with a sigh. "That gardenia smell. You know what that meant?"

"Yeah. To get the hell out of there!"

"Yes, it was the warning of the ancients." Maile took a sip of tea and spoke gravely. "They were looking out for you."

"For me?"

"You, or you never would have smelled the warning." Maile narrowed her eyes over the steam of her tea. "Something bad's going on, Storm. I don't like this at all. That rustling in the bushes...." She shook her head.

"I wasn't as worried about the noise. Whatever it was sounded clumsy, like a human or a cow. What do you think?"

Maile got up to fiddle in the sink. "Don't know. Doesn't matter. What matters is that you were supposed to get away from it."

"And the creature? Any idea what it was?"

Maile sat down at the table, looked onto the surface of her tea, and gently blew the steam into whorls. She spoke softly in the comfortable kitchen. "Late one night when I was about ten, my grandfather and a friend of his got to talking about a god who was half man, half wild pig. Their low voices made me peek from my sleeping bag next to the beach fire. Grandad's friend sketched a picture in the sand; said it was a beast that walked partly upright, partly on its arms. He said it was Kamapua'a, and told Grandad that he would come out of the volcanic vents when he was angry."

"Kamapua'a? Pele's lover?" Like other kids growing up on the Big Island, Storm had heard tales of the various gods. She'd even seen the altar in Waipio Valley, where humans were sacrificed to placate some of them. It was said that gods, who could be either malevolent or kind, depending on their mood, could walk among the humans. But their feet didn't touch the ground. Many people claimed to have seen the volcano goddess, especially on the Saddle Road, which traveled between the two majestic volcanic mountains.

"He was also her enemy. Pele was a volatile sort." She chuckled at Storm's rolling eyes. "I couldn't resist."

Storm didn't want to be distracted with corny puns. "Why do you think he's angry?"

"It was said that Kamapua'a would come out to destroy or defend someone. He could be called by an *'aumakua*. Especially the pig."

"Aunt Maile…"

"Storm, these are old stories."

"I know, but please. You really think some old legend was out on the mountain today?"

"Listen to your gut, Storm. When we were on the mountain, you told me the creature looked otherworldly, unlike any beast you had ever seen."

Uncle Keone appeared at the kitchen door. "Storm, I almost wen' forget. You had one phone call. From a guy named Hamlet…somethin' like that. He sound pretty serious. His voice shook."

Chapter 18

Hamlin picked up his office phone on the first ring. "Storm, thank God you called. Lorraine's been in an accident. Some drunk ran a red light in his pickup and hit her while she was crossing the street."

Storm bit down on her lower lip so hard she drew blood. "Where was she?"

"At the farmer's market. About ten this morning."

Storm's knees threatened to buckle and she grabbed at the counter top. "Oh God." Her voice shook. "How badly is she hurt?"

"Bad. She's in intensive care. Storm, before she lost consciousness, she said your name."

"Hamlin, I tried to call her."

"Why?"

"Last night, someone chased me on the road to Pa'auilo. I should have warned her." Storm's voice broke as she told him about her harrowing experience the night before.

"You couldn't have changed anything." Hamlin's voice was soft. "Storm? You there?"

"Sorry, Hamlin. I'm coming back. I'll get the next plane."

Storm hung up and rubbed her eyes. She dropped into a chair and wondered if Lorraine knew about Tom Sakai's file. The file was confidential, yet Lorraine and Uncle Miles had worked together for over thirty years. She had to know something. She had mentioned that Hamasaki had started—what were the words she'd used?—to look after a cancer patient who came to see him. Then Lorraine had changed the subject.

Storm dialed the airline desk in Kona. There was no way she was going to drive the road back to Hilo. There was still a seat on the next-to-last flight, at six-thirty. She called Hamlin back. "Can you meet me at the hospital? I should be there by eight."

She looked at Uncle Keone and Aunt Maile. "I've got to go."

Keone nodded. "We know. Storm, be careful. Please."

Maile's eyes were dark with worry. She left the room, then slipped back in. "Come on, I'll help you pack. I've got the plants boxed for you. Just stick them in the refrigerator when you get home. Maybe you can take them to Bebe tomorrow."

Ten minutes later, Storm spewed gravel down the road to Honoka'a where she would connect with the paved two-lane highway to Kona. Although narrow and curvy, the route had fewer hairpin turns and no sugarcane scum to slick the blacktop. Storm drove five miles over the speed limit and prayed that the few local cops on duty were on the Hilo side of the highway that afternoon. When she turned south at Kawaihae and the road became flatter and wider, she sped up and prayed harder.

An irate car rental company agreed to call Chief Mendoza for the police report and turn the damage issue over to its insurance company, which left Storm free to get into one of the lines of happy, relaxed tourists. She stood there numb, and wondered if she'd ever again be able to share their sunburned nonchalance. In her seat, she observed the perfectly coifed guy and girl duo go through their flight attendant duties with the sincerity of Barbie and Ken dolls, and forty minutes later, the plane glided into Honolulu International. Storm watched the sun bleed its dying rays over the Wai'anae Mountains and wrestled with guilt over Lorraine's accident. Instead of sleeping until eleven, she should have gotten up and called her.

Hamlin stood in the almost deserted lobby of Queen's Hospital, arms folded across his chest, and gazed into the yellow-lit parking lot. When Storm stepped through the wide-open door, she moved to within a couple of feet of him before the drawn expression on his face melted in recognition. He wore a Thai silk aloha shirt that was coming untucked from his pants. The gabardine trousers, a nice cut, bagged at the knees. Deep lines bracketed his mouth.

"How is she?" Storm asked.

"No change. She hasn't regained consciousness." Hamlin led Storm to a bank of elevators.

"I thought she called me."

"One of the doctors reported that she said something about a coming storm. We thought she might have meant you." They got on an elevator and Hamlin pushed a button.

"How'd you find out about the accident?"

"Her husband called the office. Meredith was there, so she called me at home." He stared into the blankness of the stainless steel doors.

"So Lorraine was alone when it happened?"

"Ben was waiting in the car for her, reading the paper. Looked up in time to see the truck go through the light. Poor guy's a basket case."

"That's horrible." Storm's throat tightened with sadness.

"I saw her hand you something before lunch on Friday. A half-dozen people were standing around the office."

"Who was there? I can't even remember."

"A handful of us. Another associate was with me, a couple of secretaries, Ed Wang, Meredith...wasn't Cunningham coming out of your office, too? What's this list about?"

"Phone calls to Hamasaki. Mostly about a family disagreement over David and the will. There were some calls from clients, I guess."

Hamlin's eyes were bloodshot when he looked at her. "I want you to be very careful. A few days ago, I thought some addict broke into your house. I don't think so anymore. We have to tell the cops about all of this."

"I've been in touch with them."

"Does HPD know about the driver on the Big Island?"

Storm looked at the toes of her tennis shoes. "Chief Mendoza and I go back a ways. He'd love to pin the accident on me."

"That's all you need." Hamlin held the elevator door open for her and they got out. "Have you talked to Detective Fujita about it?"

"I haven't had time, but I will." The breath snagged in Storm's throat. She pondered telling him about the herb-gathering incident with Aunt Maile, but stopped. It was too bizarre.

"If I'd got hold of Lorraine yesterday, I might have been able to stop this." Storm's voice shook.

"Storm, you can't blame yourself. She goes every week." Hamlin sighed. "The cops are sure it's a hit and run."

"But if I'd told her about the guy who rammed me?"

"You think she wouldn't have bought her groceries?" Hamlin looked at her with sad eyes.

Storm didn't answer and Hamlin shoved open a door that stood ajar. They entered a room lit with the greenish glow of monitors. Backlit by a screen, Lorraine's husband sat by the bed with his head bowed. Storm thought he might have been dozing, but he raised his face slowly to them. His eyes were glazed and swollen.

"Any change?" Hamlin asked softly.

The neck wattles trembled on Ben Tanabe's neck when he shook his head silently from side to side. Storm moved to the bedside and involuntarily took a step back.

She would never have known the person in the bed was a woman, let alone Lorraine. Clear tubing ran from the purple mottling on the shaved scalp; other tubes of varying sizes ran into her nose, her mouth, under the sheet to hidden parts of the lumpy form. Her facial features were swollen and dark, flecked with darker material at the corners of eyes, nose, and mouth.

Storm couldn't breathe; her chest had seized in an inflated state and wouldn't move. She swallowed three times in a row, and then forced herself to take a step closer to the bed.

"Oh, Lorraine," she murmured. "Lorraine, please get better." Storm reached out to the older woman's arm, then withdrew it when she connected with an IV line. She wasn't sure where the real Lorraine was. She stepped back and knelt down next to Ben Tanabe.

He glanced at her only once and positioned his gaze back on the bed. When he mumbled, Storm leaned closer to hear him.

She opened her mouth to say, "Pardon?" but he began to speak without being prompted. With a little start, she realized that he spoke to himself. "I didn't know, I didn't know..."

Storm's eyes filled with tears. She looked at Hamlin, whose face was dark in the shadows of the room. "What can we do for her...for him?"

"Say a prayer," he whispered. He squeezed the old man's shoulder and moved toward Lorraine's still form. Hamlin reached out, snaked his hand under some clear tubing, and squeezed Lorraine's hand. He closed his eyes tight, opened them, and turned to go.

Storm stumbled after him.

Halfway down the hallway, neither of them had spoken a word. The tapping of high heels echoed closer and closer on the tiles. Meredith Wo turned the corner. With a brief nod to Storm, she put her hand on Hamlin's arm and stepped close to him.

"Has she spoken again?" Her head was tilted back to look up at Hamlin's face. Storm watched the sleeve of her gauzy shirt flutter against Hamlin's chest.

Hamlin shook his head. He could have taken a step back, Storm wasn't sure. Meredith looked at Storm, her almond eyes so dark that Storm couldn't read them. "She wanted to tell you something, Storm."

"We don't know for sure, Meredith," Hamlin said.

"That's what you said, Ian."

"She has a terrible head injury."

"I see." She shook her head. "What a shame. Is there anything we can do for Mr. Tanabe?"

Storm answered, though Meredith had addressed the question to Hamlin. "The firm needs to support him. We should send flowers, bring him food. Each person should visit when they can."

Meredith and Hamlin looked at Storm. Wo spoke first. "Good idea. Why don't you send a memo around the office Monday?"

"We need to start now. Could you talk to the other partners?" Storm said.

Meredith cocked an eyebrow, looked back at Hamlin, and walked away. Hamlin walked with Storm to her car. It had rained while they were in the hospital and the yellow streetlights reflected dully from the wet blacktop. The air hung motionless around them, dragging their moods to the level of the mists that hovered below their knees.

"Will you be okay to drive?" Hamlin looked past her shoulder to ask the question.

"Yes, thanks." His face looked gray in the shadows. "Uh, could I buy you a beer? Or a sandwich?"

"No thanks. I'd...I'd better get going." He gave her a little wave and headed toward the other side of the parking lot. Storm lost him in the shadows of the big monkey pod tree that spanned the area. In the day, it shaded cars from the scorching sun. Tonight, it dropped tears into the darkness.

Storm stopped by Leila's house to pick up Fang, but she declined Leila's invitation to spend the night. "It's too late. Leila, Hamasaki's secretary was in an accident. I'll call and tell you everything tomorrow."

With Fang tucked under one arm and a bag of goodies from the bakery that Leila insisted on giving her under the other, Storm headed for home. She was glad she had company when she opened the door to her dark little cottage.

She was doubly glad Fang was with her when she heard the knock on the door ten minutes later, not that the cat could do anything to protect her. She wondered if Fang would be offended if she were to add a Doberman to their tiny family.

Storm flicked on the front light, relieved that she'd locked the door behind herself, and peeked through the window. "Hamlin! Are you okay?" She opened the door to the aroma of hot pizza.

"I got to thinking about the break-ins in your neighborhood and thought I'd make sure you got in all right." His eyes looked green as a forest at twilight in the glow of the porch lamp. "Is it too late to take you up on dinner?"

"Come on in. I've got beer." It was the one thing Storm could count on not having grown green fuzz in her refrigerator.

Hamlin left a trail of delicious aromas as he walked to the living room and plopped the box onto the coffee table. Storm hurried from the kitchen with a couple of plates and two bottles of Beck's. They sat on the couch and scooped melting cheese, black olives, and onions back onto thick wedges with their fingers.

Storm sat back with a sigh. "I was hungrier than I thought."

"Yeah, me, too." Hamlin took another bite and wiped his mustache with a paper napkin. He chewed a moment, then spoke. "You were right about supporting Tanabe. And Meredith should approach the partners, not you."

"Didn't look like she liked me suggesting it."

"She's pretty strong-willed," Hamlin said.

"You know her well, don't you?" Storm asked, then hoped the floor lamp next to them wasn't bright enough to show her reddening face. She shoved a piece of pizza in her mouth.

Hamlin picked stray black olives out of the box and popped a few into his mouth. "Yeah. She was the one who lured me away from the prosecutor's office into private practice, though it was Miles who solidified my decision."

"How'd it happen that Meredith was working with the prosecutor?" Storm asked.

"She had a medical negligence case, a strong one, but Meredith wanted to get criminal charges approved so that the doctor would be tried for wrongful death instead of just malpractice or negligence."

"Wow, the guy must have really screwed up."

"He did, but he didn't deserve to be tried as a criminal." Hamlin shoved a few onions back onto a wedge of pizza. "He was seventy-two, a neurosurgeon who should have retired a decade before this case, but he was famous for developing this technique for fusing cervical discs. He was also one of those guys who live on past glories. Drove a big Mercedes with vanity plates with the name of this technique on them. He even had special tools patented for this surgery. The manufacturer used his name and often called him in to work certain cases and run seminars for residents and other doctors.

"Anyway, he was doing a case and nicked the patient's spinal cord. Unfortunately, it was a forty-five-year-old woman with four young kids who ended up quadriplegic."

"God, that's awful."

"Yeah, it was tragic." Hamlin sat back with a sigh and rearranged some olives on his pizza slice.

"But how could Meredith turn it into criminal negligence?"

Hamlin took a long pull on his beer. "Meredith comes from a big Chinese family. She's probably related to half of Chinatown. Her first cousin's son—is that a second cousin?—was a resident anesthesiologist on the case and observed the whole thing. Said the doctor's hands shook like he'd been on a three-day binge. Another of her uncles was a major in the police department. The department was getting bad press lately and wanted a big collar."

"I can't help but feel a little sorry for the doctor. Was he really drunk?"

"That's what Meredith's family was convinced of and she set out to prove it. Drunkenness would justify criminal charges."

"What do you think?"

"No one thought to take blood alcohol levels at the time of surgery. I doubt very much he was drunk. The guy's hands trembled because he was old and nervous. He shouldn't have been doing the operation, and he knew it.

I think the prosecutor's office made a mistake in allowing the charges, but by this time, there was a volcano of emotion ready to blow. There should have been compensation for the family and all that, but because of the criminal charges, the case got huge publicity."

"I remember reading about it. Didn't the doctor have a stroke during the trial?"

"Yeah, he was devastated. You could tell he felt betrayed. All these people who had used his fame and skill backpedaled so fast they were falling over each other. His lawyers got the charges reduced. There was no proof of drunkenness, but the damage was done. He's in an institution and Meredith got a big out-of-court settlement."

"And became the youngest partner in my uncle's firm."

"That's right. And I came on board soon after." Hamlin did not sound proud of the fact.

"You helped her get the criminal charges?"

"She didn't get the charges, remember?" Hamlin met Storm's eyes. The scar on his chin stood out white in the lamplight. His mouth was tight under the bushy mustache.

Storm suddenly got it. "When did you break up with her?"

"Right after I joined the firm. I tried to resign, but Hamasaki talked me out of it. He said Meredith would act like the relationship never happened and that I shouldn't sacrifice my position if it was where I wanted to be."

Storm sat back and chewed on a bite of pizza. This rang true. It also explained Meredith's familiarity with Hamlin. And Meredith had phoned his home to tell him of the accident. Storm watched Hamlin reach for another piece of pizza, then pulled her eyes away from the athletic slouch of his body on the couch.

She wished Hamlin had told her about this earlier, though when she thought about his actions, Storm was fairly sure that Hamlin was no longer Meredith's lover. But something else was bothering her. Hamlin had been more upset at the hospital than she would have expected, as if being there had touched a deep source of sadness in him. In the parking lot, he had seemed downright depressed.

The living room lamp threw a comfortable arc of light across his face and half of the pizza box. Though subdued, he no longer looked as pinched and gray as he had earlier.

Storm plucked at a string of cheese that drooped from a bite she'd just taken and sorted through a barrage of thoughts. Hamlin drew on his bottle of beer, caught her eye, and raised his eyebrows at her as if he wondered what she was thinking. She gave him a little smile. She knew he was a good lawyer who, like the others in the firm, made a living convincing people. And she hoped he was telling her the whole story.

Chapter 19

The ringing phone was a surprise intruder on their melancholy peace. Storm started, then reached for it with a sigh. Hardly anyone called her after ten, and it was much later. "Hello?"

Meredith's voice came over the line. "Storm, Lorraine died about twenty minutes ago. Is Ian there? I tried his apartment, but no one answered."

Storm handed the phone to Hamlin. She was aware that her face had telegraphed anguish to him. His jaw muscles were clenched when he took the phone from her. After a few monosyllabic responses, he hung up.

Storm's eyes spilled over. "Oh, no."

Hamlin draped one arm over her shoulder and turned her to face him. He rested his cheek on top of her head. The prickly hairs of his mustache brushed her forehead and she leaned against his chest, soothed by its sporadically uneven rise and fall. In a few minutes, she looked up at him. His eyes were dark with pain and he stared into a dark corner of the living room.

"Good grief, Hamlin, what's going on?" she whispered.

"What was on that list?" His voice wavered a bit.

"I told you what I remember." Storm looked up at him. "The only unusual conversation was an argument between Hamasaki and his wife about David's diabetes."

"A family problem."

"Right." Storm sank into her seat. "What do we do now?"

"We try to help Tanabe, hope he's got good friends and family to lean on."

"Do we need to talk to the police again?"

"We can try." Hamlin lowered her into a chair. "The guy who hit Lorraine ditched a stolen truck and got away. He even left an empty vodka bottle rolling around on the floor. Cops don't suspect drunks of having a plan other than getting from one bar to the next. This was the kind of accident they see way too often."

"I suppose." Storm took a deep breath.

Hamlin stroked her hair. "You need some rest," he said.

She nodded under his soft touch, glad for the comfort. She felt so guilty she couldn't look up at him. Could she have prevented Lorraine's death?

"Storm, did you find out who Hamasaki was meeting with on Tuesday night?" Hamlin whispered into her hair.

"Not exactly, but I found the appointment book."

"No kidding? What'd it say?"

"Some initials, I couldn't decipher what he meant. And I had to send it to Fujita. Good grief, I'd forgotten about it." Storm shook her head. "I'm exhausted, Hamlin. I can hardly remember what day it is."

"Would you feel safer if I slept on the couch?"

"Here?"

"No, at the neighbor's."

Storm had to smile. She could feel the warmth of his body from a foot away and she looked up at the scar on his chin, white against the tawny skin. Someday she'd have to ask him how he got it, but tonight she didn't trust herself. Those sympathetic arms felt too good. "No, go on. You need a good night's sleep, too. I'll be all right."

When she closed the door behind him, though, the room was so still she could hear the kitchen faucet drip. When Fang padded around the corner of the kitchen, she scooped her up in both arms. "Want to keep my feet warm tonight, furball?"

Despite her sadness about Lorraine, Storm slept as if the pizza had been laced with sleeping drugs and when the cat woke her up by sitting on her chest and purring into her face, she was surprised to see that her clock radio said nearly ten o'clock.

Fang had been patient, but once Storm was vertical, the cat demanded attention. By the time Storm pulled on shorts and a tee-shirt, Fang had given up on mere meows and had left for the kitchen where she batted her bowl against the refrigerator door.

"All right, all right." Storm dumped a can of fishy stuff into Fang's bowl, then stood with her hands on her hips. The cat's purrs were punctuated by gulping noises. Maybe Fang had the right idea. Though she didn't have much of an appetite, breakfast would help her face the day, too.

Two cups of coffee and a bowl of Cheerios later, Storm noticed the message light blinking on her answering machine. She pushed the play button and listened to Aunt Maile's voice give her Bebe Fernandez's phone number and ask Storm to call back as soon as she could, she had something she wanted to tell her. The time of the message was shortly before she'd arrived home from the hospital the night before.

Maile's phone number was busy, so Storm dialed Bebe's. A warm, older woman's voice sounded delighted to hear from her and invited her over. She gave her rather complicated directions which involved driving all the way up the Wai'anae coast, then taking a couple of gravel roads back toward the mountains. It was going to be an hour and a half drive each way.

Some O'ahu folks would spend the night if they had to drive that far in one day. Storm had spent her college undergraduate years on the mainland, though, where people drive an hour and a half just to go to a movie. She looked forward to it, as the coast was beautiful and she hadn't been on the leeward side of the island for several years.

When she hung up the phone, it rang. Leila was on the line with an invitation for tennis, then dinner. Storm smiled. Her friend's proposal sounded like a ray of sunshine poking through the black cloud that had been following her around. She hadn't seen her tennis friends or worked out for over a week, not since Uncle Miles's death. It was just what she needed. "I've got to drive to Wai'anae. What time were you thinking of playing?"

"How about four? We'll play for a couple of hours, then meet here and cook burgers on the grill."

"I'll meet you at the courts." Storm hung up and looked at the kitchen clock. She had time, but she had to get moving.

She was twenty minutes out of town, barreling west on the H-1 freeway, when she remembered that she hadn't connected with Aunt Maile. She'd call her later from Leila's.

Storm always found the Wai'anae coastline to be one of the most beautiful stretches of beach in the Hawaiian Islands. Massive lava rocks were strewn from the mountain-tops as if Pele and another Hawaiian goddess had been playing jacks. The great boulders marched across hot white sands to the sapphire ocean. The beaches were wide and interrupted only by the jet-black boulders and a few fishermen, surfers, and the ubiquitous coolers of beer.

Storm had to force her eyes back to the flat two-lane highway before her. In her bartending days after college and before law school, she'd spent the early mornings and late afternoons surfing. She still felt the pull of the cool, azure waters. She would have enjoyed stopping to chat with some of the attractive young men and women who stood on the dazzling sand, waxing their boards and studying the break, but she didn't have time.

She found the first turn back toward the mountains, but when the road surface eroded to gravel, then to a dirt two-track with potholes the size of the calves that grazed lazily behind dilapidated fences, she consulted the notes she'd made.

Banana trees brushed the right side of the car. Their tattered leaves drooped around the vulgar purple flowers that preceded the heavy bunches of dangling fruits. An aroma of decaying vegetation filled the air. Between the cows, buzzing bees and flies, and the water-retaining banana stems, the fecundity of the jungle was almost oppressive.

The right front wheel of the VW dropped into a hole and splattered black mud over half the windshield. Storm nearly bit her tongue with the clonk of the undercarriage hitting dirt. "Shee-it," she said with the bump of the car's climb out of the pothole. But the VW still putted onward without any new rattles of protest.

She peered around and looked for the old bunker Bebe had described. There it was, a concrete pillbox, flaking with what must have passed for camouflage green in World War II. It was mottled chartreuse, a sterile wart among teeming grasses and flowering plants. At least she was on the right track. Boy, she'd have a great excuse for leaving early. She'd never find her way out of here at night.

Fifteen minutes farther down the trail, Storm saw a neatly painted, square cottage whose *lanai* stretched along the front and around the sides of the house. Neat bundles of plants hung at regular intervals beneath the eaves. A porch swing swayed among the drying herbs as if a benevolent spirit relaxed on it with a good book.

The homestead had a warm, inviting air. The wheel ruts of the trail ended at the rear of a vintage Jeep, painted bright pink. Storm pulled up behind the vehicle and turned off the VW at the same time a woman about Aunt Maile's age trotted down the front steps.

Bebe Fernandez showed white teeth in a big grin, her walnut face framed by wisps of short gray hair. Her cheeks and eyes were creased into permanent smile lines like Aunt Maile's. From there on, the resemblance ended. Bebe was tiny and thin. She was dressed in an oversized tee-shirt painted with outrageous red and pink floral designs. It covered all but the bottom three inches of neon green bike shorts. Knobby-kneed mahogany legs ended in a pair of what looked like wooden Dutch shoes.

"You made good time," Bebe said. Her dark, sharp eyes scanned Storm's face as if they could read her personality from her skin.

"Thank goodness for your directions." Storm grabbed Maile's wrapped carton and got out of the car. Mud seeped up the soles of her tennis shoes, sucking at each footstep. As she got closer to Bebe, she noticed that the bright yellow shoes were rubber. Bebe was a practical woman.

"Come on in." Bebe took Storm's elbow and led her on higher tufts of soggy grass to the house. "It's really nice to meet you. I can see the family resemblance between you and Maile."

"Did you know my mother, too?" Storm asked.

Bebe's dark eyes met Storm's squarely. "Of course. She was a beautiful person." Bebe took Storm's box and opened the front door. "I'll get you a glass of iced tea. It's a dusty drive, isn't it?"

"Either dusty or muddy."

"I still prefer it to the bustle of the city."

"I would too, if I could. Does Tom Sakai come out here?"

"He used to, his wife would drive him. They'd bring the kids along, too. But he's weakening and they have a baby now." Bebe shook her head sadly.

"So he's still really sick?"

"Yes. All I can do is ease his pain with *lomi* and *ho'oponopono*, you know, massage and spiritual comfort. I help him with his diet, too, when I can get him to eat."

She showed Storm to a comfortable koa rocking chair, handed her a tall glass of iced tea, and took a seat opposite her. "Maile told me you wanted to talk to him."

"Yes, I want to ask him if he knew Miles Hamasaki, the lawyer. Hamasaki died recently and I'm trying to wind up some cases he was working on."

"Tom's being treated by Unimed. Is he going to sue them?"

Bebe's directness would have surprised Storm if she hadn't known Aunt Maile. They were similar in personality, if not looks. "Not that I know. Hamasaki left some papers with me and I'm tying up loose ends. Tom's doctor was trying to get a bone marrow transplant for him and I thought maybe I could help." She sighed. "You know, I started out with just trying to take care of Hamasaki's affairs, and then I read Tom's file. He's just a little older than I am, he has kids, it just struck me that maybe I could do something to help."

"I went to see him yesterday and asked him if he felt up to talking to you. He said he'd try to help, but he didn't know much. He's a friendly type when he's feeling all right. If he's not, you'll have to try another time."

"How about if I take his family dinner? At least I can do something for them."

"Lani would like that, I'm sure. So would Tom, for Lani's and the kids' sake."

"You think tomorrow would be all right?"

"Why don't you give them a call and ask?" Bebe went to an old roll-top desk and jotted down a number, which she handed to Storm.

Before Storm left, Bebe explained how she and Maile shared plants that they could only find in their own locales, increasing each other's repertoire of treatments. They also shared their experiences. "Your aunt is a talented *kupuna*." Bebe handed Storm a dried coconut husk. "Did you know the ashes of this husk heal burns and cuts?"

"She told me you were the best healer in the islands."

Bebe's dark eyes sparkled. She reached for Storm's hand. "And you, you may have the gift, too." She ran her own warm, dry palm over Storm's, along her fingers. "Maybe someday, you'll come and learn. There are too few of us left."

Bebe led Storm around her garden behind the house, a large tract of lovingly cultivated land arranged in quilt-like blocks with different greenery. Bebe showed Storm plants that Storm had seen discarded by landscapers in Kāhala. How many people knew that they had powerful medicines growing in their yards, around their mailboxes and dog dishes? Kailua dump was piled with coconut husks. Storm was going to look at plants with a more respectful eye.

The trip to see Bebe Fernandez left Storm with a lighter feeling, respect for the earth's generosity, a feeling that humans participated in a bigger whole than they usually acknowledged.

She drove back to the city and noticed that Lorraine's death did not rest on her quite so heavily, though from time to time, the image of Mr. Tanabe's hunched and grieving figure returned to her. She'd try to go see him this week, but right now she was looking forward to some physical exertion and lighthearted competition with friends.

Storm's timing was perfect; she pulled into the parking lot at Diamond Head tennis courts ten minutes early and dashed to put her name on the list of people waiting for courts. Leila had already staked out a spot and was sitting on a bench, smearing suntan lotion onto her freckling arms. Two more of their team members ambled in and the four sat and chatted while they waited for an available court.

Two sets later, the women drove their cars to Leila's house where they showered and set out their contributions to the potluck dinner. The evening, on top of the uplifting trip to the country, was exactly what Storm needed to escape the feeling that catastrophe followed on her heels. She drank three beers over the course of the night and insisted on staying to wash dishes with Leila after their other friends left. Not only did she want to make sure she would be safe to drive, she wanted to tell Leila about the weekend's events.

As soon as she finished the part about the car-chase, Storm's hand flew to her mouth. "Shoot! I forgot to return Aunt Maile's call." She looked at the kitchen clock. "Almost nine. I guess I can still do it."

"Be my guest." Leila gestured to the phone.

Maile picked up on the second ring. "Honey, you all right? I was scared to death."

"Yeah, I tried earlier, then got busy and forgot. Aunt Maile, Bebe Fernandez was a joy to visit."

"Storm, remember that guy in Hilo?"

"You mean the one that went off the road?"

"No, the other one." Storm could hear a newspaper rattling. "Tong Choy. Yeah, that's his name."

"The guy whose car was stolen."

"Yeah, that's it. Some guys found him up near where we picked the *koali*. He was dead, had a broken neck."

Chicken skin crept up Storm's arms. She sat down on one of Leila's kitchen chairs with a thud. "Who found him?"

"Some locals, looking for *pānini*, they said. Huh, fat chance they were looking for prickly pear with rifles. They were hunting wild pig. That's illegal on private land. I'm glad we didn't run into them." Maile snorted her derision.

"For once, I'm kinda glad they had guns. How do the cops think it happened?"

"They're saying he fell. You know Chief Mendoza, can't find his ass with both hands. Storm, you know those fields. You could break your ankle, but your neck?" Maile's voice dropped to a near whisper. "And he had scratches on his chest. One of the deputies told Keone it was like he'd been scored, raked by claws. Mendoza says he slid on some rocks before he hit his head." Aunt Maile finally had to take a breath.

"Maybe he did."

"Honey, he didn't have any marks on his head. Uncle Keone asked the deputy. Storm, there was some ancient magic up there. It was Kamapua'a."

"Now, Aunt Maile...." Despite her conscious rejection of the idea, the hair on the back of Storm's neck stood up. "Kamapua'a had hooves," she said. "How could he make claw marks?"

"With those teeth." Maile sounded exasperated.

Storm caught her breath. There had to be other explanations. "Aunt Maile, some animal probably tried to eat him. There are lots of dogs around the area, some hawks, even the *pueo*..."

"No, the marks were different, and they were bleeding, so they were caused in a struggle before he died. This deputy is one Hawaiian guy whose family's been here since Kamehameha I's time. He told Keone those marks were different than a scavenger's. And they found him last night, around sunset," Maile continued. "The rain had stopped by then."

"Right after I saw that thing." Storm made an effort to breathe deeply, calmly. "Aunt Maile, what have the police said about Kwi Choy? Why did he go off the cliff?"

Storm heard more rattling of the newspaper and Maile cleared her throat. "Well, they said he had a blood alcohol level above the legal limit."

"See, it was an accident." Storm felt marginally better.

"Storm, Kwi's friends said he came to Hilo only to visit and drink beer with his friends. That deputy that Keone talked to? He told him that Kwi had deposited a big check a few days ago."

"He got a better job?" Storm's voice sounded weak, even to her.

Maile didn't even bother to refute that comment. "Something bad's goin' on, I feel it. I'll do a chant to your *'aumakua,* then talk to that deputy again."

"Aunt Maile, thanks, but I want you and Uncle Keone to stay out of this. I'll tell the police here."

"Listen to me, Storm." Maile's voice had the tone Storm remembered from her early teens. She wasn't going to heed any young upstarts. "I've been around a long time and there are some things which are real hard to explain with modern logic. Sometimes the old legends do a better job."

"Aunt Maile, you've given me some ideas. I've got to look into some things over here."

"You watch out, young lady. Or I'm gonna come over there and take care of you myself."

"Aunt Maile, really, I will. I'll talk to you later this week. And Aunt Maile? Thank you." Storm hung up the phone and stared, wordless, at her reflection in Leila's kitchen window.

Chapter 20

Leila placed a cup of coffee in front of her friend. "You don't look so good. Someone else get hurt?"

"Got dead, you mean." Storm kept her eyes on the blankness of the window.

"Jesus, who?" Leila dropped into the chair across from Storm. "What does Aunt Maile say?"

"It's a guy from Hilo. He knew the guy who was driving the car that chased me. But Aunt Maile is taking her Hawaiian spirit thing too far this time."

"She's usually got both feet solidly on the ground." Leila raised an eyebrow at Storm.

Storm tried to smile. "It's hard to imagine a woman her size getting adrift on us, isn't it?"

Leila grinned. "So, what does she think is going on?"

Storm knew she could tell Leila about the strange sights on the mountainside without Leila thinking she was nuts. Leila knew her family; she also paid attention to Hawaiian lore. Aunt Maile adored her. Storm related the rest of the story, including Aunt Maile's conclusion that Kamapua'a had protected her from Tong Choy.

Leila sipped at her cup of coffee. "I don't blame Aunt Maile for being worried. Why was that guy on the mountain with you? You need to tell Detective Fujita the whole story."

Storm suppressed a shudder at the memory of that lonely road and the crash. "Leila, this has to do with something Uncle Miles discovered."

Leila's eyes were dark with worry. "You mean something that was on Lorraine's list?"

"Someone has stolen or attempted to steal whatever papers Hamasaki might have given me."

"And it all started with his death?"

"Yup." Storm chewed a thumbnail. "Leila, it would be just like Hamasaki to make some subtle but threatening comments to Sherwood Overton at Unimed."

"Why?"

"To get Tom Sakai better treatment. On the other hand, O'Toole probably swore him to secrecy." She rubbed her eyes. "I don't know! I'm too tired to think clearly anymore. I've got to go home and get to bed." She pushed herself slowly to her feet.

Leila walked Storm to the door. "Are you okay to go home?"

"Yes, I asked Hamlin to drive by. He'd call if he saw anything suspicious."

"Drive carefully, you hear?" Leila hugged her friend.

Storm's sleep was disturbed with dark dreams. Hamasaki tried to talk to her, but she couldn't hear what he was saying. Then she sat in a doctor's office, where someone like O'Toole waved a syringe and ranted on a topic that made all the blood vessels in his neck stand out under his florid skin. Lorraine was there, too, with papers that Storm couldn't read because for some reason, she couldn't take her sunglasses off.

When the birds outside the bedroom window began to announce first morning light, Storm opened her gritty eyes with relief. Lorraine had been sitting right on her shoulder, whispering some message into her ear. But Lorraine was speaking a language Storm couldn't understand and Storm's heart was pounding with frustration and fear.

She hauled herself upright and shook her aching head. It was early, but she wasn't getting any more sleep. She'd be better off at the office, distracted by work.

Storm didn't even bother to turn on the lights in the reception area. In another hour, the rest of the staff would arrive. Let them handle it. Without looking at the chair Lorraine had occupied last week, Storm went to her office and closed the door. She dumped her laptop case on the desk, fired up the espresso machine, and slumped into her chair.

Twenty minutes and a half-cup of coffee later, she began reading and preparing for her morning meeting with the partners. She was halfway through a list of questions for them when the pen she was using ran out of ink. Digging in her purse for her favorite pen, she came up with the Montblanc Uncle Miles had given her. When she pulled it out, a piece of paper was stuck under the clip.

Tom Sakai's phone number. Oh brother, of all nights to have suggested taking dinner over. With a sigh, she checked her watch. Eight o'clock: with a baby, they'd be up. She picked up the phone and dialed the number. Maybe this wouldn't be a good evening for them, either. On the other hand, seeing his predicament might jolt her out of her own self-pity.

A woman who introduced herself as Lani answered the phone and cheerfully accepted Storm's offer. She mentioned that Bebe had told them Storm might call. "It'll be nice to meet you," Lani said. Storm could hear children laughing in the background.

She hung up. Lani sounded nice; the visit might not be so bad. She ruffled through a stack of papers and sighed. Maybe she'd make another cup of coffee before she got back to work. No, she'd be wired by the time the partners came by. Tea would hit the spot, the kind she always shared with Uncle Miles.

Somewhere in the corner of the office, she had stowed the box with Uncle Miles's hand-painted mugs. She found it under a counter with a stack of files piled on top, a sprinkling of dust already covering them. She pulled out a mug and peered inside to see if she needed to wash it out. She did. In fact, coffee residue had formed a sepia stain over the white ceramic and she peered with disgust at what was certainly a cluster of cockroach turds in the goo at the bottom. "Yuck." She could still smell the sharp odor of stale coffee. She pulled out the others. They were clean; she'd use one of those and soak the dirty one.

In the kitchenette, she ran the tap and waited for the water to get hot. Suddenly, she turned the faucet off with a slap. Wait, if the other cups were clean, then this was probably the mug Uncle Miles had been gripping when he'd died.

But—he didn't drink coffee. She stuck her nose in the cup. Definitely a coffee smell.

Hamasaki drank his strong Oolong or Keemun tea with cream and sugar, or honey if it was around. A tingling started at her fingertips and passed up her arms to the back of her neck and scalp. When she'd gathered the mugs from his recently unlocked office a couple of days after Hamasaki's death, the used one was on his desk and three clean ones were in his lavatory. Except for one that she'd used, she'd piled them into a box and shoved them under the counter, out of sight.

Of course they were all mixed up now, but this was the only dirty mug, so it had to be the one he was holding. Fujita had mentioned coffee, come to think of it. At the time, she thought he had mistaken what was left in the cup for tea. With cream in it, they were practically the same color. You'd have to be looking for tea to notice the difference.

Fujita was right; it was coffee in the mug. So why had Hamasaki been holding a mug of coffee? Storm put a kettle of water on the small stove to boil and wandered back to her office with the dirty mug. Maybe he needed a picker-upper and his guest was drinking coffee, so he decided to have some.

But he'd never done that in the past, and he knew where she kept their communal stash of loose tea, in glass jars in the back of a beat-up filing cabinet in her office.

They started that practice a couple of years ago when someone kept dipping into the tea in the kitchenette and leaving the jars open. The flavor dissipated when the tea was continuously left exposed to air and light, so they ordered a new batch and hid it.

No, he wouldn't have drunk coffee. She was sure of it.

Storm carefully put the cup back in the box and re-checked the others. Except for some dust, they were clean. She sat still, then got up to check the tea supply in the file cabinet. There was plenty of both Oolong and Keemun tea. Storm filled an infuser with Keemun, went back to the kitchenette and finished making the pot. She poured some in one of the clean cups and stood by the narrow window in the small room, sipping while she thought.

In a few minutes, she rummaged through a drawer for a plastic food storage bag and took one back to her office. She sealed the dirty mug in it, placed it back in the box, and stowed it under the dusty files and the countertop.

Meanwhile, she had about twenty minutes to finish her questions on Wo's and Wang's project. She'd have to think about Hamasaki's mug later.

Meredith met Storm in the conference room and Wang's secretary, Diane, brought in a fresh pot of coffee. Cunningham came in a few minutes later.

"Mr. Wang called from his car to say he's running fifteen minutes late. The nurse was late this morning and his mother is agitated, so he couldn't leave her alone," Diane said.

Meredith sipped noisily from her coffee mug. "Poor Ed. The cost for all that home care is more than a nursing home." Her eyes were bloodshot. But then, Storm thought, mine probably are, too. Everyone in the firm had to be distressed about Lorraine.

Cunningham took a phone call and carried on a quiet conversation in the corner. Wo seemed to be more interested in the coffeepot than in exchanging pleasantries. Ten minutes later, Wang bustled into the room.

"Thank you for waiting." Wang sat down at the table, let Diane serve him a mug of coffee, then dismissed her.

All three of the partners seemed subdued. Wang, who usually directed the office staff, asked what time Lorraine's funeral was that afternoon.

Meredith glanced at him out of the corner of her eyes. "Five o'clock. We'll dismiss everyone at four, if you think that's all right." Meredith's voice had a grim note that drew Storm's attention, though Wang didn't even look up from his notes.

"Sure," he said. "You have any questions on what information you need to take to the Department of Health, Storm?"

"I'll look through the file and see what data I need, then call Unimed for their statistics." Storm's pulse picked up. This would give her a great opportunity to see if Sherwood Overton had visited Hamasaki the afternoon of his death.

"Good, let's get going on this." Wang closed his file and stood up. Storm left for her own office.

Ten minutes later, Storm walked down the hall on her way to the washroom. She heard Meredith's voice in Wang's office. "You all right, Ed?" Wo sounded concerned.

"It's just too much," Wang mumbled. "Both her and Hamasaki."

"Hang tough, old man," Cunningham's voice responded. "We'll make it through."

Diane was standing outside the door with a sugar bowl, but she caught Storm's eye and shook her head sadly. Both women, without a sound, moved down the corridor.

Storm went back to her office and was gathering what she needed for a trip to the law library when the phone rang.

"Hi, are you all right?" Martin asked.

"I've been better. Martin, when do you have to go back to Chicago?"

"I get a week off for Dad's death. But I've been thinking about some things. You free for lunch Wednesday?"

"I've got a meeting. How about tomorrow?"

"David and I are going over some things. How's tonight?"

"No can do."

"Busy social life."

"Hardly."

"Well, maybe I can cheer you up. Remember that financial data Dad and I were looking over? I got to thinking. Maybe between you, me, and David, we could scrape together enough to buy a hundred shares. We've got to get right on it, though. Do you have sixty-five, sixty-six hundred bucks?"

"Sure, my purse is stuffed with it," Storm snorted. "You gotta be nuts, Martin. I'd be lucky if I had half that in my entire savings. I'm still paying back student loans. Didn't you just tell me I need a new car?"

"Storm, in a year you could pay back the whole debt and buy a Mercedes. The company went up nine points since we had lunch four days ago." Martin's voice rose with frustration. "You sound like Dad."

"Martin, I just can't afford to make a risky investment."

He let go of an audible sigh. "Storm, I make my living advising very rich people how to make more money. Don't you think I can do my job as well as you? Or Dad? This company got picked up last week by one of the biggest mutual funds in the business. At least let me show you the data I was going to show Dad."

"I'd love to see it," Storm said. "And I do trust you, I'm just poor."

"Look, why don't you meet David and me tomorrow? Meet at David's restaurant at twelve thirty. I'll tell him you're coming."

Storm hung up the phone slowly. She hadn't seen David since the reading of the will. Given the circumstances of their last meeting, he wasn't going to be turning cartwheels when she joined the brothers for a discussion of finances. Including her had sounded like a last resort on Martin's part, but he'd done it.

Storm sunk her chin in her hand and pondered the last two exchanges she'd had with Martin. Since high school, he had struggled for credibility and acceptance in his parents' eyes, and for years she'd striven with him. In fact, she had always been the black sheep. In the two years after college, she had, to Hamasaki's distress, lived with her boyfriend and worked the evening shift at a Waikiki bar. In those days, Martin worked at a graphic design office. He and Storm had shared some rollicking good times. When the design office lost its downtown lease and went out of business, Martin moved to the higher-profile financial business. And as she got more secure in her profession, he seemed to withdraw.

Lorraine had hinted at the Hamasaki children's envy. It had never entered Storm's mind that she would be a threat to any of them. She had always assumed none of them had wanted anything to do with the legal profession and that their own careers gave them security and satisfaction.

Not all of this discomfort could be due to her, though. If she thought about it, there had been strife about Hamasaki's patriarchal role for a while. That's what Aunt Bitsy's phone call had apparently been about, David and his father's purse strings. These problems had been festering over time. She didn't know all of them, or how long it had been going on, either. She just knew, now, that she'd been excluded.

Still, she had a hunch that a more recent ripple of unease was underfoot. It seemed odd that Martin was pushing a stock purchase so soon after his father's funeral. Was a few days, a week even, really that important? Maybe. This was Martin's realm, not hers.

Storm looked at Hamasaki's cheerful mug, which still sat on her desk. She was on the outside looking in at the family with whom she'd grown to adulthood. She thought about how she'd often shared an afternoon cup of tea with Uncle Miles. He'd related stories about early days in the firm, they'd told jokes and imparted confidences. She would miss him terribly. The days when she'd found support in the company of siblings and under the tutelage of a wise and powerful man had ended. Her throat constricted with the thought.

Still, she was more fortunate than many. She had Aunt Maile and Uncle Keone. That might be more comfort than Martin had right now. Insecurity had shown in his voice, almost a tinge of desperation. Perhaps in his mind, this stock deal was proof of his professional competence. Though he struggled to prove himself to a ghost.

Storm knew emotions such as these were rarely ruled by logic. She still had to show she wasn't like her mother, didn't she?

If Martin was hurting, he needed her. After all, he had stuck by her through some very rough stretches in their teen years and she wanted to help him through his hard times, too. Losing a parent was bad. Losing one during a period of discord or alienation was worse.

Chapter 21

Storm sat in the back of the Buddhist temple at Lorraine's funeral and tried to swallow the constriction in her throat. Ben Tanabe looked like a lost child; Storm could swear that his hair was thinner and grayer since she'd seen him in the hospital. Two women, one with a toddler on her arm and one following close behind, supported him. Storm remembered that Lorraine had daughters and was glad to see the family together.

After the ceremony, Storm drove home to change out of the clothes she'd been wearing all day. She didn't want to visit the Sakai family wearing a funeral suit. Something brightly colored and appropriate for playing with children would go a long way toward shaking the sorrow that sat on her chest.

Fang pranced along the path to the cottage and Storm was glad she'd made the trip home. While the cat told her all about how hungry she was, Storm pulled on jeans and a striped tee-shirt. Each meow was lasting longer and longer. The animal could do *La Bohème* if she kept practicing.

"All right, all right," Storm said. She went to the kitchen, placed a full cat dish on the floor and the caterwauling came to a dead stop. A purr rumbled noisily. "Sheesh. What would you have said if I'd come home after the Sakais?" Storm asked the cat. Fang ignored her.

Storm picked up the phone and called Robbie's favorite Chinese restaurant. She requested two orders of minute chicken with cake noodles (Robbie could eat two by himself, so Storm figured this dish was a good bet), shrimp with caramelized walnuts, won bok with tofu, *opakapaka* in black bean sauce, and an order of fried rice. She hoped that she had covered the kids' and the adults' tastes and headed out the door. Her own stomach was already gurgling in anticipation. This was looking like a better and better idea.

The restaurant was on the way to the South King Street address Lani had given her. The food was waiting, neatly boxed and bagged, and Storm was back in her car in a matter of minutes. Ala Moana Boulevard was still fairly busy with people escaping the downtown office buildings, but Storm escaped the bottleneck going to Pearl City and the airport by turning up Alakea Street to the heart of downtown Honolulu.

South King Street was a one-way street going the opposite direction, so she had to guess at the street numbers by traveling along a parallel street. The business area of the city wasn't very big, just five or six blocks, and by the time the street numbers were in the vicinity of the one Lani had given her, she was in the middle of Chinatown.

Chinatown had always appealed to her. She watched with interest while last-minute workers scurried across the streets, locking the doors of travel agencies, acupuncture and herbal specialty shops, and lei-makers. The food markets were already closed up tightly, the bright red chickens' and pigs' feet taken from their hooks to be stir-fried with red pepper and ginger and consumed that evening.

The night population, which transformed the neighborhood, was just beginning to stretch its gaunt arms and peek from behind dark curtains. Korean bars and strip joint proprietors flicked on their neon signs, one by one. A whippet-thin creature in a clingy white dress leaned against a dark storefront and smoked a long cigarette, her sloe eyes following certain men's progress along the sidewalk. Storm, at a stoplight, noticed that she didn't bother watching shop-owner types or the white-shirted fellows who scurried home to their families.

Storm searched for a street sign to confirm whether she was in the right area. There weren't going to be any nice condominium parking lots around here. Bebe hadn't told her that the Sakais were poor. To Storm's knowledge, only immigrants and the penniless lived above the garlic or liquor-infused shops in Chinatown.

A cop car from the Chinatown substation crawled toward her and she felt the gaze of the two uniforms inspect her old car and, she hoped, clean and honest face. The narrow streets were lined with "No Parking" signs. She was going to have to head a couple of blocks *mauka*, or toward the mountains, to the municipal lot.

Ten days ago, she wouldn't have thought twice about walking the streets in the rosy sunset. Who would bother an athletic-looking woman in jeans and tennis shoes? Especially one carrying a stack of aromatic take-out boxes. Storm pulled into the parking lot and looked into the back of her car. Now she wasn't as confident about safety. She'd tuck her tennis racquet under her arm for extra protection.

Except for the beery vapors left in the wakes of a few people on the sidewalk, Storm passed mostly working folks. She walked two blocks down Mauna Kea Street, past the tuberose-scented air that surrounded the lei-makers, and rounded the corner to South King Street. The Sakais lived above a travel agency, their door a neatly varnished, barely noticeable passageway adjacent to a plate glass window covered with posters of Beijing.

Storm rang the bell on the street and was buzzed in. When she got to the top of the stairs, two beautiful *hapa haole*, or half Asian, half Caucasian, children greeted her with smiles. "Aunt Bebe told us about you. Your aunt is a healer, too." Their eyes followed the boxes in her arms.

Lani Sakai, a petite blonde, appeared behind them and guided Storm into the apartment. "Thanks for coming over. I left the office about an hour ago and picked up the kids on the way home, so it's hard to make dinner and get everyone organized. Tom is looking forward to meeting you."

She gestured for Storm to set the boxes on a hardwood dining table that looked like a family heirloom. She shouted toward the older child, who looked about eight. "Brandon, do you have homework? If you want to eat with the rest of us, you'd better get busy."

Storm put the boxes down and looked around at a noise behind her. She was standing in the living/dining room area. From across the room, a very thin man with a few wisps of black hair that sprouted haphazardly from his scalp pushed an afghan from his lap and stood up from a lazy-boy recliner. His black, almond-shaped eyes, huge in a drawn face, crinkled and warmed the air between them. Strong white teeth shone in a grin against his yellow-gray skin. He steadied himself for a moment by taking the hand of the little girl who had greeted Storm at the top of the stairs. "I think you've met Stephanie," he said. Tom offered Storm his hand. His grip was cool and firm, his skin dry as a flannel nightgown. The little girl, who looked about six, hugged her father round the hips, then led him to a dining room chair.

"Nice of you to come by and bring dinner. Takes a burden off Lani." He smiled in the direction of his wife, who had headed toward the kitchen and the noise of a fussing baby.

Lani came back out a minute later with a tray of water glasses and two milks. She glanced toward her husband and Storm saw her blue eyes darken momentarily.

Storm helped her set the drinks out, then rummaged in the bags and set out the dishes in the middle of the table, to be eaten family-style. The older children laid out place settings.

Lani put the baby in a high chair at the table, then sat down with the rest of the group and joined the chatter. Brandon wolfed his meal, then asked his sister for her last morsel of chicken. When she covered it with both hands, he went instead for the container and, with a swift glance at his mother, dumped the remainder of the cake noodles on his plate. Storm stifled a grin.

Lani, also, ate everything on her plate, but Tom picked walnuts from around his shrimp, ate a few chunks of tofu, then pushed food around on his plate to leave bare spots. Storm would have bet her favorite tennis shoes that Lani noticed it, too, though she couldn't catch her watching him with anything but pleasure. For a few moments, the knot in Storm's throat wouldn't let her swallow.

She looked around the apartment, surprisingly comfortable in its incongruous neighborhood. An air conditioner in the living room window insulated the home from the downtown noise. Wood floors gleamed and though the area rugs were far from new, they were Chinese wool, and lovely. The furniture was comfortable and clean, books and family photos covered the shelves on which perched a small color television.

It was a home where people loved each other. Storm blinked hard a few times and looked at Tom, who was speaking.

"I met your uncle, you know," he said. "A real nice guy. Dr. O'Toole sent me to talk to him."

Here was the information she'd sought, yet all she could think to say was, "Yeah, I miss him." Storm could have kicked herself, but Tom beamed at her.

"He had a good sense of humor. I could tell. Bet he was fun to work with," Tom said.

"He was. He's the reason I went into law." Storm bit the tail from a shrimp. "Did Dr. O'Toole send you to meet him after he told you that you needed a bone marrow transplant?"

Lani made a snorting noise and Tom's mouth twisted. "O'Toole didn't tell us," he said. "We found out on the Internet. There are chat rooms for people with cancer. When we asked O'Toole about it, he told us the procedure wasn't covered by my insurance policy. He said the HMO wouldn't pay for it."

Lani was practically sputtering. "We knew by then how much they cost. Could be a couple hundred thousand dollars! I told him we'd sue him and Unimed, that we were cheated out of time we couldn't afford to lose. They'd let us go for months without telling us what Tom needed."

Tom smiled in his wife's direction. "I didn't have the energy to protest, but Lani did." He took her hand and his eyes glowed. "And when she gets mad, watch out!"

"I'll say this for old Dr. O'Toole," Lani said. "He looked more nervous and ashamed than mad. I thought he'd tell us to find another doctor, but he sent us to see Mr. Hamasaki."

"What did Hamasaki say?"

"He said he'd try to talk to some people, pressure them a little," Lani said. "If that didn't work, then he'd start a lawsuit. He was worried about the stress of the trial for Tom."

"He knew I didn't have time to sue," Tom said quietly.

Lani glanced at him, her eyes shadowed with worry. "He pointed out that Unimed makes it very clear, in the fine print, that they're under no legal obligation to pay for certain procedures. He warned that a lawsuit might take years."

"And having the transplant is probably my best chance at beating this." Tom took a deep breath and pushed won bok around on his plate. He looked tired. "Dr. O'Toole told us that Hamasaki's firm does some of Unimed's legal work. Your uncle was going to see what could be done, if some strings could be pulled. He thought maybe I could be Unimed's first bone marrow transplant here in the islands. He said that it would be great publicity for the company."

"What happened?" Storm asked.

Tom looked down at his plate. "He died."

"Did O'Toole talk to you after that?"

Lani spoke up. "Dr. O'Toole told us that Hamasaki met with the CFO of Unimed, Hawai'i. His name is Dr. Overton. But he doesn't know what they decided."

"Maybe I can find out for you," Storm said. "Meanwhile, do you have any other options?"

Lani's eyes gleamed. "We've been working with the local Bone Marrow Registry. When they find a match for Tom, they'll help us with a fundraiser. We've already had two bone marrow drives for potential donors." Her chin jutted slightly and she set down her fork. "We're going to do it. It just would have been a whole lot easier if Unimed had helped with the cost, or at least been up front about the whole thing."

"Do either of the children match his blood type?" Storm asked.

"No," Lani said. "They're too much *haole.* You know, Caucasian from me. Tom is mostly Japanese, with a little Hawaiian and Portuguese."

"I'll try. I'm half Japanese, half Hawaiian," Storm said.

"Every little bit helps. Even if you can't help Tom, your blood type'll be in the registry for someone else who may need you later."

"I'll ask around to see who was supposed to talk to Overton, too."

Lani reached over and squeezed Tom's knee. "And we'll keep you healthy and strong, meanwhile. Especially with friends like Bebe and your Aunt Maile."

Storm unwrapped little boxes of almond float for dessert. Brandon and Stephanie were delighted, but she could see that Tom was beginning to tire. Lani got up to make a tea for him that Bebe had prescribed, then tucked her husband into his reclining chair. Storm cleared the table of dinner dishes.

When Lani came back, Storm handed her untouched pudding to the older children. "Why don't you two share this? I've got to go, and if my jeans get any tighter I won't be able to sit down."

Lani walked Storm to the door and gave her a hug. "Thanks so much for visiting us and bringing dinner. It was great."

"I'd like to do it again," Storm said. She saw the split-second hesitation in Lani's eyes. "I'll call you first and see how Tom's feeling."

"Thank you."

Lani closed the door quietly and Storm walked down the stairs to the street. She couldn't stop thinking about

Tom Sakai's eyes. Luminous when they rested on Lani. Scared and sad when he thought no one was looking.

On the sidewalk, a different world from when she'd entered the Sakais' apartment bustled around Storm. South King Street glittered with activity, lit by the hanging paper lanterns of Chinese restaurants that let aromatic clouds of garlic, seafood, and cilantro escape to the street. Neon flickered above the heads of the people who meandered between bars. Light spilled through open doors, but the alleys between buildings were opaque in their darkness and the people, mostly men, who sauntered into them disappeared as if they'd passed into a parallel universe. Only the embers of cigarettes glowed to show that the barrier wasn't physical.

Storm stopped on the corner to wait for the traffic light and tightened her grip on her purse and her tennis racquet. A quartet of sailors, their white suits still fairly clean, sauntered by and saluted her in a Slavic language. They were good-natured boys who were out for a good time and might need a hipful of penicillin in a few weeks. The loners were the ones who concerned her, the lowlifes who roamed in and out of the blackness between the strip joints.

She could feel their eyes crawl down her body, take in the racquet, and move on. She made herself stand tall and gaze around, get a good look at her surroundings. Somewhere she'd read that prowlers looked for women who looked down and away when they passed a man. Fear and submissiveness attracted predators.

Directly across from Storm was a tattoo parlor where a heavyset man stood in the door and scanned the street. His arms were painted so heavily that at first, Storm thought he wore a long-sleeved shirt. She looked again and realized that, except for an earring, he wore only a denim vest and baggy jeans.

His eyes rolled past her without pause. She was probably better off crossing to his corner. He was marginally less threatening than the tall woman in white who leaned against the streetlight on the opposite corner. She staked a territory in front of the dark doorway to a bar whose name, The Geisha's Lair, was displayed in hand-painted calligraphy.

Lair, indeed. Storm had no desire to cross into a hooker's domain. She glanced at the long, painted nails of the woman's hand. Haloed by cigarette smoke, they traced an arc to her maroon lips in the yellow cone of the street lamp. Her wrist was thick and strong. Storm glanced down at her stiletto-heeled sandals. The feet and ankles in the strappy shoes were too large-boned to be a woman's.

A group of chattering Japanese tourists, all male, surged around Storm like a school of sardines. Right before the light changed, the female impersonator in the white dress caught her eye. He cocked a fine, arched eyebrow at her and allowed one side of his lip to curl. Caught staring, her scalp prickled with embarrassment. Storm jerked her eyes forward and stepped off the curb. She picked up her pace, but could feel White Dress watching her. She squared her shoulders and lengthened her stride.

Mauna Kea Street got darker as Storm walked toward the municipal parking lot. The bars were dim; no paper lanterns hung out. A couple of the streetlights were broken. Fewer people walked along the sidewalks and those who did mostly shuffled along, their eyes to the ground.

A clanking of glass drew Storm's attention across the street. Otherwise, she would never have seen the neatly dressed man who walked by the tattered woman rummaging in the dumpster. His face was buried in the evening paper, though his black leather vest gleamed dully in the dim lights, showing the lean curve of his body. Storm stopped in surprise and backed against the bricks of a dark building. Her heart pounded, partly with dismay. She watched Martin's gold earring reflect the available light and listened to his leather heels click on the sidewalk.

Chapter 22

Storm's first thought was that he shouldn't be down here alone this time of night. Of course she was there, too, but she was leaving as fast as she could. And she had a tennis racquet to protect her. Storm stepped to the curb and opened her mouth to shout a greeting. Then she stepped back. Martin's posture, the newspaper, his averted face, all told her he didn't want to be recognized.

Storm looked around. No one was nearby. Martin's back was still visible, that kidskin vest of his gleaming against the dull black of his shirt. His step bounced a little, as if with anticipation.

Storm darted across the street, about a half-block behind him. She slipped along the dark sidewalk, oblivious to the yawning black doors every ten to twenty feet. She could hear the buzz of voices inside, the bursts of laughter, but she ignored them. Apprehension and curiosity pushed her after Martin.

For a moment, she wondered if he knew Tom Sakai. No, she was sure the Sakai family expected no more visitors this evening. She'd felt Lani draw her shields around the family for the night, making Tom's tea, hustling the kids through dessert and to finishing their schoolwork. Plus, why would Martin know them?

Storm's stomach did a little pirouette. God, don't let him go into The Geisha's Lair. The lustrous black hair of

White Dress gleamed from a distance in the neon of the street, right outside the entrance to the bar. But White Dress was faced away from Martin and Storm, toward South King Street, where the heavier traffic passed.

Storm focused her attention back on Martin, just in time to see him turn into a dark doorway only twenty feet or so from White Dress's corner. Storm slowed, made sure her feet slipped silently along the grimy concrete. Look casual. Sure, like a woman wearing jeans and carrying a tennis racquet would fit in. There were only two other women—that she thought were women, anyway—hanging around, and they wore false eyelashes and lycra dresses which barely covered their bony rear ends. They were so thin, you could hit a tennis ball between their legs even when their knees met. A flurry of emotions bombarded Storm: curiosity, embarrassment, sorrow at the women's professions. She felt as conspicuous as a Great Dane at a poodle show—and kept her eyes straight ahead and on the spot where Martin disappeared.

Strips of brocaded silk, impossible to see through, veiled the door where he'd entered. A plate glass window abutted the door, but heavy curtains, surrounded by the kind of little white lights interior designers put on Christmas trees, were drawn tight. Several feet above her head, the eight inches of uncovered window was crowded with hanging plants.

Eyes were on her, she could sense them. Storm peeked to her right, toward the lights of South King Street. There stood White Dress, hands on cocked hips. He shook his head slowly at her, like a kindergarten teacher monitoring the rowdies at recess. Storm looked away quickly, back to the veiled window and the name of the bar across its face. The Queen Bee was spelled out with tiny bamboo spears.

Storm felt a flush cover her cheeks and neck. She felt like she'd just awakened to discover that the recurrent nightmare that she was naked in school wasn't a dream after all. The Queen Bee couldn't mean…Martin couldn't… unless he was meeting some old friend. That was it. Martin had old friends who still played live gigs at nightclubs. From the corner of her eye, she could see White Dress. He shrugged, went back to his post at the corner.

Storm stepped through the silk into a smoky vestibule. She stood for a moment, tennis racquet dangling from her hand, and waited for her eyes to adjust to the darkness. Voices hummed around her; it was a busy place. But her eyes were as disabled as if she'd stepped from the noonday sun into a cave. She could sense a crush of people. This might be fun. It was the kind of place she and Martin used to go to back when they enjoyed being rebels.

She dragged one hand along the wall and crept ahead, toward the laughter and music, into a big room. The only light seemed to come from the little white Christmas bulbs that encircled the ceiling. They continued around large objects in the corners, which in a few moments she made out to be big potted plants. Ficus trees, probably.

The room was crowded with little wrought iron tables, packed with guys. Many of them embraced or touched each other shyly. The tables were surrounded by so many standing men that Storm couldn't get a feel for how deep the room was; she could barely make out a bar against the left wall. The bartender, dressed entirely in black leather, had a few more lights around him. So he could tell what bottle to grab, she guessed.

Her mind ground to a halt, trying to deal with the data that her eyes were sending. There were no women in this room. Two men were locked in a fervent kiss ten feet to her right, pelvises grinding together. She looked away, quickly. It wasn't the kind of place they used to go after all.

Expensive colognes blended to a heady musk and the temperature of the place was at least fifteen degrees warmer than on the sidewalk. Still fixed on her rationale for Martin having entered a gay bar, she looked around for the band. No band. Instead, David Bowie blared from speakers over the bar.

Heat and concentrated perfumes were making her dizzy. She took quick, shallow breaths, and felt with one hand for the wall. She was immobilized, unable to back out or go forward.

"The courts are closed, honey." A very tall, broad man with a nose that went in three directions before it ended in a flattened knob smiled down on her. He had been sitting on a stool by the door, hidden in the shadows.

"Huh?"

He raised his bushy eyebrows and looked down at her tennis racquet.

"I'm looking for someone."

"We all are."

Storm stared at him. Though his face was pockmarked and lumpy, his eyes were rimmed with thick, black lashes. They were dark and kind.

The synapses in her brain were finally sputtering out of their frozen state and her gaze swept the room. "It's my brother...he's got something I need..."

In the middle of the room, sitting at a table and holding hands with a broad-shouldered man who faced away from her, was Martin. Despite the number of bodies between them, his eyes locked with hers as if an electrical current had joined them.

Storm saw a spectrum of emotions cross Martin's face. Later, she would try many times to relive that moment and change it. She recognized shame, fear, and indignant fury. His eyes, dark and fierce, burned into her.

"Maybe you could get it tomorrow, dear." The sensitive voice of the giant at her elbow broke the spell of those angry orbs.

Storm tasted blood from where she'd bitten her lower lip, first in shock, then to keep it from trembling. She looked up at the long-lashed bouncer. Wordlessly, she backed out of the dark, steamy place and onto the sidewalk.

In the neon of the street, a few feet from the doorway to The Queen Bee, she leaned against a No Parking sign. She felt as if she'd been hit in the chest. Breathing hurt. Her vision swam and her neck felt like a great band of steel had been tightened around it.

Why had he never trusted her? Did David and Michelle know? They were his blood brother and sister. And Bitsy, she probably knew, too. Everyone but her. The real family stuck together again. Storm drew a ragged breath.

A pang of fear struck her. Did he use a rubber? Did he ask his lovers to use them? He could die, for Christ's sake. She stared at the filthy sidewalk without seeing. When a pair of splitting, run-down cowboy boots appeared in front of her own shoes, she didn't even look up.

"Hey, baby." The rancid odor of rotting teeth and metabolizing alcohol pulled her back to the street. Storm looked up, but her mind still whirled around Martin. "Come with Uncle John." He clutched the biceps of the arm with the tennis racquet and squeezed, hard. "Wanna get high? Forget your troubles?" He flipped open a shirt-tail to reveal the hilt of a large knife against the pale, flabby skin of his stomach.

Storm stared, numb, and hung onto the signpost with her other hand out of sheer instinct. The pressure of his grip was shifting her state of mind from grief and confusion to anger. She couldn't move the tennis racquet; he was pressing on a nerve that immobilized her arm. His unshaven leer moved closer to her face. She could see the broken capillaries in his nose, the ropes that coiled inside the loose skin of his neck. His eyes were the color of dirty ice, close together and red-rimmed.

"Get away from me," she said and tried to pull back. Asshole, she thought. I've got bigger problems than you.

"C'mon, we'll take a little walk." His fingers dug into her flesh with such viciousness that involuntary tears of pain sprang to her eyes.

"Ouch. Let go!" she shouted. Her arm and her alleged weapon were useless. A surge of panic washed over her. He saw it and moved his face to within two inches of hers.

"Let's go, now. Be a nice girl." She tried to hold her breath against the reeking pungency that came from him.

"Help!" Her voice squawked like a sleepwalker's. She reared back against the signpost. Her arm hung helplessly in the vice of his thick fingers. The tennis racquet clattered to the cement.

She saw the change in his eyes without knowing why it was happening. When the chain struck his face, she was so startled, she staggered to one knee. The first strike was a glancing one. The next time, the half-inch links wrapped around his neck.

He let go of her arm and grappled with both hands to get free. His bloodshot eyes bulged and she watched, shocked, from below. When her adrenaline-soaked brain finally gave her the signal to run, she struggled to her feet and scrambled backward over the curb.

"Watch out!" A young man's voice shouted in her ear. Stumbling to avoid a collision, Storm turned toward her rescuer. White Dress jumped out of Storm's way and toward the lout who scuffled to escape.

White Dress's shapely arm was raised again, the weapon incongruous in the manicured hand. "Scram, you piece o' shit." An accent of the Far East broadened White Dress's vowels. His narrow, expertly made-up eyes glinted with the anticipation of another strike.

The attacker scuttled into a dark alley. White Dress reluctantly lowered his swinging arm and kept his eyes on the shadows where the man disappeared. "He no come back."

"Thank you," Storm gasped.

"Welcome. Now go home." White Dress looked at her forehead instead of her eyes. He was shorter than she'd thought, about the same height as she in her tennis shoes. Without his heels, he would be shorter. And he probably weighed less. Storm swallowed hard. What kind of life had this boy led? How could she thank him?

"Could I buy you a beer?" she asked.

He looked at her sharply. Only when the skin around the flat black stones of his eyes softened did Storm realize her words had been those of a prospective john. She grimaced.

"No, t'ank you. Go home." His maroon lips twitched in what might have been a smile.

"Right. You're right." Storm picked up the useless tennis racquet with the arm that didn't throb and started up the street. She stayed close to the curb, in the light, away from the shadows of the buildings and the gaping maws of doors and alleyways. Her legs felt like Jell-O.

"Storm!"

Storm jerked around. There was Hamlin, in a black tee-shirt and black jeans. Storm stood agape. His outfit was similar to what Martin had been wearing, though not as elegant. Why in the world was he here? She was besieged with another disappointment, on top of everything else. Those terrific legs...

"You shouldn't be down here alone," Hamlin said.

"Huh?"

"Well, it's not a great neighborhood at night." Hamlin still looked concerned, but his eyes held many questions.

Storm sputtered. "Why didn't you help me a few minutes ago?" Storm's nerves were stretched to their limits. "I don't need shitty advice right now, Hamlin."

Now Hamlin looked perplexed. "Help you? Storm, why are you here? It's not safe."

"Why am I here?" That was the last straw. "Why are you here? Men! You're a bunch of opportunistic, manipulative bastards, playing your games at anybody's expense." Her voice was thick and hoarse.

"Hey, Storm." He reached a hand out and she batted it away.

"Leave me alone. All of you." Her adrenaline surge was fading and she felt weak and shaky. "Go back to the Bee's Knees, where you all belong." She panted with exertion.

"The Queen Bee, I think you mean. I wasn't there, though I think maybe I should have been. I was looking for a client."

"Right. That's what Martin's gonna tell me, too."

"What?"

"I've gotta go. It's been a busy night." Storm turned away. "You've got friends to meet."

"Mind if I see you to your car?"

Storm squinted at him. She didn't know how much mileage her quivering legs had left in them. The two dark blocks to the parking lot looked like a mile. Good sense overcame pride. "If you want."

She started out stomping up the sidewalk, then slowed and resisted the urge to use her racquet like a cane. She kept her eyes front and center. Hamlin was quiet. After a few minutes, Storm spoke. "So, you didn't see that guy grab me?"

"No, but now I know why Jasmine was stalking that dirtbag who ran into the alley." Hamlin sneaked a peek at her out of the corner of his eyes, his jaw set with concern.

"Jasmine?" Storm asked.

"Yeah. Tough kid, that one. Used to be Ming-shan."

Storm looked sideways at him. "You know him?"

"From my days in the prosecutor's office. We kept trying to rehab him, but he wasn't having any. Didn't want to send him back to Cambodia, either." Hamlin shrugged. "What were you saying about Martin?"

"Nothing."

"Um, Storm, did you by any chance see a good-looking guy, big, with dark hair in a pony-tail?"

Storm gave him a poisonous look. "I've had it with surprises tonight." She shook her head and felt irrational tears sting her eyes. "Sounds like the guy Martin was with," she whispered. She fired her next words at him. "Why don't you go back and join them?"

"Cause I think you need a drink before I take you home."

Chapter 23

Storm's knees still quivered and she knew she wouldn't be able to sleep for hours. Hamlin's suggestion to stop at the Ama struck her just right. A low, weather-beaten hut that squatted between million-dollar condos along Waikīkī beach, the Ama was named for the outrigger float on the traditional Polynesian canoes. It was an old favorite of hers. Years ago, back when she had to use a fake ID to get in, she and Martin and a few choice friends used to go to the one-roomed, salt-crusted tavern.

Not much had changed in the past couple of decades. The place was still decrepit and the Ama's tables were almost all filled. Two ceiling fans stirred the humid air. The bouncer who hovered inside the front door was a big Hawaiian guy who wore his hair in a long ponytail with a headband of traditional fabric. Hamlin nodded at him when they entered. "Hey, Kimo," he said in a soft voice.

Kimo's teeth shone brilliantly against his dark skin. The smile sent slivers of light flashing from his dark eyes. Then he bent his head down and resumed plucking the slack-key guitar he held on his lap.

Hamlin led Storm around the island-like bar, still draped with the same musty rope, fishing nets, and glass ball floats Storm remembered from years ago, to a small table at the front window. The window extended the length of the room and opened directly onto the beach. Hurricane shutters were propped up by gray, weathered two-by-twos at regular intervals along the face of the small building. Neither glass nor screens hindered the briny trade winds that whispered through the place.

The Ama persevered on the "gold coast" of O'ahu, smack-dab in the midst of some of America's most expensive real estate, because well-connected *kama'aina* and long-time residents had pooled their considerable resources and made an offer on the property. They were making a last-ditch attempt to save it from the foreign developers who, with ringing pile drivers and stacks of cash, built twenty-plus story hotels and condos along one of the most beautiful beaches in the world.

They'd not been able to out-bid the Japanese national who planned another luxury hotel, but they had had enough money to satisfy the original owner of the place, who grew up in the Waikīkī that bordered the pig farms of Kāhala. Fortunately, he accepted the lesser millions with glee; he merely wanted to retire with enough to take his wife to Vegas twice a year. He could still take his grandchildren and all their friends, too.

The Ama endured. The new *hui*, or partnership of owners, left the place with sand and shells on the floor, apparently replaced only what threatened to collapse, and continued to encourage homegrown musicians to come for impromptu jams.

Storm felt a surge of nostalgia. She liked the fact that it hadn't changed and remembered how she and Martin would show up, not knowing if it would be a quiet evening or whether Peter Moon or George Winston would be working out harmonies, their groupies in tow. One time, they'd seen Eric Clapton. Rumor was that the owners made just enough to cover expenses, and no one wanted to look too closely at how they afforded the property taxes on that oceanfront land. It was one time that the widespread nepotism in the islands seemed to actually work for the people at large.

Storm dropped into a chair that wobbled a bit and turned her face to the incoming breeze. Hamlin did the same. Neither of them spoke for a while. Storm closed her eyes to the soothing breeze off the ocean, took a deep breath of the cleansing air, and let it out slowly. She felt like she could sit here all night and watch the gentle surge of the Pacific, let its hidden powers soothe her anguished thoughts. The tension seeped from her shoulders. Just being near the ocean had a purifying effect.

When the waitress set down their draft beers, Hamlin took a grateful quaff and sat back in his chair. "What were you doing down there, anyway?"

Storm drew her eyes from the foam that skittered along the hard, fine sand. "Chinatown, you mean?"

"Sure. You scared me to death," Hamlin said.

"I scared you?" Storm snorted. "What were you doing there?"

Hamlin narrowed his eyes and gave her a half-smile. "Okay." He took another sip of beer. "I was looking for someone."

"You told me that part already."

"Yeah, well, it's a client."

"Sounds like what I was doing," Storm said. She looked back out at the ocean and wished that the lights from the Waikīkī strip a half-mile down the beach weren't quite so bright. She could barely see the phosphorescence of the waves.

"It's also a friend," Hamlin said.

"Same here."

Hamlin put his mug down with a crack. "Christ, Storm." He sighed. "It's this guy I've known for years. He's gay."

"No shit, Sherlock." She tilted her head at him and raised one eyebrow.

"He was my college roommate. He knew about my... my family and encouraged me to move here after law school."

"That's a long time to be with someone. Kind of like a marriage. How'd you sandwich Meredith into that relationship?" Storm sat back in her chair.

"Storm, he's not my lover. Never has been. Whether you can accept it or not, he's a friend." Hamlin frowned down at the table. "And he's got some problems."

Storm stiffened. "He has AIDS?"

"We don't know, yet. You saw him with Martin, didn't you?"

She nodded.

"I suspected that."

Storm bristled. "What do you mean?"

"I wondered about Martin—" He swirled his beer in the mug. "You didn't know, I take it?"

Storm turned her head to the beach, away from Hamlin's gaze. The city lights looked like stars in the prisms of her tears.

Hamlin looked away, out at the water. "Want to take a walk?" His voice was soft.

Storm nodded without taking her eyes from the ocean. Hamlin laid a ten on the table and stood up. She rose, too, and he draped one arm casually across her shoulders. It felt good, supportive and warm.

On the beach, both of them stopped to take off their shoes and socks. They left them in a little pile by a deserted lifeguard stand and let the cool, damp grains of sand drizzle between their toes. Storm dragged her feet and enjoyed the pull on the muscles that ran down the fronts of her legs.

Hamlin kept pace while Storm, her arms wrapped around herself, meandered into the gentle waves that licked at her insteps, then her ankles. The water seemed to drain away some of her distress, carry it out to be feasted upon by the night scavengers of the reef.

Storm looked at the swath of moonlight on the dimpled water. So peaceful, lulling, illusive. Just a foot below the surface, life teemed with a ferocity that could be alarming. As a child, she had thrown pieces of fish and crab shells onto coral at the water's edge after the sun had set and watched moray eels emerge from where people had swum all day. Three and four feet long, they came with their mouths open and razor teeth glinting, until the sand writhed with them. Sharks fed when the sun's light faded, too, along with hundreds of species of carnivorous, cannibalistic fish. She understood the rules here better than in nighttime Chinatown.

"It must be a devastating secret for Martin." Hamlin's soft voice broke into her thoughts.

"What makes you so sure?" Bitterness colored Storm's voice. "I'm sure his family knew. I'm just now realizing the secrets they all kept."

"I know because my friend wouldn't tell me who he was seeing," Hamlin said when he caught her sharp glance. He picked up a piece of coral. "You're right, the Hamasaki family has secrets, but I think Miles Hamasaki might have just discovered this one."

"What gives you that idea?"

"I think Martin would have told you first." He looked at her. "And the part about Hamasaki finding out is an idea I've been pondering the last few days."

"Why?" Storm drew deep troughs in the sand with her toes.

"Look, families keep secrets from each other." Hamlin kept his eyes on the running lights of a container ship, just visible on the horizon.

"Not the Hamasakis."

Hamlin's voice was flat and low. "Everyone." He was quiet for a few minutes while he skipped a few pieces of coral into the water. "Remember how I thought Hamasaki was preoccupied?"

"Sure, but that was because of Tom Sakai."

"I don't think so. This was personal."

"What makes you so sure?" Storm kicked a clump of seaweed, hard.

"The look on his face in the elevator one night after work." Hamlin still wouldn't meet her eyes. "It corresponds with Chris telling me about his new love."

"The artist? Is Chris the guy I saw in your office?" Her voice became hard. "Why didn't you tell me before I saw them in the bar together?"

"I thought about it. But I figured it was up to Martin."

"Okay." Storm's voice was gentler. "Chris was your college roommate?"

Hamlin nodded.

"How did they get together?" Storm asked. "Martin was in Chicago until we called him about Hamasaki's death."

"So was Chris. He had an exhibition at the Museum of Contemporary Art in Chicago. And he met this guy from Hawai'i. He was very happy because they had so much in common." Hamlin smiled, but his eyes were sad. "I was glad for him. He'd had so many disappointments."

"You were worried about AIDS," Storm said.

Hamlin kicked at the sand. "About two months before Chris left for Chicago, he was raped. He'd gone to a bar to meet some friends for a farewell party. According to Chris, one of the guys, somebody's friend's friend, no one can really identify him now, made a pass at Chris. Chris gently rebuffed him, he says. Then he woke up in some rat hole on a mattress on the floor, hemorrhaging from rectal tears. Somehow, at four in the morning, he made it back to the bar and called me."

Hamlin and Storm had wandered from the end of Waikīkī Beach around Diamond Head crater to Diamond Head Beach, where the reef met the sand and peeked from the water at low tide. Here, the beach was wilder, untamed. Storm preferred it to the manicured stretch of Waikīkī. Coral-encrusted lava rocks, deposited by bygone storms, littered the coarse sand. Honolulu's city lights were visible as a far-off blush in the sky. Moonlight and phosphorescence in the water illuminated their footsteps and each other's faces. Every few seconds, the lighthouse flashed a beam far out to sea, probing the blue velvet of the night. Even the trade winds gusted untamed and buffeted Storm's hair free of her braid. Hamlin's shirttail whipped around him.

Storm sat down and leaned against a boulder in the lee of the wind. She tucked a loose strand of hair behind one ear and rested her chin on her knees. "That's awful," she whispered. "Did you take him to the hospital?"

"Yes. They did a drug screen and found that he'd been given this stuff dubbed the 'date drug' by the media a few years ago." Hamlin sat down next to her.

"That sounds familiar."

"Yeah." Hamlin didn't hide the disgust in his voice. "It got some press a few years ago when frat guys were doping their dates in order to take advantage of them. It's called Rohypnol."

"God," Storm whispered. "Poor Chris. Did he ever figure out who this person was? Did anyone see him leave with this guy?"

"No, that's the really frustrating thing. I guess no one really knew who he was. He'd claimed to know someone who wasn't actually there that night and everyone believed him. Chris's friends had had a few drinks themselves and thought Chris was fine." Hamlin let a handful of sand slip through his fingers. "Apparently, they kind of wandered away with their own romantic prospects and left him there."

"I can see how that would happen," Storm said. "It goes on pretty often with women."

"Yeah, I bet."

Storm swallowed hard. "Did he get an AIDS test?"

"Yeah, I made him get the test, and told him to get tested again, in about six months."

Storm watched his eyes follow a ship's lights on the water. The thought flashed through her mind that not even a week ago, she'd thought of Hamlin as rakish in his expensive suits, tough, climbing the firm's ladder to a partnership. She'd also decided that anyone who could bed and maintain a relationship with Meredith Wo was off the charts on her own scale of alleged opportunism. She remembered Rick's betrayal with the owner of the lace g-string panties. And Rick wasn't as smart. Now she was observing a different side of Hamlin. He showed a sensitive streak and talked of a relationship that was not professionally expedient.

"You're worried," she said. Her eyes dropped to a long thigh whose musculature was delineated by tight black denim. She jerked her eyes higher, to safer territory, only to find his face inches from hers. The warmth of his body surrounded her in the cool night air.

"Just my nature, I guess," he whispered. With the crook of one finger, he tilted her chin up, paused for a second while he searched her eyes, and then kissed her. His lips were soft and searching, the mustache tickled her nose, and she responded. Her blood sang through her veins, while somewhere in the back of her mind, a little voice tried to chirp a warning. She ignored it.

She wound one arm around his shoulder. He smelled of warm skin, the sea, and night air. The second kiss was even sweeter.

When he lowered her a few inches to the sand, she pulled him close and kissed him again. "Hamlin," she whispered. "We have enough problems already."

Chapter 24

Hamlin grazed her lips with his and pulled back a millimeter. "Let's clear up one of them. Call me Ian."

She kissed him again, relished the warmth of his thigh against one of her legs. "Not yet," she murmured.

"You won't call me Ian?" He leaned on one arm and smiled down on her.

"No, I mean I need to slow down." She ran two fingers down his cheekbone.

"You? The woman who neutered her mugger?" He kissed her lightly on the lips and cocked an eyebrow at her.

She drew back a couple of inches. "I'm a cautious person."

Hamlin chuckled. "Right." He pushed a lock of hair behind her ear.

Storm pushed up on one elbow. She gazed into Hamlin's face, then rolled over on her back and looked up at the stars. She could feel Hamlin's warmth next to her. One of his legs lay nearby and she moved hers a fraction to touch it. "Well, I'm trying to change my habit of barging into things. You know, bulldozing ahead before I think."

Hamlin laughed out loud, kissed her on the forehead, then dropped down so that they both lay flat on their backs, hands behind their heads. The heavens spread above them like an indigo dome. "I saw a shooting star," Hamlin said.

"Did you make a wish?" Storm's voice was husky.

He rolled over toward her. "A couple of them." He took her hand. "One of them is that you get home safely. It's after one."

Storm sat up with a start. "Oh God, I was going to get to the office early."

"Me, too. I've got to be in court before eight."

They strolled back to the Ama in comfortable silence. The bartender's bulky frame was silhouetted in the tavern's dim lights as he lowered the hurricane shutters. One by one, they snapped closed like eyelids.

Hamlin walked Storm to her car, watched her unlock the door, then put an arm on each side of her body. He leaned in close. "Drive carefully." He brushed her lips with a kiss, then turned away. Storm watched him go back into the shadowy bar, then she bumped the VW out of the potholed parking lot onto the street.

She was glad no one was around to see her grin, all by herself at one o'clock in the morning. They'd think she was drunk, driving up Diamond Head Road, beaming like a fool and popping her head out the side window so that she could see the stars. The same stars she'd stared at with Hamlin.

The tickle of Hamlin's mustache and his warm kiss stayed on her lips. She ran the events of the evening through her mind, and even the sad parts didn't seem as bad as they had earlier. The scumbag on the street was exactly that, a pile of garbage not worth any more thought. Next time, she'd remember to put her knee in a vulnerable spot, hard. And Martin would get over his surprise. After all, she had. Plus, they were having lunch together tomorrow. She even had hope for Tom Sakai. Maybe she could help with the bone marrow drive or some of the fundraising. Put some signs up at the courthouse, get some publicity going.

Storm's cavorting mind halted. Tom Sakai? She had mentioned Tom to Hamlin by accident and Hamlin had taken it right in stride. He'd said Hamasaki wasn't depressed over Tom, that it was something more personal. Maybe Hamlin was right, but who had told Hamlin about Sakai and his illness?

Storm's fingertips chilled on the steering wheel. She pulled into her carport, turned off the car and sat for a moment, thinking. Had she mentioned Sakai to anyone other than Bebe and Aunt Maile? How about Lorraine? And why was Hamlin so knowledgeable on the subject of family secrets?

Storm heard Fang meowing outside the car. She stepped out of the VW and leaned down to stroke the cat. Lorraine knew about Sakai; in fact, Hamasaki himself had probably told several people in the office, especially if Meredith, Cunningham, and Wang were counsels for Sherwood Overton, the Unimed honcho.

She'd seen Overton himself hanging around the reception area. Absently, she walked into her house and flicked on the lights. Fang rubbed against her legs, trotted over to check her dish, then went back to Storm, purring like an outboard motor. Shoot, Overton was a fat cat who had probably been in everyone's office in the firm. Storm collapsed in a chair with relief. That's how Hamlin knew about Tom Sakai.

She dragged herself down the hall to brush her teeth. When she peeled off her jeans and tee-shirt, sand fell out of the pockets. Storm looked at the grains on the bathroom floor, shook her hair out of the French braid and listened to more sand skitter across the tile. Hell with it. She'd bathe in the morning and clean up the house after work tomorrow. She wasn't going to get enough sleep as it was.

When the radio alarm blasted some DJ's giddy voice at her, Storm pried open sticky eyelids. The guy should be muzzled, whooping like that at six o'clock in the morning. She pulled a pillow over her head, snuggled down, and tried to recall the remnants of a dream that still teased her. Something about O'Toole and his hypodermic needle again. Of course, O'Toole was a doctor. He probably gave dozens of injections every day. He gave her a flu shot last fall at Hamasaki's insistence. But Hamlin was in the dream, too. Telling her about Chris. There was something she needed to ask Hamlin about Chris, but she couldn't drag the thought back. Storm tried to burrow deeper, but sand in the sheets rasped against her arms. With a sigh, she threw back the covers, squinted against the light, and staggered to the shower.

In the office, Storm pushed aside files so they wouldn't get grease spots from the pastries she laid out on the blotter. The two chocolate chip scones smelled so good, she could hardly stand it. For some reason, her office smelled like good, rich coffee, too. Well, what do you know…a hot mug, with exactly the right amount of cream in it, sat on her desk. She picked it up and took a sip. Right amount of sugar, too, and still hot.

She set it down and walked into the hall. The light was on under Hamlin's door. She had a hand in the air, ready to knock, when he popped out, walking backwards while talking to his secretary. His briefcase was tucked under one arm and a stack of files under the other. "I'll be back before noon with luck."

"How'd you know I'd get here in time to drink it?" Storm asked.

He grinned. "You're not so unpredictable, you know."

"Huh. I'd better think about that." She walked through the reception area with him and opened the door to the corridor. Her dream flickered back to her and she waited until they were alone in the hall. "That drug, the one the frat guys gave to girls in their drinks. It's tasteless?" She spoke in a low voice.

"Yeah, the ER docs figured it was in Chris's beer. He never knew."

Storm turned around. "Thanks," she said over her shoulder and walked with purpose back to the office. The elevator door nearly closed on Hamlin, who stared after her.

Storm closed her office door, sat down and took a big hit of the coffee Hamlin had made her. It was in his mug, the Wild Bill Hickok one. Storm would have taken time to appreciate Wild Bill's raffishness, but this morning she needed the stimulating properties of the caffeine on her brain cells. She dropped to her knees and pulled Hamasaki's cup in its plastic bag out from under the stack of dusty files. She was still stuck with the question of why

Uncle Miles would drink coffee. That was a question that needed to be faced, but right now the idea of sedatives was bugging her.

Storm punched Detective Fujita's number into her phone. It was seven-thirty, but she could leave a message for him to call her back. She put her feet up on her desk and leaned back in her chair.

"Fujita." He barked into the phone as if he'd spent the night at his desk. Maybe he had.

"Hello, this is Storm Kayama. I know you're busy, but I wondered if you could tell me a good laboratory for analyzing substances."

"What're you up to, Ms. Kayama?"

Storm told him about the cup and how Hamasaki never drank coffee.

There was a second of silence on the line. "There was coffee in that cup he was holding."

"I know. Was there any left in the cup when you found it?" Storm asked.

"Maybe a few drops and a couple of dribbles down the outside. Some had spilled on his desk blotter."

Storm put her feet on the floor and leaned forward on her elbows. "This coffee business is bothering me. I'll pay for the analysis, of course."

Storm could hear a huff of air being pushed from his nostrils. "Try Chem-Tox. It's a subdivision of one of the big pharmaceutical companies." He gave her a phone number. "And Ms. Kayama, call me back, okay?"

"If you call me Storm. Thanks for your help." She hung up just as someone knocked on her office door. She shoved Hamasaki's mug between her knees under the desk.

"Yes?"

The new receptionist poked her head in. "Martin Hamasaki called, but he wouldn't hold. Said he can't meet you for lunch today." She closed the door again.

"Dammit." Storm took a gulp of coffee, and narrowed her eyes at the wall opposite her. She snapped the phone up, and rang the Hamasaki house. Her aunt answered.

"Aunt Bitsy, is Martin there?" Storm gritted her teeth at her own rudeness. "Uh, how're you doing today?"

Aunt Bitsy remained unruffled. "I'm all right, dear. How are you?" She paused while Storm mumbled a few platitudes, then went on. "You just missed Martin. He ran out of here about five minutes ago." She sounded like she'd been caught in the vapor trail of his escape.

"Oh. Did he take your car? Do you need a ride anywhere?"

"Thanks, honey, a friend of his picked him up. Michelle is picking me up for lunch. Then we're going to the temple to start *shojingyo* for Miles. Would you like to come?"

"Thanks, Aunt Bitsy, but I'd better stay in the office and catch up. Is Martin meeting you?"

"No, he even canceled lunch with David. He didn't say when he'd be back."

Storm hung up and sat back with a deep sigh. The bagged mug started to slip from between her knees. She grabbed it, set it on her desk, and stared at it. Martin had never run away from her, even during their few sibling fights. In fact, she was the one who would go lock her bedroom door and leave Martin banging away outside, swearing at her for burying her anger. Maybe she could track him down through Chris DeLario, but she'd have to wait for Hamlin to get back for that. The sculptor didn't have a listed phone number.

She finished the last swallow of Hamlin's coffee, which was lukewarm, grimaced, and stared at the bottom of the mug. Written in rambling script on the inside was, "Hedge your bets and keep your back to the wall. Congrats, Chris."

Wasn't Hickok shot in the back during a poker game? Must be a private joke. She'd have to ask Hamlin. Clever buddies, those two.

She set the mug down and thought about the Hamasaki family. Jumbled thoughts without any conclusions fizzled through her mind. Loads of questions, no answers, and Martin avoiding contact. She was going to have to stay calm, collected, and exercise patience. A tough order.

Storm puffed out her cheeks and blew out the breath she'd been holding. At least she could call Chem-Tox and get one question off her mind.

One of the analysts answered the phone himself, to Storm's delight. He sounded enthusiastic about her questions and looked forward to seeing her around noon. He'd wait before he went to lunch. Storm put the receiver back and felt the muscles between her shoulder blades unclench a centimeter or two. Martin's broken lunch date at least gave her time to check the mug.

Storm jotted the Chem-Tox address in her date book. She had the same kind of date book that Hamasaki had used, the one she'd found in his briefcase. The one where he'd written "S.O." at six-thirty on the night he died. Another loose end she needed to follow.

Right now, she had to forget about coffee-stained mugs and get to work on the file Wo and Wang had given her. It was another thread that led to Unimed. Storm scrutinized the front of the document. Dozens of yellow Post-it squares, covered with Wang's cramped handwriting, poked from between the pages. The guy must own stock in 3M.

She leafed through the file. Nothing electrifying. Unimed was petitioning the state for a "Certificate of Need," a requirement in the state of Hawai'i for any multi-million dollar medical expenditure. The health maintenance organization wanted to purchase a magnetic resonance imaging scanner, one of the big diagnostic tools that medical centers clamored to have.

Storm could find information on state policy at the law library. She vaguely recalled that the state of Hawai'i had set limits on the numbers of certain expensive machines to be purchased within the state, with the idea that hospitals could share them. Maybe the bureaucrats believed that frivolous use of the insurance-guzzling diagnostics would be reduced, or maybe they felt the millions could be better spent in other areas. Storm wasn't sure.

She knew that having certain equipment gave a medical center an aura of progressiveness, which in this day and age attracted patients. When medical centers competed for contracts with the state and other large employment groups, they vied for millions. Storm flipped to the last page. Both Wang and Wo's names were on the contract. They needed her to do some footwork with the state, call the people in control, use Hamasaki's name to grease the wheels so that the agreement slid through without any hitches.

Storm went through the papers carefully, writing her own notes on a legal sheet. Sure enough, there were some holes that she knew that the Department of Health would want filled. The people in the DOH were number-crunchers, MBAs, CPAs. She needed to know a few more details before she took the contract over to them. It was a great reason to see Sherwood Overton and ask him if he'd met with Hamasaki one evening about this or a related topic.

A knock at her door caused Storm to raise her head. "Come in."

Meredith Wo opened the door. She looked a little more alert than she had yesterday, though her makeup wasn't covering the gray smudges under her eyes.

"Have you had a chance to read over the Unimed file, yet?" Wo asked. "Overton wants to get it to the DOH by Wednesday."

Wo's eyes traveled from the file on Storm's desk to the bagged mug next to it. "Isn't that one of Hamasaki's mugs?" She peered over the desk at it. "What're you doing with it, having it bronzed?"

Storm shrugged with what she hoped looked like nonchalance. Damn, she'd forgotten that she'd left it on the desk. "I'm giving it back to the Hamasakis," she lied. "And I'm working on your file right now."

Wo sniffed and pointed at the paperwork on Storm's desk. Either Wo didn't give a damn about the mug or she was an excellent actor. But then, most trial attorneys were.

"How soon can you get the DOH to clear this contract?" Wo asked.

"I need more information, like what other purchase requests has Unimed submitted?"

"For crying out loud, Unimed just opened its Hawai'i hospital a little over two years ago. They've had all kinds of interaction with the Department of Health. In fact, we got a Certificate of Need for a renal dialysis unit just last February. The state's probably got all of it on file."

Storm cocked an eyebrow at Wo. "How fast do you want this?" She tapped her front teeth with her pen. "They'll take at least a month to look it up."

"Okay, what do you need?" Wo thrust out her hand. Storm handed her the notes she'd taken. Wo looked down the list. "I'll get back to you," she said and turned to leave.

"If you want, I can drop by Overton's office and pick the data up after lunch," Storm called after her.

Wo squinted back at her. "I've got to be in court all afternoon. Let me ask Edwin and get back to you." Her stockings swished out of the office and Storm picked up the next file on her desk.

A few minutes later, her office line buzzed. "Wang's busy, too," Wo said. "Can you get to Overton's office around one? Go to the tenth floor, Bishop Wing."

"No problem," Storm answered. "If I get what I need, I can take it over to the DOH tomorrow."

"Great, let me know." Wo hung up.

Storm dragged the next file in front of her and turned her attention to a lawsuit against a local supermarket chain. Some fifty-year-old bus driver, already on disability leave from the city for back pain, wanted to sue the chain for ten million because he swallowed part of a crab shell. He claimed he had an allergic reaction. Why was a guy on food stamps eating crab?

It was Hamlin's case. Storm called the state office that handled worker's compensation claims and found out that the guy's disability income ended in three months. She couldn't wait to tell Hamlin whom their tax dollars were supporting. Let the freeloader find another lawyer.

Fifteen minutes later, after dropping Wang's files on his desk, Storm was on the H-1 freeway. Hamasaki's mug sat on the seat beside her, safely wrapped in a brown paper bag from the same supermarket Hamlin's client was trying to sue.

Chapter 25

Paul Andrews was a Ph.D. in chemistry who asked Storm to call him Paul. By his conversation with an employee whom he sent to lunch, Storm figured he either owned the company or was chief manager. Andrews had to be nearly seven feet tall with arms hard as ironwood and skin the color of bittersweet chocolate. Storm figured he weighed at least two-fifty, none of it fat.

He put on a pair of reading glasses and sat down with smooth, athletic grace on a stool so that he was at eye level with Storm, who, standing, was five-eight. This guy made her feel petite.

With unconcealed enthusiasm, he unwrapped the mug. "Now tell me what we're looking for. It helps me decide which chromatography separation to use." He peered inside. "I gather you want qual rather than quant?"

"What?" Storm blinked.

He grinned at her. "Sorry. I meant qualitative versus quantitative analysis."

"Right. I was wondering if there might be sedative in the coffee." She touched the handle of the mug with obvious sadness. Andrews peered at her over the top of his reading glasses and waited patiently.

"A friend of mine died recently," she said. "He was seventy-seven, so maybe it was a heart attack or stroke." She frowned at the mug, then looked at the tall chemist. "But he was holding this, and he never drank coffee."

"It's his mug?" Andrews asked.

"Yes, it's his tea mug."

"Who took it out of his hand?"

"The police, but they don't consider it to be a suspicious death."

"Oh?" Andrews's eyebrows rose in neat arcs. He sniffed at the cup. "Black coffee. That's good, no lipids." He thought for a moment. "I'll look for tea, too." He got up and took the cup to a counter lined with labeled bottles. He poured a liquid into the cup. "I'll probably need to run a couple of chromatographic separations." He looked over at her. "It'll probably take a few days. That okay?"

"Sure, okay. I'll look forward to hearing from you."

Storm walked out the front door and wondered about the truthfulness of her last statement. If Andrews found a sedative, she would be faced with the fact that someone had definitely killed Hamasaki. The fact that she'd know for sure made a hard knot in her stomach.

It was hard for her to think about anything other than Uncle Miles's mug during her drive to the large Unimed complex. Even after she wandered through the front door, she was distracted by the thought of his grip on that cup. It took an extra ten minutes for her to find her way to the plush, corporate office wing of the multi-storied hospital. She knocked on a door marked by a brass plaque with Overton's name, his M.D., Ph.D., and position. Impressive—she'd not known he was a physician, too. When she knocked, a woman's voice called out, "Come in."

Storm entered a small reception area with a thick rug and nice artwork on the wall. Very nice artwork. She recognized a local Chinese artist's trademark pen and ink horses. Small ones went for a few thousand and the painting of three horses cavorting across the wall in front of the woman at the rosewood desk was probably four feet wide before it was framed.

"I'm Storm Kayama to see Dr. Overton, please."

The woman, an attractive blonde somewhere between thirty-five and fifty, smiled. Her face was smooth and tight, just like her body. "Storm? I have a packet for you."

"He's not here?"

"No, he had a meeting downtown with one of the bank boards he serves on. Did you have a question?"

Storm kicked herself mentally. How had she been so deluded to think he'd see her personally? She looked down at the nameplate on the woman's desk. "Oh, Ms. Robertson, I thought of a few more questions after Meredith Wo called you. But then, you know how nit-picky these state offices are. Every *t* has to be crossed."

"Call me Marilyn, honey. I know, we have to deal with those types constantly. Hospital accreditation boards are even worse. I went through all of that just last week. What do you need to know?"

"Last week? Was that why he had the six-thirty appointment last Tuesday with Miles Hamasaki?"

The woman frowned. "Six-thirty? He usually oversees rounds with the residents first thing in the morning."

"No, six-thirty p.m." Storm chuckled. "I guess Dr. Overton is really busy."

"You couldn't begin to fathom." Marilyn sighed. "I moved here with him from California." She tried to maintain her perky attitude. "But he has to work harder than ever, now." She ducked her head, licked her thumb and leafed back a week in a large appointment book. "No, I thought so. He was with the Hospital Accreditation Board that evening."

"Tuesday last week?"

"Yup, no doubt. That was one of those tough weeks." Marilyn closed the appointment book. "Is that what you needed to know?"

"Um, did you include data on the other Certificates of Need you've applied for in the last couple years?" Storm peered down at the large envelope she held. "I got the impression Dr. Overton wanted this rushed."

"I'm sure all the information is in there." Marilyn gestured to Storm's packet and showed off some expensive dental work in a practiced smile.

"How about info on how many patients are using your new renal dialysis unit on a weekly basis?"

Marilyn's hand fluttered across her desk. A flash of something, anxiety or irritation, Storm wasn't sure, passed through her bright blue eyes. "Of course, honey. Why don't you read through the packet, then phone me with any questions?"

Storm strolled slowly down the carpeted hall that led to the main hospital. When she got to the tiled floors, her heels tapped a pensive beat. She looked around. She stood in a wide, busy corridor right outside a big swinging door marked Radiology. Gurneys rigged with IV lines, like ships powered by nurses and orderlies, sailed by her. Renal Dialysis was right across the hall. Wo said the hospital had applied for some new dialysis units. Maybe she should pop in and see them.

In truth, many of these departments intrigued her. She found the combination of the latest scientific technologies applied to the complicated human mechanism fascinating. Even the unfaithful Rick had delighted her with a look at his new Physical Therapy Department when it opened.

Speak of the devil, there he was, walking down the hall toward her. Aunt Maile would say that our thoughts call back unfinished business to be dealt with. Storm's first impulse was to bolt, but before she could get her feet moving, Rick saw her. Storm's heart skipped a beat or two, but she managed to wiggle her fingers at him.

To her surprise, he gave her a shaky smile and walked toward her. When they were within ten feet of each other, they both blurted, "I'm sorry," then stuttered again on top of each other's words.

"I really am," Rick said. "I fu...blew it big time."

"You were a real shit," Storm said. "But I wasn't exactly great company. And about that mess. I feel bad, now."

"Yeah, it was a pretty strong way of getting your point across." Rick shuffled his feet. "I was pissed as hell at first, but the next day, I told one of the P.T.'s I work with and she told me that she would have opened the bathroom door and dumped the chili right on us. Then she would have..." Rick winced and his hand fluttered below the waist of his scrub pants.

"Let's forget it," Storm said.

"Yeah, okay. Uh, what're you doing here? Work?"

"Just some legwork. Looks like Unimed is getting an MRI. Will you get to use it for your patients?"

Rick looked disgusted. "I'll believe it when I see it. The Unimed honchos say they're more efficient than public hospitals, but that's a crock." He snorted. "You'd think the CT scanner would be top-of-the line, right? It's being repaired half the time. Piece of shit. They're going to get another one, though. So they say."

"What about the new dialysis units?"

"I have this friend who works in dialysis." A flush began at the v-neck of his green scrubs.

Storm cocked an eyebrow. The owner of the lacy g-string.

Rick forged on. "There are twelve functioning dialysis machines and only a couple of them are modern. Those just got here last week, but there are supposed to be, I don't know, four or five more on the way." He shrugged. "Maybe the manufacturers can't keep up."

"Must be frustrating," Storm said.

"You bet." He shoved his hands in the pockets of his pants. "Hey, it's good to see you. Maybe we should have a drink and talk."

Storm stared at him, then grinned. She was surprised at the sense of relief that flowed through her. "Nah, let's just let things go for a while."

"Yeah, I guess so."

Storm gave him a wave and sauntered down the hall. She felt unchained. Rick's departing grin had been friendly and free of rancor. Maybe Aunt Maile was right about unfinished business.

She followed the signs to the lobby, remembered her parking floor without any glitches, and picked up a box lunch, or bento, of tossed salad, shoyu chicken on rice, and guava juice on the way back to the office. Back at her desk, Storm refrained from licking the Styrofoam plate. No one was around to see her, but it was a matter of dignity. She slurped the last of her juice, popped the top off her paper cup and knocked an ice cube into her mouth.

With a satisfying crunch, she doodled on her legal pad. *MRI*, the initials *S.O.*, *dialysis unit, Tom Sakai*.

What were Tom's chances of surviving his cancer? How had Hamasaki planned to help him? Sherwood Overton was going to be hard to talk to, but she could get hold of Sidney O'Toole. Perhaps he knew whom Hamasaki had spoken to, and what agreements, if any, had been made. Storm chewed thoughtfully on the tip of her pen.

Her eyes widened. For the first time, she noticed that Sidney O'Toole's initials were S.O., also. Aside from her own father, O'Toole was Hamasaki's oldest friend. A frisson of emotion she hadn't felt for years passed through her. She wished she could call her father and tell him about this whole mess.

Her father had never been close to O'Toole and now she wondered why. Storm remembered a trip she and her father had taken to O'ahu when her dad was supposed to meet Hamasaki. After arriving, he'd discovered O'Toole was going along with them, sat quietly for a moment, then asked her if she'd like to go to a movie. She remembered asking him why he'd changed his plans and he'd said that he and Hamasaki were going to a VFW meeting the next night. As if they hadn't rushed to make the three o'clock plane so that he could be on time for that evening. She was so excited about doing something with him alone that she'd accepted his explanation.

She had savored his attention like a seedling starved for water. Her strongest recollection of that night was how they had laughed together. She had peeked away from the comedy to watch his face, crinkled with mirth in the dark theater. It was a precious memory, and a rare occurrence since Eme's death.

A pang of regret pierced Storm. She missed her father, and for once, the emotion was not stained with resentment and sorrow at his withdrawal. A glimmer of awareness danced on the edges of her mind. What Storm had interpreted as estrangement had been his own struggle with helplessness, grief, and failing energy. When her mother died, he had allowed Aunt Maile to "handle the woman-to-woman stuff." Older now, she realized that many men were uncomfortable with women's issues. Hamasaki used to talk to her about his philosophies: his hopes, fears, education, his ideas of what made a good human being. Not exactly chitchat about menstrual cramps and what to do if your date groped you, though. Given her father's burdens and illness, perhaps he hadn't been as aloof as she remembered. And he'd made sure that she was surrounded with love.

Storm stared across her office, unseeing, and wondered if his grief could have been eased if she'd overcome her own distress and anger at her mother's death. She could have at least approached him more often. Her eyes burned. She always figured this stuff out when it was too late.

She dumped another ice cube into her mouth; this time a block of cubes hit her nose and water streamed down the sides of her face onto her blouse front. Damn. She brushed away droplets and gazed at the spreading spots on her desk blotter. It was a cold wake-up call. Okay, this was today; yesterday was gone. What did she need to do about her current problems?

For one thing, she could call O'Toole and ask about Tom Sakai's prognosis and Hamasaki's actions. She might also ask him if he'd seen Hamasaki the night he died.

O'Toole's office number had the same three-digit prefix as Unimed. He'd given up his private practice entirely, it appeared. She dialed and gave her name, then carefully ate another ice cube while the receptionist put her on hold.

A moment later, a gravelly voice said, "Storm, Sid O'Toole here. How are you holding up, my dear?"

"It's hard to accept that he's gone, Dr. O'Toole. These questions keep whirling around in my head."

"Normal mourning process, honey. Do you need anything to help you sleep?"

"No, thanks." Good old O'Toole. She wondered if he ever recommended exercise or another holistic alternative to Prozac for his depressed patients. His concern seemed genuine, though. She'd try to show a little gratitude.

"Dr. O'Toole, I was going through some of Uncle Miles's papers and found a file on Tom Sakai."

O'Toole did not respond for a few seconds. When he did, the warm doctor voice had disappeared. "They're extremely confidential. I need to have those returned right away."

"Certainly. But, what are Tom's chances of beating this? Criminy, the guy's so young. And he has little kids."

"I shouldn't have bothered Miles with all that. Nothing he could do, apparently. Hope it didn't contribute to his, uh..."

"No, Uncle Miles had a lot of experience with people's troubles." Storm thought about Hamlin's belief that Hamasaki had been preoccupied with a crisis closer to home. "Is Tom's case hopeless?"

"His chances are pretty slim, but I'd never tell him or Lani. Hope is sometimes the best medicine we have."

"She seems strong," Storm said.

There was a long pause on the phone. "You've met her?"

"Uh, yes. My aunt is a Hawaiian healer, working with Bebe Fernandez. I brought some herbs from Honoka'a last weekend." Storm wanted to shift the subject back to Sakai's treatment. "Are the Hawaiian methods helping him?"

"More than I thought."

"But he's still undergoing traditional Western treatments, isn't he?" Storm asked.

"Yes, he goes over to Queen's Hospital for a CT scan once a month, then back to Unimed for his blood work. He had a bad time around March or April, but he's fairly stable right now."

"Queen's?" Storm asked.

"Temporarily, of course. Unimed has a very good radiology department. We just had a temporary breakdown in our new machine and the older one doesn't have the resolution I wanted for Tom. I want to see the tiniest shadow, a hairline fracture, any hint of a new tumor. You know. We're following him like a hawk."

"I know you're trying to do everything you can for him."

"Yes." His voice was tinged with weariness.

"Dr. O'Toole, did you by any chance drop into Hamasaki's office on Sunday, the night he died?"

Two or three seconds of thick silence met her question. "The police asked me about this already. Storm, you need help. Obsessional bereavement is not unusual, believe me. Unimed has a psychiatrist who specializes in grief management. His name is Dr. Edelstein. I'll refer you."

"Just a minute, Dr. O'Toole. You did see him, right?"

"Certainly, we met for a few minutes, as we often did," O'Toole barked. "Miles was trying to get Overton to pay for a last-ditch effort to save Sakai's life. That afternoon, he gave me a short progress report. When I left, he was chatting cheerfully on the telephone."

"What time did you leave?" Storm asked.

"I told the police that and I'm not going to discuss it any further," O'Toole snapped. She heard him take a deep breath. "Storm, you need to talk to someone about this obsession."

Storm could imagine the hue of his face. His nose was probably the color of an Okinawa sweet potato, a mottled and veined purple.

"I'll have Edelstein's receptionist call you for an appointment." He slammed down the phone.

Chapter 26

Storm sat back in her chair, rubbed her hands over her face, and tried to sort through what O'Toole had just said. He'd revealed a lot. First, he'd been very defensive when he mentioned the police. Still, O'Toole had been Hamasaki's doctor. Second, he said that Unimed owned two CT scanners and one was old. A couple of hours ago, Rick told her that Unimed had only one, which needed a lot of repairs. Of course, Rick might have been distracted.

Rick's comments about the dialysis unit were illuminating, too. The information that Marilyn, Overton's secretary, had given her was a recap of what she already had; there was nothing on any other high-cost equipment requested by Certificate of Need, which should include both dialysis machines and CT scanners. When she'd mentioned them, Marilyn had waved her question away. Storm gritted her teeth. With Wo and Wang putting on the pressure, she didn't want to have to chase down this data.

Storm picked up the phone, dialed Unimed's central operator and started to request Overton's office, then changed mid-sentence and asked for the renal dialysis unit.

"Hi, my mother's diabetic and needs dialysis. I'm looking for a facility..."

"Hold on a minute, please."

Muzak crooned into her ear and Storm held the phone a foot away from her head while she paged through the Unimed data again to make sure she hadn't missed anything.

"Hello, this is Stephanie Oishi, head nurse in the Unimed dialysis unit. May I help you?"

Storm repeated her ailing mother story and asked how many dialysis machines Unimed had available. Oishi spewed some interesting information in her sales pitch. "...Twenty modern dialysis stations, nationally accredited technicians, evaluation for transplant potential, blood typing and access to a national organ donor data bank, ten more new dialysis units to be set up in the next six months..."

"Thank you, Ms. Oishi. I'll get back to you." Storm hung up the phone and stared at an industrious spider in the corner of her ceiling. Rick had said twelve machines, and some of them were old.

Storm punched in the number for Overton's office, and as she hoped, Marilyn's cheerful voice responded. "Hello, Marilyn. It's Storm Kayama. I'm going through your paperwork and I still need some information. Can you tell me how many CT scanners and dialysis machines Unimed has presently and how many were acquired in the last year? It would expedite this application...Sure, you can call me back."

Storm was filling in what blanks she could on the Unimed application when Meredith Wo rapped once on the door and burst in without waiting for a response. "Have you got that application filled, yet?"

"I'm working on it right now."

"What is taking so long? Storm, if you're going to be anything other than a pencil pusher, you've got to take some initiative. Fill in the goddamn blanks." Meredith paused for a breath and stood with her hands stiff at her sides, fingers splayed. Her face was covered with a sweaty sheen. "You tell those pimply-assed anal-retentives down at the Department of Health what you expect from them. Today!" Wo sprayed the words across the room. What was all this? Could Unimed be threatening to transfer its business to another firm?

Wo would have flounced out the door and left her derision ringing in Storm's small office, but she caught her high heel on a loop of carpet. It was just enough time for Storm to speak up, with such calm strength in her voice that she surprised herself. Wo stopped dead in her tracks, though she jerked her foot about a bit.

"Meredith, think of the government like an elephant who's lying on your car keys. You have to give it peanuts to get it to move. It works better than pushing."

Wo's eyes narrowed. She opened and closed her mouth once, then turned on her heel.

When Wo was out of sight, Storm let out a pent-up breath. That was no fun at all. However, she was proud of remembering one of Uncle Miles's lessons, especially when she needed it. Perhaps other confrontational types would back down when faced with calm strength, too. Of course, Uncle Miles had had a wonderful intuition about people. And she, the perpetual hothead, had finally had enough presence of mind to try it. Of course, that loose thread on the carpet had helped, too.

Storm rubbed her face. The implacable front may have worked this time, but she hoped the confrontation wouldn't come back to haunt her. Meanwhile, she had to get through a stack of files before she went home this evening. And it was already well after three.

Over an hour and most of the pile later, Storm responded to a tap on her door. "Come in," she said.

Hamlin stuck his head in. "I wanted to get your take on that guy who's suing the supermarket."

"That maggot? Don't tell me you're thinking of taking the case."

"Someone else will if I don't."

"Yeah, well, let 'em. Hamlin, maybe I'm just naive, but I wouldn't want to wake up and know I helped a guy like that rape the system."

"Why did I think you'd say that?" He leaned against the door frame.

"Cause you thought the same thing?"

"I suppose." Hamlin shook his head in mock resignation. "Hey, how did things go with Martin?"

Storm put her pen down with a thud. "He canceled on me. Hamlin, it's not like him to do that." Her forehead creased with concern. "Could we call DeLario?"

Hamlin came in and sat down. "Don't you think it's a better idea to let him contact you when the hurt wears off?"

"Look, Martin used to force me to talk to him when I was upset. And it helped. I'm at least going to try to get in touch with him."

Hamlin winced. "This is different than a teen-age snit. How do you think Hamasaki reacted when he found out Martin was gay?"

"Snit?" Storm glared at Hamlin, then took a deep breath and sat back. "I'm glad I wasn't around for that confrontation. He probably lectured him, told him it was a choice." She grimaced. "It would have driven Martin up the wall." She glowered again. "*If* Hamasaki knew."

Hamlin ignored her last comment. "That's what I thought, too." He got up to leave. "How about if I call Chris and try to arrange a get-together?"

Storm held out her phone. Hamlin shook his head. "I'll have better luck in an hour or two."

Storm watched him go. He was more protective of DeLario than most guys were of their brothers. Hamlin probably finished his undergraduate training twenty-plus years ago. Most roommates lost track of each other in graduate school; the close ones sent Christmas cards across the continent once a year.

Storm finished her paperwork and took the stack to Wang's office. His secretary waved her in.

"I've got a meeting with Sherwood Overton in five minutes," he said when he looked up from some papers on his desk. Storm couldn't read the expression in his eyes because of the reflection of his desk lamp in his thick-lensed glasses. "I'll try and get the answers to your questions. Meredith gave me your list."

"Thanks, Mr. Wang."

On the way back to her office, Storm turned at the soft sound of splintering wood and saw carpenters prying the brass plaque from Hamasaki's door. One of them smoothed putty into the screw holes; a can of wood stain sat on the floor.

Storm dashed down the hall, closed her door, and dialed the Hamasaki household. "Hi, Aunt Bitsy? Some workmen are taking Uncle Miles's name off the door."

"I know, darling. Edwin told me that they needed the office space." Her voice was low and resigned.

"We haven't even gone through his things."

"I know, we'll have to get to it. One of the partners has her eye on it." Aunt Bitsy emphasized the word "her." She always had thought Meredith was too pushy.

"When does Wang want the room available?"

"By next Monday. He was very polite about it, Storm. I got the feeling he didn't want to do it, but as managing partner, he's stuck with the dirty work. I think it's just hard for us to accept that Miles is not coming back."

"It is for me." Storm fought to keep her voice steady.

"Me, too. But we've got to face it," Aunt Bitsy said. "Let's see if we can get a truck and move the furniture in the next day or two. I want to be sure some of the prints on the wall stay in the family. They're quite valuable. And he'd like you to have some of his wonderful old books. Is there any chance you could go through the files before then? Save anything that pertains to the house or estate for me and keep the legal ones for yourself. Throw out the rest. I don't think I could stand...." This time, Aunt Bitsy's voice shook. "I'd really appreciate it, dear. And I'll ask the other kids to reserve some time to help move the heavy things."

Storm hung up and walked back down the corridor to Hamasaki's office, but the door was locked and smelled of fresh varnish. The locks had been changed, too. Her old key to the office was useless, even though the room was still filled with Hamasaki's things. Storm jerked on the shiny new doorknob and drew back her foot. "Damn them!" she muttered. A noise behind her stopped her from shattering her toe and any remaining dignity.

Diane, Wang's secretary, was locking the door to their office. "If you don't tell anyone, I'll give you the key," she whispered. "Ms. Wo shouldn't have had the lock changed so soon." She glanced down the hallway. "Mr. Wang can't say no to her."

Storm felt her face flush. "Thanks, I'd appreciate it. I'll start getting his things out of the office after work tomorrow."

When she returned to her office, she slumped into her chair. Tears burned her eyes and she took a couple of deep breaths.

When the phone rang, she picked it up slowly. "Yes?"

A pause responded to her lugubrious greeting. Then a syrupy voice began, "This is Dr. Edelstein's office. Your internist, Dr. O'Toole, referred you for grief management."

"What?" Storm sat up straight in her chair.

"We'd like to schedule you for tomorrow morning at nine."

"Wait a minute. O'Toole isn't my internist."

"You'll have to take that up with Dr. O'Toole. Hold on please."

A new-age guitar arrangement of "Raindrops Keep Falling on My Head" played in Storm's ear. Right as she was about to slam the receiver down, a man's voice came on. "Now, young lady. Plenty of normal people benefit—"

"Are you Dr. Edelstein?"

"Yes, and we have arranged an appointment for you that—"

"Dr. Edelstein, there's some confusion."

"Confusion is part of the problem. Depression skews your whole perspective."

"Listen to me, Edelstein. I am not—"

"Unless you let us help—"

"Depressed!" Storm crashed the receiver down. She launched to her feet and stomped across the room to the window. Her breath steamed the glass. If Edelstein or O'Toole had been in the room, she would have breathed fire.

The sound of a clearing throat caused her to turn.

Hamlin was peering around the doorframe. "Care to go out for a little hot spiced Valium?"

"What?" Storm snapped, then sagged against the window frame. "You heard that?"

"I think the stevedores down on the docks heard." Hamlin tiptoed to her window and made a show of looking down to the street. "They're cheering for you."

Storm couldn't stand it; her scowl cracked into a smile. "What's with him? What did Hamasaki see in O'Toole, anyway?"

"A depraved friend makes a guy feel better about himself, didn't you know?" Hamlin said. "O'Toole needed him."

She looked at him for a moment. "If we can substitute a good red wine for that Valium, I'll take you up on it."

"Now that sounds like a reasonable woman." He plopped some papers onto her desk, then tucked her arm into his and steered her down the hall.

"What's the rush?" Storm asked. "You think the men in white coats are coming?"

Hamlin squeezed her arm. "Hell, no. Edelstein wants nice, placid neurotics who pay their bills on time."

Storm threw back her head and laughed. In the elevator, they collapsed against the walls in stitches. When the elevator stopped on the fourth floor, two potential riders stared at the howling couple. They let the doors close. You never know these days.

Chapter 27

They were still chuckling when Hamlin led her into a cozy downtown tavern. The aroma of grilled meats and vegetables made Storm's mouth water. Her head swiveled to watch a waiter with a heaping plate of nachos, smothered in guacamole and cheese, while Hamlin steered her to a large corner table

"I just realized that I'm starving."

"I called ahead for a reservation for four."

"Four?" Storm's smile faded. She dropped into the deeply cushioned booth. "Why didn't you tell me?"

"I did." Hamlin sat at right angles to her in the booth.

"Sooner, I mean. I might have composed myself faster."

Hamlin grinned. "I got distracted."

"Right." Storm looked up at the waiter who had appeared for their drink order. "Cabernet, please."

Hamlin spoke up. "I'll have one, too. Just bring a bottle of the Clos du Bois."

When the man left, Storm leaned toward Hamlin. "How hard was it to persuade them to come?"

"I let Chris pick the restaurant. My treat."

Storm narrowed her eyes at him. "Does Martin know I'm going to be here?"

"Chris will tell him."

Storm drooped in her seat. "Are you sure?" She regarded him glumly while the waiter appeared, opened the wine, and offered a taste to Hamlin. Hamlin nodded to the fellow, who poured wine in Storm's glass, then Hamlin's.

Hamlin bobbed his head in greeting at the first of two figures following the maitre d' around the corner. DeLario walked single file in front of Martin, who looked up to negotiate his way around a table. His face froze in shock at the sight of Storm. He pivoted to flee, but DeLario grabbed his arm.

"Wait, please. We need to talk to her."

"Why didn't you tell me? Can't anyone tell me anything straight anymore?" Martin spoke through clenched teeth. Heads turned toward him.

Storm clutched the stem of her wineglass. DeLario kept his hand on Martin's arm. His low, comforting voice reached her in unintelligible phrases.

She looked up at Hamlin with flashing dark eyes. "I didn't want to bushwhack him!"

"It's not what I expected, either," Hamlin said.

Storm stood up. "I'm leaving." She looked at Martin. "I'm sorry. I didn't mean to surprise you, either time. Call me when you want to talk."

"Wait." Martin walked away from the table with her. He stopped and wiped a shaking hand over his face. "I've been having a hard time, lately."

Storm became aware of a table of four people who were fastidiously studying their sashimi. "Martin, let's sit down," she whispered. "Or should we go someplace alone, where we can talk?"

Her eyes flicked over to where DeLario and Hamlin sat. Hamlin was addressing DeLario, his face serious. DeLario grasped a wineglass with long, delicate fingers and moved it around in small circles while he listened. His hands were incongruous with the tanned ruggedness of his face and the frayed jeans he wore. He must wear gloves to work with the bronzes he sculpted. She was struck by his height and looks. From their glances, she could tell other people were impressed, too.

DeLario was oblivious to the attention of the other diners. His head bobbed in tiny, begrudging movements to whatever Hamlin was telling him.

"I could use a drink," Martin said. He looked at DeLario. "We might as well stay here."

When they got to the table, DeLario stood up and took Storm's hand. His fingers were damp and cool. "My apologies for the surprise." He stopped just short of kissing her hand in an old-fashioned, European manner. His dark, steady gaze settled on Martin. "My friend, I am so sorry. I thought this meeting would help all of us understand each other."

Martin nodded without a word and took a seat next to DeLario and facing Hamlin. Storm sat next to Hamlin. For a long second, the silence had a palpable density. Martin studied the weave in the tablecloth and DeLario's expression was as frozen as one of his statues'. Storm thought she could feel an electrical current pass between the two men. She and Hamlin were invisible to them at that moment. She glanced toward Martin and saw that his downcast eyes were hooded with anger.

DeLario's face was craggy and intense. His dark wavy hair, streaked with gray and pulled into a ponytail, contrasted with Martin's jet-black, short razor cut. DeLario's eyes appeared aged ahead of his years, though the lines around his expressive mouth added to his looks. The hand that held the stem of his wineglass trembled.

Storm looked at Martin and her heart squeezed with emotion for him. All signs of last week's sunburn had faded except for a few freckles that stood out against the white of his nose. It was he who loved more deeply. She knew how that felt.

"I'm glad to see you, Martin," she said softly, to break the spell. She felt Hamlin's feet shift beneath the table, probably with relief.

Martin tried to smile. "I'm glad to see you, too. I was planning on phoning you tomorrow."

Storm wasn't sure if that was true after his behavior ten minutes ago, but it was no time to argue. "I guess you were worried about my reaction?"

Martin's eyes dulled. "Of course. I thought you were checking up on what Dad told you."

"He didn't tell me anything. Come on, we had lunch last week. Don't you think I would have said something if I'd known?" Storm asked.

"I wasn't sure." Martin flushed. "You were so close to him." He took a drink from the glass of wine Hamlin had poured.

"I know." Storm picked at a thread on the tablecloth. "And I'm not even his real daughter."

"I didn't mean it that way."

"It's okay. I promise Uncle Miles didn't breathe a word about you and Chris. He wouldn't, you know. It was private," Storm said. "How did he find out? Did you tell him?"

"I wish I had." Martin took another belt of wine and glanced toward DeLario. Storm followed his look just in time to see the sculptor shake his head, then look away.

"He called a couple of weeks ago and Chris answered the phone." Martin didn't bother to disguise the pain in his eyes when he looked at her this time. "When I got on the line, he asked me if 'that man' was my lover."

"And you told him?" Storm asked.

"I...I didn't know how." Martin examined the base of his nearly empty wineglass. "No one said anything for what seemed like a long time, then he changed the subject to stocks, asked my advice about some purchases. I told him about Unimed and asked him if he'd release part of my trust fund or at least invest it for me. He hemmed and hawed around for a minute. You know how tight he could be. He said he'd check some things and call me back."

Storm frowned. Though Hamasaki hadn't handed out money without a reason, he hadn't seemed tight. Of course, she'd had different expectations than his own kids. When she thought of where she was headed with her old high school gang, she was grateful for the opportunities he offered her. Better not bring up that bag of worms.

"What happened when he called you back?" she asked. "He didn't."

Martin's eyes flicked to DeLario again. Storm looked at him, too. The artist's gaze was on her and his eyes were filled with a darkness that she didn't understand.

Hamlin was taking in the whole exchange, his expression as blank as a poker player's.

"What else did he say?" she asked, then wished she hadn't. She could feel DeLario's glare burn her face.

"It was his voice, the sarcasm in it," Martin said. Storm thought she saw DeLario nod briefly in her peripheral vision, but Martin continued without looking in his direction. "When he said he'd get back to me, I knew he was really talking about my lifestyle and what he would do about it."

"Martin, could he have been upset about something which had nothing to do with you? Maybe he was upset about David. Or me, for that matter," Storm said.

"Storm, you don't understand." Martin's lip curled at her. He emptied the wine bottle into his glass, then held the bottle up to catch the attention of a passing waiter.

DeLario brushed Martin's hand with his fingertips. "Martin, we have to tell her." He spoke to Storm. "A couple of days after Hamasaki called Martin, I returned to Honolulu. Right after I got back, he phoned me and told me to stay away from his son." DeLario's eyes flattened with anger. "He called me...names."

"Oh, no." Storm whispered.

Hamlin spoke up. "Chris, he was reacting out of shock, trying to protect his son. He might have understood if he'd ever had the chance to meet you."

"Come on, Ian. You know better than that," DeLario said. Martin kept his eyes down and twirled his wineglass with trembling fingers.

At that moment, a waiter appeared and waved a white napkin at them. "Hello folks, would you like to hear about our specials?" Without a pause, he launched into a long list of complicated dishes. Then he announced that he would give them a few more minutes to decide and sashayed away.

"What'd that guy say?" Martin gaped after the departing waiter.

Storm's front teeth clanked on the edge of her wineglass and she sputtered. She and Hamlin snorted at the same time. Martin sat stunned for another moment, then began to laugh.

"What the hell is so funny?" DeLario asked.

Martin patted his arm. "We're laughing at that bozo. And the unpredictability, the randomness," he waved his hands around in the air, "of life. God, Chris, we've got to laugh. What else can we do?"

DeLario looked around the table, took a swallow of wine, then nodded. Slowly, the angry gleam faded from his eyes and he chuckled, his voice uncertain.

"Okay," he said. He raised a glass. "To spontaneity, everyone."

The four of them clinked glasses. Storm let a smile of relief cross her face. Indeed, spontaneity was harmless. No sharp edges, right?

The waiter returned and Martin looked up at him. "What are the specials again?"

They all burst out laughing. The waiter raised a haughty eyebrow, then recounted the long list once more. "I'll give you a few more minutes." He turned on his heel.

They choked back their laughter and buried their faces in the menu. When he came back, each person ordered the same fresh catch, though they got a few different side dishes. The waiter just shook his head. He kept his chin tilted so high that they could have counted nose hairs, if they'd wanted. They didn't.

The evening became more lighthearted, filled with the sharing of past experiences. Hamlin and DeLario talked about how, as freshmen, they'd had rooms across the hall in a dormitory at the University of Michigan. One of DeLario's best friends was a soprano that Hamlin had briefly lusted after. DeLario had an art scholarship and

Hamlin a track one, though DeLario was on the wrestling team until his studio time demanded too much of him. "Come on, Hamlin. Those guys were afraid I'd grope 'em." He laughed while Hamlin shook his head and rolled his eyes.

"That's not why you won, Chris."

DeLario announced that on that note, he'd better visit the men's room. When he returned, he jumped back in the conversation to tell a funny story about how the elastic in Hamlin's shorts had been through the dryer too many times and fell lower and lower during a track meet. DeLario had finally sent Neil back to the room for another pair.

"Who's Neil? Another roommate?" Storm asked.

"No, my brother," Hamlin answered. "That wasn't my best meet, Chris."

"Not that day, but the next day, you set a new NCAA record for the two hundred meter," DeLario said. He watched his friend's eyes. "You should have seen him fly."

"This guy is known for artistic hyperbole, you know." Though his tone was jocular, the skin around Hamlin's eyes was tight. Storm watched Hamlin and wondered why she'd never heard him speak of his brother. Hamlin forged ahead with his anecdote. "He was dashing over to my races between his wrestling events. He was the only guy I ever knew who wrestled on a full art scholarship."

Hamlin grinned and Storm saw relief pass through DeLario. The sculptor beamed and twirled his side of linguine with pesto around his fork. "What we both had to learn was how to interact with people who didn't put their faces down in their pasta and inhale."

Hamlin laughed and flagged down the waiter for another bottle of wine. He directed his comments to Martin. "See, we both came from inner city Detroit and had simple, immigrant parents. They spoke a little broken English outside the home, but even the neighborhoods were ethnic so they could get away with not speaking English for a week or two."

DeLario chuckled. "All of a sudden, we were in classes with these guys who took off their army surplus jackets and put on monogrammed shirts when their parents drove the Mercedes in from Grosse Point. Hamlin and I took the bus back to the old neighborhood together." DeLario's eyes became wistful. "And dug through the barrels of olives at the open market," he said.

Hamlin laughed. "Remember the time you got thrown out of that stall for dipping too many? We couldn't speak a word of Greek, but we knew the meaning of every gesture that guy made." All four of them laughed.

Martin and Storm shared how, while in college on the mainland, both of them had been asked by other students if Hawaiians had electricity in their grass shacks. "They thought we surfed to school," Martin laughed. "I never did admit that I couldn't swim until Mom put me in a class at the YMCA when I was twelve." He poured more wine into his glass.

"That's about the time I got my first pair of closed shoes," Storm added.

"For a Big Island girl, that's early." Martin tossed a piece of bread at her from across the table.

Storm stuck out her tongue, then popped the bread into her mouth. "Yeah, still is, I bet." Her voice was thoughtful.

When the four finished the last bottle of wine and stood to leave the restaurant, Hamlin draped his arm over Storm's shoulders. Martin and DeLario bumped hips, the turbulence of their earlier troubles dissipated. DeLario steadied Martin's passage through the maze of tables.

On the street, the four paused to say goodbye. "Are you on the motorcycle?" Hamlin asked.

"We walked," DeLario grinned. "My apartment's only a half-mile from here."

"Good." Hamlin looked at Storm. "We should take a cab. I'll get my car later."

The cab driver was a Vietnamese immigrant who held the door and showed bigger holes in his grin than a six-year-old. Storm and Hamlin tumbled into the back seat, holding hands. Storm leaned back in the seat and closed her eyes. "You know, I had a great time." She peeked at him, then her watch. "Four hours and gallons of wine ago, I thought I'd be crawling home in tears."

Hamlin pulled her closer. "I was pretty worried, too."

"I've been thinking, though…"

"Uh oh."

Storm punched his arm hard enough that he winced. "Come on. Remember that phone conversation you told me about? When Hamasaki was talking to Martin about stocks?"

"Yeah."

"When was that?" she asked.

Hamlin looked out the window and frowned. "It was a couple of weeks before Hamasaki died. I'd had to rush from court to make the appointment with him and I was kind of glad to see him on the phone. You know, not waiting for me."

"Hamasaki had plenty of time to get back to Martin," Storm said.

"Yeah." The car pulled to the curb in front of Storm's cottage.

"Hamasaki was known for his promptness."

"Maybe he was checking on the stock."

The cab driver stepped out and opened the back door. Hamlin helped Storm out. "Wait a minute," he said to the cab driver. "I'll be right back."

Storm leaned into the cab and handed the driver his fare and a tip. "It's okay, you can go."

The cab driver showed that he didn't have many molars, either. Hamlin looked from Storm to the driver and back, then shrugged. The little man waved at their departing backs, then hopped back into his car and squealed away.

Storm looked up into Hamlin's face. "Don't you need a cup of coffee before you go?"

"Uh, sure," he said. "That would hit the spot."

Chapter 28

"So why did you wait so long to get your first pair of shoes?" Hamlin asked Storm. He breathed in the aroma from her coffeepot.

She got a couple of mugs out of the cupboard. "Like Martin said, twelve was early." She poured coffee and handed him one of the mugs.

"Really? Kids in Honoka'a don't wear shoes until they graduate from high school?"

Storm shrugged. "It depends on what you mean by shoes. I got patent leather shoes to go to my mother's funeral."

"She died when you were twelve?"

"Yeah." Storm turned off the kitchen light and Hamlin followed her into the living room. "DeLario mentioned your brother, Neil. How come you never told me about him?"

Storm plopped onto the couch, but Hamlin remained on his feet and concentrated on his coffee mug.

"He died of AIDS when I was in college." He sat down next to her, his eyes shadowed with sadness. "What happened to your mom?"

"She took about thirty Seconal."

Hamlin's eyebrows popped up and he looked at her, but it was Storm's turn to inspect the surface of her coffee. "That must have been tough," he said. "Neil used to have what I called his black furies."

"He got depressed, too?"

"Yeah," Hamlin said with a sigh.

"Because he was sick?"

"No, AIDS actually mellowed him. I guess it made him more philosophical. It definitely took the course of his life out of his hands. And DeLario helped him, too." Hamlin took a sip of coffee. "My father had the furies, too, but his were directed outward." The softness of Hamlin's voice did not hide the underlying resentment.

"Oh no."

"Dad was harder on Neil than me. He must have suspected Neil's inclination." Hamlin shook his head. "I was too frightened to intervene." Storm saw the shine of tears in his eyes before he looked down at his mug.

"How much younger was Neil?"

"Not quite two years."

"So Neil followed you to college?"

"Not exactly. Neil left for New York when I graduated from high school."

"You told me your dad left, too. Do you know where he went?"

"No, but that was a relief." Hamlin shrugged. "Neil got his GED in the city and started writing plays. One of them actually was performed off-Broadway. I was really proud of him, told him he could do even better if he went back to school, maybe got a degree under his belt."

"And he came to Ann Arbor."

Hamlin nodded. "He'd been taking some courses at a community college and doing well, so he decided to give the big U a go. By the time Neil came to Michigan, he had the virus. It was kind of a last shot at self-respect, I think."

"What about treatment?"

"AZT and some of the better drugs weren't around yet."

"He sounds like a brave guy."

"I wish I'd told him that." Hamlin kept his eyes down.

"I'll bet he knew how you felt."

"Maybe, toward the end. But I wish I'd spent more time with him when he was healthy."

"Yeah, I know what you mean." Storm's voice was sad.

Hamlin looked at her out of the corner of his eyes. "You were very young when your mom died."

"And a combative little piss-ant."

Hamlin half-smiled. "Listen to us, full of self-recriminations. Let's think of some of the good times, okay?" He took a deep breath. "You know that track meet DeLario was talking about? By then, the three of us were sharing an apartment. I had some of the best times of my life with those guys. I brought dates back that couldn't believe that I lived with two gay men. We'd laugh and party until the wee hours. There was so much talent packed into those rooms. Neil sang and acted, too. He and DeLario were an amazing duo."

"My mom was a singer!" Storm grinned at him. "She tried to teach me, but my voice always cracked when I got nervous. The only tunes I could sing with confidence were limericks."

Hamlin started to chuckle.

"You got it." Storm laughed. "When we were alone, Mom and I used to do them in duets. If I got down in the dumps, she'd start the first line and I was supposed to make up the second. We'd fall down, we laughed so hard."

"You were twelve?" Hamlin asked.

"Hey, I lived on a ranch. The facts of life were pretty obvious to anyone who had eyes. Come to think of it, there was a blind boy in fifth grade who told dirty jokes..."

"Did you ever tell your mother the jokes?"

"As a matter of fact, I did. She said it was okay if they were funnier than they were dirty and if I left out certain words."

"Which of course you did."

"Of course." They both laughed.

"My brother told great jokes," Hamlin said. Storm ran her finger down the side of his face, around the bushy mustache.

"Tell me one of them."

Hamlin pulled the corners of his mouth up. "I can't remember any right now. What perfume are you wearing? Just the slightest hint of spice..."

"Volupte...I put it on hours ago..."

Their lips touched, warm, mustache prickly, coffee-rich. "I like it," he murmured. "Oh, God. I've wanted to do this."

"Me, too," Storm whispered. She put her arm around one hard shoulder and pulled him closer.

He folded her in his arms. Storm ran the fingers of one hand through the fine hair over his ear and slid the other hand down the length of his back. He sighed and let his mouth melt into hers. They slipped lower into the couch cushions.

His shirt was untucked in back and Storm let her fingertips dance over the fine hairs at the base of his spine, just above his belt. Hamlin moaned and pressed closer.

Storm's skirt was riding up her thighs and she wanted to remove it, peel away the layers between his skin and hers. He kissed her lightly, then rubbed his nose against hers. His hand was at her back, just above the zipper. Caution and desire merged in his eyes.

"It's okay," she whispered.

The warm aroma of his skin, the heat of his yearning, melted away her inhibitions. She stretched so that her entire body length pressed against him. A sob of desire caught in her throat and she pulled away from his lips so that she could look at him, the fervor in his green eyes, the tawny mustache hairs mixed with gray, the five-o'clock shadow. She wanted to inhale all of it, keep it, and slow this moment into eternity.

And a crash from the kitchen froze them both. Hamlin raised his head, his eyes icy and focused on the darkness beyond the cone of warm light that shone near them. The muscles in his right arm quivered against Storm's side. He slipped off her with the slightest hiss, friction between their clothing, and crouched, ready to spring. The void left by him chilled her. She shuddered, sat up slowly.

"It sounded like a dish," she said.

"Did you lock the door?" Hamlin whispered.

"I don't think so."

Hamlin crept toward the dark kitchen doorway. Storm picked up the only object she could use as a weapon, a flower vase from the coffee table, and followed him. So close that her legs moved in time with his, she tiptoed through the doorframe, ran her hand along the wall molding, and flicked on the wall switch to the overhead light. Both of them stared at the countertop next to the coffeepot.

There sat Fang, calmly licking her paws. She glanced at them, blinked her wide yellow eyes, and looked down at the shattered cream pitcher on the floor. She looked back up at the two pale-faced people, stood up and stretched. "Mrww," she burped, and walked away with a cat-sigh of disappointment. All that waste, just because the cream pitcher wouldn't sit still.

Storm sagged against the countertop. "Jeez." She set the vase down with a clunk.

Hamlin ran a hand over his face. His dress shirt, flawlessly pressed a few hours ago, hung partly out of his trousers. Buttons were askew, and his stocking feet were still splayed in a fight-or-flight stance.

She took two steps toward him and wrapped one arm around him. She used the other hand to turn off the bright ceiling light.

"That's my guard cat."

"He's guarding your chastity?"

"He's a she. Just making sure I don't rush into anything. We gals have to watch out for each other."

"Yeah?"

"Let's go back to where we were." Storm kissed him. He enclosed her with his arms, let his lips brush hers lightly, then put one hand on the back of her neck and pressed his lips against hers as if he'd never let her go.

When he finally did, she gasped. "Hamlin..."

"Yeah?"

"Will you stay?"

Hamlin looked into her eyes. "If you call me Ian."

With a grin, Storm turned and locked the front door. Then she led him to the bedroom, picked a pile of clothes off the bed, and threw them onto a rocking chair in the corner. Silvery moonlight flowed through the window, illuminating the two of them. Storm was suddenly shy. She turned toward her closet and undid a button of her blouse.

"Wait," Hamlin said. He scooped her into his arms and deposited her onto the bed. He lay next to her, then kissed her neck gently, moving from under one ear, under her chin, to the soft skin under the other ear. His mustache tickled, enticed, made her yearn for his kisses on her lips, harder, faster. He slipped the blouse off her shoulders before she knew he'd unbuttoned it.

His body lay lean and hard next to hers, the warm sweet aroma from his skin blended with her own. They moved concurrently, gentle, warm, tingling, together.

Storm woke when morning's light caressed her face. She smiled, burrowed into the pillow, and smelled Hamlin on the sheets around her. She opened one eye. A note and a sprig of mock orange from the fragrant shrub in the garden lay on the pillow next to her. She raised her head. The warm lump lying along her leg was Fang. Damn.

She picked up the note. "Couldn't wear this shirt to court—might get confused with my client. Love, Ian. P.S. Love your pig."

Storm snorted, then sat bolt upright. She laughed out loud and twisted around to regard the tattoo she'd told him he'd never see.

The light coming in the window was brighter than usual and the clock said seven fifteen, an hour later than her usual wake-up time. Thank God she didn't have any appointments, but Wang would be dropping in around eight, stacking file folders in her in box, wanting to check the status of the Certificate of Need for Unimed.

A half-hour later, Storm was fluffing her still-damp hair with the windows down in the VW and applying her mascara at the traffic lights along Kapi'olani Boulevard, thinking how much easier all this would be if she had an automatic transmission. Or if she'd not overslept. Or if she could wear shorts to work. And so on. Not that she would have passed up last night for anything.

It was quarter of eight and she would be pushing her luck if she stopped at Leila's bakery for goodies, but if she didn't, she'd be practically shaking with hunger in an hour, scavenging for stale donut crumbs or the petrified caramels that sat next to the office coffeepot in a Santa Claus jar. Maybe Bruce, Leila's baker, would put some of their fresh-squeezed orange juice into a paper cup to go.

That did it. She swerved into the alley, crawled around the delivery trucks, and blocked the back door to her friend's shop. Ten minutes later, she was holding the rolled rim of the paper cup in her teeth to turn the knob to the front door. The aroma of the sticky bun in her laptop briefcase made her salivate.

She turned on the office lights and set down the orange juice, her purse, and the heavy case and sighed. A stack of files sat on her desk, covered with little yellow notes. "Rats, he beat me," she muttered under her breath.

"I'd like to see you before my afternoon appointment." Wang's voice surprised her. She looked up to see him in the doorway.

"I have time now. Would you like a cup of coffee?"

"I have a meeting in five minutes." He handed her a folder. "How about three o'clock? Meanwhile, I need you to look up some data at the university law library." His eyes traveled over her.

Storm resisted the urge to check her zipper. "Shall I meet you in your office?" She looked him in the eye. When your knees are shaking, act like you know what's going on.

"Fine."

Wang left. Storm waited a few seconds, then pulled out her purse compact and checked her face. A little puffy-eyed, but passable. The lipstick she had applied in the parking garage wasn't even on her front teeth. She smoothed her blouse front and skirt. A tiny run in her stocking was climbing above the heel of her shoe. Damn, but Wang couldn't have seen that.

She'd have to knock his socks off with her research. She also needed to buy a new pair of stockings before her lunch with Ray Tam, the union man. Storm downed her orange juice while she scanned the reference list Wang had given her. His lists were invariably incomplete; they were jumping-off points. He hadn't been in the university law library for years.

She'd better get going. As it was, she was going to have to return to the library after her lunch, jam for another hour, then dash back for her three o'clock appointment with Wang. Storm sighed, gathered her laptop, and hoped she could eat the sticky bun undetected in the library stacks, where no food was allowed.

On the way out the door, her direct line rang. Storm paused and glared at the phone. Few people had that number; most of her calls were routed through the front desk. It might be Martin, Leila, or Paul Andrews with a report on the coffee mug. She picked it up. The crackle of a long distance call greeted her.

Chapter 29

"Don't you ever check your messages?" Aunt Maile's voice teased, but held a note of exasperation. "I was worried about you."

"I guess I've been busy." Truth was, she'd been too distracted last night to check the answering machine.

"Uncle Keone and I are coming to Honolulu. We're at the Hilo airport now. He needs some new tack, so we're going to that saddle shop out in Pearl City. Then we're going to Ala Moana Shopping Center. Can you meet us for a bite of dinner?"

"Sure, it'll be great to see you." It would, but their timing could have been better. Plus, she'd bet her left shoe they'd want to eat at the Hibiscus Diner, where even spaghetti was served with a side of rice and *tsukemono*, or pickled Japanese vegetables. The vegetables were mostly daikon, which was a big, white radish and gave off a smell like swamp gas. It got worse with the digestion process. Storm stashed Tums in her purse when she went to the Hibiscus Diner.

"Let me take you to the Chao Phraya, this terrific Thai restaurant. You'll love the satay. They have sticky rice and fresh catch—"

"Oh, honey, Keone's got his heart set on the Hibiscus Diner's oxtail soup. They still serve it with boiled peanuts, don't they?"

"Probably," Storm sighed. "How about six-thirty? Can you spend the night with me?"

"I'd love to, but Keone wants to sleep at home, show up at the ranch next morning with the new equipment. Bebe's going to shoot me when she finds out we came over and didn't stay."

"When's the last plane?" Storm's shoulders were climbing with tension. She needed another deadline today almost as much as she needed another visit from one of the partners.

"Seven-thirty. Could you meet us at the Diner at five?"

"I'll try. If I'm late, go ahead and order." Storm dropped the receiver back in the cradle. She gathered her briefcase, closed her office door, and peered hopefully toward Hamlin's end of the hallway. All looked quiet down there; he was still in court.

Storm found a remote desk at the back of the stacks in the university law library and wolfed the now-cool sticky bun while she typed up pages of references and case studies for Wang on her laptop. Hours later, her growling stomach reminded her to glance at her watch. She had barely enough time to get to the Kāhala Country Club dining room. Forget about buying new stockings.

The hostess seated her and told her that Mr. Tam had called to say he would be there shortly. Storm sank into a plush dining room chair with relief. It was better form for her to be waiting for him than vice versa. This way, too, the runner in her stocking was hidden under the table.

She stared out at the golf course through floor to ceiling tinted windows. The contrast of white sand traps against brilliant greens, juxtaposed against azure waters and cloudless sky, looked like a color-enhanced post card. She took a grateful sip of ice water. It took a hot sun to bring out the blues in water and sky like that.

"Ms. Kayama, I'm sorry I'm late." Ray Tam grasped her hand warmly.

"I was enjoying the view, glad to be in the air conditioning."

Tam recommended the papaya halves filled with lobster salad. They both ordered it and Storm savored every bite. When she had scraped her papaya down to the mottled green skin and followed Tam's lead again in ordering lychee ice cream, he opened his briefcase. He slid a sheaf of papers across the table to her.

"This is the contract. Read through it in the next day or two, then we'll meet for your signature. I want you to do the work for us."

"Mr. Tam, I appreciate your confidence. I'm sure you realize that there are others in my firm with more experience."

"You'll be gaining experience daily." Daily? It would certainly beat sitting in the library stacks. She should genuflect with gratitude for this show of trust. Wang would be delighted, and the steady, lucrative jobs coming through the powerful Hawai'i labor unions could give her a solid position in the firm.

"We trust your maturity," he smiled, "and your former mentor, Mr. Hamasaki."

Storm put out her hand. "Mr. Tam, thank you. I'll work very hard for you."

He shook her hand and stood up to leave. "I know you will."

Storm nabbed a great parking place back at the law library, which was a rare find. A good omen. She had an hour and a half to finish her research for Wang and get back for her meeting with him.

In an hour, she had finished with the resources the library had to offer on Wang's cases. She scanned through her notes again. Great, she had time to go back and plug the laptop into the printer. She'd be able to hand a neat hard copy to Wang at the meeting.

The office was quiet. No clients sat in the waiting room and the receptionist was busy transcribing dictation while she fielded the phone. She merely nodded a greeting instead of stopping Storm with messages.

Storm plugged the laptop into the printer cable, flicked the on-switch, stood back, and sighed when nothing happened. It wouldn't be the first time the after-hours cleaning service used the outlet to run the vacuum, then forgot to replace the printer plug. She dropped to her hands and knees and rummaged under the counter that ran along the wall. Sure enough, the plug was dangling.

"I like the view from here."

Storm jerked back and up, nearly clonking her head on the underside of the shelf. Hamlin had put out his hand in anticipation, though.

"You scared me to death." She clambered to her feet.

"I was afraid of that. It's difficult when you walk into a room and discover only someone's backside." He glanced toward the cracked-open door and made sure no one was standing outside, then pulled her to him. "Will you have dinner with me tonight?"

Storm looked toward the door, too. "Careful, what would Meredith do if she saw us? Or Wang?"

"Maybe we'd have to open our own practice."

Storm shook her head with a smile. "I'm a lowly clerk, remember? Let me gather a few more clients." She planted a kiss on his chin. "Dinner last night was wonderful."

"Did we eat dinner?"

Storm chuckled. "I have to meet my Aunt and Uncle tonight at the Hibiscus Diner. Want to join us?"

"Hmm...why there?"

"It's their favorite place. Every time they come to Honolulu, they go at least once." Storm chuckled at his expression.

"What time?"

"Five."

"I can't."

Storm burst out laughing.

"No, really, I'll still be in the office."

"Nice try, Hamlin."

"Tomorrow. We'll go tomorrow."

"They're leaving tonight." She shook her head and grinned at him. "You got off easy."

"Tomorrow, anyway. Just us."

"We'll see." Storm gave him a push. "Get outta here. I'm meeting Wang in five minutes."

Hamlin brushed her lips with his and slipped out the door. Five minutes later, Storm stood outside Wang's office and paused to make sure she'd stifled her goofy grin.

Diane, Wang's secretary, smiled at her. "He'll be ready for you in one minute. He's on the phone." She lowered her voice. "You want the key to Hamasaki's office?"

"I've got to meet family for dinner tonight. I'll do it tomorrow after work."

"I'll leave the key in an envelope on your desk tomorrow when I leave. Can you get it back to me first thing the next morning?"

"Sure."

Diane glanced down at the phone. "Go on in, Storm."

Wang gestured to a chair facing his big rosewood desk. Silhouetted against the setting sun outside his huge windows, he looked small behind it.

She sat down and handed him a folder with the recently printed references. "I did a computer search and found almost all of the volumes in the stacks."

Wang ran his eyes down the first page. He settled back in his chair and got out a gold pen, which he used to make marks next to certain lines. There were eleven single-spaced pages. He flipped the first page over and proceeded as if he were alone in the room.

Storm gazed around his office. The top of his rich, rosewood desk was clear except for the papers he was reading, a fine leather blotter, a leather penholder, and a matching notepaper holder. A rosewood cabinet filled the entire wall to her left. The doors were fitted with glass panels so that one could admire the jade pieces displayed on the shelves, which were also glass. The back of the cabinet was a mirror, so that Storm could see under and around each item. Some of the jade carvings looked crude to Storm's untrained eye, like animals one would see in cave paintings, their large forms recognizable, but without detail. They had to be thousands of years old. On another shelf, hummingbirds, dragons, and mythical creatures in rare dark green hues were perched, every scale and tooth distinct. Below them, daggers with highly decorated blades were arranged in parallel rows. On the bottom shelf sat big slabs of apple green stone, carved into landscapes. The color variations in the stone were incorporated into the scene.

She glanced at Wang and found him looking at her. "Your collection is beautiful."

"Thank you." He gestured to the cabinet. "Some of those pieces just got back from the deYoung Museum in San Francisco. My mother started it years ago and I've continued it. I'm expecting another landscape to arrive any day now from Hong Kong." He bobbed his head in the direction of one of the larger carvings. "There are still pieces in mainland China that survived the Revolution, but they're hard to find. Citizens are holding on to them, now."

"They didn't always?"

"Ten years ago we could pick up a dragon like that one from black marketers. I could pay about a thousand U.S., which was more than two years' income to most people. It could mean the survival of a family in those times." He sounded as if he'd been performing a service. "Now, the Chinese government is trying to collect them, too. Prices have increased exponentially. People use the pieces as bargaining chips. Collectors like me have to bid against the government."

He shook his head as if disgruntled by the inconvenience and picked up the papers she'd given him. Storm stared at the dragon he'd pointed to, wondering just what the families got in exchange for their heirlooms.

His voice dragged her back from thoughts of struggling refugees. "This looks good." He pulled another file from his desk drawer and handed it over to her. "Meredith got some numbers for you. Should be all you need. I'd like to have it in the Department of Health office by tomorrow morning."

"I'll get right on it." Storm stood up to leave.

"Please notify me when it goes over to the state office."

"Okay."

It was quarter after five when Storm got to the Hibiscus Diner. She hugged Aunt Maile and Uncle Keone, then dropped onto the bench across from them and picked up the tattered plastic menu from its spot between a big bottle of soy sauce and a refilled ketchup dispenser hand-labeled "Chili Sauce." Storm wondered if the fumes from the chili bottle had hastened the disintegration of the cracked and yellow menu.

She looked at the dishes in front of Aunt Maile and Uncle Keone. The service here was fast and friendly; she'd hand them that. Aunt Maile was having what was probably described on the menu as barbecued ribs. Islands of meat sat in a swamp of sauce. Even her two scoops of rice were surrounded by molasses-hued liquid.

She was using a fork and spoon with enthusiasm. Uncle Keone slurped his oxtail soup, which had peanuts floating like drowned flies in the broth. His side dish of macaroni salad had no vegetables, just swollen pasta and mayonnaise. This was the sustenance of her childhood, Storm thought. Oh, well. Keone and Maile were full of love, support, and unsolicited advice. And whose family was perfect, anyway?

Aunt Maile used a tiny paper napkin to blot her lips. She had four or five crumpled beside her plate already. "I called Bebe to say hello and she scolded us for being in such a rush."

Uncle Keone shrugged. "I like to sleep in my own bed. No offense, honey. Just want to get the plane trip over with."

"It's okay, I understand," Storm said.

"Bebe wants me to send her *noni* leaves from the Big Island," Maile continued. "But I know a farm in Waimanalo where they grow lush and healthy. I told her I'd ask you to help her pick 'em. They'll be fresher."

"Aunt Maile, work is really busy right now."

Maile's big brown eyes looked sad. "Her arthritic hip has been bad lately."

"Then I have to drive them out to Waianae. That'll take a whole day."

"No, no. I asked Bebe to meet you in Waimanalo. She just can't climb some of the rocks where they grow."

"Is this for Tom Sakai?" Storm sounded resigned.

"Yes, him and a boy with leukemia."

"How old is the boy?" She should never have asked.

"Four." Maile shook her head sadly. "You would be helping them a great deal."

"Okay, okay. Can she meet me out there tomorrow at four-thirty?" Storm felt her shoulders droop. Now she'd have to leave the office early and return after leaf-picking to go through Hamasaki's files. Not only would it be a long day, but she'd have to turn down Hamlin's offer of dinner. Plus, she'd be a muddy mess when she got back to the office. Aunt Maile gave her a smile that made the sacrifice worthwhile.

Storm's chef salad arrived and she picked at the strips of ham on top. It was the processed kind, nether pig parts pressed into a pink mass and sliced. The colorless iceberg lettuce was flooded with Ranch dressing. But that might be a blessing, because it hid a lot. Storm took a few bites and told herself not to be such a snob.

"Honey, do you want to get a doggie bag?" Uncle Keone asked. "It's time for us to leave for the airport."

Storm put her fork down. "No need. Can I give you a ride?"

"No, we've got to turn in our rental car," Aunt Maile said.

"Then let me get dinner." Storm reached for her purse.

Uncle Keone patted her arm. "I already paid. You changed your busy schedule to see us."

Storm walked with them to the meter where they'd parked their car. "Spend a few days with me next time, okay?" She gave Uncle Keone a huge squeeze, then walked around to the other side of the car to help Aunt Maile get her large self into the small rental. She hated to see them go. "Take care of each other. I'll call soon."

Aunt Maile wrapped her arms around Storm. "You watch out for yourself, hear?" She pressed a tissue-wrapped object into Storm's hands. "Take this with you everywhere 'til this business with Hamasaki is over."

"Aunt Maile..."

Aunt Maile frowned at her. "Keep your eyes open." She pointed to the package. "Directions to the farm are in there."

Storm waved at the back of their disappearing car, warmed by their love and happy that she'd met them for dinner. Maybe next time, she'd convince them to try the Thai restaurant.

She poked at the wrapping paper and recognized the eight-inch wood figure. It was her *'aumakua.* She stood on the sidewalk and unwrapped the carving enough so that she could see the funny face of *pua'a*, the pig, so full of Big Island memories that despite his ferocious appearance, he made her smile.

Aunt Maile was getting a bit carried away, though. She wasn't going to be able to carry the pua'a around with her all the time. It wasn't the little one Maile used to let her wear around her neck. Storm stuffed him in her handbag, which would no longer zip closed. The purse was now considerably heavier.

Chapter 30

At home, Storm fed Fang and plopped into her reading chair only to fall soundly asleep after reading one page of Roy Tam's contract. It was two a.m. when Fang leaped into her lap and rumpled the papers. Muttering and groggy, Storm staggered off to bed.

When her alarm went off at six, she was pretty sure that she hadn't moved the entire night. One arm was completely asleep, a wooden bat filled with pins and needles, and the face in the mirror was puffy and lined with pillow creases. She was still paying for the night with Hamlin and yes, it was still worth it.

Once she got her arm working, Storm showered and hustled to her car. She braided her hair and put on a little eyeliner, mascara, and lipstick at red lights on the way downtown. She stopped at Leila's bakery for orange juice and a cherry strudel to go and gave Bruce, who must have been waiting by the back door, a cheerful peck on the cheek. By ten of seven, she was firing up the espresso machine in her office.

She wanted to go through Ray Tam's contract before the day got busy. Then she would hand-deliver Unimed's equipment request to an old high school friend at the DOH, a workaholic who Storm knew to be the most efficient person in the department. Maybe even the state.

She thought about her plans for the day. If she were to meet Bebe at the *Hāwanawana Lā'au* farm in Waimanalo by four-thirty, she had to leave the office at three. She'd slipped Aunt Maile's directions out of the pua'a's wrappings and noted that the place was at least five miles off the main road, or Kamehameha Highway, toward the Ko'olau Mountains. Beautiful country, but remote.

A tap at her door interrupted her thoughts. When she saw Hamlin, she grinned. He leaned over her desk and kissed her. "So, tonight? Seven o'clock?"

"Hamlin, Aunt Maile asked a favor of me. I've got to pick *noni* with a friend of hers this afternoon in Waimanalo."

"Waimanalo? When are you meeting her?"

"Four-thirty. I have a hunch it will take a while and I'm going to be pretty muddy afterwards. People grow a lot of taro back there, have pig farms, that sort of thing."

"Sounds refreshing." Hamlin chuckled. "What's *noni*?"

"A medicinal plant. Some kind of mulberry, I think."

"You know what it looks like and she doesn't, is that it?"

"No, she knows it better than I do. But the terrain is rough and Bebe's got an arthritic hip. She must be in her seventies." Storm remembered the lime green bike shorts. "Though she doesn't act like it."

"Want some company?"

Storm's face lit up. "Could you get away?"

"I'll try. Let me get back to you later." He disappeared.

Storm gazed happily at the back of the door for a few seconds and went back to the contract. She made a few notes, questions for Tam, and dialed his office. The secretary told her that Tam would meet her for coffee at three o'clock tomorrow afternoon. Would Starbucks be all right? Of course.

The minute Storm hung up, her direct line rang. Paul Andrews' rich bass came over the wire.

"Storm, do you have a few minutes or would you rather come over to the lab?"

"We'd better talk now," she said. "The rest of the day is going to be rushed."

"Okay. As we knew, there was black coffee in the cup. But there were traces of tea, too. Like maybe he'd had a cup of tea first, then a half-cup of coffee. There was more of the tea residue on the walls of the upper half of the mug. Here's the interesting part. I found butabarbital sodium, traces of calcium stearate, cornstarch, and dibasic calcium phosphate in the cup. There was a much lower concentration of the butabarbital in the coffee, but there was a substantial amount in the tea residue around the top of the cup."

Storm felt as if her heart stopped. When it resumed, it pounded with dread against her chest wall. "What is that stuff?"

"Butabarbital sodium is a barbiturate, a sedative. The calcium stearate, calcium phosphate, and cornstarch are binders, commonly used in the manufacture of tablets. You know, to make the pill hold together."

"Oh." Her jaw was moving as if it had rusted. "Was there enough buta...barbiturate to put him to sleep?"

"I won't bore you with the calculations, but if he drank 250 cc's, or about a cup, of tea with the concentration I found, he consumed approximately four 100 mg tablets. You told me he was an old guy, right? Was he overweight?"

"No, he was about my height and maybe a hundred fifty pounds."

"Storm, this dose would have knocked me out and I'm twice your size."

"Could it have killed him?"

"It could if he had any unusual reactions." Andrews paused. "I thought of something else, though. Could he have been using it medicinally over a period of time? Did he have trouble sleeping, was he suffering from an emotional shock?"

"I don't think so." She would have noticed if he'd been distraught. And it wouldn't have been like him to get a prescription for a sedative even if he were upset about his son and DeLario.

"Wouldn't that be a big dose even for an emotional problem?" Storm asked.

"Yes, but if he took it over time, he'd be habituated to it. He'd need more to get the same effect. But he would

have had to take it for months." Andrews sounded thoughtful, almost sad. "People can surprise you. There are some
very unlikely users running around. In expensive suits,
with the best educations money can buy."

Storm stared across the room. "No, I'm sure he didn't
use it regularly. Assuming that he wasn't accustomed to
taking it, how long would the drug take to put him to
sleep?"

"Fifteen, twenty minutes. He'd be out of it pretty quickly."

"Thanks, Dr. Andrews."

"You're welcome. I'll mail you a print-out of the
analysis."

Storm hung up the receiver and sat unmoving in her
chair for several minutes. Slowly, she picked the phone
back up and dialed Detective Fujita's number. She let out
a silent breath of relief when he answered gruffly. "Fujita."

"There was a barbiturate in the coffee mug."

"Oh boy. You got the analysis in front of you?"

"No, Paul Andrews just called me."

"He did it himself?" Fujita paused. "You mind asking
him to release a copy to me?" Storm could hear him
sipping something, probably coffee. "That changes things
a bit. Interesting, I wanted to talk to you, too. The truck
that killed Lorraine Tanabe was wiped down."

"You mean someone planned to hit her?"

"Makes you wonder. We found fibers from canvas
gardener's gloves, the kind Long's Drugs sells by the
dozens. The only fingerprints were on the vodka bottle
rolling around on the passenger's side floor."

"Could you trace them?"

"No problem. They belong to a homeless guy who
sleeps next to the public restroom in Kapi'olani Park. He's
been picked up once or twice for vagrancy."

"Is he still around?"

"Sure. Gave him a coupla Big Macs, sat him down for
a talk. He claims he saw some Oriental guy, a little on the
husky side, with glasses, digging around in the dumpster
where our homeless friend throws his trash." Fujita gave

a rueful chuckle. "Sounds like he's describing me. Or a few thousand other guys."

"You believe him?"

"Yeah. We also found fibers from new J.C. Penney's blue jeans and a red plaid flannel shirt. This guy would love to have clothes like that. He hasn't had new rags since the Vietnam War."

"Would he run someone down for money?"

"Unlikely. He's the kind of guy who raids dumpsters next to restaurants and shares the food with stray cats. Plus, he's not organized enough. Someone put some thought into this job. Every fiber in there was traceable to about twenty sources."

"You think it's connected to Hamasaki's death?"

"Hard not to after what you told me about the coffee." He paused. "Ms. Kayama, what made you think about getting the coffee in the cup analyzed?"

"Someone told me about a date-rape drug. It was unconnected to Hamasaki; it just got me thinking along those lines."

"I see." Fujita sighed. " Did Lorraine have access to all of Hamasaki's cases?"

"As far as I know. She knew his long-term clients. He'd go ask her what their wives' or kids' names were. She even kept notes on personal stuff, like if they were vegetarians or had seafood allergies, so when he took them to dinner, he didn't go to the wrong restaurant."

"I could use someone like that," Fujita said.

"Me, too."

"Where are her notes?"

Storm chewed on her lower lip. "I don't know. We cleaned out Lorraine's desk already. There was only one hanging file drawer and there wasn't any client or business information in there, just manuals for office machines, that sort of thing. Nothing confidential."

"Discreet of her."

"She was protective of Hamasaki, yet she pulled it off without making you feel as if you weren't on the inside track."

"Sounds like a smart woman," Fujita said.

"Yeah." Storm's voice was sad.

"I'd like to take a look at his files. Could you arrange that?"

"I think so. I've got to go through them myself."

"Thanks for your call," Fujita said. "I'll get back to you."

Storm sat holding the humming receiver, then slowly lowered it into its cradle. Hamasaki kept files on more than his clients' food allergies. A month or two ago, she'd seen him with a letter from David's doctor about the change in his insulin doses. She'd asked Hamasaki about it and he'd muttered that he kept track of David's health because David wasn't responsible enough.

She wondered what else Hamasaki kept track of. Her own teen-aged scrapes with the Waimea police, or details of her mother's death? And what about Martin? Even if her history had made it to the shredder, Hamasaki's discovery of Martin's homosexuality was recent.

Another, more urgent reason to use Diane's key tonight. Meredith had been carrying boxes into the office this morning, moving her own items into the new space. Storm didn't want those papers, if they existed, to get outside the family circle. Neither members of the law firm nor the police needed to know some of these personal secrets.

Chapter 31

With considerable effort, Storm shoved thoughts about Paul Andrews' report and the conversation with Fujita out of her mind. Wang and Wo were going to be banging on her door about the Department of Health approval.

She forced herself to concentrate on rechecking Unimed's contract for the last time, then put it into a manila envelope. She walked to Hamlin's end of the corridor and popped her head into his office. He was on the phone, but his eyes flickered in her direction. His voice was low and soothing. "Come on, you know better than that. Listen, I'd better go." He hung up.

Storm cocked her head at him. He'd curtailed that call quickly. "I'm going over to the state offices," she said. "Thought I'd check on our outing this afternoon."

"I canceled an appointment just for you," Hamlin said. He stuffed some papers into his drawer and closed it. "What time you want to leave?"

"Can you make it by three? We're supposed to meet Bebe at four-thirty," Storm said. "You're going to need old sneakers. And jeans or shorts. Don't even think about wearing a suit. We may be walking through fields of water."

"Oh yeah. Taro farms, right? Do we have time to run to my apartment and change?"

"If you're fast," Storm said. "It'll take about an hour to get there."

"I'm fast." Hamlin grinned.

Storm rolled her eyes. "What have I gotten myself into?"

"Great times, sweetheart."

"I'm gonna hold you to that." Storm gave him a wave and headed down the hall.

"Meet you here at three," he said at her disappearing back.

The state office for the Department of Health was about four blocks from Storm's office building. It was more trouble for Storm to drive her car out of one underground parking lot and into another than it was to walk. The day was beautiful; wisps of clouds blown by the brisk trade winds tumbled across a cerulean sky. And the expedition to Waimanalo was looking a lot less like an obligation. Storm walked three blocks before she stopped grinning like a schoolgirl playing hooky.

When she walked into the DOH and asked for Mark Suzuki, the receptionist smiled at her. Back in his cubicle, Suzuki looked up from behind three shoulder-high piles of quadruplicate forms and squinted at her. "You either got a raise or you're getting laid." He pushed his wire-rimmed glasses up the bridge of his nose. They were crooked, as usual. His office reeked of old-fashioned copy machine fluid.

"The fumes in here are getting to you, Suzuki. You need a break." She pointed at a stack of documents that looked like the IRS had printed them in batches of a hundred thousand or so. "I'm taking you to lunch."

"What do you need this time?" Suzuki said. He sneezed.

"Cynicism can give you allergies." Storm took the pen from his fingers and dropped it on the desk.

"You didn't walk over here to make fun of me." He blew his nose on a tissue.

"I never make fun of you." Storm peered at him seriously. "I need you to look over a contract for Unimed."

"I knew it." Suzuki sneezed again. "What are you getting a poor innocent like me into?"

"If you're innocent, then I'm Snow White." Storm went around his desk and grabbed his arm. "What you need is a cheeseburger."

Suzuki drew back in horror. "Hey, I'm not cheap, sweetie. You have to spring for lasagna, at least. Maybe I should hold out for lobster..." He stood up with a dreamy expression and tucked a shirttail into drooping pants.

Storm gave him a push and laughed. "Let's try that deli on the corner of Queen and Alakea. I hear they've got a good Philly cheese steak."

Suzuki's eyes gleamed with interest. "No kidding? The real thing?"

"You'll have to tell me."

On the way to the restaurant, he extolled the virtues of authentic Italian rolls and whether or not he believed the real thing could have made its way to Honolulu. "It's all in the bread, you know."

After all the commentary, Storm had to eat one, too. They sat on rickety white wrought-iron furniture practically in the middle of the downtown sidewalk. She figured Suzuki was happy because, undistracted by the surges of pedestrians around them, he wolfed down the huge sandwich, then picked strands of cheese from the paper wrapping.

He sat back in the fragile chair, which creaked. "I owe you one, Kayama. That was good."

"Just read my contract by this afternoon."

"Strings, strings." Suzuki picked a morsel of onion off his already spotted tie.

"You love it. That's why you stay with the state."

"Don't tell anyone," he said.

"Your secret is safe with me." Storm patted his arm. "I've got to get back to the office. Call me when you've looked it over, okay?"

"I'll talk to you tomorrow," Suzuki said.

"Wonderful."

The receptionist handed Storm a batch of messages on the way to her office. The work was piling up and she had two hours before she met Hamlin to go to the farm.

Storm made all of the client-related calls, but saved the one to Martin for later. She hoped he planned to help her pack up Hamasaki's furniture this weekend.

She looked down at the last message. It was from Marianne Watanabe, Aunt Bitsy's sister in Hilo. Bitsy had been staying with her the night Hamasaki was killed. Storm liked Marianne and knew her to be a direct, efficient woman. This call wouldn't take long. Storm dialed the long distance Big Island number.

"Storm, I'm coming over this weekend to stay with Bitsy. She's getting more depressed, you know. I guess the shock of everything. And I still have her overnight bag. It has her address book, her needlepoint, toothbrush, all the everyday little things. She left in such a hurry that morning. I'll bring it with me. But I need someone to pick me up at the airport Friday afternoon. David and Michelle will be between the lunch and dinner shifts at the restaurant and Martin is leaving the same morning. I hate to bother you, but..."

"I'll be happy to, Marianne. What flight will you be on?" Storm wrote down the information, but her mind was on what Marianne had just said. Marianne had mentioned that Bitsy left her house, which was in Hilo, in the morning. The desk clerk at the Hilo airport had told Storm that Bitsy had left Kona in the afternoon. Pieces of the puzzle were beginning to fall into place.

"Um, she, uh...left her bag because she was upset about Uncle Miles's death?" Storm asked.

"No, we didn't even know yet. What a day that was! She left to meet Martin and his friend. They called from one of those big hotels in Kona. No one even knew he was here," Marianne said. "Bitsy found out about Miles after she landed in Honolulu."

Marianne's last sentences bounced around Storm's stupefied brain cells. Martin had not only been in the Islands without telling anyone, he had been in Kona when Uncle Miles died. And he told Storm that he got his tan on the beaches in Chicago. The little weasel.

"Storm? You there?"

"Uh...I swallowed my coffee wrong." She coughed a few times and drew a deep breath. "I'm okay, now. Were they at the Lani Wai Resort? It's such a nice place."

"No, I think the one down the coast a bit. You know, the one with private bungalows. The Hualalai. That's how we knew it was a special friend." Marianne chuckled.

"Bitsy knew about him?" Storm asked.

"Martin let her in on the secret a couple weeks ago. He was terrified of telling his father, though, and Bitsy was trying to help him, encourage him," Marianne said.

"Why was Bitsy out of sorts Friday morning, though?"

"I'm not sure. Martin's call got her all upset. The boys had been planning to go to Honolulu to tell Miles the whole story when he died. Such a sad thing." Marianne sighed. "I've got a call coming through. See you Friday, okay?"

Storm hung up the phone and dialed the number Martin had left the receptionist. She got Chris DeLario's answering machine and left a message for Martin to call her back. She was rubbing her temples and staring at her desktop when Meredith Wo knocked at her door.

"Storm, what's the news on that contract?" Wo asked.

"He'll call me about it tomorrow. He's doing us a big favor since he's two weeks behind on state work. A couple of people are on vacation."

Irritation crossed Wo's face and her eyes narrowed. "When tomorrow? This is a billion-dollar project. And it's probably where that nerd gets his medical care."

Storm glared at her. "Everyone who brings a contract to this nerd has a billion-dollar project."

Meredith snorted, then handed Storm a thick file. "I need you to go to the U.H. law library."

Storm took the folder. "I'll do it first thing tomorrow morning. I have a meeting this afternoon." She glanced at her watch and prayed that Hamlin didn't choose that moment to come through her door. It was ten of three.

"Storm, your procrastination may be a problem for you here in the firm."

Storm drew in a long breath and began to count to ten. She got to four. "What procrastination, Meredith?" she snapped. "I keep careful records of your requests and how long I take to get your work back to you. Would you like to look over the last week?" She prayed that Wo didn't.

"We'll talk about this later. With the partners." Meredith walked briskly away.

Storm stared after the woman's vapor trail. The last few days, Meredith had been acting like Tonya Harding on steroids. Did she suspect that Hamlin and Storm were having a fling?

The silk of Storm's blouse stuck to her sweating sides like sliding wallpaper. One thing was sure; she didn't need any more conflict right now. She was starting to feel like she had one foot in her mouth and one sinking in quicksand. She was afraid to take a step for fear of burying herself in errors or finding out something that she was scared to know. Martin's deception hung even heavier on her mind than Meredith's threat.

"You look like you've been through a shitstorm." Hamlin leaned against the doorframe.

"Let's get outta here." Storm used both hands to push herself to her feet.

"Okay. I already picked up my clothes." He held up a gym bag.

"My stuff is in my car. I'll drive," Storm said.

"You sure? You look like you could use a rest."

"Let's just go. I'll tell you about it on the way."

Chapter 32

Storm drove in silence until the freeway ended at Kalani-anaole Highway. She ignored Hamlin's curious glances. At the first red light she drew a deep breath.

"Did you know that Chris and Martin were on the Big Island when Hamasaki died?" she asked. From her peripheral vision, she saw Hamlin's jaw muscles flex. Shit, he knew.

"Why didn't you tell me?"

"I just found out. I was talking to Chris when you came into the office this morning."

"Why didn't you tell me then?"

"You were in a hurry, so I thought I'd wait until we were outdoors, in the soothing company of pigs."

Storm cracked a small smile. "The pigs are behind fences. We're going to be up on the slopes of the Ko'olau Mountains."

"Okay. That's where I was going to talk to you."

"Talk to me now. Why did Chris wait until today to phone you?"

"I phoned him."

Storm frowned and turned her head to stare at him. "Why? I thought you didn't know they were in Hawai'i when Hamasaki died."

"He was being evasive and I had some questions about his recent blood test."

Dread crept from Storm's fingertips up her arms.

"I've seen him like that before." Hamlin's voice drifted off. His eyes narrowed, unfocused, on the distance.

Storm felt a jolt of fear for Martin and a surge of sorrow for Hamlin and his friend. "How sick is he?"

"He's HIV positive, but not sick. Not yet." He looked over at Storm. "And he told Martin. They've been careful."

"Oh, God, Ian. I'm so sorry."

"Me, too." He sighed. "The drugs are better now than when Neil died. No one even understood the virus, then." He stared out the windshield.

Storm had passed through Hawai'i Kai and was at the road's high point above Hanauma Bay. She followed Hamlin's gaze out over the extinct volcanic crater, half-collapsed millions of years ago and filled with azure water and spectacular reef life. It was an underwater park, a favorite of tourists from around the world. Every time she drove by, she slowed down to relish the panorama. She rolled down her window and let the salty breeze pass through the car. Hamlin lowered his, too.

"I never tire of this route," he said. The muscles of his face relaxed and the breeze ruffled his hair. "Thanks for bringing me along. I needed this."

"Me, too." She breathed in the briny air. A strong summer swell pounded the lava cliffs below them and sent billows of salt spray drifting over the sinuous road.

By the time she and Hamlin had rounded the point at Makapu'u and wound their way along the coast to Waimanalo, she had told Hamlin about Wo's threats. He waved his hand. "Don't worry. Wang may be a pawn, but Cunningham is wise to them and he likes you."

"He does?" Storm remembered his leg against hers and his scotch-laden breath. She had been sure she'd burned her bridges in that department.

Hamlin looked at her out of the corner of his eye. "Yeah, he respects you. And the word is out that Ray Tam has asked you to do some work for the union."

"Boy, no secrets on an island."

"I guess not." His voice was heavy.

Storm looked over at him, but he was staring out the window again. Before she could say anything, he pointed out the turnoff she'd asked him to watch for.

Someone had dumped gravel into some of the deep ruts of the dirt lane to make it more passable, but it still was like driving in deep sand, then rock-strewn dust, then another gravel pit. They passed a nursery on their right, fields of purple dendrobium orchids protected from the full onslaught of the sun by semi-transparent tarps. After the nursery, banana trees lined both sides of the road and sheltered the land from the trade winds that had blown so briskly along the south shore.

Storm crept, hunched over the steering wheel, and hoped that the frame of her old car would hold up to abuse for the second time this week. Dust rose and coated the windshield, making it even harder to see what was in front of her. It was some consolation that someone had passed along the road not long before them; she could follow the cloud of silt that hung in the sluggish air. But Storm eyed the woods covering the base of the mountains ahead and remembered the strange creature she saw on the last herb-gathering outing she'd taken. Anxiety about traipsing off into the taro fields flooded her.

They bounced along another mile and a half before they saw a shack, then a small single-wall house. A sow that weighed at least five hundred pounds stood in the front lawn. Her teats hung nearly to the ground and she merely glanced toward the car when Storm applied her noisy parking brake. The hog had more important things to attend to. Bebe was scratching her ears.

Hamlin peered through the dusty windshield at the huge animal. "I thought you said they'd be in pens."

Storm shrugged. "Must be a pet."

"A guard pig, sumo-sized," he muttered. "I'm glad you don't have one of those."

Bebe waved at them, her brown face a collection of laugh lines. Hamlin grinned in spite of himself.

"Sam will be right out. He went after some coconut husk." She gestured to the pig. "Hortense has mastitis.

Storm, you're going to stay with me and help make a poultice for her while the men pick the *noni.*"

Storm felt a rush of relief tinged with irritation at being told what to do. Bebe certainly was bossy. However, now she wouldn't have to go tramping through muddy, flooded terraces, worrying about improbable hairy creatures. And perhaps she would learn some healing tips from Bebe, which would make the trip even more worthwhile.

"How many babies is she nursing?" Storm asked.

"Thirteen," said Bebe.

"Ouch," said Hamlin.

Bebe laughed and held out her hand to Hamlin. Storm introduced them. She could see Bebe's eyes, still sparkling with amusement, sweep over the man. "Thanks for helping out. We've had rain and the paths are slippery, so it's better if Sam doesn't go alone." She took in the expensive suit and loosened tie, then pointed to the bag he carried. "You better change. Go on in the house."

When Hamlin and Storm came back out in their old sneakers and shorts, Bebe and Sam were rubbing the sow's belly. Hortense, who lay on her side, looked as if she were smiling despite three red, tender-looking teats.

Sam stood up and offered his hand to Storm, then Hamlin. He had a tanned face with a strong, broad Hawaiian nose and liquid black eyes. His dark, wavy hair was streaked with gray and pulled back with a faded bandana. The seat of his denim overalls was white where it had been worn to single threads.

He grinned at Hamlin, pulled some berries from his pocket, and held them in a rough, callused paw, the hand of a farmer. "We gone look for these, yeah? They mostly past the *kalo* terraces, see?" He pointed down a narrow, muddy dike, a raised path between flooded taro fields. "Where the path run out, we need climb a little more. Then we see the shrubs. Little guys." He held his hand a couple feet above the ground. "Try pick some leaves, too, yeah?"

Hamlin took a few berries and examined a leaf. "I'll follow you."

Storm looked at the berries in Hamlin's soft, clean hands and felt a surge of apprehension. What had she led Hamlin into? The sun was dropping fast behind the Ko'olau Mountains and the Waimanalo farm would soon be deep in shadow.

Get a grip, she told herself. Hamlin was with Sam, who knew this land better than she knew the floor plan in her cottage. Plus, that strange beast she'd seen on the Big Island was hundreds of miles away. She shifted her purse under her arm. She'd stuffed her stockings into it and with the *'aumakua* she'd forgotten to take out, the bag was nearly bursting. Everything poked out of the open zipper.

Bebe pointed to the *'aumakua*. "That's an old one. *Pua'a,* the pig. May I look?"

Storm nodded. "He was my great-grandmother's. Aunt Maile gave him to me yesterday."

"Really?" Bebe pulled it out a bit, then looked at Storm, her dark eyes bright. "Your aunt's a wise woman." Bebe nestled it carefully back into Storm's purse and shot a glance toward the men. "We need to talk," she said softly to Storm.

Hamlin and Storm took their work clothes to the car and Storm bent the front seat forward so that they could drape their good clothes over the back seat with minimal wrinkling. Hamlin even found a coat hanger stuck between the seat cushions and draped his suit pants over it. Storm jiggled her bulging handbag down into the narrow spot behind the driver's seat, out of the way of Hamlin's neatly arranged clothing.

Storm's eyes followed him as he trailed Sam along a slippery, dike-like path between irrigated taro patches. Grass-covered, it was barely wide enough to go single file and the walls of the passage fell steeply into muddy water. As she watched them disappear, Bebe spoke.

"What do you know about your friend?"

The two women moved towards Hortense, who lay snoozing on her side a few feet away. Bebe sat on a little stool while Storm squatted next to a bowl on the ground and stirred water into the ashes of a burned coconut husk.

"A lot. Why?" Storm bristled at the question. "Should I add more water to this paste?"

Bebe splashed in a few tablespoons and went on, oblivious to Storm's tone. "You work together, yeah?"

"Yeah."

"He from the mainland?"

Storm looked over at Bebe. She squelched the "duh" and said, "Yes."

"City person, yeah?"

"Yes."

"Like you are these days, yeah?"

Storm glared outright at Bebe. "Yes, that's where I work."

Bebe raised one eyebrow at Storm. "Your aunt told me about what you saw on the mountain that day."

"We don't know what it was." Storm sat back on her heels. "I was kind of upset about other things at the time."

Bebe just nodded. "That paste is perfect. See how it clings to the skin?" Bebe put a bit on her own arm, smelled it, checked the color, and smiled. She dabbed a spot on Storm's arm where a mosquito had bitten her. "Feel better?"

Storm attempted a smile. "Yeah, it does."

"Let's see how Hortense likes it." Bebe smiled at her. "Remember Hortense from Dr. Seuss?"

"The elephant that sat on the egg?"

"Yup. Couple years ago, Hortense nursed six kittens. Their momma got hit by a car on the highway." Bebe pointed in the direction of the road that ran along the ocean, the same one Storm and Hamlin had driven. "Hortense wasn't much more than a teenager herself."

"Is that one of the kittens?" Storm pointed at a fat gray tiger who sat grooming himself under a nearby tree.

"Maybe. I can't keep all of Sam's animals straight. You'll have to ask him." Bebe stood up slowly and walked over to Hortense, who lay resting in the grass. Storm followed with the bowl of paste. "You could ask Sam about some of those old legends, too. He'll be very interested in hearing about what you saw."

"My imagination got the best of me that day. It was rainy, foggy, and we were halfway up a volcano that's steeped in old myths."

Bebe spread the paste gently on the sow's tender underbelly. Hortense gave a big sigh and Storm thought her mouth turned up at the corners. "Tell me more," Bebe urged. Stifling impatience, Storm took them both through that misty morning, ending with her finding Aunt Maile sidelined in the barbed wire and their speculations about the eerie events. It took much longer than she expected. Her irritability must have showed.

"Listen to what your aunt tells you. She's a wise woman." The edge in Bebe's voice made Hortense raise her head and flick her ears.

Storm gritted her teeth. "I always—"

A shrill scream rent the air, a shriek that made the hair on both women's arms stand on end. Storm leaped to her feet. Bebe was beside her, a light hand on Storm's arm.

"Hamlin," Storm cried out. "Ian!" she shouted, louder.

"He's with Sam."

Storm didn't find that fact as reassuring as Bebe obviously did. Someone was in trouble behind the kalo terraces.

Both women jogged toward the watery fields. Storm, just ahead of Bebe, scanned the area for signs of movement. The wide, lush taro leaves swayed placidly above the muddy water. A mynah bird hopped along the trail between the patches, then took flight when Storm splashed through a mud puddle and onto the narrow path.

Bebe was less than ten feet behind. "Careful, it's slippery."

"Right," Storm said and slowed slightly.

On the other side of the irrigated terraces, the path widened a few inches and the women increased their pace. Tree roots snarled the trail, their sinews criss-crossing the path like bulging veins. Storm jogged along, her gaze bobbing from placing her feet to watching for the two men. "Ian," she called. "Sam?"

Bebe's footsteps sounded behind, but Storm could also hear movement through the foliage ahead of her. With a flood of relief, she caught a flash of white clothing. Both men had been wearing white shirts. "Ian," she shouted and dashed ahead.

She never even saw the root that caught the toe of her sneaker. When she went down, she skidded for half a foot on her belly, plowed her chin into the soil, and bit her tongue so hard that her eyes watered from the pain. She lay for a moment, stunned. When her eyes cleared, she got to her hands and knees and stared at the muddy path a few inches from her face.

"Storm!" Three voices shouted at once. Hamlin dashed to her and helped her get shakily to her feet. "Are you all right?"

Sam, who still carried enough greenery to start a small nursery, was right behind him, while Bebe took less than two seconds to join the group.

Pain shot up Storm's leg and she leaned against Hamlin, but she kept her eyes on the ground. "Yes, I just took a header. But look. Is that a hoof print?"

Sam leaned down first. "Sure is. Looks like a big pig." He looked straight at Bebe.

Storm peered closer. "That's a cow's hoof. It's even bigger than Hortense's feet."

"Looks like a pig to me," Bebe said softly. "Let's get back to the house."

"The pig wen' *holo*, Bebe. We heard it." Bebe looked at Sam, her eyes wide. "But it sounded like it was chasing someone." Sam moved off the path and into the undergrowth.

Hamlin looked at Storm with a question in his eyes. "Ian," she said softly. "What did you see?"

Chapter 33

Hamlin looked uncomfortable. "I'm not completely clear what happened…"

"Come on, Ian, you've had years of practice dragging testimony from witnesses. Pretend you're in court."

"Okay." He looked at the path. "Sam and I walked away from you up the dike…" Hamlin's voice sank as he moved into the story.

"How deep is it?" I looked out over the acres of rich green leaves rising above the surface of the terraces.

"A foot or two. Hawaiian term for taro is *kalo*, you know." Sam sounded proud. "All hand-harvested. My brother and his wife work with me." He waved his arm in the direction of the perfect lines of stems. "Hard work. Not too many people do this anymore."

"*Poi* must be expensive."

Sam nodded. "It is, at the store." He gave me a rueful smile. "We don't make the money, though, the middlemen do. You like eat poi?"

"Uh, well, I'm getting used to it. I like it with *lomi* salmon."

Sam looked back and grinned. "Me, too. You try the leaves, yet? Really *'ono*. Delicious." His smile faded. "Usually a family profession, you know, passed on. This was my father's farm. But my son, he move to the mainland."

"Maybe he'll come back one day." I didn't know exactly what to say. My feeling is my mother and Sam would have some sentiments in common. Still, even I had seen young, well-educated Hawaiians leaving for better job opportunities. I can't blame them, though. Law, medicine, and business usually paid better than farming.

"Maybe. Never know about life, yeah?"

"That's for sure."

We were out of the taro patch and on rocky, steep terrain. At one point, I needed to use both hands to climb up a four-foot vertical rise of lava rock, so old and worn that its face was smooth, with natural footholds.

Sam scrambled up the embankment with surprising agility. "We better hurry. Sun's going drop behind the mountains soon. We got to get the noni for those poor sick boys."

"I'm right behind you." I was enjoying the woods and the exercise, but knew we didn't want to be out here in the approaching dusk. Even with Sam's knowledge of the area, the path had its steep, rocky sections. And the shadows were already deep.

I followed Sam through a stand of tall ironwood trees. Their long, delicate needles cushioned the path and hid the hard, round little seeds. The last of the sun sliced through the trunks in streams of gold. My foot slipped on a hidden seed and I braced myself against a tree trunk. "It's beautiful in here."

"Sure is." Sam pointed to a lone shrub, standing among the undergrowth, about ten feet off the path. Dark berries shone among the satiny green-black leaves. "There's a noni bush."

"I'll pick that one."

"Good. We need a few more, though. Noni usually grow in clusters—you know, the birds spread seeds around the same area." Sam pointed ahead. "I'll go up the path a couple of feet."

"Okay, I'll walk ahead when I'm done and find you." I pulled one of the plastic grocery sacks that Sam had given me from my pocket and picked my way around the thorny low kiawe, which grew next to the path. In a few minutes, I had stripped the shrub of its ripest berries and taken a few sprigs of glossy leaves. My bag wasn't even a quarter full.

So I started up the path, scanning the lengthening shadows, but didn't see any more of the berry bushes. Nor did I see Sam. I put a couple of fingers in my mouth and blasted a short whistle. A whistle answered. I marched ahead a few feet and caught sight of another noni bush, this time off the path to the left.

"Sam," I called out. "You find a patch?"

"Yeah, big bunch." Sam's voice came from my left.

"Got one here, too."

"Good, we almost done," Sam answered. I could hear him rustling through the undergrowth.

I made my way to the bush and filled the bag to nearly three-quarters full. How much of this did they need, anyway? I wasn't sure if the leaves were used to make tea or for a poultice like the one for Hortense. I walked ahead on the path and whistled again, but got no answer. "Sam?" I heard rustling and what might have been a grunting response, so I followed the sound.

The woods were growing denser with the huge leaves and thick vines of plants that required the rainfall of higher elevations. No rays of sun penetrated the jungle vegetation and I thought that I'd probably passed out of the habitat of the noni. The path had dwindled to a game trail that disappeared in the dense foliage.

"Sam?"

"Be right there," came the answer, but from farther away than before.

I looked around. Sam's voice had come from deep in the woods, so I stood still and waited for a moment, shifting my weight from foot to foot, feeling foolish standing in the middle of the woods holding a grocery bag of leaves and berries. I decided to count to twenty, then head back down the path.

...Nineteen, twenty. "Hey, Sam, I'm heading down."

"...found something good...catch up..."

I started down the trail, but in a moment or two stopped to check around. I hated to leave the fellow in the woods, even though Sam did know his way around. The shadows had lengthened and though the path was still visible, the undergrowth beside it was dark, too dark to make out individual plants ten or fifteen feet away.

"Sam?" I was shouting now.

Only the whisper of wind ruffling the tops of the tall ironwoods answered. The path seemed steeper going back than it had been coming, probably because I was alone, but a gradual climb is easier than walking downhill. I took off again and slipped on the tough, round kernels that were the ironwood's version of a pinecone. I grabbed the branch of a nearby shrub for stability.

"Yow!" Spiky kiawe thorns pierced my palm, leaving two deep scratches. The damned plant had kept me from falling on my ass, but now I needed Neosporin ointment and a Band-Aid. Or some of Bebe's herbs. I wondered about the noni, but didn't know if its medicine worked on scratches and abrasions. I made a note to ask Bebe later—the knowledge might come in handy.

Then someone started smashing through the thorny underbrush. Sam's overalls were going to be shredded. At least the Hawaiian was wearing long pants. My legs would be in ribbons if I ran right through the thick foliage like that.

"Hey, I'm over here." I shouted in the direction of the crashing noise, but it suddenly stopped. Absolute silence. No birds sang, no crickets chirped, no bees buzzed in the honeysuckle patches.

For the first time, I felt truly uneasy. The shadows beside the trail were now nearly impenetrable. Some light leaked through the tops of the tall ironwoods, but it was the murky haze of dusk. I stood stock-still. Why hadn't Sam answered my shouts? Maybe he'd taken a tumble, or a branch had fallen on him. I looked up the tree trunks. The woods here were very different from the hardwood forests of Michigan; no heavy branches hovered overhead. But then, I had no idea what pitfalls these seemingly

benign jungles held—Hawai'i doesn't have snakes, but
there are wild pigs and though they aren't big, they have
nasty reputations. I'd heard stories from local hunters.

"Sam, you okay?" The silence was thick; even the wind
was holding its breath. The hairs on the back of my necked
lifted and I felt cold, even though the evening was warm.
Something was wrong.

The crashing noise had moved across the path and into
the woods on the right, so if it was a pig, there was a good
chance the animal was still in front of me. It would be better
to go back and try to find Sam. But I was increasingly uneasy.

I told myself that an escaped farm animal had most
likely made the noise. The birds had stopped singing
because of all the shouting. I moved back up the path,
walking quietly, avoiding twigs by rolling the soles of my
sneakers along the needle-cushioned trail.

The air was sultry and unmoving. Sweat began to run
down the side of my face. The air felt charged, like it did
before an electrical storm.

I rounded the next corner and climbed a small rise,
watching my feet to avoid slipping. And there was Sam,
cheerfully coming toward me with a full grocery bag and
an enormous bunch of thick-stemmed plants that were
five to six feet long. He could hardly see over the mess.

Relief washed over me. "Here, let me give you a hand."

"I found this *'awapuhi.* Bebe gone be so happy. The
sap good for shampoo and the flowers, they—" Sam's
mouth dropped and his dark skin lightened three shades
before my eyes.

I whirled. A dark shadow, about my height, glided
across the path about fifteen feet away. The atmosphere
grew so still that not even a mosquito hummed.

That was a funny-looking character, hunched over like
that, but he seemed to be alone, so why was Sam so
startled? We had the guy outnumbered.

"You know him?" Sam hadn't seemed like the type who
would spook easily. For some reason, the smell of the plants
Sam held had become overwhelming. Way too sweet for my
taste. In fact, they smelled like dying gardenias.

Sam dropped everything on the ground and gave me a hard shove. "Quick," he whispered. "Into the woods. Lie down flat."

We pressed into the earth and heard the crash of foliage again, just a few yards from where we lay with our faces nearly buried in the moist, composting soil. The sound stopped, then began again, farther away. At least the guy was moving on.

I felt Sam stir, then sniff the air. I sniffed, too. The strong flower odor had gone. We rose to our knees. Then a loud shriek followed by the sound of breaking wood and tearing branches ripped the syrupy air. Sam and I flattened ourselves once again and lay absolutely still.

The noise choked to a stop and stillness rolled through the woods as if a thick blanket had been pulled around the trees. A muffled thud and choking sound reached us through the undergrowth.

Several minutes passed before I felt Sam stir. I lifted my head and followed Sam's lead in getting slowly to my feet. Sam placed a gentle hand on my arm. "One minute," he said. He crept to the path and I watched him look around and test the air. Then he gestured to me. "Hurry, let's get back to the farm."

We gathered the harvested plants that lay undisturbed where we'd dropped them. Sam led the way down the path. I stayed close behind, keeping an eye on the woods beside us. From time to time, Sam would slow and check the air for odors.

After a few minutes of stealing nearly soundlessly down the path, Sam increased his pace. I let myself gradually unwind although I could feel my muscles grow heavy with spent adrenaline.

I wanted to ask Sam who we had seen and why they had hidden, but it wasn't the time. The cords in the Hawaiian's neck still stood out and his head swept steadily from side to side. Every now and then, he slowed to examine a shadow in the nearly dark woods. But he didn't stop, and he moved with a stealth and silence that impressed me.

Chapter 34

Storm bit her lip as Hamlin ended his recital. Bebe had moved closer to hear his words. In the silence, four sets of anxious eyes looked into the forest.

"Try wait one minute," Sam said. His eyes were on an object nestled in the broken branches and crushed leaves several feet from the path. When he stopped six or eight feet into the woods and peered down, Storm saw his jaw muscles tighten. Already unnerved by Hamlin's vivid recital, she gripped his arm tightly. Sam came up with a grim expression on his face and an athletic shoe dangling between his forefinger and thumb.

"It could have been there for days," said Storm.

Sam looked doubtful. "It's dry. And it rained this morning."

"We need to leave this place, go back to the house. Right now," Bebe said.

"What if someone needs help?" Hamlin asked.

"That's what I'm thinking, too." Sam looked worried. He shouted into the woods. "Hey! Anyone there?" All of them stood, looking into the dark trees. The woods, which now looked like a wall of impenetrable tree trunks, seemed serene. The placid songs of birds settling down for the night drifted to them.

Sam, who had stood listening to most of Hamlin's recital, now looked at Bebe and shrugged.

"It would be silly to chase after a noise in the dark," she said. "Let's go back." Bebe set out first, with Sam close behind her. Storm and Hamlin walked side by side. Her foot and ankle sent out an occasional twinge.

"We heard a terrible scream," she said.

"So did we."

"Describe again what you saw," Bebe commanded.

"Something very strange. Like a pig, but…" Sam's voice was low and uneasy.

"Yes, what was that thing?" Hamlin asked. "I thought someone was following us."

"It was following the guy who lost his shoe." Sam jerked his head toward the woods. "Poor sucker sounded like he was running for his life." Sam looked back at Hamlin again. "You smelled the flowers, yeah?"

"Yes, but you had an armload of them." Hamlin gestured to his white ginger.

"The *'awapuhi* smells different." He plucked a flower and handed it to Hamlin. "The odor back there was a warning," Sam said.

Bebe looked back at Storm with an eyebrow raised and steel in her gaze. "This sounds like your afternoon on the mountain. Sam, would you mind making some coffee? We need to talk."

Sam glanced over his shoulder at Storm and Hamlin's eyes followed, full of questions.

The dark brew Sam conjured from his tiny galley was delicious. He also brought an ice pack for Storm's foot. She propped it on a stool and drank a whole cup of coffee before Bebe stopped blowing on her first cup.

Bebe turned to Hamlin. "You know much about Hawaiian legends?"

"Just the common ones, I guess. Don't take bananas in a boat or drive over the Pali Highway with pork in your car. If you see an old woman beside the road, give her a ride because she might be Pele…" Hamlin shrugged.

"That's a start." Bebe nodded her approval. "Did you know that the ancient Hawaiians believed that the spirits of dead people entered into animals?" She took a sip of her coffee and regarded Hamlin.

"I don't think I've heard about that."

"These spirits, or *'aumakua*, became helpers of the people."

Hamlin looked at Storm. "Like your pig?"

Storm rolled her eyes at him. "They're old stories," she said. "They were imagined by people who stared into fires and had no scientific way to explain or avoid events that terrified them. A couple hundred years ago, parents lost half their children to illness before their first birthdays. Hurricanes and volcanic eruptions were whims of the gods."

She ignored Bebe's glare and gazed into her coffee cup. "Anyway, Kamapua'a would have hovered above the ground," she said. "He wouldn't have left a footprint." From the corner of her eye, she saw both Hamlin's and Sam's heads whirl toward her.

"What?" Sam asked.

"Like the creature you saw on the mountainside? The one who left a dead man behind you?" Bebe's voice was impatient and she gave Sam a significant glance.

"A dead man?" Hamlin's voice showed his dismay and Storm was afraid to look in his direction. Bebe didn't know about Lorraine, and maybe not even about the guy who had chased Storm on the road to Laupahoehoe, but Hamlin did. And he was adding up the bodies. Hamasaki. Lorraine. Kwi Choy. With Tong Choy, the fellow who had died on the slopes of Mauna Kea, the count was up to four.

She should have told Hamlin about the herb-picking incident earlier, but the story had seemed too implausible to repeat, especially once she was back in the city. Plus, at the time, they had both been too upset about Lorraine's death for her to bring up some flaky legend-in-the-mist. Now she regretted her silence.

"The police say that he fell and broke his neck," Storm said. Her voice sounded unconvincing even to her own ears.

"Storm, you are not paying attention to the ancient signs." Bebe's sharp voice chastised her. Storm ignored the flush of anger that reddened her cheeks and took a deep breath. Instead of a defensive retort, she chewed her lip. Uncle Miles would be proud that she'd thought before firing off her mouth. She needed to gather more information to get to the bottom of this. It all started with Uncle Miles. And perhaps the answers lay in his private files.

Sam broke the heavy silence. "Anyone want more coffee?"

Storm shook her head. Hamlin got to his feet. "I'm sorry everyone. I've got to get going." He turned to Sam. "Could I use your phone for a minute?"

Storm looked at him in surprise.

"I have to call Chris. I told him I'd meet him at eight and it's eight-thirty now. I'm going to ask him for a raincheck," he said to her.

Storm got slowly to her feet. She thought she would be the one calling off their evening in order to go through Hamasaki's files. Since the incident in the woods and the following conversation, she'd been trying to think up a way to search the office another time. Problem was, Meredith would be in there tomorrow and she had to find those private files before anyone else did. She couldn't put it off.

"I'm going outside to say goodbye to Hortense," she said. She wanted to see if the coconut husk poultice was working, and she also wanted to look at the animal's hooves. She was sure that the huge sow's feet were much smaller than the print in the mud.

The small shed was lit with warm, yellow lights and Hortense lay on her side in a pile of clean straw. She raised her head when Storm walked through the door. Lots of little piglets swarmed around her teats, so many that Storm not only couldn't count them, she couldn't see the infected nipple.

Sam came in behind her, humming softly. "She much bettah, yeah?" he said softly. He patted her arm. "You no worry about Bebe's scoldings, okay? She gets carried away. You one fine Hawaiian gal."

Bebe arrived and went to the hog. "Sam, I'll put one more poultice on her. I left the paste in your sink."

"I'll get it for you." He gave Storm a wink and ambled toward his house.

Bebe looked up at Storm. "Thank you for bringing your friend to gather the noni for me." She put her hand on Storm's arm. "Be aware, though, your friend is hiding something."

Before Storm could respond, Hamlin called out, Storm?" He popped his head into the shed.

Storm turned away from Bebe. "Did you get hold of him?"

"Yes, we're going to meet later." They walked toward the car, slowly because Storm was limping.

"He should understand, after the day you've had," she said. "Wish I could go home, too."

"You can't?"

"I have to go to the office."

Hamlin looked at her and frowned. "No way. Don't worry about Meredith. She gets grumpy under stress. She's really okay."

Storm looked at him. "Really? She's taking over Hamasaki's office. Tomorrow." Despite Bebe's warning, his brush with primitive spirits convinced Storm she had nothing to fear from him. "I have to go through Hamasaki's old files, clean out the desk and stuff."

"I know she can be impatient." He sighed. "Look, just ask for a few more days."

"She's already started moving stuff in."

"You need to go home and pack that ankle in ice. You can't go to the office alone."

Storm put her hand on the door of the old VW and faced him. "Hamlin, I have to. All these weird events started with Uncle Miles's death. With his murder. I've got to see if he's left any answers to so many questions. What if someone else is injured or died because I didn't bother?"

"How long will it take?"

Storm thought for a minute. If she could just find those private files, she could do the rest later. Lorraine would have kept his filing system well organized. "Maybe an hour."

For a moment, his eyes showed anguish. "I'm going with you then."

"Hamlin, are you sure?" Storm felt a rush of gratitude. Her foot and ankle throbbed and she had not wanted to go alone.

He sighed. "Yes. I'll phone Chris again. If he needs me, he knows where I'll be. You ready?"

"Sure. And thank you," she said.

Hamlin just shrugged and Storm started to duck into the car. With a gasp, she backed up and stepped squarely on Hamlin's foot. He grunted and peered over her shoulder with a frown.

Her *'aumakua* rested on the driver's bucket seat. Storm stared at it while her mind whirled. She had stuffed it into her purse, then jammed both behind the front seat. Now it leaned, its piggy snout and folded arms facing belligerently forward, against the upholstery.

"What's wrong?" Hamlin asked. The dark carving covered most of the beige seat.

"It...it was in my purse." Storm picked it up. "You didn't get it out, did you?"

"I haven't been out here."

"It's my *'aumakua.*"

Hamlin paused a beat. "I know, the pig. He looks pretty ferocious."

"It's supposed to be protective. You know, like a totem or fetish."

He watched her stuff it back into her purse, then walked around the car to get in the passenger's seat. He looked warily at Storm. "This has been a very strange afternoon."

"I agree."

Hamlin pulled out his cell phone, left a message. Then neither of them talked during the drive down the pot-holed gravel road. When the silence got so dense that Storm didn't know how to begin to break it, Hamlin finally spoke. "Why didn't you tell me about the dead man on the Big Island?"

Storm chewed her lip. She hadn't because it had sounded too incredible at the time. Now, the edges of believability blurred in the darkness. The sea was ten feet from the side of the road, but she couldn't see it in the blackness of the night. They could hear the rumble of pounding breakers, though, and a salty mist covered the windshield. Under the infrequent street lamps, she could see the tension of Hamlin's jaw.

"I didn't want to believe that it had anything to do with me."

"How could you find another body and not think so?"

"I didn't find it. I didn't even see it. Aunt Maile told me about it." Storm took a deep breath. "But I think I saw what you saw today."

She looked over at him and saw the flash of his eyes in the dark car.

"Would you have believed me if I told you? The link is the smell, the gardenias." She paused. "What exactly did you see, anyway?"

"I'm not sure. I thought it was a man, but it seemed to glide rather than walk. And yet, you saw that big hoof print." He shook his head. "Sam got a better view than I did. So, do you believe in those old legends?"

Storm shrugged. "Not really, but right now I wouldn't discount them. What do you think?"

Hamlin sighed. "I don't know, Storm. I really don't." He looked out the car window. "Ask me tomorrow when I'm not so tired."

She nodded. He was right. The blackness of the night surrounded them and the surf pounded the beach like some ancient drum. Salt spray shot up in billows and clouds from the sea wafted around the moving car— another reminder of the earth's unpredictable forces.

Both of them were shaky and the conclusions they reached tonight might change when they were surrounded by city daylight, in presumed control of their world. Hamlin stared out at the ocean. He rolled the window down and took deep breaths of the tangy wind.

"I'm glad we're back near the water again. Those cliffs, the humidity back in there, the air sits on you." He gazed out the window for a few long minutes. "I'm also tired and I can't help worrying about the scream we heard."

"You must be worried about DeLario, too."

"I guess that's part of it."

"Is he upset about the blood test?"

"That and his...his relationship with Martin."

"Artists don't have to worry about their sexuality, do they? Not as much as a stockbroker, I'd think."

"A lot of his commissioned work comes from wealthy widows. He told me once that his income would drop drastically if people knew he was gay."

"He didn't hide it in college, did he?"

"He was pretty discreet, though people guessed. The only time he didn't care was when Neil was in the hospital."

"You were there, too, weren't you?"

"Yes. But Chris spent as much time with him as I did, maybe more."

"Were they still lovers?"

"No. By the time we all shared the apartment, Neil had moved on to another relationship. Chris, too."

"And Chris still stayed in the hospital with Neil?"

"Yes, Chris would give him sponge baths, even administer his medications. By then, Neil's veins were collapsing and the IV sites needed to be changed often."

"That must have been terribly hard," Storm said.

"There were days when I could hardly bear to see him, watch his deterioration. When he got pneumonia, he couldn't talk because of the respirator, but his eyes seemed to plead with us. I wondered on more than one occasion if he were begging for life or death."

"I imagine the patient considers ending it," Storm whispered. She reached across and touched his hand.

"We talked about it, once." Hamlin looked out the side window, his voice very soft. "I told him I couldn't, that he'd beaten infections before. And he pulled out of that one, came home for a couple of months."

Storm didn't know what to say. She doubted that she would be able to give a final injection, especially if the tiniest shred of hope remained.

"My mother tried to kill herself twice before she succeeded. When she finally did it, I was furious with her." Storm's eyes burned with a surge of familiar emotion. She kept her gaze locked on the sinuous solid yellow line of the road and thought about the complexity of the feelings she had for her mother. For the first time in her life, she was able to sort through and separate some of them. One of them was guilt.

"Want to hear something crazy?" she asked. She could feel, rather than see, that Hamlin had turned his head to watch her. "I felt I had failed her because I couldn't make her happy, and at the same time, I felt rotten because I kept her from her version of relief, which was death."

"I know. I would be devastated one day, angry at Neil the next." Hamlin spoke softly. "Dealing with your mother would be even worse. She gave you life. She was your teacher and defender. And you were a child. You still needed her."

Storm nodded, her throat so tight that she couldn't speak. Yet some of the burden she had carried for fifteen years lifted just a little. Though she'd never stop missing her mother, she was beginning to forgive herself.

Chapter 35

Storm used her after-hours pass to get into the underground garage and parked next to Hamlin's Porsche. Going back to the office was the last thing she wanted to do and she could tell by looking at Hamlin that he felt the same way. He appeared to be gazing with longing at his car. His face was muddy and scratched; leaves clung in his hair. Bless him for coming along with her.

She felt like the day had lasted a week. If any of the security guards saw their muddy sneakers, torn shorts, and bedraggled tee-shirts, they would probably think it had been that long since the two of them changed clothes. With luck, they could avoid running into any of them. She was going to do this as fast as she could. Just find the private files tonight. She could save moving the rest of the stuff for later.

The elevator whirred them to the eleventh floor and softly ka-chunked to a stop. "Hey, Joe," Hamlin greeted the guard who was strolling down the corridor.

"Hey, boss." He looked them over. "Where you guys been?"

"In a taro field," Hamlin answered.

Joe laughed loudly. "Right. Have a nice evening." He wandered down the hall.

Hamlin raised his eyebrows at her. "See? Tell the truth and no one believes you."

"Right." Storm shook her head.

"You're just feeling vulnerable this evening," Hamlin replied.

"Wonder why."

Storm used her keys to open the elegant koa door of the office suite and shook her head in dismay when she caught sight of her reflection. Mirrored in the shining brass that proclaimed Hamasaki, Cunningham, Wang, & Wo, Attorneys at Law, was a mud-splattered face, frizzy hair, and eyes circled by fatigue.

She avoided looking at Hamlin, who followed closely, and marched through the dimly lit reception area to her office. She unlocked the door, flicked on the lights, and left Hamlin standing in the doorway. He watched her open her desk drawer. Sure enough, there was a lumpy envelope that made a key-jingle noise and had her name on the outside. Hamlin's eyebrows shot up.

Storm said defensively, "Meredith changed the locks already."

"You have a friend here in the firm, don't you?"

"Not everyone thinks Meredith walks on water."

"Right. I guess I'll do some paperwork, too, while you work." He turned away.

Storm heard him unlock his own office door and saw the lights of his office illuminate his end of the corridor. She sighed loudly, then left her own office, closing the door behind her. What was his problem now?

She locked her door and stomped down the hallway, unlocked Hamasaki's office, and turned on the lights. The custom recessed lamps set the room aglow with soft, warm light. Storm stood for a moment and looked around. The tall mahogany cabinets that held his case files were still along one wall, too heavy to be moved until they were emptied. She also noted with relief that Hamasaki's antiquarian books were still undisturbed.

She jingled her old key ring in her shorts pocket. Hamasaki had given her keys to his files when she started to clerk for the firm. What she was not accustomed to was the stacks of folders on the floor, cardboard cartons spilling over with papers, frames, and doo-dads. Meredith's junk. All over the place, making dusty rectangular impressions in the thick carpet.

Storm frowned and moved over to the mahogany cabinet. She tugged on a drawer. Good, it was still locked. She wondered if Meredith planned to make the Hamasaki family an offer on the furniture or just figured that possession was the better part of ownership.

Storm unlocked the cabinet at the top, which released the four vertical drawers. She started at the highest drawer and worked her way down. Each file was labeled, usually typed, but occasionally printed in a tidy hand that Storm recognized as Lorraine's. Many of the cases were familiar to her. In fact, there was a file on Ray Tam that would probably help her in getting background on some of his projects. She ruffled through the thick stack of papers. It went back to 1985. The file behind it was labeled 1975-1984. This was great. Storm took them out and piled them in a corner. She'd take them with her when she left.

She sat down on the floor to look through the bottom drawer. It was jammed with cases that were older than the files in the top drawer. Nothing of a personal nature, though. She didn't even recognize most of the names on the folders.

Storm wiped a dusty hand across her forehead and sighed. Meredith's boxes surrounded her like tree stumps in a clear-cut forest. They made her about as sad.

Storm couldn't resist poking into the closest box. Stuff was spilling out, anyway. There was a law school diploma, a chipped porcelain cat, a bunch of desk clutter, and hundreds of spilled and rusting paper clips. Under all this was jammed a stack of stained and ruffled files. Hamasaki would shudder.

Storm snorted with disgust and turned around to look at the room. She got to her feet, grimacing at her aches. She was so damned tired. Walking over to Hamasaki's desk, she sank into the comfortable leather chair, then stood up abruptly. That was where she had found him.

A click and the thrumming sound of the air conditioner coming on brought Storm back to her present imperative, the search for Hamasaki's personal files. She shivered in the draft of chilly air and loosened the fists she had unconsciously clenched. Her fingernails had made deep crescents in the palms of her hands. She sat down on the carpet to think.

If someone had been sitting in the office chair, she had just assumed the posture of a fawning dog at its master's feet. With her legs crossed in a yoga position, she squared her shoulders and took several deep breaths. She didn't have time for distracting emotion. Maybe later, after she got things out of Meredith's new domain.

She got to her knees and tugged on the wide, shallow desk drawer right below the desktop. It was locked. She settled back down on the carpet and frowned. From where she sat, the drawer was slightly above her eye level. And there was a metallic glint of a slightly different brass than the bottom of the drawer runners. Storm reached up and felt around, then unhooked a small key.

L.T. was etched onto the key. She'd found Lorraine Tanabe's private key, which she left where she needed it. Hamasaki probably carried his in his pocket.

She fit one key into the pencil drawer and opened it. Inside were Hamasaki's good pens, including an elaborate gold number that had been a gift from a grateful and wealthy client. The drawer was arranged neatly and held Hamasaki's personal stationery, a checkbook, small office items like a stapler, a staple remover, a bottle of white-out, and personal odds and ends: a little bottle of mouth-wash, nail clippers, and a pair of reading glasses. Nothing outstanding, though the reading glasses flooded Storm with nostalgia. He'd worn them whenever they went over papers and contracts together. Everything looked exactly as Hamasaki would have left it.

Storm paused. If he'd been reading when he died, he would have been wearing those glasses. He must have had time to put them away and lock the drawer before the drug took effect. Maybe as he was talking to the person who killed him.

She relocked the drawer and tried the little key in a deep drawer to the side of the desk. It not only didn't fit, the drawer wasn't locked. It slid open with the pressure of her hand on the handle. Inside was a hanging file, neatly arranged with big phone books: Honolulu, Los Angeles, Manhattan, Chicago. Nothing personal.

Storm turned the little key over and over in her fingers. Why did he lock the pencil drawer? Because Ed Wang kept borrowing his Montblanc and forgetting to return it? Maybe, but...She opened the drawer again and started to poke around. She knocked against a box of extra staples and felt an unexpected weight.

Inside were a few staples and a ring with two keys: a tarnished old-fashioned one, three inches long, and a small, modern, stainless steel one.

Storm sat back down and swiveled in the leather chair to survey the room. The antique bookcase looked like it would match a key like the large one. And it did. With a little jiggling of the key in the big hole, she felt the bolt slide. Not much of a security system; she could have opened it with a bobby pin. Storm pulled a couple of legal volumes off the shelf. Dusty old things.

She knelt down to the fiction shelf, where some of Hamasaki's favorites rested. *A Connecticut Yankee in King Arthur's Court* and *Huckleberry Finn* were bracketed by a couple of William Faulkner's novels. He had used them often, consulted them for inspiration or humor, depending on his mood. The bottom shelf of the old case held what looked like a complete set of Ogden Nash. Storm smiled; these represented Hamasaki's sense of humor. *You Can't Get There from Here*.

She picked one off the middle of the shelf, and opened it. It was signed by the author. Storm pulled another out. It was a signed first edition, too. Hamasaki had little bookmarks stuck between some of the pages. She could probably find some of his favorite witticisms here. She felt close to him, in a happy way, for the first time since he'd died.

Storm reached for *You Can't Get There from Here*, set it down, and glanced up because the rest of the books on the shelf started to lean. The shifting line of books left a triangular gap, in which Storm saw a metallic glint. She pulled out Faulkner's *Absalom, Absalom*. A small, stainless steel inset was concealed at the back of the shelf.

She pulled out a few more books on each side of the gap she'd created and picked up the little key. It fit easily in the hole and turned with the click of modern, well-designed carpentry. The base of the bookshelf glided toward her knees. It was a drawer, its cracks completely hidden in the curved wood of the old case.

The drawer was heavy, stuffed with hanging files labeled only with initials. There was "S.K." Storm pulled it out.

In the folder was a stack of letters from Hamasaki to Sergeant Mendoza in Waimea. Surprise slammed into Storm's chest. This was the material she'd been searching for. But it was her own history, a chronicle of her own missteps. And now that she'd found it, she was afraid of what she'd see. Chewing a hangnail on one thumb and barely daring to breathe, she began to read.

Hamasaki, in order to keep her from being tried in juvenile court for the alleged cultivation of marijuana for sale, had filed semi-annual reports to Waimea Police Chief Allen Leong and Sergeant Mendoza. The letters, complete with academic records, stopped after her second year of college.

She remembered those days. Hamasaki used to harangue her to make the dean's list. She had bitched and moaned, complained about his nit-picky obsessions, and done it. Now she knew part of the reason he'd bugged her so relentlessly.

Tucked into her college records was a hand-written report signed by an E.L. Benning. Storm had never heard the name before. Dated the fall of Storm's junior year in college, the notes documented an affair Mendoza was having with a twenty-year-old woman he'd arrested for shoplifting at Safeway.

Storm gulped. The woman's name was familiar. She had been a high school classmate. Wow. Hamasaki had gotten dirt from this guy Benning. And used it.

She drew a ragged breath and stuffed the file under the stack she planned to take home. Steadying herself, she peeked back into the drawer. "U." Who would that be?

Her eyes grew wide when she saw the Unimed logo on the first page. Hamasaki, as a potential investor, had requested an auditor's report of business at the Hawai'i hospital. The letter Storm read referred him to corporate headquarters in Seattle for the annual report to the stockholders.

The next pages revealed that Hamasaki had seen this as a brush-off. Several sheets from a legal pad were covered with his hand-written notes, in his own version of short-hand. Lorraine and Storm were among the few who could decipher it. Lorraine was a lot better at it than Storm, but Storm could make out most of the words.

Hamasaki commented on O'Toole's reaction to Hamasaki's questions about the lack of functioning large diagnostic equipment at the hospital. "O'Toole clammed up when I asked him. After March's incident, he's hanging by a spider web. They only know about the booze. How many more lives, in addition to our long friendship, do I ruin if I blow the whistle on his addiction to codeine analogs? Two young kids. Poor Arlene." Hamasaki had written the last five words in an anguished longhand.

Storm gaped at the notes. So Hamasaki did know O'Toole was incompetent. Her father had been right. Hamasaki had held on for old time's sake and for O'Toole's family. His first wife and Bitsy were friends. It was a sad story, but not enough of a reason for creating this file.

She turned to the next page. More notes, in different handwriting. Storm flipped to the end. The last page was signed by E.L. Benning, apparently Hamasaki's spook.

The man had written his conclusions in a four-page summary with an invoice attached. According to his report, Unimed filed requisitions two years ago to fund large equipment expenditures. They did it again in January of this year. As before, they requested eight and a half million dollars for an MRI scanner, two CT scanners, and salaries for five technicians. Benning found by checking the diagnostic radiology department and talking to several hospital staff members that the hospital had never received any new machinery.

Over eleven million dollars had been deposited in one of Unimed's accounts in February, after the most recent membership drive for the Hawai'i branch of the health maintenance organization. Corporate headquarters had kicked in another five million, designated for the purchase of hospital equipment. Benning noted that Unimed used several accounts.

He related that of the recent deposit, all but $12,000 had been transferred to Unimed's purchasing department. According to hospital records, the money was then wired to manufacturer's accounts, but when Benning checked with the equipment manufacturers themselves, they claimed to have never received it, neither in February of this year, nor two years ago.

The last page reported that Benning couldn't find the money. His instincts told him that it had been wired out of the country, possibly to Hong Kong, but he had no proof of this having happened.

The money was missing. And it was a staggering amount. Storm stopped to think. So many people close to Hamasaki needed money. His older son, stressed about keeping his restaurant going. But how could David have had anything to do with Unimed? Same for Martin. He urged a major investment in Unimed stock, wanted his father to be forced to admire his acumen, but where did Martin fit with some kind of purchasing scam?

Someone at the office? What about Wang and his twin obsessions: keeping his mother at home, giving her dignity, and his jade collection. Both drank up dollars. Wang could have pulled this off, could have drugged Hamasaki quite easily.

But maybe the money was merely a distraction. Martin had another reason for anger toward his father, his relationship with Chris DeLario. If Hamasaki had his own private investigator track her life, wouldn't he have turned Benning loose on his own children as well? Setting the "U" folder aside, Storm thought for a moment, then turned back to Hamasaki's desk.

Chapter 36

There was a quicker way to track Hamasaki's actions. Storm pulled open the pencil drawer again and withdrew the checkbook she'd seen. The checks were printed with only Hamasaki's name. Chances were good even Aunt Bitsy didn't know about this account, though Lorraine probably did.

Storm thumbed through the balance record. The account wasn't new; the checks went back fifteen years. He didn't use it often, and E.L Benning's name appeared again and again. She'd been right. Storm went to the most recent entries and looked for Benning's last bill.

Surprise checked her next breath. The check for $1375.06 was made out to the Hualalai Resort and dated June twentieth. The $500 was to cash, as she'd suspected, but there was another check, made out to Benning for $616.88 and marked "expenses." It was dated June twenty-second, the day before Hamasaki's death.

She sat back in Hamasaki's chair. Hamlin was correct. Hamasaki knew about Martin and Chris. In fact, he had sent Benning to spy on them during their stay at the Hualalai Resort. Even as Bitsy went to help Martin and Chris confront Hamasaki with their "news," Hamasaki was ahead of them.

Storm sat unmoving, listened to the hum of the air conditioner, and shivered. The office seemed very cold. She ruffled the check register numbly and thought, not for the first time, that Hamasaki should have let his children live their own lives. He had taught her the value of information and getting the scoop in business, but he hadn't separated work from family. He hadn't learned to trust his children's decisions, to allow them to make their own mistakes and recoup their own losses.

Of course, his intervention had probably saved her from doing time in some juvenile home. But according to Michelle, their father was harder on the three of them than he had ever been on her. Storm had come to the family as a teenager with a well-developed personality. One which, according to Aunt Maile, Hamasaki felt was similar to his own.

Michelle was right. After his children left the house and started to pay their own way, their father should have backed out of their affairs. Storm sat back in the deep leather chair. With a flash of insight, she was struck with one of the enigmas of parenthood. How does one learn to let go? He was a manipulator by nature. And he wanted the best for his children.

Fatigue hit Storm like a rogue wave. She felt flattened; her temples pounded and her limbs moved like cast iron. She dragged herself back to the bookcase drawer and flipped through the tabs on the files. There was one labelled "M." Must be either Martin's or Michelle's. Storm sighed. More stuff that she probably didn't want to know about. She was going to have to pull out the whole bloody drawer and take it home.

She sighed. Reading through this was going to be no fun at all. Maybe she should burn the stuff without ever looking at it. With a sigh dredged from the bottom of a melancholy heart, she knew that she couldn't do that. The key to Hamasaki's killer lay here. It was time to pack them up and go tell Hamlin that they could leave.

Storm stood up, certain that she'd heard footsteps in the hallway. She'd left Hamasaki's door partly open in case Hamlin checked on her. She didn't want even him to see this file, though. Shoving the drawer closed and locking it, she checked the floor for anything she might have dropped, and went back to the desk. She crammed the checkbook back into the pencil drawer and locked it, too.

Of course, it could be Meredith, coming by to do some moving after office hours. According to Hamlin, she loved to work nights. Too late to close Hamasaki's office door, she sat under the bright lights at the desk and decided on the excuse she would give Meredith for having the keys to her new office.

She squinted in surprise at the swaggering approach of a broad-shouldered shape in the dark hallway. Definitely not Meredith, or even Hamlin. Tight jeans, black leather jacket. What in the world was Christopher DeLario doing here?

With a jolt, she realized that she still held not only the key to the desk, but the two keys to the bookcase. She shoved them into her shorts pocket.

"Chris, what are you doing here?"

"Did you find it?"

"Find what?"

DeLario looked as if he hadn't slept in a week. His face was grim and pale and no longer held the handsome warmth she'd noticed merely two days before. The tremor in his hands was even worse. Strands of hair had come free from his ponytail and fell in unkempt strands across his forehead. His bloodshot eyes darted around the room, then fell on the mahogany file cabinet, where Storm had left the bottom drawer open.

"Let's get Hamlin. He's right down the hall."

"Yeah, I know." He turned away and knelt before the file drawer. "He hasn't told you?"

"About what?" Storm walked over to him. "Hey, Chris, those are client files. They're private. What are you looking for?"

DeLario stood up and faced her. His jaw muscles were knotted with anger and his powerful shoulders hunched under his jacket. Storm tried not to back up.

"Maybe the same thing you are. The files Hamasaki used to make everyone dance to his chosen tunes." His voice shook with barely controlled fury.

He squatted again and ruffled through the bottom drawer, then stood and opened the top drawer.

"Stop." Storm put her hand on his arm.

DeLario recoiled as if she'd used a cattle prod on him. He swung at her hand, batting it away with a smack.

Storm lurched backward. "C'mon, you wouldn't want someone going through your private things." She tried to keep her voice calm.

"Get out of my way, Storm."

"Look, Chris. I have to move his stuff out of this room. If I find them, I'll call you or Martin."

After the last entry in Hamasaki's checkbook, she didn't doubt that DeLario had a file. It was probably in the "M" folder, which she'd just crammed back into the hidden drawer. Maybe she should just give the file to him. But then he'd see the rest, the information on Unimed and incriminating details she hadn't even read through yet.

He turned back to the file drawer, shrugged out of the leather jacket, and threw it to the carpet. The armpits of his tee-shirt were stained with perspiration and the acrid odor of stale, unhealthy sweat saturated the room.

"Chris, I won't show it to anyone else. I promise."

He turned back to her and stared. "He hated me. Why should I believe anything you say?"

"Because I like you and I love Martin. And I don't agree with some of the things Hamasaki did, even though I, well, I loved him, too."

DeLario locked his bloodshot eyes on hers. Storm swallowed hard. His hands shook as he reached down to pick his jacket up from the floor.

Hamlin's voice caused both of their heads to turn. "She means it, Chris. Let's go, I'll call Martin to come get you." He leaned against the doorframe, his face pale and miserable.

"Why would you help me?" DeLario's voice cracked.

Hamlin gazed back at DeLario and Storm could feel a current pass between the men. She had ceased to exist for them at that moment.

"Chris, some people would find your actions merciful," Hamlin said softly.

"Not you."

"You're right. I couldn't do it."

Storm looked back and forth, openmouthed, from one man to the other. What the hell was this about?

"You called me a murderer," DeLario whispered.

"I was wrong, Chris." Hamlin's voice shook. "Forget it, please. He was dying. What was a day or two? We've both got to go on from here."

"I can't." DeLario made a choking noise. "I came here last Sunday to talk to Martin's father, to explain about Neil. The old man's mind was closed. He only saw what he'd guessed as a means of turning Martin away from me. He wouldn't listen, hardly seemed to hear me. Maybe he's succeeded anyway." DeLario, voice cracking, stumbled out of the room.

"Chris," Hamlin called out. The door down the corridor banged closed and Hamlin sagged against the wall.

"Jesus," Storm said. "He told you he killed Neil. And Hamasaki knew it?"

Hamlin nodded. "With an overdose. It would have been so easy to do. Neil was on enough morphine to finish off any of us." He wiped his face with a shaking hand. "I should have guessed, but I didn't want to know. What difference would it have made, anyway?"

Storm couldn't answer. It might have made a difference. It might have saved both Hamlin and DeLario a lot of suffering. And now Martin.

Hamlin looked sick. "Storm, I need to go home. Can we leave soon?"

"Sure, give me ten minutes. I need to gather up all these things to carry to the car."

"I'll be back to give you a hand. I'm going to phone Martin and tell him Chris is in a bad way."

A flash of understanding hit Storm. "What's he using?"

Hamlin looked at her with gloomy, shadowed eyes. "Probably crystal meth. Who knows?"

"Does he do it often?" She was sure she'd seen him when he was perfectly straight.

Hamlin's shoulders slumped. "Often enough, especial-ly if he's depressed. Maybe that's in Hamasaki's file, too." He gave a sigh that was almost a moan. Storm watched him leave the glow of light from the office and head down the darkened hall.

Chapter 37

Storm paced around the office, her thoughts whirling. Why would DeLario lie? Could he in fact lie in his present shape? So, rule out DeLario and the family. Who killed Hamasaki? He'd written S.O. in his daily planner for the meeting the night he died. Maybe Hamasaki had confronted Sidney O'Toole about the effects of his drug addiction on his patients and family. God knows, O'Toole had access to barbiturates.

O'Toole didn't strike her as organized enough to cover his tracks after murdering his life-long friend, though Storm could see him doing it as an addled act of desperation. But what would O'Toole have to do with fraudulent purchase orders? Plus, she didn't think he would have been able to sit and commiserate with Aunt Bitsy if he'd done the killing. His grief and confusion seemed genuine the morning of Hamasaki's death. Still, Storm reminded herself, he hadn't wanted an autopsy. Maybe she wasn't giving him enough credit for deviousness.

She rubbed her temples. A headache was probing the back of her eyeballs and moving across the crown of her skull. Contemplating the motives of people she'd once trusted was making her nauseous.

It was easy to get drugs on the street if one had the contacts and knowledge. Anyone could have gotten hold of the pills. She didn't know about Meredith, but Wang, O'Toole, and Sherwood Overton were all familiar with drugs and their administration. For that matter, David Hamasaki knew about injectable drugs, too, and was desperate for the trust fund he thought was due him. Even Hamlin knew how to use a needle. And Bebe had said he was hiding something. But now she knew what it was.

She was missing an important piece of information. Like Benning, she still needed to follow the money. Unlocking the desk drawer again, she reviewed the checks written to the P.I. Then she walked over to the hidden files and reopened them. Where were his P.I.'s notes? Right, in the file marked "U."

Reading the pages she'd skipped, Storm saw that Benning had found a loose end that disturbed him. Tipped off by a source in the Unimed purchasing department, the investigator wrote that he'd gone through plane reservations to Hong Kong back to January of this year. Meredith Wo's name turned up. She had reservations a week from the date Benning filed his report. The Unimed account with the $12,000—now $7,632.19—picked up the tab. With dread creeping through her, Storm ran her eyes down to the dates of the reservation.

The dates included the day of Hamasaki's death. Storm bit her lip and turned back to the beginning of the report. It was dated three days before his death. Certainly Lorraine had not known about Meredith's trip to Hong Kong then; Storm remembered her running around the office the day he died, asking how to find Meredith in Australia.

With a flash of insight, Storm remembered the cryptic letters following Wo's and Cunningham's names on the list Lorraine had given her. Lorraine had probably asked enough questions about Meredith's whereabouts to alarm someone. If "DC" meant Washington—where Cunningham claimed to be and there was no evidence to the contrary— then Lorraine was telling Storm in her list that "HK" meant Hong Kong.

Wo's flight plan was paper-clipped to the last page of Benning's report. She left Hong Kong on Sunday, June twenty-third, at 2:50 p.m.

The day Hamasaki died.

Storm drew in a sharp breath. She flipped to the first page of Benning's report. Hamasaki had received this on Thursday. According to Benning, Meredith left Thursday night.

She let the notes flutter into her lap. Two invoices, one for $1,375.06 and one for an even $500, floated after the pages. Storm stared at the bills from the detective, dated the day of the report, and felt her brain tangle with whirling thoughts. Were these bills for the investigation of Unimed? Five hundred sounded like a cash payment. What was that for? But most important, how would Hamasaki have handled this knowledge?

He would have been appalled to discover Meredith's apparent involvement in the purchasing deceit. Did he have time to approach her before she left? Did he threaten her with exposure or try to talk her out of her involvement with Unimed? If Meredith had left before Hamasaki read the report, whom else did he approach?

Storm wondered if Meredith would kill if she were cornered with enough evidence to ruin her career and send her to jail. Possibly. But she was out of town when he died, even if it was Hong Kong instead of Australia. Storm was sure that the flight from Hong Kong to Honolulu took at least eight hours. Plus, the coffee didn't fit. Meredith would know that Hamasaki didn't drink coffee. She'd shared tea with him.

Putting back the family and Unimed files, Storm locked up, thinking about the grief she'd seen in Hamlin's eyes. Some secrets were like poison, like carcinogens that lurked and destroyed over time. Some of them our bodies seemed to know on a cellular level before our brains could cope with the truth. It was too late to dig any further. She needed to grab a little sleep. She'd come back very early and remove the whole set of files when neither Hamlin nor anyone was around.

With a sigh of her own, she turned to the effort of packing up the books. She began slowly stacking Hamasaki's old books by empty cartons. For her, the fragile old volumes brought memories of laughter and shared humor.

She longingly eyed the Mark Twain and the little markers that Hamasaki had left in it. Too bad that the books she loved also hid secrets in their own way.

A Connecticut Yankee in King Arthur's Court was still in her hand when she saw the door open slowly. She flushed with irritation at another interruption. The need to finish this task was even more urgent, now. Storm made sure the books covered the hidden file drawer and sat leafing through the Twain. She waited, but whoever had entered remained silent. Her pulse rate jumped when she saw the slender, wiry figure before her. Oh, shit.

"Hi, Meredith."

"Storm, what the fuck are you doing in here?" Meredith stood with her hands on her hips, feet planted wide. She wore a black sweatshirt and loose, dark-gray silk cargo pants.

"I'm cleaning out Hamasaki's stuff so you can move in. Wang told me to get it done." That was true, last week. "Bitsy will come in this weekend to finish—"

"You have no right to break into this room."

"Me? Break in?" Storm glared at her through narrowed eyes. "You had no right to change the locks." She stood up and faced the fuming attorney.

"Tough shit. It's mine, now." Meredith took a step further into the room. Her flat black eyes met Storm's. "What have you taken out of here?"

"Nothing, yet. Meredith, no judge on earth is going to let you walk into this office and take what's in here."

"How would you know? You're such a legal expert?" Meredith sneered and stepped closer. "I asked you a question."

"I'm busy, Meredith."

"Did you find the papers I asked for?" Wo's eyes flicked around the room.

Storm made herself take a deep breath, ready to defuse this situation. She hoped Wo meant the file she'd been asking about since Hamasaki died. "You mean for that cancer patient?" Storm pointed at the mahogany file cabinet. A couple of its drawers were still ajar. "I haven't found anything, yet. If it's earmarked for you, you'll get it."

Wo's slitted eyes settled on the book Storm held. "What's that?"

"An old book Uncle Miles and I used to read together. You caught me reminiscing."

"How sweet." She looked at the title of the book, over at the open bookcase, then let her eyes roam over the room. "Have you touched any of my things?"

"Of course not."

Wo squinted as if contemplating that statement and walked to the file cabinet. Storm had never seen her dressed casually. In fact she'd never seen her in anything but high heels. Wo moved with a cat-like grace in her running shoes. Storm wondered if she ran marathons. She had that gaunt look, but she must do them when normal people were sleeping. The rest of the time, she worked.

Storm strolled over and sat down at the desk, placing the Twain novel in front of her. "Meredith, leave me to finish up and I'll look for the file and leave it for you."

Without saying a word, Wo walked to the front of the desk and picked up the book. She ignored Storm, and leafed through it, pausing frequently. When she passed one of the bookmarks on which Hamasaki had made notes, she stopped and read it slowly. Then she snapped the book closed and tucked it under her arm.

Storm was about to demand that Wo put it down when the woman's calculating expression stopped her. Wo wasn't just looking for Hamasaki's old cases. Like DeLario, she was looking for the personal files, the ones with secrets that could hurt if uncovered. Of course, longtime members of the firm might have heard rumors of the secret files and certainly knew the boss's habits well enough to believe them. Perhaps they even knew about Benning. But Meredith apparently suspected that Hamasaki might have left clues in his favorite books as well.

Storm spoke with a light tone. "I just got here a few minutes ago." She pointed to the book under Meredith's arm. "I'd like to keep some of these old books. He often used quotes from them in his talks." It was time to get some help. She reached for the phone. "We could ask Hamlin if he knows about any files. Want to talk to him?"

"No!" Wo dropped the book to the floor and jerked the phone from Storm's grasp, then hurled it across the room. Barely checked by the wire, which tore free as if it were a thread, the projectile flew into the antique bookcase. Glass shattered with such force that shards struck Storm's legs fifteen feet away. Storm rocked back in Hamasaki's chair with shock. She had never expected that kind of explosiveness from Wo.

Wo's eyes glittered at her. Storm stared at her with wariness as if regarding a swaying cobra.

Wo's eyes, flat and black as buttons, flitted around the room. Her breathing had accelerated with this last effort and Storm could see the quick rise and fall of her chest. Jesus, the woman was wound tightly. Where the hell was Hamlin? The breaking glass should have brought him running.

Wo's gaze slithered to Storm, darkened, and slid away. She took a step closer, appraised Storm's position at the desk, then moved on across the room to the filing cabinet. Storm felt anger overcoming fear.

Storm got to her feet. "Go through the files, Meredith, if you must. I'm going to the restroom. I'll be back in a minute and pack the books. Then I'm gone."

Meredith lunged across the room, her slick face inches from Storm's nose. "Sit down, Storm," she hissed.

"Like hell, Meredith. You're being an asshole."

Meredith struck fast, a stunning blow with the back of her hand. Her heavy jade ring sliced across Storm's jaw. Storm sat, stupefied, and reached up to her face. Her hand came away with a trace of blood. "Christ, Meredith. You're crazy."

The blackness of the woman's irises was indistinguishable from the opaque tunnels of her pupils. It was like looking into the one-dimensional, amoral gaze of a rodent.

"You're not leaving, you conniving twit." Wo spit the words at her. "You're just like the almighty Hamasaki."

Storm recoiled from the saliva Wo splattered in her rage. "I'm not going to beg. I won't negotiate with the likes of you."

"Negotiate what?" She knew it was critical to defuse Meredith without sounding afraid, and at the same time, without being threatening. She straightened with what she hoped was confidence in Hamasaki's deep chair. Meredith's eyes jumped from the files, to Storm, and back again.

If she hadn't so carefully locked her own office door, Storm would have bolted down the hall to sanctuary. But she knew she wouldn't be able to outrun Meredith and unlock the door in time. More than the ten minutes she'd promised Hamlin had passed and she was starting to get a bad feeling about why he hadn't shown up. She strained to hear footsteps in the carpeted hall, but the smooth hum of the air conditioner was the only sound in the office. With a gulp, she forced her clammy hands under her bare legs for warmth.

One thumb encountered a hard round object, sunk in the deep leather crease between the back and seat of the chair. What could Meredith have done to Hamlin? She closed her fingers around the little round item and tried to swallow away her apprehension.

As if Wo read Storm's thoughts, she turned toward Storm, forcing her to meet Wo's poisonous gaze. Storm knew if she showed fear, she'd merely feed this madness. Wo looked away and Storm glanced down at her own clenched fists. Inside one of them was the hard, round object she'd found in the seat of the chair. It was an imported mint.

Meredith had offered a candy just like it to Storm when she had come seeking information about the cancer patient. With a bolt of comprehension, Storm was convinced that Wo had done the same thing to Hamasaki.

Like Hamasaki, Wo worked long hours. No one would think it was surprising that she was in the office on a Sunday. Plus, most people thought she was in Sydney. Only Benning and Hamasaki, and perhaps Lorraine, Storm remembered with a lurch, knew that she was in Hong Kong. It still didn't explain why Benning's information on Meredith's departure time didn't jibe with Meredith being in Honolulu on Sunday night.

Storm was certain that Hamasaki, with a practiced graciousness, would have taken a mint from the proffered box. A skillful courtroom adversary, he would likely have had a confident, perhaps arrogant manner. So he'd sat toying with the mint on the desktop and made Wo stutter out her explanations.

People like to fill silences, Storm. Let them. You discover the best information that way. It was one of her mentor's favorite interrogation techniques. He would drop a nugget of information, let Wo begin her story, then fill in the gaping holes left by her lies with Benning's information.

The cup of tea was probably sitting on Hamasaki's desk when she entered. Somehow she had been able to drop the barbiturate into it without his noticing. Paul Andrews had said that the barbiturate would knock out a horse, but probably not kill. So what had she done next?

Storm regarded Wo's flat, cold eyes, the smirk that marred the smooth mask of her face. Wo looked back as if she were connected by an electric current, the same filament of knowledge. And slid her hand into one of her cargo pockets.

The syringe must have been carefully placed there where she could slip it out without even turning it around. Not a particularly big syringe, maybe ten or fifteen cc's. She held it up and let Storm eye the pale liquid within. "You've got the Unimed files, don't you? You know the whole story."

Chapter 38

Storm hunched down in the chair. She couldn't believe what she saw. Was this how Hamasaki had died? She opened her mouth, closed it, tried again.

"All his files are over there." She gestured toward the mahogany cabinets and gulped. "Don't be stupid, Meredith."

Wo flicked off the needle guard and tapped the barrel as if she had done this a hundred times. The stainless steel gleamed. Her eyes fell to Storm's bare legs.

Storm looked down. No one would ever notice a puncture wound among the scratches she'd picked up from her dash into the taro fields that afternoon.

"Bullshit. You're a lousy liar, Kayama."

Storm swallowed hard. "What's in that?" She forced the words through numb lips.

"Succinylcholine. You'll be paralyzed." Wo curled her lips into a scornful smile and glanced toward the desk drawer. "You can watch me search."

Storm's throat closed convulsively. She'd heard about succinylcholine. It was like curare. Her classmates in law school loved to drink beer and theorize about the "perfect" murder. Curare caused such complete paralysis that the victim couldn't breathe. Unconsciousness occurred in several minutes due to lack of oxygen, and death followed soon after. Those few minutes of consciousness, though, would seem an eternity of terror. The victim was cognizant and completely helpless.

Succinylcholine was metabolized in the body and therefore virtually untraceable. It was frequently used in hospital operating rooms for administering anesthesia. With oxygen, of course.

"I don't know why you think there would be a separate file for Unimed—"

"You're pathetic, Storm. After all, you're the big man's protégée. He told you everything." Her voice was cold and not much louder than a whisper, like the susurration of a snake in sand. "Martin will be the one who goes through your things, won't he? You're so close." Wo chuckled. "There must be a record of his and DeLario's secrets. I'll leave it behind. We'll see if he or the police find that file first."

Storm sank back in the chair, her fingers curved into stiff hooks on the arms. Martin would find the file, all right. And he would find out that it was hidden in his father's favorite bookcase, which he would perceive as another betrayal. He would also believe that Storm knew all about it.

Wo took a step toward her. This time her eyes were on the pale liquid in the syringe. She adjusted her thumb on the plunger. A drop of liquid ran down the side of the syringe and oozed down the length of her thumb. She smiled.

Storm forced herself to breathe and waited for Wo to take one more step toward her. She forced herself to think of the woman as a rabid animal, one that had to be out-witted. She could not think of her as the colleague who'd offered a badly needed crumb of support by subtly acknow-ledging Cunningham's lechery. She couldn't even think of her as human. So Storm scrutinized her as one would a slavering wolverine, and willed her to approach from straight ahead, without moving to either side of the chair.

Wo's eyes were busy moving along Storm's exposed flesh, the bare arms and nicked legs. When Wo lunged, she struck like the wild animal Storm imagined. She grabbed Storm's upper arm with a grip that made Storm gasp.

It also pushed Storm's building fury over the edge. "No!" she shouted. She kicked out with both feet at Wo's kneecaps.

She connected with one of them and felt a gratifying pop before her shoe slid from the fabric of her slick pants. Wo yelped with pain and surprise and fell back. It was enough to break her grip on Storm's arm. Storm leaped to her feet and spun the chair so that the high back was between them.

Caught between the chair and the wall, Storm used the heavy chair to parry Wo's advance. Wo's expressionless mask folded into a vindictive mug of fury. With a will that deepened Storm's fear, the woman ignored the obvious pain in her knee. The black eyes, instead of glittering, were dulled to a focus so intent that Storm had to look away. Instead, Storm watched the gleam of the needle wave mere inches from the back of the chair.

Meredith was going to pounce any second. If Storm were to make a break around the desk, Wo would have her. And all Wo had to do was snag her long enough to inject a small amount of the drug. She could do it even through Storm's clothing.

How much stuff did it take to paralyze a person? How much time would Wo need to inject it? How much time did Storm have after the injection? Her mind spun through questions, skittering around the terror, the unknown.

Storm watched the needle. An intramuscular dose might only take minutes to act. Maybe five. If she stayed perfectly still. Already her heart galloped with fear. It would speed the drug to her vulnerable nervous system.

Part of her wanted to succumb to tears, but the survival part of her mind shrieked at her. Think, stay fluid. Fight her. Do the unexpected.

Storm forced her limbs to relax, then leaped to the desktop. The move surprised even her. She was amazed that her tired legs had launched her without faltering. Wo gaped at her, astonished. It was the first break in her icy composure.

Then Wo's hand shot out and hooked the laces of one of Storm's sneakers. Thrown off balance by the grip on the shoelace, Storm toppled to the floor on the other side of the desk. Her shoe came off and Wo lost her grip, but the fall knocked the wind out of Storm.

The desk was between them. In the few precious seconds while Storm's chest heaved reflexively, Wo scurried around the desk. By the time Storm began to wobble to her feet, Wo loomed above.

This was the harridan who had killed Uncle Miles and Lorraine. Letting this witch triumph would be an anathema. So Storm concentrated every aspect of her fury on the woman above her. She loathed the dank sheen of her hair, the stony pallor of her face. She abhorred the arrogance, the manipulative deception of the woman. This was a killer who hid behind false intellectual authority and aloof superiority.

Storm couldn't allow Wo to win. She couldn't let Wo's demented insolence steal any more from the people around her. Storm's world narrowed to a super-focused tunnel of anger. Her blood raced hot and fast. She pulled together anything she'd ever known about fighting. A cop had once told her that women were better off fighting from the floor because a woman's legs were much stronger than her upper body.

Jesus, God, please let it be true. If she stood up, she'd be a bigger target for that lethal needle. She rolled to one side and raised the foot with the shoe as if to hold Wo off. And the woman ignored the thick-soled sneaker. She bent over Storm, features frozen in concentration, her breathing labored with her recent exertion. The needle quivered in her grip.

Storm suspended breathing and waited. She stayed still, poised until the needle was inches from her bare calf, though the skin of her leg crawled with dread.

Wo aimed her shot. Storm's eyes nearly crossed with her focus on the glinting stainless steel. Another half inch, nearly grazing her flesh.

Storm forced herself to exhale and fired the coiled piston of her leg. The bottom of her shoe smashed into the hand holding the syringe. Wo's face contorted with pain. She grabbed her injured fingers and the syringe tumbled to the floor.

Storm scooted along the floor so that the syringe was inches from her other foot. For the first time, Wo showed an expression other than condescension. Fear flashed in the rictus of her lips, which hardened into a homicidal grimace. She swung one arm at Storm and reached toward the syringe with the other.

Storm used a swollen vein on Wo's forehead as a target. Like a battering ram, her leg slashed out and the shoe connected with the woman's head. The muddy sole hit with a dull thud and Wo crashed to her rump.

Storm tried to wobble to her feet, but her right ankle buckled. She stifled a moan of pain and rolled away. The syringe had been knocked farther from Wo's reach when she fell, but it remained only a few feet from either of them. Storm's only chance was to get to it first.

A slurred voice came from the doorway. "You fucked up, Meredith. I wasn't much in the mood for coffee."

Wo swung her head like a viper whose attention was momentarily distracted from its prey.

"Hamlin, help," Storm gasped. "Call the police."

Hamlin, pale, stared as if he couldn't believe what he was seeing.

"Hamlin, she attacked me," Wo said. "She wants to keep her beloved uncle's office, push me out."

"Bullshit, Meredith." Hamlin shook his head as if to clear it. "Get over there and sit down." He pointed at Hamasaki's desk chair. "Now."

Wo sat where she was. "Hamlin, you never could separate reason from your emotions."

Hamlin ignored her. "Storm, are you okay?" He reached down to help her stand up. At the same time, Wo got to her feet and backed slowly toward the chair.

Hamlin blocked Storm's view of Wo, but her view of the carpet was unimpeded. The syringe was no longer on the floor.

"Hamlin," Storm shouted. "She's got a drug."

Storm watched Hamlin try to focus his eyes. "I know, she put it in my coffee." His words blurred together.

From the corner of her eye, Storm saw Wo strike. The rest of the scene seemed to proceed in slow motion. Storm cried out a warning, too late. Hamlin, still confused, reached for the sting in his hip.

Panicky, Storm shoved Hamlin with all her strength. She had to break his contact with the lethal syringe. Hamlin staggered backward, still holding Storm's arm, and stumbled against one of Meredith's boxes. He fell to his knees. Storm, dragged off balance, sat down hard beside him.

Hamlin looked up, dazed, at Wo, who still held the hypodermic. "Meredith, stop this now. You're with your colleagues. We can work out whatever—"

"Shut up," Wo said. She circled around the two and readjusted the plunger.

Staggering to her feet, Storm got between Hamlin and Wo and moved with Wo, mirroring her feints. She wanted to scream, to spew the frustration and terror that she felt.

But that was just what Wo wanted. She loved this. Ever the combatant, she relished seeing Storm's fear and the impotent rage with which she smoldered. She cherished the sight of Hamlin, vulnerable and failing on the floor, bewildered by her attack. Wo laughed.

She held up the syringe so that Storm could see that it still had fluid in it. Hamlin was leaning on an arm, one leg out straight, the other tucked beneath him. He opened and closed his mouth from time to time, but made no noise.

Storm wanted to run to him, prop him up. But she had the feeling that Wo was waiting for her to do just that. So she kept her eyes on Wo, who watched Storm, then Hamlin, then Storm again. The satisfied smirk on Wo's lips grew. She knew time was on her side. Hamlin was weakening.

Wo circled and Storm moved with her, still keeping her body between Wo and Hamlin. Wo held the syringe safely out of Storm's reach, poised for another shot.

"You don't have a chance," Storm whispered to her.

That made Wo laugh out loud. "Wrong. It's you who has no chance."

"You think the cops won't figure this out?"

"It won't matter."

Of course, she would go to Hong Kong. Or China, for that matter. They'd never find her, even if they could get an extradition treaty.

Wo took a step closer to her and instinctively, Storm backed up. The moment she did, she knew she'd made a mistake. She'd had to go to the side to avoid stepping on Hamlin's outstretched leg. Now, Wo not only had an opening to Hamlin, Storm was grazing one of Wo's overfilled boxes with her leg. One more step and she'd be backed against the wall.

Wo chuckled. "I admire your zest, Storm, but the game's up."

Hamlin rustled beside her, but Storm didn't dare glance away from her opponent. And she was afraid to look for another reason. Her hopes dropped with each passing second as the drug took effect. Perhaps three minutes had passed since he'd been injected, but it seemed to Storm like three hours. Once he stopped breathing, what could she do to save him?

Wo watched her face and slightly relaxed. Storm feared that she transmitted every emotion to the woman, and each one fed her sense of impending victory.

Hamlin moved again. This time, he dropped on his back to the floor and Storm's heart fell with him. She didn't dare take her eyes off Wo, but desperate and furious tears sprang to her eyes, nearly obscuring the projectile that flew by her head. Hamlin used the last of his strength. The ceramic cat that had perched on top of one of the boxes caught Wo squarely on the cheekbone.

Wo shrieked and froze in her circular path. Storm backed one step toward the wall, where Hamasaki's family portrait hung, and prayed. Wo moved in on Hamlin just as Storm lifted the picture, gratified to feel the weight of glass instead of Plexiglas in the frame. It was damned awkward, but Wo was enjoying her moment of power over the man sprawled on the floor too much to notice Storm's move.

Wo was watching Hamlin flop desperately like a grounded trout, each movement becoming weaker. With all her strength, Storm slammed the frame over Wo's head. The glass cracked loudly and Wo looked at her, amazed. She paused, then stumbled to her knees.

But Storm's attention was drawn to Hamlin's twitching foot. With horror, she saw a paperweight roll from his limp fingers. His eyes met hers, then jerked twice and were immobile. His foot stopped moving.

"No!" Storm screamed with rage. She took a quick step toward Wo. Like a big square discus, she swung the picture frame in a two-handed backhand, up from her waist to the woman's jaw.

The glass, already cracked, shot out in long shards at impact. With a grinding noise that Storm realized with a rising gorge was flesh and cartilage in addition to wood, the frame crumpled. Wo's hands flew to her throat and she bent over, retching and choking. Storm stood rooted in shock at what she'd done, frozen with horror and in anticipation of Wo's next move.

Wo dropped to her knees, then her side, and curled into a fetal position. Her breathing came in rasping gulps, interspersed with a keening whine, which faded away.

Storm leaped over Wo and even kicked her out of the way to get to Hamlin. "Ian, Ian," she cried and threw her weight against him. She got him onto his back, crushing the box next to him.

Hamlin was a dead, limp weight. His lips were turning blue. She knelt beside him. "I'll breathe for you," she gasped.

She raised her head from his mouth and felt her own eyes fill with tears when she read the terror in his. She pinched his nose closed and blew between his slack lips. She gave him ten good breaths and watched the blueness begin to fade from the fingernails of the hand splayed across his chest. She thought even the expression in his eyes had softened, but it was hard to tell. He was like a rag doll.

"You look better." Storm wiped a trickle of sweat from her forehead. She lowered her mouth to his and blew again, then came up to gasp for her own oxygen.

Hamlin's eyes again held a look of dread. She frowned down at him. His fingernails and lips were pinker than when she'd started. "What's wrong?" she asked, then felt a pain in her left thigh.

Stunned, she looked over her shoulder. The syringe, empty, wobbled in the flesh of her leg. She pulled it out and stared at it in horror. How much had been left in it? How much did she need to be paralyzed?

Frantic, she blew the air she'd inhaled into Hamlin's mouth and sucked in another breath. Then she realized that she couldn't open and close her mouth very well. Her jaw was starting to hang. She could barely close it. Her neck felt weak, too. She gave Hamlin another breath, drew in more air and staggered to her feet. She had to get to a phone.

Storm made it to the doorway, then felt her overtaxed ankle give with a searing pop. Like a marionette whose strings were cut, she dropped. With her face pressed to the floor, she commanded her legs to rise, and could not do it. There she lay, her nose pressed into the plush carpet while the chemical smell of whatever rug shampoo had last been used tormented her. Fibers pressed painfully into the sclera of one eye and she couldn't even blink.

Dizzy nausea washed over her. As the darkness crept in from the sides of her vision, Storm hallucinated a room full of violent, angry shouting creatures. A wild man with red piggy eyes who tossed her helpless body onto its back. The wild boar on the mountainside had finally found them.

Chapter 39

Something dropped on Storm's chest, a thud on her hollow lungs. The shouting continued, her lips felt swollen and bruised, her jaw was in a vice. Noise shrieked around her. She tried to scream, but worse than any nightmare, she couldn't move her lips. She tried to roll from her back, but again she couldn't move, even though she could feel the fierce arms of the beast that trapped her. Tears ran down the sides of her face, and pooled in her ears.

The tears, though, cooled her burning eyes and Storm began to see a blur of white above the black mass that crouched on her face. Her heart lurched, then pounded with dread. A man's gentle voice broke through to her. She could hardly make out the words over the screaming of a siren.

"Hey, you're all right. Gonna be okay. You hear me?"

A woman's voice shouted from behind Storm's head. "You think she's back?"

"I think her eyes are more focused." The man's face peered into hers. Storm could smell his aftershave.

"Sure," said the woman's voice. "And you know what she's thinking, too."

"Marty, you have no imagination. Her PO_2 is pretty good. She's got enough oxygen in her blood to be conscious now. What else do they want us to do?"

Storm heard the static of a radio and recognized the movement of a vehicle. The siren warbled a more frantic refrain.

"We're almost there. Rob and Francine are right behind us with the guy."

She felt the restraints on her arms; bands across her chest kept her from rolling off the stretcher. She must have passed out from absolute exhaustion. The ambulance lurched to a halt and the big doors at Storm's feet were thrown open by a flurry of people. She bumped helplessly on a gurney through a mechanical door where lights shone fuzzily overhead. She was okay. But Hamlin?

People moved around her with efficiency. A woman in green scrubs leaned over her and spoke, waving away a syringe. She put her face in front of Storm's and touched her hair. "Your friend is being treated. We'll send you down to X-ray for that ankle. Can you tell us if you took anything, if you were given anything?"

Storm croaked out, "Nothing."

The woman hustled away. Hovering in the background, behind a nurse who pricked Storm's arm with a needle, then connected it to a clear plastic tube, Storm saw the round bespectacled face of Detective Fujita. He looked worried. The nurse spoke to him. "Detective, you'll have to stand back now. She's doing pretty well. We don't know about the guy, yet."

"We don't do CPR too often." Fujita's voice was anxious.

"You did great, Detective. We'll take over from here."

"I'll call later. I need to talk to them."

Fujita faded out of Storm's vision. She tried with all her might to keep them open, but her eyes closed.

Then light inundated her eyes again. Her heart was hammering in her chest and clammy sweat poured from her face. An attendant trotted to her side with his eyes on the monitor beside the bed.

The nurse rushed over and patted Storm's arm. "You're okay. You're exhausted and you fell asleep." The doctor returned, checked a gauge by the bed. The worry lines faded.

Storm realized that her eyes were following the doctor's back. She wiggled her arm and felt the sting of the needle to the IV line. She moved her hand, then tried to jiggle a leg. It worked.

"You feeling better?" a man's calm voice asked.

"Yeah. Hamlin?" Storm's voice rasped, dry and painful.

"He's still intubated. Just relax, now. I'm going to give you something to help you sleep."

"No!" Storm tried to rise to her elbows. Dread swept through her. "I don't want it. Nothing else, please."

The fellow put his hand gently on Storm's shoulder. "Okay, okay. But you need to rest and you may want some painkillers for that ankle. We'll keep you here overnight."

Storm hadn't known she was asleep until she woke herself with a shout. Her face hurt, her whole leg throbbed, and she couldn't remember where she was. The sun streamed through Venetian blinds behind a dark head. Another person stood on the other side of the bed, silhouetted against the light.

Aunt Maile leaned over the bed and hugged her. "They called us last night. We came over on the earliest plane."

Uncle Keone's voice rumbled. "We got plenty scared, honey."

Storm's eyes filled. Their lined, brown faces had never looked so loving or welcome to her. "I'm so glad you're here." She looked first at Maile, then Keone. "Who's they?"

"First the police, then someone from the office. One of the lawyers, had a *haole* name." Aunt Maile looked at Uncle Keone, who shrugged.

"Oh." The only Caucasian partner was Cunningham. The breath caught in Storm's throat. "Have you heard anything about Hamlin?"

Aunt Maile opened her mouth, but a light knock on the door interrupted her. "She's awake, Detective." She sounded pretty happy to see the cop.

Fujita paused at the threshold and fiddled with the plastic top of a paper Starbucks coffee cup. "Mind if I talk to her for a minute?"

Aunt Maile patted Storm's hand. "We'll go get a cup of coffee and come back."

Fujita sat in the chair next to the bed, pushed his glasses up on his nose, and slurped through the little hole in the top. Storm could smell the rich brew. It was making her salivate. All of a sudden, she was starving.

"What time is it?" she asked.

"Two o'clock."

Storm looked at him with surprise. "In the afternoon?"

"Yup."

"You gave me CPR."

"You had a pulse. I just breathed for you." He tucked his chin and peered into the little hole of his coffee top.

"What made you come to the office when you did?"

Fujita peered over his glasses at her. "Your stepbrother called 911. He was frantic."

"Martin, thank God." Storm paused. "You gave Hamlin CPR, too?"

"No, Officer Roper did that." Fujita smiled a little. "Sandy claimed she never caught anything from him when they dated a few years ago. She was willing to lock lips with him last night." He flushed. "Her terms, not mine."

"Where is Hamlin?"

Fujita looked away. "He's on another floor. You'll have to talk to a doctor."

"Detective Fujita, is he okay?"

He seemed to be avoiding her gaze. "He's a little more beat up than you. It's lucky we got to him when we did." He met her eyes.

She looked at the cop, longing to believe him. "What made Martin call you?"

"Wo blasted by DeLario in the parking lot on her way in, nearly knocked his motorcycle into a concrete piling."

"Oh, no. Was he hurt?"

"He made it home. Who did this to you?" he asked.

Storm looked at him, startled. "Meredith Wo wasn't there?"

"No, she wasn't. Did she give Ian Hamlin an injection of succinylcholine?"

"Yes, but I thought she was badly hurt, unconscious. I mean, I tried to stop her..."

"That would be the smashed picture frame?"

Storm nodded.

"Looked that way." Fujita swirled his coffee in the cup, then regarded her with raised eyebrows. "We found some interesting stuff in the box under Hamlin. Does the name Tong Choy ring any bells?"

"Yeah," Storm said slowly. "He's the guy who died on Mauna Kea, right?"

"Yes, and we found immigration paperwork for him and his brother on the floor of Hamasaki's office."

"His brother?"

"Kwi Choy. Kwi has an apartment here in Honolulu, right off the freeway. It's a crummy neighborhood, but he has one of those huge TV screens and a closet full of new clothes. You ever heard of this guy?"

"That's the guy who tried to run me off the road."

The detective pushed his glasses up on his nose. "Right. They were Wo's clients. Maybe Wang's, too. We're going to search his files, too. Any ideas about what happened to Choy on Mauna Kea?"

"I think a boar chased him."

"They have tusks, but they don't usually break necks." Fujita squinted at her. "Storm, what were you doing in Hamasaki's office last night?"

She looked down at her fingernails, still dirty from working on Sam's farm. It seemed like she'd been in Waimanalo weeks ago rather than only yesterday.

Fujita waited and Storm drew breath. "I heard about some private files that Hamasaki had kept on his family and probably some other people. I was trying to get them out before Meredith moved into the office."

"Are these the ones you told me about?"

"Probably, but when I told you about them, I had no idea they held so many secrets. He used a private eye to get his information." She picked at a hangnail. "I didn't want any more people hurt."

"And Meredith Wo knew about these secret files?"

"I believe so, but I don't know how, or when, she found out."

Fujita drained off what was left in his coffee cup. He stood up. "I'm glad to see you're okay. I'll drop by later on."

"Detective, Meredith Wo killed Hamasaki."

"We're trying to find her now...and we're looking into that possibility." He gave her a little wave and walked out the door.

Storm clamped her teeth together in frustration. Why was Fujita so bloody nonchalant while that murderous bitch was still running around? And where was Hamlin? She looked around for a hospital official. Anyone—nurse, orderly, whatever. When she was trying to sleep or find a little privacy in the bathroom, they were all over her.

She swung her legs over the side of the bed and gritted her teeth at the throbbing ankle. A wave of dizziness toppled her back to the pillows. She closed her eyes to stop the whirling room.

Aunt Maile popped her head through the door. "I brought you a papaya. Good food for healing." She gave Storm a cellophane-wrapped piece of fruit on a flimsy plastic plate. "Keone's down in the snack shop. Some people from your office are with him. Everyone's worried about you. You feeling better?"

"Yeah, I'm okay." Storm sounded grumpy even to herself. She softened her voice. "Aunt Maile, would you find the doctor who took care of me last night? Or someone who knows how Hamlin is doing?"

"Sure, honey. I'll find Uncle Keone and we'll be back in ten or fifteen minutes."

If Uncle Keone's in the snack shop, you can make that an hour, Storm thought. She set the papaya on the bedside table and stared at the blank TV screen on the wall opposite her bed. Her ankle was killing her. She looked around for a button to call the nurse. Weren't they supposed to be right nearby? What if she fell out of bed? Or had a seizure? Or died of boredom? Sighing, she lay back and was shortly asleep.

Chapter 40

Storm awoke to a darkened room. Someone had turned out the light, closed her door. She pushed the call button. The hospital aide, switching on the light, told her that her aunt and uncle were in the cafeteria and would return soon. And, if she was awake, that policeman was back. She was.

Fujita, smiling, walked in. A steaming cup of Starbucks went to the bedside table. He sat, perching another cup on his crossed knee.

"You think your doctors will mind?" he asked. "It's decaf."

Storm inhaled the aroma. "I hope not."

Fujita sipped. "You're better. I've been back to Hamasaki's office. Talk to me more about the files you saw. Not the family stuff. We're still getting a handle on how Wo knew—"

"I think I can help."

A low voice from the doorway caused both of them to turn their heads. Hamlin sat in a wheelchair and one side of his face drooped. The lower lid of one eye was pulled down by the weight of the paralyzed cheek to show bright pink lining. Now it pooled with tears. "Storm, I'm so sorry."

"Oh, Ian, I've been so worried about you." She struggled to sit up. "What happened to you?"

"Seventh cranial nerve damage. From the lack of oxygen." He held a hand in front of his mouth when he spoke, but Storm could see that one side of his mouth hung flaccid and his proud moustache straggled above the loose lower lip.

"Why are you sorry? I'm sorry I didn't knock her out better." Storm tried not to stare at his stricken face. "Will this go away?"

"Maybe, time will tell." He wiped at an eye. Storm could not tell if the tears were the result of sadness or injury, but he went on. "I'm sorry that I ignored all the signs that pointed to Meredith. I should have known. Remember her big lawsuit against the neurosurgeon?" Hamlin looked at the detective, who looked down at his coffee cup.

"She was going after twenty million. It was not only going to make her reputation, her retainer was forty percent." He met Storm's eyes. "When we were dating, she was in the middle of the case. She talked about the hospital's involvement and whether to name Unimed in the lawsuit, too. She went to Ed Wang, who was the personal attorney for Sherwood Overton, CFO of the company. After ranting in my office one afternoon about how she'd been stonewalled, she completely shut up about it." Hamlin looked at Fujita, then Storm. "She got a two million dollar settlement. A few months later, she was asked to be a full partner at the firm."

Fujita interrupted. "She never filed suit against the HMO?"

Hamlin shook his head. "No. We broke up soon after." He paused. "A couple of years passed and I didn't think much more about it. But then, in the way unresolved issues keep popping up, I overheard Hamasaki arguing with someone the afternoon he died. They were really shouting at each other.

"I would have closed my office door, but the word 'Unimed' kept coming up. So I left the door open, and about ten minutes later, Sydney O'Toole stomped out of Hamasaki's office. Edwin Wang must have heard it, too, because he dropped in right after O'Toole left. Soon after, Lorraine Tanabe took Hamasaki a cup of tea. A few minutes later, Hamasaki went to the men's room, then returned to his office."

Hamlin's sad eyes went back and forth between Fujita's and Storm's rapt faces. "All was quiet and I left soon after. Lorraine was pulling covers over the office equipment, so she apparently was planning to leave soon, also." Hamlin looked miserable. "Next morning Hamasaki was dead."

Storm's eyes narrowed. "When you told me Hamasaki was preoccupied, you knew he was upset about Unimed."

"No, I still believe it was about Martin. I just didn't tell you about the quarrel with O'Toole."

"Why not?" Fujita asked. "And why didn't you tell the police?"

Hamlin glared at Fujita. "You have to ask?"

Fujita picked at the top of his coffee cup. "Okay."

"Okay, what? What are you talking about?" Storm sat up straight.

Hamlin looked disgusted. "The careers of the good detective, here, and I both benefited from Meredith's lawsuit. The police, the prosecutor's office, even the hospital administrative bigwigs hopped around and said they'd long ago suggested he stop cutting. We jumped all over that poor surgeon looking for criminal negligence. He was a big target to bring down." The lines in Hamlin's face dragged on his mouth and his drooping eye filled with tears again.

"The doctor had a stroke in the middle of the trial," Storm said.

"Right. I was damned if I was going to ruin another guy in the twilight of his profession. I thought it would be better to ask some questions, first. After all, I saw O'Toole leave and Hamasaki was still fine."

Fujita regarded Hamlin from the corner of his eyes. "And then what?"

"I took O'Toole out for a drink a few days later." Hamlin looked sheepish. "He wanted to talk. He thought he'd stressed out his old friend and given him a heart attack.

"After about four rounds of Jameson's, he loosened up quite a bit." Hamlin shook his head. "That guy can drink. I wondered if I was going to stay sober enough to remember what he told me. He said he'd started the whole mess when he went to Hamasaki for advice about a patient of his who needed a bone marrow transplant. Seems the HMO wouldn't pay for the procedure, though they talked a big story about how they were building a state-of-the-art cancer treatment clinic. O'Toole was frustrated because their equipment was obsolete and continually under repair.

"Hamasaki picked up on this right away. O'Toole chuckled about how no one ever could pull the wool over his friend's eyes. Hamasaki talked to hospital department heads, listened to the company line, then looked up the purchasing orders on his own. He found the discrepancies, then went back to O'Toole to find out what was going on."

Hamlin took a deep breath. "This is where O'Toole got fuzzy. And it wasn't just the booze. He was nervous, like someone was threatening him. He tossed back the rest of his drink and got up. I threw some money on the table and followed him out of the bar. Had to practically chase him down the street. He wouldn't let me call him a cab, either, the crazy fool. Last thing he said as he shuffled off was that he'd told Hamasaki to clean his own nest. And he told me to do the same."

Fujita looked thoughtful. "So, not just Wo, Wang was in on this, too."

"Of course. That wimp never could say no to her," Storm said.

"That wimp is dead." Fujita's voice was grim. "He died yesterday afternoon, while you were up in the Ko'olau Mountains. Looks like a heart attack. His face was a mask of pain—or maybe fear—hard to say."

Fujita looked puzzled. "The odd thing is, he was wearing just one tennis shoe. We couldn't find the other."

Storm and Hamlin both gaped at him. "Jesus," Storm whispered. Hamlin opened his mouth, but no sound came out. Storm knew she'd have to talk to Aunt Maile and to Bebe and Sam. Later. Storm forced herself back on track. "Did she get the files?"

"Where were they kept?" Fujita asked.

Storm told him about the hidden drawer in the old bookcase.

"The glass was broken, but no books were moved. She would only have had a minute or two before we got there."

"It's real private stuff." Storm's eyes slid to meet Hamlin's. "A lot of it Hamasaki shouldn't have kept."

"But you found information about Unimed?" Fujita asked.

Storm nodded. "Overton, Wang, Meredith, and Unimed are all connected." She looked at Hamlin. "Like Ian said, Hamasaki found out that money was being diverted from one of Unimed's accounts." Storm sighed. "I think he approached her or Wang with questions about the equipment purchasing orders. O'Toole virtually told him the problem lay within the firm, right?"

"Makes sense." Fujita took off his glasses and rubbed the bridge of his nose. "Storm, I need to see those files."

"I knew you would say that." She pointed to her bagged clothing in a corner of the room. Fujita handed them to her and she dug out the key. "Could you leave the family files behind? Please?"

Fujita shook his head. "I have to go through them, but I promise we'll bring anything unrelated to this case to you. I'll do it myself." He gestured to someone in the hall. "You and Hamlin have twenty-four-hour guards until we find her."

A nurse walked into the room. "Mr. Hamlin, you've got an appointment with neurology."

Hamlin nodded and turned his chair slowly.

"Ian, I'll come see you," Storm called after him.

Fujita jingled the keys in his hand. "You think Wo blackmailed Wang?" he asked Storm.

"Maybe. Or maybe he just couldn't face up to her, even in the end." She watched the door for a minute. "Do you know if Wang had any Chinese immigrant clients?"

Fujita's eyebrows shot up. "Yes, the papers we found on Tong Choy showed he was Wang's client. We're getting a search warrant right now for Wang's office."

"I was thinking. Wang had this incredible jade collection. He talked to me about it, once. He loaned it to museums, you know."

"And?"

"People came to him to sell their family heirlooms. He talked about how it was tougher these days to get good pieces."

Fujita stared at her.

"Maybe he offered sponsorship to the United States for jade."

"Immigrants do need guaranteed employment. Yeah, we can check that out. What's the connection to Meredith?"

"She would have known."

"Maybe Wang had Meredith do his paperwork?"

"Wang got everyone to do his paperwork."

Storm slumped back on her pillow. Sadness and fatigue had drained her. Fujita gave her a pat on the arm and walked slowly from the room.

Storm thought about all those hidden documents. She believed that Fujita would keep them private, but she was embarrassed to have anyone else see what was in them. A tangled mess of family skeletons and betrayals ensnared them all. Faith had been an elusive quality in the Hamasaki family and she couldn't help but feel that Miles Hamasaki himself had set the first example. He had been unable to relinquish his power, and by striving for new ways of control, he'd doomed the foundation of trust for which he'd worked so hard.

Chapter 41

Aunt Maile and Uncle Keone came into Storm's room and vowed not to leave her side until she was discharged. Well, except for an occasional trip to the cafeteria, one at a time. The hospital even rounded up two cots for the night. All three clung to each other's presence.

The lines in her aunt's and uncle's faces looked deeper than she remembered. Their bones looked more prominent and Uncle Keone's jeans bagged more on his flat bottom. She noticed for the first time that the once-deep brown irises of their eyes were ringed with blue. The three of them shared the evening paper; Aunt Maile and Uncle Keone passed a pair of reading glasses back and forth. And she could see the knowledge of human fragility reflected in their eyes.

She knew they partly blamed themselves for her close call. They felt they should have warned her more strongly, or been with her after Hamasaki's death. Uncle Keone apologized for not spending the night when they came to O'ahu for a saddle.

"What could you have done?" Storm asked them, and she meant it. But they were deflated, worried about their own judgment and weaknesses. They were afraid they'd contributed to her pain.

Storm felt a gap widen with their reticence, like the one she'd felt with her father. It was up to her to reach out now. She began by explaining what she and Fujita thought had happened, that Wo had been covering up a large-scale embezzlement of Unimed. She told them how she and Fujita figured either Wang was involved or being blackmailed by Meredith. The Chinese immigrants had done Wo's bidding, afraid of losing their sponsorship and being sent back. One of them had tried to run Storm off the road and one followed her on the slopes of the mountain. Both were dead. It was up to Fujita to find who had actually carried out the violence against Lorraine.

Storm picked at the bed covers. "Aunt Maile, I still don't understand how Tong Choy broke his neck on the mountain. There were no footprints, no signs of struggle. And what was that strange animal we saw?"

Aunt Maile glanced at Uncle Keone. "The old legends say that the *'aumakua* protects. The spirits of dead ancestors call on whatever god is needed to defend the family," Maile said. She shrugged. "Some of the *kahuna* would say that the creature was Kamapua'a, half-man, half-pig."

"I remember the songs and dances that tell his story, but do you really believe those old legends? I'm not convinced Wo didn't hire someone to clean up after the Tong brothers," Storm said. "And to remove Ed Wang before he betrayed her."

Her aunt and uncle looked alike in that moment, gray hair and wizened brown skin, and they reached for each other's hands. "I don't think we'll ever know for sure."

Aunt Maile looked at Storm with steady dark eyes. "But I'm sure she didn't conjure up a wild boar," she said. "Did she even know about your *'aumakua*? That it is *pua'a*, the pig?"

Storm shook her head. "No."

Uncle Keone leaned forward on his chair, his elbows on his knees, and rested his warm, dry hand on Storm's. "Some of the old teachings are metaphors for life and nature. Like what the Bible says, 'whatsoever a man soweth, that shall he also reap?' Can you explain why that happens? Yet it does, doesn't it?"

His eyes twinkled. "The old Hawaiians believed in the forces of nature, that they took human form." Uncle Keone sat back next to Aunt Maile with a smile and nodded at Storm. She no longer felt distance between them. Instead, they felt part of a bigger whole. And it was comforting.

She was still terrified of falling asleep, being out of her own control, but her doctor visited her during a physical therapy session and told her that these fears were normal and should fade. Her body demanded sleep for healing, though, and she took frequent naps that became less and less fraught with anxiety. Except for two empty bags of Mrs. Field's cookies, a half-eaten jar of kim chee that left a strong garlic aroma throughout the room, and a rubbish can full of banana and papaya peels, she might have believed that Aunt Maile and Uncle Keone never left her side.

After one long nap, she woke to find Aunt Bitsy and Michelle waiting with flowers. Aunt Maile and Uncle Keone slipped away for a visit to the cafeteria. Bitsy looked fragile and tears welled in her eyes. "Thank you for getting to the bottom of this mess, dear."

"How's Martin?" Storm asked.

"He'll come see you later this afternoon," Michelle answered.

Storm took a deep breath. They had all broken promises and made painful mistakes. Keeping secrets and harboring resentments had been as damaging as a direct assault, but it was time to try to learn and move on. "He saved my life, you know. I want to give him a big hug."

"He'd like that," Michelle said. "David couldn't leave the lunch crowd at the restaurant, but he knows you're going home tomorrow. He'll bring dinner over for you."

"That would be great. I'd like to see him."

When Michelle and Bitsy had hugged Storm and left, Storm settled back on her pillows. She must have dozed off again, because when she opened her eyes, Uncle Keone was sitting nearby, well into the newspaper. Aunt Maile and a smiling nurse stood by the bed. The nurse was chewing what appeared to be a chunk of *pipikaula*, the spicy Hawaiian beef jerky.

Fujita came in as the nurse departed, licking her lips. Storm was glad to see he wasn't eating *pipikaula* or kim chee, too. She was getting the feeling that it was about time to go home, lie around on the couch with Fang.

He sat down and propped his forearms on his knees. "You feeling okay?"

"Better. I'm sleeping a lot."

"That's normal. It's the effect of the stress on your body and the drug." He jiggled one leg. "We picked up Meredith Wo at the airport. She was booked on a flight to Hong Kong. She won't talk to us and she called an attorney, from outside the firm, by the way. But we've got Hamasaki's Unimed notes and access to bank accounts belonging to her and Wang. They both made deposits that hint at huge commissions on those Chinese-manufactured machines. The equipment cost a fraction of the amount the Unimed purchasing director had been told. Wo alone pocketed two and a half million from each of the two deals Hamasaki discovered."

Both of Fujita's legs were jiggling, now, and he could scarcely keep the glee out of his voice. "I have a hunch it's just the tip of the iceberg, too. We're getting subpoenas for all of Overton's files."

"What about Lorraine? Why did they kill her?" Storm asked. She couldn't share Fujita's merriment at the big bust. It was just too hard to overlook the arrogant and wanton disposal of human life perpetrated by greed.

"She knew whatever Hamasaki knew," Fujita said. "According to Wang's secretary, a few days after Hamasaki died, Lorraine confronted Meredith. Seems like Lorraine didn't believe it was an accidental death, either." He peered over his glasses at her. "And Wo saw her give you a list before you left for the Big Island, didn't she?"

Storm nodded sadly. "Poor Lorraine. If she suspected someone had killed Hamasaki, why didn't she think they'd kill her, too?"

"She did. She prepared two copies of Hamasaki's papers." Fujita sat back in his chair and his feet came to a flat standstill. His voice lost its levity. "She gave two envelopes to her husband. If anything happened to her, he was to mail one to you and a copy to us.

"But Wang visited him. Mr. Tanabe's bank account grew by two hundred thousand dollars three hours after Lorraine got hit. She wasn't even dead, yet." Fujita slumped in his chair. "Poor Mr. Tanabe broke down when we visited him last night. Wo threatened the Tanabes' married daughter and her two kids on Kaua'i. So he gave both sets of files to Wang, who believed he had the originals."

"Did Wang or Wo kill Hamasaki? Did Wo take an earlier plane from Hong Kong?" Storm asked.

"Meredith was on a JAL flight that left Hong Kong at 2:50 p.m. on Sunday. But because of the International Date Line, she actually got into Honolulu at 9:20 a.m. the same day. We found a couple empty syringes in a locked desk drawer in her office. Apparently, she got the drug from Wang. His private nurse said that they keep succinyl-choline around in case his invalid mother needs to be intubated."

Storm wondered if her dizziness was due to distress or the remnants of the succinylcholine in her system. "How could Hamasaki sit still for an injection?"

Fujita sighed. "Hamlin said Hamasaki left the office for a minute after Lorraine brought him the tea. Plenty of time for Wo to drop the sedative into his cup."

"But why was coffee in the cup? She knew he drank tea."

"We can't check this now, but it's likely that Wo used potassium instead of succinylcholine to speed up Hama-saki's death. When you called us, we found his hand gripping the mug as if he'd had a seizure or heart attack. We think that when Wo couldn't get the mug out of his clenched hand, she used coffee from the kitchenette to rinse the cup."

"Do you think Wang knew that Wo killed Hamasaki and Lorraine?"

Fujita's eyes glittered behind his glasses. "Some of the office personnel said he was very upset this last week."

"Have you talked to Sherwood Overton yet?"

Fujita pressed his lips into a thin line. "He's gone. His secretary claims that he left the office right before lunch yesterday. He had a board meeting downtown, but he never showed up."

Silence passed between them. Storm swallowed hard and picked at a hangnail on her thumb. "How do you do this day in and day out?"

He regarded the floor for a few seconds, then looked up. "I have to believe that I'm keeping others from getting hurt. But some days…" He stood up slowly, as if his knees ached. "I'm going to take my nephew reef fishing this afternoon. Don't care if I catch anything, either."

Fujita slipped away. Storm was still gazing into her lap. "Aunt Maile, Uncle Keone, would you mind if I went to Hamlin's room for a few minutes?"

Hamlin was writing on a legal pad and looked up in surprise. His first reaction was a crooked smile. Then he put his hand up to cover the side of his face that drooped.

"You look better, you know," Storm said. "It's going to disappear."

"The experts can't tell yet." Hamlin looked down at his paper and kept his eyes there. "I'm stronger, though."

"See, it's not even been two days."

"Yeah."

"Has Fujita caught you up on what happened?"

"I haven't seen him since yesterday," Hamlin mumbled.

"He's probably on his way, but I'll fill you in." Storm told him about the scam with Unimed. She tried to keep the anguish out of her voice as she related how Lorraine had tried to protect her family by copying the files. Hamlin looked very pale. They both knew how close they had come to being Meredith Wo's victims, too.

He listened carefully, but kept his eyes down and his face in shadow. The lamp over his bed was carefully aimed to shine on his lap.

"How is DeLario?"

Hamlin picked at his moustache. "He came to see me."

"You could have told me about his drug problem. And that he'd euthanized Neil."

"I would have, eventually, but I was trying to work through it. My feelings swung between guilt and anger. It brought back all the sadness I felt back then, too."

Storm nodded; this was something she understood. She limped closer to Hamlin's bedside and took his hand. "Were you trying to protect Meredith?"

He looked up from the papers in his lap and met her eyes. "No, never. I always knew she was selfish. I just never had any idea how desperate she was."

Storm smiled at him. Neither of them spoke for a few minutes. When the nurse came through the door, they both started and Storm let go of his hand. The nurse looked kindly at Storm. "Time for his physical therapy. We'll have this guy back on track, soon."

"Yeah, I know." Storm shuffled toward the door, then looked back. "They're going to let me go home tomorrow. How 'bout if I bring pizza for dinner?"

Hamlin didn't answer and kept his eyes down.

Storm went back to his bedside. "Hey, it's your long legs I hang around for, not your face." She punched him lightly on the arm.

Hamlin let his gaze slide to meet hers. There was a hopeful light in his eyes.

"Six-thirty. Black olives and Maui onions. Extra cheese," Storm said.

He almost smiled.

To receive a free catalog of other Poisoned Pen Press titles,
please contact us in one of the following ways:

Phone: 1-800-421-3976
Facsimile: 1-480-949-1707
Email: info@poisonedpenpress.com
Website: www.poisonedpenpress.com

Poisoned Pen Press
6962 E. First Ave. Ste 103
Scottsdale, AZ 85251